HARRY'S ARK

Christmas, 2010

Dear Gary & Carol,

Adele and I thought you might enjoy reading my novel, which Adele finished last week. So, here it is; with my best wishes for the Holiday season and a great 2011. Hope to see you soon.

Love

HARRY'S ARK

David Newcomb

To order additional copies of this book, contact:
Xlibris Corporation
1-888-795-4274
www.Xlibris.com
Orders@Xlibris.com
18393

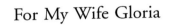

For My Wife Gloria

Credits and Acknowledgment

The cover collage of HARRY'S ARK was designed and created by Tom Gladden Graphic Design.

Author's photograph by Marci Bauman; edited by Tom Gladden Graphic Design.

The Tuskegee airman pictured in the cover collage is 1st Lt. John H. Leahr of the 301st Fighter Squadron, 332nd Fighter Group, USAAF.

The senior officer pictured in the cover collage is Lt. Col. Augustine Warner Robins, one-time Commander of Wilbur Wright Field. The source photograph appears in FROM HUFFMAN PRAIRIE TO THE MOON: THE HISTORY OF WRIGHT-PATTERSON AIR FORCE BASE, by Lois E. Walker and Shelby E. Wickam, Air Force Logistical Command, 1986, at page 61.

The helicopter pictured in the cover collage is a realization by Fernando Hernandez and Scott Szoko of an original design by David Newcomb.

The author thanks Barry Lerner, translator of LOVE'S LAST MADNESS: POEMS ON A SPIRITUAL PATH BY DARSHAN SINGH, for his friendship, support and counsel during the writing of HARRY'S ARK.

CHAPTER ONE

Ponce, Puerto Rico,
Friday afternoon, March 7, 1947.

The locals were sitting on the fence. They came out to Baird Field every day the ship flew; unemployed men, and boys playing hooky from school. They watched, even stared, as Alice's car pulled onto the field, and watched the more intently as Alice's niece, Patty Symms, got out. She was new in town, and the locals always stared at someone new. But Patty had earned her success in the world at large. Now twenty-four, she worked for *Life Magazine*.

Alice drove off.

The first sounds Patty heard came from the blades of Harry's aircraft, which beat the air with a peculiar, concussive *whapping* that was audible even though the ship was out of sight, more than a mile distant to the east. Harry had built a helicopter, and today would be Patty's first shoot of the new class of aircraft: rotary wings.

A hundred yards from Patty, Harry stood, with the others in the company, as they looked out from the mouth of the hangar. Alice had told Patty about Harry, as much as Alice knew. He had retired from the Army after serving forty years at Wright Field. In retiring, he had taken with him one fellow officer and four civilian employees, including a draftsman, and these were the men who, with Harry himself, had built the rotary wing aircraft that Patty had come here to shoot. Harry's ship, she understood, was the largest helicopter ever flown, and was now in trials, the very thing that people like to see.

In England, where Patty spent the war years from 1943 on, she had seen few, very few, helicopters, none of which stood next to a B-17. Times had changed.

Now the locals turned toward the east, across the scrub flats that extended back toward town, and they waited for the ship to reappear.

She loaded her Speed Graphic.

One of the boys yelled, *"Viene!"* and all of them looked, men and boys, together as one. To Patty, they were like birds, perched on a fence, and she shot them as such, using the fence as a diminishing perspective. She got them, all pointing together and looking in the same direction at Don.

Harry's pilot, Don Perry, was flying Harry's aircraft nap-of-the-earth, in an effort to impress the passenger on board, Harry's guest from Wright Field. Lt. Colonel Glen Anderson, beside Don, was not impressed. Harry hoped the Army would offer to buy. The colonel felt certain he would not recommend that it should. As the ship flew west to the field, downdraft from the rotors raised dust in its wake. Don was flying at full throttle, ninety miles an hour, so low to the ground that the wheels clipped brush. The colonel found such stunting absurd, and were he not himself afraid of dying in a ridiculous crash, he would have laughed at Don. "Go higher," he yelled. But Don wouldn't. The colonel had been maintenance chief for all the Sikorsky helicopters the Army Air Forces had flown in air rescue operations in the Pacific. He knew helicopters, and he knew what they could do. At war's end, Anderson was transferred to Wright Field, where he was now in charge of rotary wing development.

When the locals saw Don approaching so low, buzzing the field, they cleared the fence. Patty, reloading film, stood her ground. In England, she had often positioned herself at the threshold of runways to get shots of bombers coming back. And more than once she had seen a B-17 crash at her feet.

Overflying the fence, the wheels of the ship cleared the top rail with inches to spare. The ship's fuselage passed to Patty's left, so close that the whoosh of its passing turned her around. But she shot. Years since she'd been buzzed like this, but still she caught the grim look on the face of the colonel, and the smile of the pilot looking back, right at her. It was one thing to risk death, but another if you took something home for your efforts. She got Don's smile, and, even more, to her surprise, she got her own eyes opened, for Alice hadn't told her he was black.

"God dam!" said the colonel, meaning Don had nearly killed them.

"Not close," said Don, who knew what he could do.

Fed up now, Colonel Anderson disembarked onto the concrete apron by the hangar. Then Don and Julio lifted off again, resuming their demonstration. Julio was the flight engineer.

"Never going to happen," the colonel told Harry.

"What?" Harry shouted in reply.

"You had your choice of white pilots," yelled the colonel, for, he knew, when the war ended, there were qualified white pilots everywhere, including white helicopter pilots. The colonel himself could have set Harry up with any Sikorsky pilot who had been flying air rescue in the war. But Harry had picked that dammed *nigra* instead. "You're a fool, Harry," the colonel told him.

"May be," Harry said.

"You're like a man who shoots himself in the foot. You're your own worst enemy." But such had been Harry's reputation at Wright Field; that he was a maverick, who always went against the grain.

"Go to hell," Harry said, after thinking about the colonel long enough to realize that the prospects for a sale were *kaput*. Don Perry was Harry's draftsman, and Don had had ambitions to fly, so that, when Harry offered Don the drafting job, Harry had to *sweeten* the offer in order to get Don, by allowing Don to fly. As a pilot, Don cost Harry nothing. Harry did not have to pay for a white pilot. He got a black one for free.

The ship hovered, wheels thirty-five feet above the ground,

nearly perfectly still in the rough air of the afternoon. Its shadow, projected onto the concrete apron below, was ringed by the flickering aura of the rotors. Looking down from the cockpit, down on them all—on Harry, on Colonel Anderson, and the others—Don felt God-like.

Lugging tripod, camera, and duffle bag across the field, Patty arrived at the hangar. Matching Don's bravado, and ever ready for a shot with a dramatic point of view, Patty went out to the apron and lay down, aiming up, below the aircraft as it hovered.

"Who the hell is that?" the colonel asked Harry.

"I think she's from *Life*," Harry answered. His attorney had told him Patty was coming to town. His attorney was a friend of Alice Symms.

Patty, sighting up, shot the aircraft back-lit by sun. She would get no detail, only silhouette and contrast. But that was the effect Patty wanted. She wanted the ship to show a halo, which it did, so the viewer might surmise there was grace.

The locals, having regrouped at the fence, applauded, while, out in the field, far from view, Harry's drunken machinist, Burt Maxwell, hid behind the truck, drinking rum.

"'She's a sweet ship,'" Harry said, quoting a remark Igor Sikorsky had once made about his own first helicopter. But, in the din the aircraft made, the colonel had as much trouble hearing Harry as Harry had hearing him, and he merely nodded, not having understood precisely. "Well behaved," said Harry, trying to explain.

What concerned Colonel Anderson most of all were the aircraft's size and complexity. It had a three-rotor configuration, which was a radical new design and would be costly to produce. Thus, it would take longer to develop this aircraft, to work the bugs out, and the aircraft would be a headache to maintain. In the colonel's view, years might pass, and fortunes might be spent, before determining once and for all that the project had never been viable from the start, and would have to be abandoned. The ship, in that view, would be a money sink. And the colonel feared that, especially in combat, the complexities of the ship would work against it. With two engines, three rotors, complex air flows and controls, the ship seemed to the colonel especially vulnerable to damage. But these considerations were lost on Harry, who was too proud of his creation to be reasonable. Harry had too much at stake. Ultimately, it was easier for the colonel just to blame the pilot and the pilot's race. "Your Nigra's a hot-dog," he said.

Don flew the ship, climbing, on a promenade around the field, showing off, first east to the fence, then, in a gentle left turn at one hundred thirty feet, around the northern perimeter along the fence to the west. In a slow sashay that brought the ship to mid-field, he pitted controls one against the other, front rotor differential against main rotor cyclic, producing a series of Dutch rolls, a cross-controlled roll against yaw. It was a move Don had rehearsed in his mind for a week; easily enough done in a small airplane, but unprecedented in a three-rotor helicopter.

Allemande left and allemande right, each maneuver Don completed induced the next move. He circled the company truck in turns to the left, then criss-crossed the truck in figure-eights. Don flew a chandelle, then a dip and a stay; all moves of the dance, moves of grace. He brought her about, and about sharply, then brought her about the other way. He looked upon the mountains and he looked upon the sea. He seemed to make a cradle and he seemed to make it rock. The ship was his lady. From the apron, shooting now off a tripod, Patty got shot after shot.

In mid-field, Don broke off the maneuvers and established a hover directly over the truck, a position signaling to Maxwell and the others that now the day's final exercise, to carry the truck, would begin. Moving aft to the cabin, Julio re-plugged the intercom's jack to direct Don. Operating the winch, he began paying out the cable, with the idea of hooking a steel "O" ring onto the harness of cables the men had lashed around the truck below him. But the hook jigged in the rotorblast. Forward, from his pilot's seat, Don could see down only to a fender of the truck, and only then if he bent forward, which was difficult because of the sticks and because Don could not relinquish his grasp on those sticks, even for a second. Over the intercom, Julio told Don the hook had dropped clear.

"They're going to haul the truck," Harry said.

"Be damned," the colonel said, for surely Harry joked. No rotary wing aircraft could pick up Harry's flatbed truck. "What's that truck weigh?" he asked, but Harry, too, was wondering the same thing. "Hundred dollars," said the colonel.

"You're on," said Harry.

The colonel laughed at Harry. Harry was surely screwed up. Money was tight. He had cut too many corners, trying to do too much with too little. But that was always Harry's way, according to reputation. He was a screw-up. He wouldn't have made full colonel had it not been for the war, though Anderson, a lieutenant colonel, could say essentially the same about himself.

Out in the field, Diego Viera, the only one in Harry's company not from Wright Field, signaled to Don from seventy feet in front of the ship that the ship was too high for the docking with the truck. "Come down!" Julio told Don, also seeing Diego. The hook had risen from the truck bed.

Now straddling the hatchway in the aft cabin, Julio found he could no longer reach the lever behind him to control the winch drum, so that he was unable to pay out more cable while watching the hook. "Messed up," he said to himself, referring to his own design of the controls.

"What's going on?" Don called back. But without answering, Julio jerked the ship's cable by hand. Rotor wash whipped it. Then the ship lurched. In the lurch, Julio stumbled, nearly falling out through the open hatchway.

Below them, in front, Diego threw up both hands. He couldn't see Julio, who was inside the ship, and Don was paying him no mind.

"Ease forward," Julio yelled. The ship had crept back. Don was having trouble playing gusts; the air was unstable. Don brought the ship forward and down.

Julio, paying out line again, caught the truck, not by the O ring, but by one of the lashings of cable. Then he yelled for Maxwell. But Maxwell couldn't hear him. Julio waved for Diego. But Diego couldn't see him. He whipped the line like a garden hose, made a snake with it, made a coil, made a wave. But the hook wouldn't fall free. Don felt the tug of the line. "Where's the cable?" Don asked.

"Hooked wrong!" yelled Julio.

"Tell me where to go!"

"Back up!"

Don, hearing the words "back up," thought Julio meant *climb, again,* and pulled pitch and opened throttle. The ship began to climb.

"No! Back down! Back down!" Julio yelled. "Move backwards!" he meant.

"Which way?!" Don demanded. "Back up or back down!"

"Back up! Move backwards!"

"Oh, man!" Don exclaimed. *Back up. Back down.* The hook fell clear. *Back down.*

Diego had dust in his eyes from the rotorblast, and withdrew. Standing under the ship was like standing under a hurricane.

Julio found blood in his palm. The ship was so noisy he couldn't hear himself think. Worse, he had dust in his eyes, too. He couldn't see; he couldn't hear. The ship was wallowing and the winch was leaking oil.

"Where's the cable?" Don yelled.

"Screw you!"

"What should we do?"

"I don't care!"

Then, below them, Diego returned on a run and climbed onto the bed of the truck to help hook the ring. A few feet above him was Julio, and Diego yelled, but in vain. On board, Julio had slipped in oil and collided with the winch brace, and was now sitting on the deck, holding his shin. Over the intercom, Don tried to reach him, because they had to move the truck to better ground, but Julio didn't answer. Finally, Don flicked the VHF and squawked.

Bill Pyrtle, another of Harry's engineers, dashed inside the hangar's annex, where Harry kept the field's radio, and answered Don's call. Then, Bill ran with the message out to the field, delivering it by yelling in Diego's ear: Don wanted the truck moved.

Above, Don had sidled away, retreating toward the west. Diego started the truck and drove it west, too, hunting for any decent patch of grass, which would reduce the amount of dust being raised by the rotorblast.

With the truck at last parked below him, Don brought the ship down until its struts were within inches of the cab. The rotor wash beat ripples through the grass. Julio, now back on his feet, payed out the cable once more from the winch, and, by the second swipe, hooked the ring. He returned to the drum and rewound, tightening the cable. "We've got it!" he called forward over the intercom, and locked the drum.

Don opened throttles and began to pull pitch. As the ship climbed, the truck came up, but was unbalanced, front end first, until the front end jammed between the struts of the ship, wedging there, tight against the trusses. The sound of rending metal met everyone's ears, all over the field. To save face, Don let down the load as gently as possible, cursing the hour of his birth.

Suddenly, the truck broke free, and the hood of the truck, sprung now and partly crushed, fluttered in downwash. Julio released the winch to clear the hook. The ship flew free.

Diego, who had abandoned the truck before the docking occurred, now returned and climbed quickly to the top of the cab. The hook dangled from the ship overhead. Diego looked straight up through the belly hatch above him, meeting Julio's eyes as Julio looked down. Julio looked for the moment like a fish in the bottom of a boat.

Back at the hangar, the colonel could not contain himself further. "*THESE GUYS ARE CLOWNS!*" he said to Harry, exclaiming the words as a death sentence for Harry's ship. "*CAN YOU IMAGINE THAT AIRCRAFT IN COMBAT?!*" Harry turned to face him, and, had Harry been wearing a sidearm, would have killed him right there.

"Get out!" Harry said. "Get off my property. Right now." The Army was not going to be a buyer, Harry knew that, and Harry was not going to beg.

Yet the dumb show went on. As the colonel walked away, he stopped every few feet to watch. "Drop the hook," Don yelled, keeping the ship's landing gear twenty feet off the ground. Beaten, Julio let out line to eighteen feet, and locked the drum. Diego, up on the truck, grabbed the hook, drawing it through the ring. Maxwell took over the task of signaling to Don. Diego jumped from the truck. Maxwell signaled to climb.

Don climbed until the rotor blades bit. Revived by the sound of the engines running rich, Julio staggered forward and leaned the mixture. The impact of the blades striking the air at full pitch sent shock waves out across the field, echoing back from hangar and house. The ship began to judder. Don was getting nowhere. At full throttle, full pitch, the ship couldn't do it. This was no surprise to anyone now but Don. Cylinder head temperatures redlined. Engine oil temperatures redlined. The gearboxes were cooking. Aboard the ship, from his window, Don watched the mast of the left front rotor, turning. She was pulling her guts out. Bill signaled that two wheels of the truck remained on the ground. "I think you all need a public relations person," Patty said to Lon Pyrtle, causing him to smile in appreciation of her sarcastic sense of humor. Lon, who was Bill Pyrtle's father, was Harry's senior engineer.

Don brought the ship about, facing upwind, east. "She's through!" Julio yelled. "Give it up."

"Never," Don answered. He couldn't quit; it wasn't in him. Instead, he began to tow the truck, upwind, eastbound, toward the parking lot, toward the colonel and the fence. The locals scattered, for the second time today. The truck bumped along in tow on its rear wheels. Truck and ship reached a speed of ten miles an hour. The colonel stood his ground, as Patty had before him. The headwind on the ship made the airspeed twenty, and, with gusts, twenty-five. Don tugged the truck faster, ever faster. Now the headwind made it thirty, and the gusts thirty-five.

The ship gained translational lift. It gained power. The truck went airborne. It flew. For forty yards, the ship carried the truck through the air. Patty took a shot of this.

But, then, Don ran out of field. He couldn't get the truck down in time to stop. The fence approached, the colonel, too, and now the colonel was scrambling for his life. The truck was on all-fours when it crashed through the fence. It missed the colonel, but took out two sections of fence. The colonel cursed Don. Maxwell laughed. Julio yelled. But, when the colonel got up from the ground, even he conceded the truck had been airborne. "It flew," he said to a local. The local just laughed. But the colonel owed Harry a hundred.

"We need a bigger field," said Don, after returning to land on the apron.

Out in the field, Diego determined that the truck, despite a leak in the radiator, still functioned. He started it up, then looped around and drove it back toward the apron, passing the colonel, who was going the other way, driving his jeep into town.

Harry inspected the grill of the truck, where a section of fence rail had lodged. He extricated the piece of wood, turning it in his hand afterwards, like a club. The radiator hissed. The men gathered round. Patty took a shot of Harry. His shock of white hair flogged his forehead. With the late afternoon sun in his face, he seemed aglow. No matter that he was sixty-eight, Harry was unbowed. For Don, the sight of the club Harry turned in his hand stirred archaic memories, of beatings, fed by the circumstances and Harry's cruel eyes, for Harry had the cruelest blue eyes on earth; cruel as the eyes of a rooster pecking hens.

Finally, Lon summoned the courage to ask, "What exactly did the colonel say?"

Harry answered, "He said get rid of Don, because, so long as Don is the pilot, no one will buy our aircraft." The men looked down at their shoes. They looked away, at the mountains, or the house, or the distant parking lot. "He called you guys clowns," Harry went on. "And he said our ship was too ambitious. He won't recommend it be procured."

"Well son of a bitch," Maxwell said.

"He called us clowns?" asked Bill.

"Worse," Harry answered. Then Harry turned toward Patty. "You could get killed pulling stunts like that."

"Sorry," Patty said.

"If you're here to shoot the ship, you're too late," he said, for he meant it to be obvious to everyone that there would be no story now.

"Fly it to Wright Field," Patty told him; her heart in her throat with those words. She tried to maintain her composure, but she knew her own voice sounded tight. When she looked around, the men looked stunned. "Fly to Wright Field," she repeated. "Make them notice."

"We could," Harry said.

"How could we?" asked Lon.

"I could do that," said Don.

"Can I go with you?" Patty asked, reaching for everything now.

—

CHAPTER TWO

In his fifties and a widower, Antonio Laracuente had practiced law in Ponce thirty years. His grandfather had come over from Spain, and it was his father who, in 1899, had built *La Casa Laracuente,* Ponce's pre-eminent example of Spanish colonial architecture and the house where Antonio now lived. Constructed with walls a foot thick and embossed tin ceilings ten feet high, *La Casa Laracuente* featured wrought-iron balconies, arched windows, arched transom over double front doors, and decoratively scrolled cornices and columns. It rose two stories, overlooking *Calle Unión*, the westernmost of the four streets bordering Ponce's plaza. The view from the front rooms took in the cathedral, which stood opposite, and other sights of the plaza, including walkways, benches, trees, fountains, bandstand, and the distant red-and-black-striped firehouse, the *Parque de Bombas.* The trade winds, ever blowing across Puerto Rico, entered the front windows of the house, bringing in gentle sounds of the plaza, which, in the evenings, were chiefly laughter and music.

At one time or another, Antonio had counseled most of Ponce's leading citizens, and was himself a leading citizen. He was Harry's attorney, and Alice's. His tanned, vigorous appearance bespoke his love of the sea and Galician ancestry. He owned a boat and often sailed. At home, he preferred the informal company of friends on the patio to dining in the *comedor* and tonight he was hosting a party to welcome Patty to Ponce. His patio was a world apart from the sounds of the street and the plaza. Ensconced within high walls covered with brilliant yellow *canaria*, and suffuse with the fragrance of jasmine, the patio glowed with the light of Spanish lanterns. Hibiscus bloomed, and bougainvillea. In jest, Antonio once said that, in the cloister of his patio, his worst intrusion was the neighbor's cat, which sometimes patrolled the high walls. When Patty and Alice arrived, Harry and company were already there, and Agustín, Antonio's man, presented the women to the assembly below by leading them through the house to the back door, thence to a landing that stood above the patio, thereby giving their entrance the air of drama. At first Patty, then Alice, appeared. Patty created an abrupt contrast to the figure the men had seen that afternoon. Tonight, she had let down her flaxen-hued hair, and worn an off-the-shoulder, peach-toned, silk faille dress and matching shoes. Abashed, the men admired her.

Then came Alice, whereupon Maxwell blurted, "Like the filly, like the mare." The men laughed, of course, but not at Alice. Although in her fifties, nearly twice Patty's age, she was a silver-haired knock-out, whose presence gave rise to the inference each man drew concerning the beauty she possessed at Patty's age, for she possessed it even now. Her regal blue eyes gave them pause. No one whistled in the silence ensuing their brief laughter, but several sighed.

Alice had settled in Ponce after years of living in India, where she had been a writer and where, in the thirties, she had written a book, *Empire and Isles*, that predicted, among other things, the coming war. When war broke out, she moved to Puerto Rico, where, by war's end, she found herself in reduced circumstances. Events the book had predicted had in fact come true, leaving a world so changed the book was no longer current. As her royalties ran out, she began to teach school. Harry had asked if she would write about his project, but Alice had declined to accept his invitation. On the other hand, she did invite her niece to visit Ponce, enticing Patty with the promise of a story.

Patty took advantage of the party to make better acquaintance of the men, including Don, whom she found photogenic. In that regard, Don's hair was close cut, nappy; his eyes large, heather-hued, and very observant. His forehead was broad. Although reserved, he was direct in manner with those with whom he spoke, and quick to smile. Though he was not accustomed to speaking freely with white women, he indulged Patty by allowing her to glean the facts that he had been married and divorced, that his ex-wife lived in Maryland, of all places, Patty's home state, and that his mother had been a school teacher. Don's family was well established in Dayton, and Don was the only one of the five Perry children who had not gone to college.

Antonio showed Patty a drawing Don had made of two birds in flight, which Don had presented to Antonio as a gift and Antonio had hung in his study. Don was more than Harry's draftsman, and more than Harry's pilot. He was an artist.

While Patty enjoyed attending to Don, Don equally enjoyed the admiration she bestowed, but recognized the limits it entailed. Ponce was liberal by comparison to the United States, excepting, perhaps, New York City; and Ponce was a city where Negroes and whites were generally integrated, even to the point of racially mixed marriages, but Patty brought her past with her, and so did Don. They had three hundred years of North American history to wall off the one from the other. Whether in Ponce or Dayton, whether *Boricua* or Yankee, the women Don dated were Negro, and the men Patty dated were white. He reminded himself any interest he had in Patty Symms was for the publicity, for the fame she could bring to the project. He never lost sight of the fact that she could put him in *Life*.

In that, Patty's interest in Don mirrored his interest in her, for *he* could put *her* there as well. Don Perry was the first Negro test pilot. She hadn't known that until today, but the first of anything meant a story.

"I gave him his break," Harry said, to curtail what seemed to be the undue attention Patty was paying to someone other than the star of the show, which was Harry himself. "I gave them all breaks," Harry said. "They wouldn't be anywhere without me."

"We aren't anywhere now," said Maxwell.

As if to demonstrate she was not stuck on Harry's pilot, Patty circulated, asking Harry's youngest employee, Diego Viera, who was a native of Ponce on a one-semester leave from MIT, why *he* had wanted to work for Harry. Answering, Diego explained that he wanted the once-in-a-lifetime privilege of working with one of the pioneers of rotary wing flight. At MIT, Diego was studying aeronautical design. Where else but here, in Ponce, he asked rhetorically, could he learn from one of the giants. As he spoke, Patty glanced at Harry, whose chest seemed to inflate before her eyes. Continuing, Diego claimed he could feel history being made, and explained Harry's work, *their* work, followed the lineage of Juan de la Cierva, the Spaniard who had invented the autogyro and cured the problem of asymmetrical lift; of Igor Sikorsky, the Russian who had mastered production techniques, without which there could be no rotary wing industry; of Heinrich Focke, the German who had solved control problems in a lateral, twin-rotor helicopter. These were, of course, the people Patty had seen captured in portraits that hung in the front room of Harry's house. Diego spoke of Havilland Platt and Laurence LePage, who were following Focke's footsteps toward the design of a tiltrotor; and, finally, of Frank Piasecki, whose work on tandem rotors completed the pantheon of Diego's heroes, and of Harry's. Harry deigned to say that no one among his men worked harder than Diego. "He's like a son," Harry said. "We're like family."

Julio gave a wink at Patty, adding that Harry's "sons" had to work at half-wage.

Opposite Diego sat Burton Maxwell, whom no one called Burton and whom everyone called Maxwell. Thirty-six and a Kentuckian, Maxwell had served in the Navy well before the war, then worked in Detroit during the Depression. He had gone to Wright Field as a civilian at the outbreak of war. At Wright, he had worked in the line maintenance shop. Here, in Ponce, with Harry, Maxwell had welded the frame of the ship, installed the transmissions and drive trains, and helped with the engine accessories. "Little of everything," he told Patty.

"Little as possible," Julio said, knowing Maxwell could not be insulted. But, to be fair, Julio then credited Maxwell with services that were invaluable to the project.

"Name one," demanded Bill Pyrtle.

"I can't think of any," Julio admitted. Maxwell, as Julio pointed out, in contrast to Harry, to Julio himself, to Don, to the Pyrtles, or to Diego, had nothing material to gain by coming to Ponce. He might have found a better-paying job anywhere, including the job he had at Wright Field. Although not an engineer, Maxwell was a top-flight mechanic, welder, and machinist, ever in demand.

"Why *did* you come here?" Patty asked.

"I'm a drunk," Maxwell admitted.

"He's drunk now," said Bill.

"I'm not drunk now," Maxwell said, a remark testifying more to his capacity than his forbearance.

"You're dressed slovenly," Julio challenged.

As if to accept Julio's words as being premised on fact, Maxwell answered, "That's because nobody knows me in Ponce."

Deadpan, Julio rejoined, "Yeah, but . . . you dress the same way in Kentucky."

"So I do," Maxwell said. "But in Kentucky, just about everybody knows me."

Patty understood this routine had played before. She expressed an interest in the Pyrtles, who sat across the patio, and asked Lon, a Cincinnatian, second-oldest in the company—Harry was oldest—and the father of Bill Pyrtle, why *he* had come to Puerto Rico. "It seemed a challenge," Lon observed. He had been an inventor and free-lance engineer for most of his life. Tall and distinguished in appearance, with a gray Van Dyke setting him apart from the others, he also suffered from the chronic and sometimes excruciating pain of a slipped disc, for the relief of which he wore a large, corset-like brace. During the war he had worked at Wright Field, as a civilian employee designing and analyzing flight controls. He had been teaming with his son Bill for the last several years.

Bill Pyrtle, twenty-six and unmarried, had an eye toward the future in electronics. He had worked at Wright Field as a civilian employee with his father, and, for Bill, Harry's project was a throw-back, since it required little involvement in electronics. Still, it was an adventure to do a different kind of work. Bill and Lon had designed and built the flight instrument panels, electrical system, and hydraulically-assisted controls. Bill's mother—Lon's wife—still lived in Cincinnati, having chosen to remain in the family home rather than accompany her husband and son to Puerto Rico. "What's your opinion of the ship?" Patty asked Bill.

"It's primitive," Bill answered.

"His opinion is primitive, is what he means," said Julio.

"Why do you say it's primitive?" she asked.

Bill had worked on the B-29 project at Wright Field, and had begun work on the B-36 project. Against such a background, everything else was simple. "Mechanically, except for the controls, our ship is basic," he said. "The controls are not so basic. On the other hand, the aerodynamics are complex. I'm sure you realize that part of our challenge has been to build a ship in what was formerly a lumberyard's shed, on a shoestring budget, using war surplus parts. To this day we don't know what our ship can do."

"It can do everything," Julio said, "except repair my marriage."

"Nothing can do that," concurred Maxwell.

Thirty-two-year-old mechanical engineer Julio Rodriguez had retired a major in the Army Air Forces, serving in Air Matériel Command at Wright Field, in the Rotary Wing Development Branch of the Engineering Division. There, he had met and become a protege of Harry. Lithe and athletic, he kept his hair close-cropped and wore a pencil-thin moustache in the manner favored by Puerto Rican men. He radiated nervous energy. Still, he was the family man among Harry's men, for he lived in Ponce with his wife, Carlota, and their five children. "Critics say helicopters don't endure in the air," he explained. "That only means the range of a helicopter is too short. We set out to build one that will endure; that will carry payload and fuel. A helicopter is a contradiction in terms. A high-endurance, long-range helicopter is especially a contradiction in terms, because a helicopter flies by opposing its own motion. It's self-limiting. It wants to tear itself apart in flight."

"It's like us," Maxwell said, a remark prompting Patty to laugh, for it seemed to her ingenious, if perverse, that Harry had gotten self-destructive and self-limiting people to build a ship whose nature was self-destructive and self-limiting. But, then, by the same token, her aunt had gotten *her* to come to Ponce to cover Harry's story. What did that say about her?

"It's true we've fallen behind our schedule," Julio admitted. "And, we're also over-budget."

"How much longer would it take to complete your work?" Patty asked.

"Years," Julio answered.

"Nonsense," Harry said. "If you had done your work right, you'd be finished by now."

But Julio blamed Harry for being remote from his own creation, for having created by fiat, like God: *Let there be, and it was*. To make Harry's design work, Julio had to test the assumptions on which the design had been based, and he found few assumptions well grounded, and much of the design needing to be changed.

"Julio strayed off the reservation," Harry said, for Patty's benefit mainly, since the others had heard this many times. "Julio deviated from my design, and that's why we're over-budget and late," he maintained.

"Did you fly at Wright Field?" Patty asked Don.

"Colored don't fly at Wright Field," Don answered.

"He owns his own airplane," said Bill.

"When the colonel heard Don owned a Piper Cub, he said, 'Cub ain't much,'" said Maxwell. The colonel's view of Don, Harry, and the project was well known.

"We should be thankful to Charlesville," Julio said.

"Who exactly is Charlesville?" asked Patty, for she had heard Charlesville mentioned by name several times.

"He lent us the money to build the ship," Harry answered. "And if we can't sell it to the Army, we have no way to pay him back. But I'm not going to let Charlesville seize his collateral, which is what the ship is, for his loan. I would rather the ship go down in the ocean."

"Yeah, but without you on board," said Julio.

"I'll be on board," said Harry. "I'll be the first to step foot on Miami's shore, at the end of a world-record-setting flight across the ocean. A thousand miles, unrefueled!" he announced loudly, for everyone. "No other aircraft of our type can do that."

"And it's hardly certain that we can do it either," said Lon, but in a very low voice.

"Our contract with Charlesville forbids flying over water," Harry said. "It also forbids flying over populated areas, or flying at night. Or flying up in the mountains."

"The man sank half-a-million dollars in his investment," said Lon. "If we crash, he's out his money."

"I'm not letting him take the aircraft to France," said Harry. "I'd rather it went down in the sea."

"Harry went to God knows how many lenders and banks," Julio explained.

"Can you make it to Miami?" Antonio asked.

"Tell him, Don," Harry said.

"Actually," Don said. "I've changed my mind. I agree with Julio that there's too much risk."

"Nobody should risk losing that aircraft," said Julio. "Not because of Charlesville."

"You just want a job in France," said Harry, well aware Charlesville had offered employment to Julio at his factory in Marseille.

"No," said Julio. "We've put too much into building that ship." They had been building the ship for over a year, and had put several years into the design.

But Harry was deeply hurt by Don's agreement with Julio, and viewed it as betrayal. "I'll fly it myself," he threatened, in a threat no one took seriously. Harry could not tolerate disloyalty, though he expected it from Julio. So destructive had been the effect of the colonel on the morale of the company that all the men were tearing at one and another as surrogates for the resentment they felt toward the colonel. "You're losers," Harry told them, when they laughed at the prospect of him flying. But, in calling them losers, Harry seemed to vindicate the judgment of the colonel, who had called them all clowns.

Patty wondered how Julio would photograph, and decided

that, despite nice features and a clean, genuine smile, he could never be handsome, because he was lacking in that sense of repose most handsome men had. He was the opposite of Don, who truly was handsome. She found Julio's thoughts, like his words, came out like darts, taut and nervous. His face wouldn't photograph the same way twice, and she wouldn't trust a photograph to say who he was. "There are two things I love," Julio admitted, turning his attention from Harry. "Our ship and my kids. I work on the ship. I play with my kids." Julio's marriage was a disaster; something everyone at the party seemed to know. The hubs of the ship's rotors were his occupational pride and joy. He was married to them. "At the hubs of the rotors lies the very heart of the ship."

"Julio's wife says he's the sixth child in their family; the one who will never grow up," said Bill.

"The one thing Carlota and I agree on is that working for Harry has helped wreck our marriage," Julio said.

"Harry, Harry, Harry," said Harry.

"She can't stand Harry," continued Julio. "In thirteen years of marriage, my wife has never once asked me how a helicopter can fly. She spends my paycheck but she doesn't care."

"What are the self-limiting principles you spoke of earlier?" asked Patty, generally.

"Getting paid," Maxwell joked.

"I didn't shanghai these men," Harry interjected, addressing Patty. "It's important for you to understand, I didn't shanghai these men."

"I know that," Patty said.

Then, Harry addressed them all, going back up that mountain. "I want to talk about the flight to Wright Field."

"There is no flight to Wright Field. It's too dangerous," said Lon.

"First Miami, then Wright Field," Harry persisted. "The Army won't come here again, and Charlesville won't allow us to leave; not until he arranges for the ship to be transported to his plant in Marseille."

"That's not the worst outcome in the world," Julio judged.

"Yes, it is," Harry said. "For me, it is." In saying so, Harry had allowed he was too old to start again. Calling the loan would sound a death knell to Harry. "Can't you try," Harry pleaded. "Rehearse for a week, to see if we can carry all the weight we'll have to carry. Then, if the ship won't do it, we'll know before the week is up, and that will be the end of it. I'll let it go to France. But see if it will fly at the weight we designed her for. If it will, then consider flying it to Wright Field. Consider setting a world's record. Do something great. Because, I swear, if we can fly a thousand miles unrefueled, we'll have something the U.S. Army will buy."

"We're the Ponce Buccaneers," said Bill.

"We could try that," Don agreed.

"*Hombre!*" Julio protested.

But Don felt sorry for Harry, and, besides, he wanted to be brave in front of Patty.

"My mother died when I was three," Harry said, his tenor suddenly changed. "My father decided he could not keep my sister and me, and so sent us to America to live with his sister, in the Lower East Side of Manhattan. Although we were Scots, my aunt was married to a Rumanian Jew. I grew up being taught by the Jews. As a boy, I worked nine-hour days, which left me some time for my studies. But, as a young man, I worked eleven-hour days, which left me no time for the ladies. That's the cost of succeeding." Harry had never married. His men were his family, and the Army had been Harry's home. "I became a mechanical engineer," he continued. "That's the price of success. Do what you have to. Stay to the end. That's the moral of the story of Columbus, when asked by his men to turn back. They complained they'd been to sea a long time, and he told them they hadn't yet arrived. Stay as long as it takes to get where you've been wanting to go. That's the point.

"Wright Field doesn't care about us!" he went on. "If we don't care, no one does. If we don't get the Army's attention, we're through! Had Columbus listened to his men, then we would never have heard of Columbus. A man who gives up on his ambition, dies." To Don he added, "You will never get another job as a test pilot, no matter what Charlesville promises. Your last chance is to fly this ship to Wright Field."

"I know that," said Don, and in fact Patty could see the weight of the decision almost crushing Don now. She set up her camera, then, and shot.

"Don't shoot," Harry told her.

"No?" she asked.

"This is private."

"They're pictures," Patty said.

"I know what they are. We're trying to sell an aircraft to the Army."

"And I'm trying to make people see." Patty blushed. Anger rose. "In the war, I saw a lot of men die, and I'm seeing that here." Her words reached the men.

"If we sell the aircraft, we've succeeded," Harry said. "That's all Charlesville wants. He'll be appreciative."

"This is true," Lon admitted.

"I was at Wright Field when they called it Huffman Prairie," Harry said. "When they called it Wilbur Wright Field. When it was McCook Field in Dayton. I was there when we went to France in '17. I was there when DeBothezat delivered the first helicopter, and got the first Army contract for doing so! I was one of the four guys who hung on to it when it flew! You talk about photographs. I'm in *that* famous photograph! I am friends with Orville Wright! Igor Sikorsky and I go fishing! Yet here I am, still waiting. I showed the ropes to a hundred young engineers, some of whom went on to do better than me. Don't let the Colonel Andersons have their way. Have yours!" His voice had become sharp, like the snapping of dry twigs.

He had them. He could see.

"I was at Wright Field, too," said Don, "when they called it Huffman Prairie. Only I was the pick-a-ninny kid who was watching from the fence. I can do it, Harry. I can fly to Wright Field. That's why I'm here."

On the way home from the party, Don stopped at a hole-in-the-wall *cafetín*, little more than an open-front bar. *Coquí's*, as it was called, had five red-leather-topped bar stools, a bar, a mirror, and blue walls. Two customers drank, a bartender kept them company, and a radio disrupted the peace. When Don sauntered to the bar, the three men turned to look at him and one of the three recognized him. "*Mira, el piloto.*"

"How're'ya doin'?" Don intoned, in his own best imitation of John Wayne. No place on earth but in Ponce would a citizen say to Don, "Look, there's the pilot." Don was home.

He bought a cold Corona, then loitered. Puerto Ricans were migrating to New York, leaving Puerto Rico in a steady exodus north. There were better-paying jobs in Manhattan, and it was often hard to find any work in Puerto Rico. Yet, here, Don was king. Here in Ponce, the Pearl of the South, Don had the pearl, the best job on earth, the first Negro test pilot, the first Negro to fly a rotary wing aircraft. "*Como va?*" asked the barkeep.

"Pretty good," answered Don, knowing it was *his* story and not Harry's that Patty ought to tell.

—

CHAPTER THREE

Saturday morning, something like panic spread through Harry's company when Charlesville called from New York to say he planned to be in Puerto Rico that afternoon. Could somebody come to meet him in San Juan? And, he was bringing Walter. Walter!

"What do we do?" Harry asked.

"Send Don to kill him," suggested Maxwell.

"How do we prepare for a flight to Wright Field, with Charlesville here watching us?" Harry asked, in a question that gave voice to the panic.

"Easy," said Don. "Tell him General Weggoner is coming here next week, and that we've promised Weggoner an air show for Saturday, specifically to demonstrate how far the ship can fly."

"Not far from the truth," cracked Diego.

"Fly around the coast, like laps. Four times around will make a thousand miles," said Don, "and that's something we can practice in front of Charlesville."

"A ruse," Harry said.

"So what," said Don. "Either way, it's for Wright Field."

——

In San Juan, Saturday afternoon, Patty and Don met Charlesville and Walter at the gate.

To Don, Walter was joyless and arrogant; a tall, awkward drag of a man, and Don was sorry to see him. During the war, Walter had flown for the Luftwaffe. Most miraculously, he had survived the Eastern Front. Even so, what had saved him seemed to have been his training as an engineer, for he had been pulled off the line before the Eastern Front collapsed. Walter had spent the last two years of the war in Bavaria, helping to develop new aircraft. As to his person, he was disliked by Harry's men because he purported to know everything, and let everyone know that he knew everything, and let them all know that none of them knew a thing. Julio called him a *sabe-lo-todo*, which in English meant a know-it-all.

On meeting, Patty liked Charlesville, because he had an interesting face. Charlesville was forty-seven, but looked younger, and only close up would one see the fine lines around his eyes. He was smooth-skinned, physically soft, somewhat unkempt, and suffered the heat of the tropics poorly. His face was flush, and his clothes somewhat rumpled, something which seemed to go with the man. He and Walter had left Marseille a week ago, traveled to Paris, London, and New York.

"I have good news," Don said, as they stood near the gate. "General Weggoner is coming next week. Saturday."

Charlesville was pleased. He knew of Weggoner, of course: Acting Chief of Procurement for Air Materiel Command, but did not indicate whether he would be staying for the week or not.

The Aeronautical Works of Marseille, founded by Charlesville's father and now called the *Société Nationale de Constructions Aéronautiques de Sud-Est*, was the business Charlesville ran. During the war he had left the business and fled France, assisting the Resistance and Allied efforts from a base in England. After the Liberation, he had reclaimed his business, long since nationalized, and continued to manage it, despite the French government. Charlesville was fond of helicopters, even though he knew little about them. He had hired Walter for that; Walter knew even less. What Charlesville did know, and knowing it was his strength, was that the rotary wing industry represented a quick, but risky, track back into economic prominence for an old, faltering, no-longer competitive firm. As the saying went, he bet the franchise on Harry. By doing so, he hoped never to have to compete with U.S. makers, such as Boeing, Douglas, Lockheed, and McDonnell, who were prominent for their manufacture of fixed-wing aircraft. Charlesville felt he might better compete in the fledgling helicopter industry now being born in the U.S. and Europe.

On the road, heading south from San Juan toward the mountains, Patty, sitting in front next to Don, showed Charlesville, sitting directly behind Don, some of her work.

Walter, not really seeing the work, dismissed Patty as a flack, someone Harry had hired. He knew Charlesville would judge her the same way, although Charlesville found Patty charming. Patty was good-looking in a healthy sort of way more typical of the Americans than of the French. She had lovely blue eyes and straight nose.

Charlesville pretended to be flattered when Patty told him he would photograph like a man in his thirties. "It is because my life has been so easy," he said, gently and patronizingly facetious. He had lost much of his family in the war.

If Charlesville was charming, it was in large part because his English accent was charmingly French. Walter, by contrast, spoke a crisp English, excellent French, excellent Castilian, and he was not charming in the least. He derogated the Spanish he heard spoken in Puerto Rico. A Bavarian by birth, he also spoke Italian and Dutch, knew some Portuguese, and had learned a smattering of Russian.

"So I have to wait a week?" Charlesville asked, bringing up the matter again of General Weggoner's purported visit.

"Yes," said Don.

"And you?" Charlesville asked Patty. "What do you think? Will General Weggoner come to Ponce next week?"

"I have no idea," Patty said.

"But if Harry says so?"

"If Harry says so, yes."

"It must be the truth," Charlesville teased.

"It must be," Patty said.

"I have a business to run," Charlesville said. "Have you ever been to Marseille?"

"No," Patty answered.

"You must come," he said. "Have you ever been to Wright Field?"

"Not there either," she answered.

"Nor I," he said. "Tell me, what do you do for Harry?"

"I work for *Life*," she answered.

"Ah, *that* I know about," he said.

On seeing Patty's work, Walter changed his opinion of her. She was more than a flack, or other than a flack. Her photographs depicted men and machines of the U.S. Army Eighth Air Force; none other than the men Walter's friends tried to kill, and perhaps had, who could say? But they were the same men who tried to kill Walter's friends, too, and perhaps had, and they were the men who had bombed Germany by day, in B-17s and B-24s, and who had flown fighters to escort those formations. Walter's sister was killed by a bomb. He looked away, out his window, at the countryside that passed.

"And Don?" Charlesville asked. "How is the drafting?"

"Few more days," Don replied, meaning soon he'd be finished with the *as-builts*, drawings that depicted the aircraft as built.

"When are you coming to France, to work for me?" Charlesville asked. "Then you can take as long as you want."

"I'm doing that already," Don said, and all of them laughed.

Charlesville had control over Harry, because his money paid for the project. And Harry had control over Don. Charlesville knew there was little of note Don would likely volunteer about Harry.

Patty turned toward Walter, directly behind her. Raw-boned, gangly, with bony cheeks and hair as blonde as straw, Walter looked older to Patty than Charlesville, although he confessed to being just twenty-nine. Walter had been a logistical pilot, supplying the German Sixth Army in the East. "It's too late for Harry to offer the ship for sale to our army," he said, in what passed for his effort at humor. When no one laughed, he explained to Patty that the German Sixth Army had fallen at Stalingrad. But she knew that, too, and still no one laughed.

Russia seemed the only story concerning Walter: the German offensives of 1941 and '42, leading to the rout outside Stalingrad in the winter of '43. The winter in which Germany had lost a million men. Mentally, as she looked at Walter, Patty posed him for a shot, getting him in a quarter-profile from the right, the better to get that head-hung blankness of Walter's eyes. She'd seen that blankness in punched-out fighters; she'd seen it in the crewmen of bombers; the face of a twenty-mission man. The RAF had that stare. It hardly mattered what men flew, or for whom. "Do you think about Russia?" she asked, as she turned him, in her mind, this way and that.

"Mm," Walter answered, for yes, and the panoply of Russia seemed to open and withdraw, behind the blue winter of his stare.

Patty turned again to Charlesville. "If you don't mind my asking," she said, "why is it you would hire a German, especially so soon after the war?"

"I got him cheap," answered Charlesville, simply.

As they drove, wind caressed her, and she picked at the buttons of her blouse. They were passing through foothills near Caguas. She found herself being drawn repeatedly to Don, who was in her eyes by far the most attractive and appealing of the three. Charlesville was photogenic, but seemed solemn. Walter was forlorn. Don, by comparison, looked regal and proud. She did like his stern eyes, and that odd, puckish mouth, with those cupid-shaped lips he kept pursed. He was thoughtful and laconic.

Don pretended he could not hear when people spoke; pretended he was invisible as he drove. He liked listening, especially *invisible listening*. It was an old role, one he had learned young. He liked hearing Patty speak. She had a pleasant, lyrical timbre in her voice.

Charlesville smiled, watching Don ignore Patty, watching Patty regard Don. Charlesville felt confirmed in the sense that Americans were just like the French.

Since he was avoiding eye contact, Patty began framing Don for yet another shot she only mentally took. She had been mentally shooting him all day. If he had chosen not to be her peer, she was making him her subject.

When she turned once more, to engage Charlesville in conversation, she saw Charlesville gazing out at the countryside. He seemed lost in his thoughts.

Challenged by the road, Don relished the drive, even in Harry's old Plymouth. As the road grew steeper, beyond Caguas, the turns were hairpin, and, having arrived at some considerable height, the road yielded on the right to a panorama of the valley and the plain. The highway served trucks, and trucks and cars alike used horns to announce their coming to the curves.

She spoke of England and the months she had spent there. This time, as she spoke, Don looked over. She had continued to study his face as he drove, and since, for some time, he had not been returning her gaze, she had come increasingly to feel an impunity. It shocked her, then, to be met once again by his gaze. She broke off, blushing. Don blushed, too. Beyond words, he saw her intent. His was to suffer, hers to pursue.

Don remembered a saying he had heard. He had heard it as a joke, albeit one that concerned the effects on a man of seeing what he shouldn't: "*El que ve es el que sufre,*" Don said, doing a fair job, Patty thought, on the Spanish.

"And what does it mean?" she asked.

"The one who sees is the one who suffers," he said.

"Your Spanish is improving," Walter interposed, condescendingly.

Patty connected the sense of the saying to the war and her job. She had gone to England thinking the war would be an adventure, and that aviation was romantic. She had come back nearly crushed by what she had discovered there. She had gotten to know many flyers, mostly combatants, mostly her age. Many of them died, and almost all died violently.

But all Don had meant to convey in suggesting the remark, that the one who sees is the one who suffers, was that he had liked what he saw when he looked in her eyes, and was sorry for it because he would have to suffer. He had found her attractive, but by no means did he include her in plans.

Patty smoked. Even with windows rolled down, the car was moving so slowly up the grade of the mountain that the smoke from her cigarette continued to remind him, not only how hard it was to quit, but, conversely, how easy it would be to resume. He had quit the year before, on his birthday; forty-one.

To her, no small part of Don's appeal stemmed directly from her sense of taboo, and that part of the appeal she found exciting. It made Don look better and better, and allowed her to rationalize away all imperfections and objections. It allowed her to exaggerate. She was with somebody she had a right to be with, but was with him in a way increasingly affectionate, and she was having to rationalize what looked more and more like an instance of having crossed over some line. She couldn't rationalize. She was giving in.

Don was her listener, captive, as it were, behind the wheel, and she aired her views. She also continued plucking at her blouse. Against the altering face of the world going by, the mountain air, that sweetness, continued caressing her from the window.

Don liked the idea of Patty's aunt Alice having moved to Puerto Rico to live. He thought Puerto Rico was the nicest place *anyone* could live, because it had the nicest people and much less racial prejudice than any place he knew. When he mentioned to Patty that he was thinking about staying on in Puerto Rico, she found herself, absurdly enough, beginning to think about staying on in Puerto Rico as well.

In the mountain town of Cayey they stopped for *merienda*, a customary, late-afternoon snack. Over rich, locally grown coffee, Charlesville discussed Indo-China. "Last October," he said, "I was in Viet Nam for the signing of a cease fire that took effect on October twenty-ninth. I was there with six other businessmen. We were not there to assess the truce. We were there to evaluate France's military needs in quelling an insurrection. While talks toward a settlement were proceeding, French forces foolishly bombed Bac Ninh, to the effect that, now, no parties indigenous to Viet Nam trust us, or our motives, or our law, all of which change, it would seem, from one month to the next.

"On that day, the twenty-ninth of October, the six of us and two pilots flew north along the coast toward the provincial capital of Hue. We flew over countryside as serene and beautiful as any on earth. Then, snipers opened fire on us from below, out of all that beauty. Their fire struck the ship. Two men onboard were killed. I was wounded. And some miles farther the ship went down, fortunately crashing on the beach. More of us were injured in the crash. The French of course came searching for us, aided by the Cochin-Chinese from the south, and eventually they did find us, or I would not be here to tell you. But it took two full days—the longest days I have ever spent—to get us to safety and medical attention. They . . . I say *they*, but we, *we* had no proper rescue craft. What do you suppose the moral of that story is?"

"Helicopters," said Patty.

"This girl is very smart," Charlesville said. "I want helicopters. France needs helicopters. And in Ponce sits the helicopter France needs." Alive to the cue, Patty set up her camera and shot his picture. "Do you have your theme?" Charlesville asked.

"Money," Patty answered, bringing a smile to Charlesville's lips. Don was pleased, too. Patty had been around but a day, and already knew all there was.

"But tell me," Charlesville quizzed her. "If I sell to the Americans, how will France get its helicopters?"

"From the Americans," she answered. "The Americans are forgiving France its war debt."

Charlesville nodded. "By the same token, I can sell directly to the French."

"Which eliminates Harry as a middleman," said Don.

"That is right," said Charlesville. "When are you coming to work for me?" he asked again. "And when is Julio?" He winked at Patty. "You should see the south of France in April."

When they resumed their drive, it rained, a brief but intense deluge typical of the mountains in the late afternoon. The rain was blinding, and all traffic, Don included, waited it out on the shoulder of the road. As they waited, Patty told them a story. There was a guy she had seen in England, carried from his bomber at the end of the day, and she took his picture. Three days later, while developing film, she realized that she had taken a picture of the very same guy, but earlier, in the morning, when he was alive and able, boarding his ship. The truly gruesome part of the story was that it had been a matter of chance, because she had hung the two prints side-by-side, that she recognized it was the same guy in both pictures. Her world had existed through the camera. The instrument she had used at one time to get in touch with her life, and reach out to people, had divorced her from life, and from the people being touched. Even today, on a bad day, she relapsed, and there seemed no world outside the scope of the lens.

"'*El que ve es el que sufre*,'" Don repeated.

"Yes," she said, but she felt better now, like old times, mostly. Not one to subscribe to the school of thought that held that the camera, and therefore the person behind it, should be invisible, Patty, to the contrary, was again using photography as a means of rejoining the world. Photography to her was eminently a social art, and she used it as such.

When the rains subsided, and they were underway again, she resumed her fascination with Don's eyes, while her own eyes kept roaming the features of his face. In profile, his nose had seemed at first unduly flat, but, by now, she had grown to like it. He seemed so at ease as he drove. Enjoying the onset of evening, he had a wonderful and quick smile, and, when he looked at her directly, it unnerved her. But, being unnerved was a sense she found sweet, and sweetness of that sort was exciting, and excitement was something she craved. It had been a long time since a man had paid Patty the attention Don paid. As they drove, he supported her conversation. He did not judge, or seem to. It had been a long time since she had boyfriends. Since England, she was mournful. "Your skin is beautiful," she said, gratuitously and so boldly that she was unnerving even to herself. But it was no lie. To her, he looked like the rock of the mountain. She could imagine his children being sweet, noble, upright, and she realized she was imagining them as hers. How utterly unrealistic she could be!

Past Aibonito, Don stopped again, on the shoulder of the road called the *Asomante*, the mountain road that, at its higher elevations, gave them a view of the southern coast of Puerto Rico. Don cherished the mountains, and knew every road. He was very much at home by himself here, and often came alone just to draw. "Do you gentlemen mind?" he asked Charlesville and Walter, asking because there would be a few moments' delay. But both were asleep; they were running on different clocks.

Outside the car, from the mountain's edge, Patty could see twenty miles, a vista that included the Caribbean.

Just before sunset, the sun appeared, as if born a second time, descending out of clouds. In an instant the entire southern coast, as far as the eye could see, from the town of Coamo at the foot of the mountain, to the blue Caribbean, to the *tulipán* tree that stood on a jut on the side of the mountain across the valley from Patty, all of it lit up. From one infolded road, through an arcade of ferns, to another, ridges, hems of clouds, flared, all bursting with the energy of light. The sun lay on the brim of the earth. Patty shot into sun. She shot into glare. She shot into aura. She shot into haze. None of these mattered. She had done it for Don.

Outside, too, while Patty had been waiting for her moment, Don had drawn a sketch of her: Patty at work. Patty intent. Patty setting up for a shot. He worked very fast, much faster than she did. She turned and discovered he had drawn her, capturing not only some semblance of her, but, also, the panorama of the coast.

"That's quite remarkable," she said, duly impressed; indeed, flattered, and only just now seeing Don cared.

On the other hand, she could see she cared a great deal. "I'd like to take your picture," she asked.

"Go ahead," Don said.

A truck came by, up the hill, slow as a river barge pushing

against current, growling away in low gear. At the approach of each turn, the driver sounded his horn, in true mountain fashion, to alert the unwary and oncoming. He hollered to Don, going by, and saluted Patty with a nod.

The *Asomante* had been hewn, blasted, and cleaved out of rock. On one side of the road, the mountain rose, topped off in sun; and on the other, the cliff plummeted, often a thousand feet, ending in shadow and ravine. Here and there, they had passed roadside crosses, simple white structures implanted by the bereaved to mark the point some traveler had plunged. "It's strange," Patty said, "that in a moment's inattention, one can fall." For whatever reason she had come to Puerto Rico, she would at this juncture and from this moment on have to reckon with the presence of Don.

She backed Don to the rock, his back to the mountain. "One becomes very light," she told him, as if suspending all consequence and time.

Respectful of death, Don's own life took its turns. Behind his head bled the spring of the rock, and the minerals of the water had reddened the face of the stone. The last sunlight in his face was burnished orange, admixed with strong yellow and red. Don's face had hardened, creased by years. But the ancient rock he stood before had softened, worn by time. For purposes of compromise, man and mountain reached accord; one had yielded the roadbed and the other dressed the wound. She shot his stillness, holding the shutter open five seconds, while, in turn, Don froze his blood.

She thought again of those white crosses. Those who came this way found one journey interrupted and another, ever longer, soon to start. "How odd," she said. "One starts out from San Juan and goes to heaven."

Don's resistance was no better than her own, despite a lifetime of preparing his reserve. He lacked expectations regarding Patty, but still loved surprise. It made him laugh. Odd, indeed. He wanted a smoke and he bummed one of hers. The truth was that years before he heard the adage, *el que ve es el que sufre,* he knew the truth supporting it. He had grown up to love being wounded;

the love of pain had nurtured him, and there was indeed another side of suffering, where what began as exquisite ended up exquisitely sweet. To be black in America Don had trained in the best dungeons on earth. One had to know nothing to learn. She loved his eyes. When she had held open the shutter of the camera he had poured out his heart through his eyes. "Will you stay in Puerto Rico?" Patty asked.

"I hope to God," he answered her. "They treat me like I'm white."

She had shot him in color, but didn't have to. In England, where she had never once used color film, there was no place like this one to compare.

By nightfall, they had reached Ponce and *La Casa Laracuente*, where Charlesville and Walter would stay, as guests of Antonio. After letting the two men out, Don drove on with Patty to Alice's, where Patty was staying. When they pulled into Alice's drive, they saw Alice was home. Buenos Aires, where Alice lived, was one of Ponce's newer neighborhoods, with modest, one-story homes of block and cement-faced construction. Several teachers were Alice's neighbors.

Patty had been invited to Ponce's *Club Deportivo* that evening. She and Alice were to be Antonio's guests, along with Harry, Charlesville, and Walter, for dinner at the *club*, and dancing. Patty wondered to herself how she might broach the subject of inviting Don to join them, since she knew Antonio liked Don, and so did Alice, and she was certain Don would be welcome.

But Don, too, had a subject in mind, equally difficult to put into words. He wanted to tell Patty how much he had enjoyed being with her through the day. He didn't want Patty to think he was presuming, but just to know that he had found her to be special. Above all, he wanted her to see him as a gentleman, but he felt at a loss, if not for the words, then the nerve.

"I had a wonderful time," Patty said, in no hurry to get out.

"I did, too," he said to her.

"It was fun," she said, and wished she hadn't used that word. *Fun* was stupid. *Fun* was dumb. *Fun* was too mild a word. Both were feeling the tug. But the words were not easy. "Would you like to join us for the evening?" she asked, summoning finally all her nerve.

"Okay," Don said, not knowing where it was they were going, and too astonished at himself to think about it. "I'll have to go home first and change."

"Antonio invited us to the *Club Deportivo*," Patty said.

"I'm sorry," said Don, with no visible emotion at all. "I can't go there."

"Why not?" she asked.

"I'm not white," he told her.

She was mortified on hearing him answer, mortified at her own stupidity, her tactlessness in having asked, in presuming; mortified that she had accepted, unwittingly, an invitation to a place that was segregated, although she would not have thought twice about such an invitation had it come to her in Baltimore. She was shocked at how insensitive her invitation to Don must have sounded. "I didn't know," she whispered back.

"I know you didn't," he said, to let her off the hook, for he was touched by the invitation, even as he was hurt by being unable to accept it. She had named what was likely the one place in Ponce where he couldn't go; the last bastion, as it were, of obvious racism. "Thank you," he said, getting out of the car. When she got out, too, drawn by his hand, he helped with the door of the house. "I did enjoy your company," he said, knowing precisely the limit and bound. "I had a wonderful day."

Forgiven, she gave him her cheek.

That night, Patty lay in bed in the back room of Alice's house, looking through the gauze of the mosquito net at the gauze-white, luminous moon, and watched its traverse through the leaves of the mango that stood in the patio outside. The voice of the *coquí* sang its two-note song, ever the same, tonic, then the octave above in rapid succession, sounding for the world like the clinking of bottles. The serenade persisted through the night, echoing the length and breadth of Puerto Rico, *coquí, coquí*, so that the *coquí* outside the window led ultimately, or responded, to one in San Juan, in the mountains, in Mayagüez or Fajardo. *Coquí. Coquí* never varied. Mixing words she had heard and had read, Patty spoke Spanish in dream, as if a fever concocted her language. In dream, she ordered in Spanish from the menu in Cayey. In dream, she spoke Spanish with Don. She told herself she did, and the sound receded to infinity. *Coquí. Coquí.* She had learned a language, taking no lessons, and yet awoke to find the words made no sense. She bobbed, like a cork on the surface of a lake, entering and removing herself from dream. *Coquí.* Which was the first *coquí* in the world? So much jasmine filled the room. Moonlight littered the eaves of the neighboring white house. The moon was *la luna. Coquí.* She drew a map in her mind, fell asleep and saw the world. Alice's cat, Fred, roamed the hall. *Coquí.* Who was she and why was she here? She rose and smoked and fell asleep with the smoke in her lap. *Coquí.* The moon's bias could reach from the window to the kitchen to the table top to the desk.

Patty sat in the kitchen drinking Earl Grey tea. Alice snored. The night knew no dawn. The clock persisted. Patty slept and she woke and she smoked. She thought and she listened. Who had told her *coquí* was a frog? She saw Don's face but, trying to see it, could no longer make it appear. The sound receded, the anvil chorus of *coquí.* Each frog knew the beginning and the end, who called, who responded, how long it should wait in refrain. The sea brought jasmine, and the desert brought bloom. If she reinvented her face, who would care? Did her nose join her forehead *too high*, did her smile cut too far in her cheeks? She could change. When she was thirteen she sat before a mirror practicing looks. Sainted Nun. Martyr. Glamour Queen. All American Girl. She practiced her *expressions*. Spicy. Naughty. Nice. Demure. Claudette Colbert. But Claudette had round eyes; oh no. And Patty's nose was too straight. She photographed best from the left, especially when looking surprised. Her lips were too thin, her cheek bones too high. Her skin was like sunshine. Her skin was like peaches and cream. The cock crowed but no sign of the dawn, and far in the distance tolled the bell of a church.

Coquí. The scents of bergamot and jasmine mixed with smoke. Her legs were her wonderful feature. She was strong. Paws of a cat on the bed. *Coquí.* The moon had gone, but now the breeze had stirred. She knew all the answers but long lost simple questions. The air was so soft and so sweet. Patty rose. She would not sleep again. *Coquí.* Love had a beginning and no end.

—

CHAPTER FOUR

Harry's house was a shuttered, wooden structure raised half a story above ground, and consisting of two rooms in back—one for Harry as bedroom and office; the other for Elisa, his secretary—a kitchen, and a larger front room that served all the men as lunchroom. Harry's cook, Minnie, did the cooking and always left a meal for Harry's supper at night.

But, on Sunday, Minnie and Elisa were off, so Harry had to arrange things himself. In a corner of the front room, he put up a tripod and pegboard, and on the pegboard pinned a chart of Puerto Rico. Red twine depicted an eight-legged course around the island.

When Maxwell and Lon arrived, they turned on the radio in the front room to hear the broadcast of the game. Ponce's baseball team, *Los Leones*, was engaged with arch rival Caguas-Guayama in the Winter League Championship, a best-of-seven series in which Ponce had already lost the first three games. Since everybody knew that in a best-of-seven series no team ever comes back after being down three games to none, Maxwell and Lon held out little hope that Ponce would break precedent.

When Julio arrived, Charlesville met him in the parking lot and accompanied him to the house. As they walked, Charlesville again offered him a job in France.

"I may take you up on that offer," Julio said, knowing Carlota would do anything to get away from Harry and out of Puerto Rico.

When Don arrived, Julio took him aside and told him about Charlesville's offer.

"Did you accept it?" asked Don.

"Not yet," Julio answered.

"Don't do it," said Don.

"Carlota will kill me if I refuse."

"Stall for time. You don't have to refuse."

The problem was, as Julio saw it, the flight to Wright Field was not only uncertain, but, if they went forward with that flight, it would mean there would be no going to France. "Do you know how much our aircraft's going to weigh when we take off to fly to Florida?" Julio asked.

Of course, Don did know. They would be carrying six tons of gasoline. "Too much," he replied.

"Who will support my widow and kids?"

"Not me, that's for sure," said Don. But, in saying so, he could also have included Harry.

"Then you'll stick with Harry, regardless?"

"I promised him I'd try," said Don.

Well into the ballgame, Walter arrived, and, finally, Bill and Diego. The meeting began. Since Harry's purpose was to mask his preparations for the flight to Wright Field, he detailed the "air show" the men would ostensibly provide for General Weggoner. "Key will be a nonstop flight of four circuits around the island," Harry said, as he pointed out the eight-legged course, marked off by the yarn on the chart, representing 253 statutory miles. "Four such circuits," he explained, "amounts to a world's record. The current distance for a helicopter flying a closed circuit course unrefueled is 621 miles, set last fall in a Sikorsky R-5 owned and flown by the Army. Come next Saturday, I propose we start by going around the coast of Puerto Rico two-and-a-half times, taking off from Ponce early Saturday morning, so that, when we arrive at San Juan in the middle of the third lap, we stage a "rescue" of sailors—prearranged of course— who will be in life rafts in the shallows off the beach." To assuage Charlesville's anxiety, he added, "This exercise will be done so near shore, there will be no danger to the ship."

He continued. "Using the winch, we will hoist twenty sailors onboard from their rafts, then fly them half-way round the island, back here to Ponce. When we arrive in Ponce, we will discharge the sailors, then embark on our fourth and final circuit."

To make things official, since Walter was a member of the *Fédéracion Aéronautique Internationale*, Harry appointed him field judge, to record the flight as an official world's record, not only for distance but also for takeoff weight, which Harry had estimated to be in the vicinity of 32,000 pounds, a figure so overwhelming for a helicopter that, by merely mentioning it, Harry caused all his men to laugh. But Harry reminded them that, nevertheless, 32,000 pounds was the design weight of the aircraft.

After appointing Walter field judge, Harry appointed Patty press secretary. At the end, he asked, "Did I leave anything out?"

"Could you explain it again?" Walter asked. He had a ferocious hangover.

Of all people in the room, Don seemed most intent on listening to Harry's plan. Even Harry was impressed by how well Don was faking. But Don was balancing his own priorities, because, ruse or no, if they flew to Miami, he would have to face the danger of taking off in that ship at the same gross weight Harry had spoken of—32,000 pounds—of which 12,000 pounds would be gasoline. Against that danger stood the potential glory of a successful flight to Wright Field. The glory was great, but the danger could cost him his life. Patty was attentive to Don.

Charlesville, sitting back in his chair, asked if they would undertake a practice flight today. "Certainly," said Harry. "We'll fly to San Juan and back, and rescue Walter."

"He appears to be in need of rescue," Charlesville said. "I am intrigued by your plan. I agree that if you can demonstrate your ship before your general, perhaps we really can, after all these months of delay and over-runs, manage to get a contract from your Army."

Don looked at Patty, having caught her in a stare at him. She blushed. Harry asked Don for the *as-builts*. "Not finished," Don said.

"Why aren't they?" Harry asked; not really a question, a demand.

"I don't draw on days I fly," said Don.

"Always something. You had more than enough time," Harry told him, and shot a glance toward Don. Don blushed. Did Harry know these things or was he just showing off for Charlesville? Don didn't ask Harry what Harry knew. The question whether Don had ample time, or any time at all, was as complex a question as any Don had ever faced. Yet, to Harry, it was simple, and Don felt his cheeks begin to burn; he felt the rage seething from within. Old words, cast as charges, implications: lazy, shiftless, floated up, not as spoken but as thought. The as-builts were not something done in a day. They took weeks, and the work on them was constrained by the work that was actually done on the ship. Harry knew that. Harry knew what he was about. Julio was right. The smarter plan was for them to go to France.

Changing tact, Harry wished them well. "Gentlemen, enjoy your flight," he said, and the briefing was adjourned.

"Harry is boss," said Charlesville to Don, outside the house, where Harry couldn't hear.

"He is," Don agreed.

"But I am Harry's boss," said Charlesville. "And I treat men as peers."

"Thank you," said Don, not at all insensitive to Charlesville's point.

Then Charlesville sided with Julio again, accompanying him as they walked. "Today we see the ship in action, no?" Charlesville asked.

"Yes," Julio said, expressing the hope that all would go well.

"You are a great engineer," Charlesville said. Julio was pleased. "France needs great engineers. You have plans for another project after this?"

"Planning's easy," Julio said.

"Come to Marseille, and I'll help you make the plans become reality. I can give you a staff, and resources. And I can give you more time."

"Time would be a luxury," said Julio.

"Plus much better pay."

"I'm listening." Julio smiled. Charlesville certainly was pitching the deal.

Don, walking by himself, looked out at the ship in the distance. His thoughts turned inward, and he began to prey upon himself. The very desperation of Harry's plan made him feel like the scapegoat for all of their troubles. By the same token, had he been white, they wouldn't have had so many troubles. The ship would have been sold by now or under contract. Don felt they were looking to him to do the impossible now, to atone for the bad luck of being black.

Don had days—many—when he hated Harry Baird, and today of course was one of them. Today was certainly that. Unable to distinguish between his fear and his hate, between his fear of failure and his hatred of Harry, who accepted no blame for any loss, Don now approached today's flight as if the ship were an enemy, too, as if the field were the place he would die. Thus he hastened his steps toward the ship, hurrying to get aboard, rushing toward the tree that would hang him.

Today was not drastically different from others. Every day Don flew he woke with icy fingers of adrenaline, tickling his guts at three a.m. Harry's plan was an excuse for his fear, nothing more, a target for hate, an everyday occurrence of self-loathing in Don. He had ridden to work on his bicycle today. On days that he flew he used that early morning, three-mile-long ride to gauge his own physiology, to correlate the effects of his fear on performance. After all, as he reckoned it, he wouldn't want to open a throttle too far just because his heart was pounding in his chest. It was not flying, but test flying, specifically for Harry, that threatened Don, or so went the argument. During his ride to the field, Don had summoned his God and uttered his prayers. The God to whom Don prayed was personal and loving, ever the Friend in Don's time of need. To Don, following Luke, the kingdom of God lay within, and he found access to peace, to the extent that he did, by turning within for God, in the stillness of his own divine soul. As to desperate Harry, Don was unable to reconcile the loving God he knew loved him with the hatred he felt at such moments toward Harry. Indeed, his hatred of Harry was so intense that he murdered Harry in thought, by hand, face to face, and eye to eye. Abashed by such violence, but never sorry he felt it, Don asked himself, "What kind of God allows for this?" And he always answered, "None."

Arriving at the ship, Don could see in his mind's eye the concatenation of thoughts that had erupted like a blaze, from spark, to flicker, to flame; from flame to fire, to roaring conflagration. Its certain sequence went: he sees Harry and, rather than submit to Harry's abuse, resigns; having resigned, he leaves Baird Field, then Ponce; he returns to the States unemployed.

Unable to find work, he's a bum. That was breakfast. As surely as the condemned counted steps, Don counted his toward the ship.

Patty loitered by herself beside the hangar, looking in through the window of the small shed that formed the hangar's annex. The glass was so streaked, yellowed, and caked with dust that the office inside appeared covered in dust. She saw rolls of drawings pigeon-holed along the back wall, aviation magazines and girly magazines on a desk, a brass spittoon, empty pop bottles grayed with dust, a Vargas girl calendar on the wall, a swivel chair and a radio.

She entered the hangar. Bill Pyrtle passed by, rolling a cart that bore four fire extinguishers, a box marked *first aid*, goggles, and ear mufflers. The first aid box bore prints left by greasy thumbs and fingers; signs, she imagined, of hurried openings. She paused at Don's drafting table, and looked at drawings he had made. She was quite taken by these, but could not say why. She concluded it was because she knew that they were his.

The interior hangar smelled of burnt sawdust, vestigial from the lumberyard. The smell raised a familiar sense, from childhood. Patty's grandfather had been a carpenter, ultimately a shipwright. When she was a child, her grandfather let her watch him use the saws, and to practice using them herself. She remembered his white hair and the smell of his cigar. Birds nested beneath the eaves of the hangar. She thought of barns, sheds, dim shop light swimming with motes of dust. She thought of hardware stores she knew as a child, towed by her grandfather's hand. About her were tools and equipment, the smell of grease and the sight of rags; projects in the midst of completion. She saw stockpiles of tube frame and pipe, torches, acetylene, scraps of paper, and notations. There were old workbenches; in back, a sofa, its springs popped and its mauve upholstery long out-of-date. Pants hung on nails on the wall. The door stood open into the toilet.

Bill Pyrtle again broke her reverie, showing her the new auxiliary tank the men had built. Constructed of aluminum, with interior baffles, the tank held one thousand gallons; filled with fuel, it weighed close to seven thousand pounds. He showed her how the tank would nestle, under the belly of the ship, between the struts. He pointed out materials they had used to build the ship: new casting alloys, tubular magnesium, aluminum, some steel. He showed her the cross section of a main rotor blade, pointing out the chord and the spar; then the chord of the pylon that supported the front rotors, the section, the spar and the truss. She looked at extruded magnesium stringers and magnesium hot-formed frames. There were needle bearings for transmissions, and lead/silver/indium bushings that had failed. There seemed no end to the nuts, the bolts, the types of screws and fasteners; boxes and bins. Bill showed her the spalls, kept in catalogued boxes, preserved like precious minerals on display. They formed a record through time of a sequence of failures, evolving to an eventual success. He held up what had been a transmission gear; the gear was missing two teeth. But when Bill removed the dentures from his mouth, he, too, was missing two teeth, right up in the front, where a car wreck had knocked them both out. "Life imitates art," he cracked.

When Patty arrived at the ship, she went around forward to the cockpit, and, looking up through the Plexiglas nose, saw Don. In part because his position was elevated as he sat in the cockpit, and in part because of the way he sat, including the expression on his face, she was seized by the resemblance between Don and the statue of Abraham Lincoln she had seen on the Mall in Washington, D.C. Don's knees protruded into the foreground of her view, as had Lincoln's when she took a picture of the statue; for what she remembered was being taken there as a child, and that, once there, she had taken one of her first photographs, using the very first camera she owned. She remembered now that, to take that picture, she had looked up, framing the shot over Lincoln's great knees, as had thousands of photographers before her and since. Only later she realized how common a view that shot was, for, given the size of the subject, and the smallness of man, no one ever looked in Lincoln's eyes.

But Don looked down, as Lincoln could not. His eyes met hers. He felt reassured she was there. It was Patty who broke off. He neither smiled nor averted his eyes.

Patty joined Julio for the preflight inspection, and Julio explained as they went around the ship that the Army had given Harry the ship's two engines after first having seized them from the Germans as spoils from the Bavarian works at Adlershof. Julio thought they were the first engines built to generate one horsepower for every cubic inch of displacement. Remarkably fuel efficient, each engine had thirty-two cylinders and a displacement of sixteen hundred cubic inches. They were air-cooled and supercharged. "We think the Germans intended the engines for a long-range bomber," Julio said.

Following Julio, Patty climbed onboard. The deck was four feet above ground. Inside, the cabin was not only hot, but the light was garish, owing to the contrast of sunlight and shadow. In the middle of the cabin stood the winch, whose purpose was to retrieve cargo, human or otherwise. There was room inside the cabin for twenty men.

The deck was plywood, an exception to Harry's claim of an all-metal ship. But the rest of the interior was trussed in aluminum, in a pattern that arrested Patty's eye. Triangles and welds repeated. Overhead, oil lines and drive trains ran forward and aft. Aft, a bulkhead separated the empennage from the cabin. Further reducing headroom on either side of the cabin, firewalls for the engines intruded. The ship, though large, was also compact, its space at a premium both inside and out.

Julio explained that most of the expense of the project involved the rotor hubs, transmissions, drive trains, and the rotors themselves, items that represented custom work. The remainder of the ship was built of surplus materials, and he led her forward, on a catwalk to the right of the bulkhead, beyond which, a step down to the left, was his own station and the engineer's panel. He squeezed into the seat, which faced aft against the port side of the ship. "My office," he said. Beside him, to *his* left, a folded jump seat would accommodate a second engineer, or at least another person. To Julio's right, a window looked out. On a small table before him, he kept his clipboard and flight log. Beside him hung a fire extinguisher. The panel housed the ship's instrumentation. Valved fuel lines ran overhead. Behind Julio's head, the bridge bulkhead shielded him from the forward gearing and transmission.

"Harry never flies?" she asked.

"Never," said Don, answering from the cockpit.

"But you will let me go with you?" she asked.

"Tell our story," Don answered, knowing that *Life* wouldn't be interested in Marseille. She stuck her head forward, through the bridge hatchway into the cockpit. Don sat in the left-hand seat, below the level of the hatchway. Given the Plexiglas nose, framed in aluminum mullions, sun shone directly in on him. He had chosen the hottest seat in Puerto Rico: in essence a greenhouse. Patty gasped. She thought the temperature was a hundred and twenty. "Hundred and thirty," said Don, dripping wet.

"You're welcome to it," she said, and withdrew.

"Want to hear a joke?" Julio asked, aft.

"Make it a fast joke," Patty said, because it wasn't just the cockpit; it was the entire interior of the aircraft that was stifling. She had burned her forearm just by touching a window ledge.

"When Sikorsky finished building his second helicopter, the model R-5, it was so loaded down with accessories that the only payload it could carry was a pilot and two oral messages."

"I don't get it," she said.

Outside, Julio continued, explaining that, during the war,

helicopters had been a low priority, because resources were tight, and because helicopters could not win the war. But now, in peacetime, it was money that was tight. The problem with the ship, as he saw it, was the scale of construction and complexity of design were too great for the money and time they had allowed for themselves.

"So you're saying that Colonel Anderson is right?" Patty said.

"Oh, he's right," Julio agreed. "What he doesn't understand is that I love this ship. So does Don. She's our baby. That's why we sit in there, in the sun. It's not entirely because we're nuts. But, truth be told, there are times when we hate the ship too."

She understood. She was pegged to her dream, as they were to theirs. Ambition drove them all. She was addicted to success. And, of course, she feared failure as death.

"Sometimes, I resent every moment I've spent here," Julio said. "Sometimes, I want to disavow responsibility for ever having worked on this ship. Just blame Harry."

"Our test flight program is compromised," Don agreed, looking out. "Everything is done in a hurry. Everything is built around selling."

"Are you frightened when you fly?" Patty asked.

"I'm not," Julio answered. "But then, I face backwards, so I'll never know what hit me."

"And you?" she asked Don, knowing that Don was frightened, but wanting to hear it from him.

"I'm frightened," Don told her, "because I'm facing forward and I see what's coming."

Patty wanted a shot of the rotors, since Julio had put so much of his time into designing and building the rotor heads. Julio told her she could shoot them best from above. To get there, she had to climb a steel scaffold, one of two that served the aircraft. The scaffold culminated in a platform nineteen feet above ground. She climbed, followed by Julio. Finally kneeling and terrified atop the platform, Patty was able to look out and somewhat down upon the rotors. Julio was right. The view was the best. The main rotor spanned seventy feet; the forward rotors, sixty.

But she was also able to see a fair distance northeast, to downtown Ponce and the tops of Ponce's buildings; southeast, to the seaport; and to the south over the scrub all along the coast to the sea. Julio chided her because she was afraid to let go of the support rail. But Patty, though she had been a good tree-climber in childhood, a good hill-climber in youth, who liked flying as a young adult, had never taken to roof tops, parapets, or platforms. She would never go off the ten-foot board at the pool. She hated high places that lacked hand-held support, and only climbed this one because she would do anything for a shot.

Julio kept chiding her. "Be like me," he said. "I'm half monkey." Then, with hardly a thought, he stepped out into space, from a rung of the scaffold across to the empennage of the ship, planting his foot below the main rotor mast and causing, as he stepped, the scaffold to recoil, just slightly, which in turned caused Patty to clutch and her heart to skip beats. "Sorry," Julio said, when he realized how much he had scared her. Effortlessly, with one hand, Julio secured himself to the hub of the main rotor, and leaned out, in the fork of two blades.

"Don!" he called. "Start the servos." Momentarily, Patty heard the whine of motors. "Just watch," Julio told her. "Left cyclic, Don!" he called down. Patty watched, then, as a vertical metal rod to the left of the mast rose; on the right side, one retreated. The rod pushed a metal swashplate that ringed the mast. The plate looked something like the bottom half of a set of drum cymbals. "See," Julio said, "the rod is attached to the ship, and therefore won't turn with the mast. The mast turns, driven by gears in the transmission."

An upper swashplate, coupled to the motion of its mate, which was now tilted up at the left, tilted too, and completed the resemblance, in Patty's view, of cymbals; the lower swashplate riding with the ship, the upper turning with the mast. A roller bearing between them mated and reciprocated their actions. *Like making love,* she thought, then caught herself thinking of Don, who was making all this happen from below.

"These rods turn pitchhorns," Julio told her, leading her

attention from one thing to the next. The upper plate transmitted its tilt through four different rods to the hub. Each rod stood apart from the others by ninety degrees. One rod thrust greatly, and one just a little; another retracted and the fourth retracted little. One pitchhorn cranked up, another down, and two barely moved. The horns conveyed their actions to the rotor blades ahead of them.

"I do understand it," she said.

All four of the blades then changed pitch.

Patty laughed. She let go of the rail and stood up, albeit shakily. Blades extended to either side of the scaffold. "I see the way a camera sees," she said. "If it's there to be seen, then I see it." Exhilarated now, she had lost her sense of fear. The scene was just impossible, not possible, absurd. She had set up the four-by-five on a tripod, installed film, wide-angle lens, and filter for the sun; to shoot a shot of casting, hinges, wristpins, flanges, blades. The hub, huge hub assembly, four feet wide, was a veritable jig of massive moving parts. Ball and ballroom, dancers, dance, and host. "Go ahead and point it out to me," she said. For Julio was the one who was insane, not her. Julio and Don. That much she saw. Their madness. Lovers' zeal.

"Rock the cradle!" Julio yelled, having a change in his day from bad to good. "Rock the cradle!" He could use another year to get it right. The pushrods pushed. The swashplates tilted left and right. The pitchhorns cranked and the blades changed pitch for the maypole dance.

She brought the Speed Graphic off the tripod to her eye in a hurry, ever ready, like a wink, and got off a good shot, handheld, of a face, two hands, and enough of the blade, enough of the hub, enough of the mast to give scale.

—

CHAPTER FIVE

Arriving in small groups, drawn as always by the prospect of a flight, townspeople had gathered at one end of Harry's field.

"Let's fly," said Don, as much to himself as to the others, for Lon and Bill had finished fueling the aircraft. The flight crew, today consisting of Julio, Don, Charlesville, Walter, Patty, and Maxwell, boarded the aircraft.

Charlesville, sitting next to Don as co-pilot, trusted Don, and, if anything, saw Don as too reserved. "You needn't be conservative," he said. "Nor treat the aircraft so gently."

"That's fine," said Don.

"Show me valor," Charlesville said. "I have my doubts about this 'air show.'"

"Sure," said Don.

In the engineering station, Julio took the seat by the window, with Patty beside him in the jump seat. Aft, Walter and Maxwell were in the cabin, sitting on the deck, leaning against the aft bulkhead. Walter was wearing Maxwell's bathing suit.

Don began the checklist. *Master switches* were set *off*. *Battery switches and inverters*—now switched *on*. He uncaged gyros. Intercom? *Intercom*. He and Julio put on headsets, throat mikes. The *air intakes* were *open*. *Waste gates—open*. Julio patted handles; no fancy stuff, all done by hand. *VHF set*—now was *on*. "There are days when I'd give anything to fly," said Don. "I still have such days, when I feel *young*."

"Gotcha'," Julio said. The *pitches* were now *bottomed*. The *rotors*—now were *braked*. "Hope today is one of them."

"Not bad," said Don. *Station frequency*—set to *station*. Really, like a brother, Julio was. "Back to intercom."

"Back to intercom."

"How 'bout you?"

"Just a kid," said Julio.

Service to gyros—was now *on. Artificial horizon*—*adjusted. Directional gyro*—was again *caged. Station elevation*—set to fourteen feet. "Relative humidity is seventy-four percent," said Julio. "Outside air temperature is eighty-nine degrees. Mark time."

"Eleven hundred twenty-two hours," said Don.

"Fuel quantity, logged at six thousand pounds in main one and two." Julio yelled from the window at Bill, who confirmed and gave the thumbs up. *Generators*—were now *off. Throttles*— *closed.* Fuel *mixture*—*rich.* Fuel *transfer valves and switches*— *closed.* "Where's your head?" Julio asked.

"I left my head in Aibonito," Don replied.

"Good enough."

"Where's yours?"

"Italy. No, in Spain. Majorca. Preferably without Carlota." *Starboard engine* clutch—*disengaged. Fuel selector*—*set by hand.*

"Prestart done," said Don.

"Prestart done."

"Fuel switch."

"Switch on." The fuel now flowed from the two main tanks.

"Fuel boost."

"Boost on." The Bendix motor pumped the fuel.

"Fuel pressure."

"Fifteen."

"Port master switch is—thrown."

"Port primed."

"All clear!" hollered Don.

"You're clear!" Lon yelled back. He stood by the extinguishers. Diego and Bill stopped work.

Don pressed the button and the port engine fired and ran. The sound was concussive, sharp, taking Patty by surprise. It shook the ship. Julio thought the engine sounded good. Quickly, the oil pressure rose to seventy-five pounds. Outside, Bill took mufflers from the cart. Charlesville, cupping his hand around his mouth, yelled to Don that the ship appeared to be long on stealth. Charlesville's mood was improving.

The starboard engine joined the port. Exhaust smoke peppered the ground and rose in a blue haze around the tail. Bill thought she was burning a little too much oil. Four pigeons flew abruptly from the eave of the hangar, and turned upwind without the slightest hesitation.

Don released the main rotor's brake to begin the exercise of rotor and turbo. At thirty-two hundred fifty rpm, engine speed, the rotor, geared down, was turning at flying speed, one hundred ten rpm, marrying the needles of both tachometers. Julio shut and opened the waste gate, engaging and disengaging the turbo, while Don pulled and bottomed pitches on the rotor. Manifold pressure surged and fell. The runup concluded with a check of magnetos.

Don concluded that Harry's evil lay in his ability to make a person think of him, even during circumstances that were otherwise pleasurable. It was an evil to capture one's attention, the way that Harry captured Don's. Julio told Don to pay attention, as they braked the main rotor, for Don's obsession with Harry could kill them. They began the exercise of the forward rotors, port engine and turbo. Julio owned the checklist, but Don was satisfied, and Don owned the flight. Forty-one was sometimes not old, thought Don. He was high. His thighs felt springy. Forty-one was sometimes a great age. He was light in the seat. He signaled out to yank the wheel chocks. He had his days.

"Hang on," said Julio, who liked to linger, or listen, while the ship was on the ground.

"You had your chance," said Don, who knew the ship was running fine. Don was *there*. The ship was *there*. He could count buttons on a kid's shirt when the kid was on the fence a hundred yards away, split hairs, read license plates of cars that sat, way off, in the parking lot. He was *there*. Bill Pyrtle gave thumbs up. Don could read the same gauges Julio read, hear what Julio heard. "Step down, you engineers," said Don. He owned the ship. She was his. And he addressed the ship directly, on her terms. "Come on, girl," he told her, and, sweet enough, she lifted off the ground.

Patty, startled at the noise, at the wind, at the difference between practice and for-real, at the change in the engines, which lost their hollow sound and sounded mottled and throaty as if seeming to dig in, suddenly discovered she was airborne, and was thrilled. With the ship only moderately loaded, Don had lifted off directly and turned directly upwind. They climbed, underway, while Julio pointed out to Patty the manifold pressure gauges, whose indications showed in the sudden surge that Don had throttled up, to thirty-eight inches of boost. Over the roar and vibration of engines and transmissions, Patty could hear the whine of the superchargers. When the ship passed the fence, leaving the field, it was already up forty feet, running at sixty miles an hour, and climbing. Ponce's seaport came into view, and momentarily, they had three hundred feet of air space below them.

En route, Julio gave Patty rules of thumb for engine performance. Every inch of manifold pressure equaled approximately 41.6 horsepower, which lifted approximately 416 pounds of weight. Hence: every horsepower lifted ten pounds. With turbo, more power, but each engine then consumed additional fuel, up to .45 pounds of fuel per hour per horsepower. With speed, the ship received a windfall of translational lift, a force sufficient at sixty miles an hour to effect a reduction in the fuel they would use of nearly forty percent. "Translational lift allowed us to carry the truck," Julio yelled, laughing, because they hadn't carried it very far.

At Cabo Mala Pascua, southeast of Maunabo, Don turned to follow the coastline northeast, toward Fajardo. Since their low level flight along the coast was smooth, Walter moved to the open hatchway of the cabin, where he could look out on Puerto Rico as it passed. He summoned Maxwell to join him. But Maxwell was queasy and intimidated by the prospect of the same open hatchway that Walter seemed so find so inviting. Walter was showing off, of course, sitting on his hands on the edge of the deck, a position all the more unnerving to

Maxwell, since, if the ship lurched, Walter would be pitched out to his death.

But Walter enjoyed sitting on the edge; he was at home there. The edge was not a thin line, but a large terrain, which, in one form or another, he found seductive. Walter should have been killed long ago, many times over, and he knew it. As a statistical likelihood, his continuing existence ought not to have occurred. He was a perseveration, a mental echo of himself.

Survival had divorced him from fear, from any actual, or real, self-preserving sense to flee death. Death was too concrete to be abstract, too banal. Walter had been inches and fractions of seconds away, many times. He liked the wind in his face. "I sleep nights," Walter yelled, apropos of nothing, really. But, he thought about death on balmy days. And he had not dreamed, not that he could remember, since the winter of 1943, the year in which all life froze in Russia.

Desperate, Maxwell pulled the safety gate closed over the hatchway, and locked it, for the gate was a device Maxwell himself had welded, as a testament to caution and an antidote to fools. Even so, vertigo and last night's drinking caught up with him, and, when he finally threw up, Walter thanked his lucky stars he sat upwind. It was not Walter's misfortune that so many of his friends had been killed. But, it was his tremendous good fortune to have sat upwind of Maxwell. After that, Maxwell retreated to the aft bulkhead again, this time to lie down. Walter went forward and told Julio.

Out in Vieques Sound, the destroyer *Buckley* was under way. Near Fajardo, everyone looked inland at the Sierra de Luquillo. It was raining in the highlands, just as Don had surmised.

"Are you coming to Marseille?" Charlesville yelled.

"I'll stay with Harry," Don yelled back.

"Why?" Charlesville grumbled, but Don didn't answer. As Charlesville viewed it, if Don stayed with Harry, Don would soon be unemployed.

Along the northern coast, heading westbound toward San Juan, the ship flew into rain. "Want me to turn back?" Don asked.

"No. Go on," Charlesville ordered. From the cockpit, the Atlantic Ocean looked majestic; gray and wind-swept. There was no confusing the Atlantic with the tranquil Caribbean. Don's choice to stay with Harry was not loyalty, but fear, Charlesville felt. Looking out his window toward the mainland U.S., invisibly distant beyond the curve of the earth and a thousand miles northwest of the ship, Charlesville considered how, if compared to France, the U.S. market represented incalculable wealth, and how only two years ago Charlesville had thought Harry would be the man who could tap it. Now, Charlesville was nearly certain Harry could not, and that he would do better on his own in Marseille. He would do better still, if he could hire Harry's men. "I want you to come to France," he said to Don. "Will you accept a job with me, if I close the project down?" Don looked nervously over. "Why should I wait for a week?" Charlesville asked. "How will that change the outcome? I can close it down today."

"Wright Field will buy this aircraft," said Don.

"Hmm. Show me valor," Charlesville said.

Below them unwound a ribbon of beach, the surf on the shore; palm trees and rain. The shacks of those who lived there passed. As with the families on the southern coast, here, too, the women, children, and the men of the coast were Negroes, the offspring of African slaves. "We're going seventy," said Don, apropos of the tail wind that now pushed them along. Nearer San Juan, the rain turned squally, the day became raw, and the sea beneath them, gray-green. Don held six hundred feet, following the line of the coast into the outskirts of the city. Rain, driven by rotorblast and slipstream, lashed cockpit and cabin, wetting Don, wetting Julio, and soaking Walter. Charlesville had free hands and closed his window. Then, the windshield wipers wouldn't work, so Don flew with his head out the window, to see. Charlesville fiddled with the wipers. The rain smeared and ran uphill when it hit the windshield. When Charlesville finally got the wipers working, Don blamed Julio for the poor design of the blade arcs. At bottom, Charlesville knew that Harry had lost control over the two men, Julio and Don, who meant most to him, who, more than anyone, were like Harry's sons. Fame had distracted Don, and money had seduced Julio. Charlesville was certain that the loss of leverage broke Harry's heart. Power was Harry's substitute for love.

Aft, Julio looked out, over Old San Juan, out across the bay, to the neighborhood of Bayamon, visible as a flat, distant vista. It was the place where he was born, and, seeing it, Julio realized that, in every literal sense, he had now risen above his origins.

Don flew along the beach and shoreline, into Old San Juan, west to the castle of El Morro. Built by the Spaniards to guard the entrance to San Juan Bay, El Morro belonged now to the U.S. Army, which had occupied it since the outset of the war. Don flew a descending left turn, bringing the ship about the opposite way, to parade it, as it were, before the castle. Gun ports, like ominous sockets, seemed to stare from the massive stone walls. As the ship turned, Patty took a picture, getting the castle, sea cliffs, surf crashing below, and the bay.

Retracing their route, Don overflew the seawall that bounded the oldest cemetery in San Juan, a place whose limestone markers stood blanched by four centuries of sun. The sight was touching, for below them, in graves, lay the bones of Conquistadors, who had followed Ponce de León. "Fountain of youth," Don called over the intercom, knowing Julio would know whom he meant. The reference, of course, was to Harry, who, like the Conquistadors, also wished to live forever. "They didn't find it," Don said to Charlesville, while wrestling with the thought that *no one does*.

A mile-and-a-half east of El Morro, having surveyed San Juan's coast and picked his spot, Don descended, hovering above rocks along the shore. Patty disembarked, to set up her camera on the beach. When she was clear of the ship, Don climbed and flew a few yards out to sea. "Go on," said Charlesville, when Don looked over to question him, for how could one show valor near the shore.

Ashore, along *Avenida Muñoz Rivera*, traffic stopped and people were gathering. When people asked Patty who she was, she identified herself as a photographer from *Life*.

Fifty yards out to sea, Don turned the ship southeast, heading toward shore but parallel to the swell, which rolled in from the northeast, and there he hovered once more, descending slowly, until the landing gear dipped into the swell. Now it was Walter's turn.

Charlesville was pleased to see so many people watching from the beach; pleased to see that the ship could draw a crowd. Nor did it hurt that the Capitol of Puerto Rico was two hundred yards away. Don had picked a good spot. Below the ship, rotor downdraft sent spray across the tops of the waves, and drove foam-green bubbles deep into the shoulders. Walter donned the Mae West and now took up the uninflated life raft. He intended to inflate the raft when he was in the water. Maxwell, lying on the cabin deck, made the sign of a "V" for good luck.

Walter leapt out the side hatch of the cabin. But before he hit the water, the raft inflated and tore loose from his grasp. Rotorblast sent it scooting crazily off like a leaf before the wind. By the time Walter bobbed to the surface, the raft was a hundred feet away to the east. Julio looked down. So did Don. Beneath them, Walter looked shocked. He had so much foam and spew in his face from the blast of the rotors that he spit water, coughing and shielding his eyes. Worse, there was no direction he could turn that would shelter him, for the blast came from three different rotors in a welter that, upon the rising, falling surface of the sea, was chaotic. From the cockpit, Don watched as this spectacle developed: Walter flailing, eyes closed, blinded, coughing up water and trying to breathe.

Disheartened, Don climbed. "What's happening?" Charlesville asked, whose position on the right side of the aircraft made it impossible for him to see what had happened on the left. Walter had swum beneath the ship, where the belly offered a lee.

"He's down there," said Don.

"Yes?" demanded Charlesville, not surprised to hear that Walter was down there, because his understanding was that Walter should be down there.

"His raft is over there!" yelled Don.

"Oh," Charlesville said, and laughed. "How will you rescue twenty men?"

Don didn't know, and never planned to rescue twenty men. He turned seaward and headed toward the raft. Suddenly, he was inspired by a memory of times during boyhood when he and other boys made money driving cows and calves from pastures to holding pens for annual culling. It was the most fun he had had as a boy; hilarious, really, running amuck in the pastures. Now, he would drive the raft back to Walter; something possible only if he got the ship out beyond the raft, then used the blast of the rotors to push the raft in, shoreward, ahead of the ship.

"I'm going to start practicing my French," Julio said, when he realized what Don had in mind.

Driving cows, Don had earned thirty-five cents for a whole day's work. But now the raft was upside down, and, even so, Walter never saw it coming. He had his eyes shut. Still, Don's skillful flying drove the raft right into Walter's face. When it smacked Walter, Walter grabbed it, and lifted one side, which let the blast in, which in turn caused the raft immediately to flip, tear loose from Walter's grasp exactly as it had before, and go scalloping off again, this time in a loop-de-loop, which put it near the beach.

Charlesville was amused, for the rescue was like a French farce, and he considered that, with twenty men instead of one, the rescue would be hilarious. The U.S. Army would not buy this aircraft. What Army would? The Italians? "Shall we stop?" he asked Don. But Don was now intent on flying, and paid no heed to Charlesville. It was too late for that. He pulled the ship up again, fearing now for Walter's safety, even for his life. Looking down, he could see once again the downdraft pummeling Walter.

Ashore, shooting from the top of a rock, with telephoto lens increasing her advantage, Patty thought Walter looked desperate. Along the roadside, others, too, sensed Walter was in peril. Still, Walter could have swum to shore, not fifty yards away. He stayed, because, like Don, Walter was at home on the edge.

Don circled to sea, wide of Walter. "We'll winch him," he told Julio.

"Lynch him?" asked Julio.

"*Winch him*," Don repeated. "For Christ's sake, don't be funny."

"I'm not," Julio said. He thought Don had said they would lynch him. In the comedy of errors it had been Don's idea to run the raft into Walter. Lynching seemed humane. Now Julio attached the rescue collar to the winch cable, and, as the ship came around, he payed out the cable, as far as it would go. Then, immediately it seemed, the cable jinked in the rotor blast and fouled around a strut. "Damn," Julio said.

"What happened?" asked Don.

"I fouled it." Julio moved to the belly hatch, reaching down in an effort to free the cable.

"What?" Charlesville asked, when Don glanced his way.

"Line's fouled."

"Show valor. It is your chance!" Charlesville cried.

Don took the ship down.

"What on earth!" Julio said. The ship touched down in the ocean. Water entered, rising to the level of the cabin. As the water washed over the deck, Maxwell jumped up, hollering, shocked by the sudden, cold intrusion. Don drove the ship forward through the swell, like a plough, creating a furrow, aiming to pass just to the right of Walter, so that Julio could reach out with the shepherd's crook and pull Walter in. The left front rotor passed over Walter's head. Walter was only feet from the hatchway. Don sidled the ship closer, and took her lower, until the sea now imparted its motion to the ship, and the ship began to roll with the swell. Walter, looking up, thought the howl was like the Russian winter. Julio, leaning out, extended the shepherd's crook. The sea rolled. A wave rolled in through the hatch, and up from the belly hatch, and rolled forward, shorting out the winch motor, which erupted into sparks and sharp smoke. The water washed into the engineer's well and over the bridge, down into the cockpit, pouring onto Charlesville and Don. Charlesville now saw his pilot showing valor. Charlesville smiled. In the midst of everything, he could appreciate Don.

The cable caught Walter, just as Julio came down with the crook. Julio watched Walter disappear. Don was watching, too, from the window and thought Julio had struck Walter down. So it appeared. "What'd you do!" Don cried out.

Walter was gone. "Where'd he go?" Julio asked. The crook was empty, and the man in the water had disappeared.

"Get him!" Don yelled.

"I didn't do it!" Julio cried, panicking, not knowing where Walter had gone. They would all drown. The ship was going down. They were all going to drown.

It's what happens, thought Don, *when you go where you oughtn't, when you do what you shouldn't.* He wished he were a kid again, in some other life; high in a maple, during summer in Ohio.

"Christ," said Maxwell, certain the ship was now sinking, and he waded to the side hatch and plunged. Maxwell was the best swimmer of them all, and swam underwater to the bottom, all the while fearing the ship would broach and come down on top of him. From the bottom, he looked up at the ship. In water as cold as November, he expected any instant a rotor blade would strike the surface, and within an instant fail catastrophically, with blades and masts flying off in all directions. He looked up through the swirl, through gray gloom, amidst the thunderous racket of gears, and he saw Walter, bolixed up in the cable, with the cable now tangled on the struts. Walter was struggling to get free underneath the aircraft, but his vest was tangled with the rescue collar, whose buoyancy, with that of the vest, pinned him between the struts and the belly of the fuselage. Serene ringing sounded from everywhere, and, hearing it, Maxwell pushed off from the bottom and swam up. Unlooping Walter, he shoved Walter forward to the belly hatch, then up through the hatch into the cabin, where Walter emerged as a sudden apparition, whose appearance frightened Julio half to death.

Walter was reborn!

Then, Maxwell, realizing that, somehow, Don was still in control of the ship, decided to re-board, entering behind Walter.

Julio called forward to Don, "Walter's here!"

"Walter's safe," Don told Charlesville.

"*Merci*," Charlesville said, as Don brought the aircraft slowly up from the ocean, allowing sea water to pour from every aperture. When the ship was aloft, Don flew it toward shore.

Patty waded out, and Julio helped her board.

Here, close to shore, Charlesville counted a U.S. Army major, two captains, three lieutenants, several seamen from the Navy, some Marines, several local *gendarmes*; and roughly two hundred civilians. "You did well," he yelled to Don, and figured that, with General Weggoner present, and some publicity, they could draw a thousand people. Charlesville had reconsidered his doubts about an air show. With a valorous pilot like Don, he was certain the air show would succeed.

Spent by his ordeal, Walter grabbed feebly at Julio. "You tried to kill me," he charged.

"Not true," Julio swore. But the ordeal had spent Julio as well, and Julio was now convinced the aircraft would not make it to Wright Field; either because the aircraft would fail, or because the men would fail it. Julio felt certain, now, his best prospect lay in France, even though, to get there, meant betraying Harry's men.

—

CHAPTER SIX

Back at the field, the men learned Ponce had won Sunday's game, salvaging at least some dignity in the series. Ponce's *Leones* now trailed Caguas, three games to one. But, for Don, the challenge posed by Charlesville's offer of a position in Marseille offset any happiness. If he went to Marseille, there could be no Wright Field.

Sunday evening, he and Patty visited the plaza to watch the *paseo*. The *paseo* was Ponce's rite of courtship, bringing young people together under the scrutiny of chaperons to promenade, men in one direction, young ladies in the other. If, in passing, a young man caught the eye of a lady, or she his, they could pair and drop out, free within the constraint of the chaperons' supervision, to stroll along the plaza's byways, where lamplight lit the way among the trees.

"Harry and I are the same," Don said at length, preoccupied and not watching. "I threaten to quit, but never do. Harry threatens to fire me, but never does. I threaten to kill him, but haven't. He threatens to die, but he won't. Maybe someday, these things will happen. The problem is, I have this insane belief that things will work out. But, then, I remind myself, there is Julio. Julio is different. He will go over to the French. He will betray us, I am sure. And there can be no flight to Wright Field if Julio does that."

A chill ran through Patty, hearing Don. "What do you want?" she asked.

"I don't know," Don confessed. Marseille was as tempting to him as he imagined it to be to Julio. At least, Marseille was a job.

"You're smoking with a vengeance," she said. At his feet, were a pile of dead butts.

They had a bench to themselves. No one paid them much mind; people passing hardly noticed, and lovers not at all. "Did I ever tell you about Lindbergh?" he asked. "I was twenty-one when Lindbergh flew the ocean. Now, there's a tale with a happy ending. Lindbergh's flight meant more to me than any other. 'Lindy' became my hero, overnight, as he did for the entire nation. I even went to New York, just to see the parade. Did you ever see four million people out to cheer one man? You're not likely to forget it if you do. That's ambition! That was mine: to have four million people cheering me. But, you know, even at twenty-one, I realized that, for me, if I were to do what Lindbergh did, I'd have to go twice as far as Lindbergh went. I realized that if I went only as far as Lindbergh went, but no farther, I would have reached only the point where Lindbergh was when he began. To come to that understanding you suddenly realize that no matter where you are, you have twice as far to go as you thought. And if you are already tired, you still have twice as far to go before you rest. If you are hungry, and I'm hungry, you have twice as long to wait before you eat. For most Negro men in America, to be Lindbergh, now, means twice the pain, and twice the grief, and twice as long, and twice as hard. And already we're like Lindbergh in disguise. We've gone his distance, never likely to be heard from or known."

"There's your answer," Patty said, for it was clear to her where Don ought to go. "You may do well in Marseille, but you of all people need someone to tell the world you've arrived. The flight to Wright Field will do that." Saying that, Patty realized how much she loved Don. It shocked her, because she could not compete with his love of the ship, or his ambition. It was her realization, matching his, that she couldn't get there from here. She, too, had twice as far to go to get to Don, and that thought was devastating to her.

Nearby, a group of Spaniards argued about *La Madre Patria*,

Spain. Their contentions drowned out a duet between a *cuatro* and guitar. What Patty faced now was the prospect of serving Don's ambition. That would be her way of keeping close to him. She knew he would never be hers. "I wish us all luck," Patty whispered, doing a star-turn of her own. Her heart was breaking, though she allowed not a sign of the pain to escape. If she served Don's ambition, and got a story, at least she would have the story to show for her grief. "I'm tired," she said at length, and rose to go. There was nothing more that would happen here tonight.

Don stayed a while, now interested in seeing the *Paseo* conclude. He was stronger than Patty, and resolved to himself he would keep himself immune to wanting her.

That night, Alice awoke at three to a sound she recognized at once as the unmuffled sobbing of her niece in the other room. Alice sighed, and, before returning to sleep, remembered lines from the Urdu poet, Darshan, whose verse, in English, went, "'All glory to the beloved for breaking my heart. The notes of its bursting sweetened the silence of the night.'"

—

CHAPTER SEVEN

The law office of Antonio Laracuente senior, and now junior, occupied the second floor of the jeweller's building on *Calle Isabel*, which bordered on the north of Ponce's plaza. From his office window Antonio could look out onto the plaza, over nearly all of his world, and back on nearly all of his life. Since Antonio loved movies, and the Fox Delicias theater was his next door neighbor below, he could joke that his life was complete, within a stone's throw of his home. He had home, work, the beloved plaza, and movies. From the window overlooking the street and the plaza, his view took in the bustling corner of *Calle Isabel* and *Calle Unión*, the cathedral, places to eat, and the facade of his own grand house. He could see across the plaza to the firehouse, to the balconies of the upper floor of the Hotel Meliá. He took comfort in the prim symmetry of the crowns of the India-laurel fig, the tree of distinction throughout Ponce's plaza. He took particular pleasure in the sight of the walkways, in their civilized traverse of the plaza, and the soft sheen of the lamplight on days when he worked into the evening. He loved the commotion of the sidewalk and street. In any fair sampling, Antonio would know a third of the people passing by. His father would have known half, but the town was smaller then.

At his desk, Antonio had drafted the instruments of countless proceedings: wills, contracts, trusts, liens, bills of sale, foreclosures and pleadings. He felt attuned through these instruments to the lives of Ponce's people. Here, too, he had drafted motions and rehearsed the arguments he argued in court. He saw Ponce in its generations come and go. It was the parade, of course, the human parade, no strange sight; the very life of a town. Antonio could predict the future, for the town moved in cycles, even as the traffic and the *Paseo* of lovers on Sunday night around the plaza. The sun always rose from the firehouse and hotel. The shadows of the morning always shrank toward the bank; the sun always set over the line of roofs that included his own. The townspeople who passed embodied the ghosts of their own parents, and essentially the ghosts of their children. If he looked out and saw two sweethearts—*novios*—holding hands, he could predict their future because he saw their parents, their past, their kinfolk, their circumstances, their status. He knew what lay buried in Ponce. His favorite argument was not legal but poetic: the child was father of the man.

Now, on a bright Monday morning, nearing noon, Antonio looked out from the window of his office and down on *Calle Unión* to see the green DeSoto he recognized as Julio's arrive at his house. Antonio watched Julio get out of the car and go to the door of the house. Antonio saw his own man, Agustín, greet Julio at the door, then turn to call someone—of course, Charlesville and Walter—who, one after the other, came out of the house carrying luggage. The men said good-bye to Agustín, and Julio opened the trunk of the car. In the trunk were rolls of drawings that Julio removed for Charlesville to look at on the way. The thought occurred to Antonio that the men were leaving town directly for San Juan, skipping Harry's. He wondered what was happening, but suspected that he knew. Always curious, Antonio wondered whether today was the day that Charlesville would succeed in stealing Julio, and, if so, whether Julio would betray Harry and the men.

All three—Charlesville, Julio, and Walter—got into Julio's car, and drove away. Still, instead of going straight and then right, which Julio would have done if he were going to Harry's field, the car went left, and Julio drove out Comercio, heading east, the road to San Juan on Route One.

Antonio called Harry, and told him what he had seen.

The news disturbed Harry so much that, at the end of the call, he went to the front room and told the men.

The news disturbed the men even more. "So," said Don.

"He did it," meaning Julio had betrayed them and gone over to the French.

"That's the end of Wright Field," said Bill.

"That's the end of our project," concurred Lon, certain Julio would tell Charlesville about the ruse, but also about the disastrous visit by Colonel Anderson.

"His wife must have driven him to do this," Maxwell judged.

"Julio's capable of betrayal on his own," said Harry. It seemed not to matter that none of the men was actually there, with Julio, Charlesville, and Walter, and it struck Patty that all of them seemed to know how Julio thought.

"Can you all be sure?" she asked.

They mocked her when she asked that question.

"I'll tell you something," said Harry, deeply saddened. "In 1939, I had a heart attack . . . ," it was a story all the men knew, but Patty had not heard before. "For three days," Harry said, "I lay in the hospital, more dead than alive. I heard them say I wouldn't make it. That was when I decided I would. Sometimes," he said, and Patty realized that now Harry had delved, and was sixty-five years in the past, "I catch a scent, like rosewater, that I don't know what it is, and it's her, my mother. It's what I remember of her." He paused. Patty looked up. Minnie, listening from the kitchen, was crying. Elisa, too, had come out from her office. It was her favorite story. "I have a piece of my mother's skirt, in a strongbox, in my office," Harry said. "My sister has a lock of her hair. It was auburn, a color I admire." Patty's own hair, in some light, had the sheen of auburn, and Harry looked forlornly her way. "She was with me in the hospital, I know she was. Of course, I thought my Army days were over. I love the Army. The Army was my mother. But when the war broke out, I offered to re-enlist, and they took me. Julio was in my first command. I met him my first day back at Wright Field. Julio. He was like a son."

"Let me go," said Don.

"Go where?" asked Harry.

"I'll find him," said Don.

"He's done this to us all," said Bill. "He gains something, but we lose in the process. It's hardly fair. It's very selfish."

"Take my car," Harry said.

"I'll take the ship," said Don.

"Do what's best," Harry said.

"I'll go with you," said Maxwell. On hearing that, Patty feared they meant to kill Julio. The men rose and left the house abruptly. Lunch had ended, then and there.

At the ship, Patty hardly knew whether to ask if she could go, or to keep her distance by not intruding on what was, essentially, the men's quarrel. Then, to her surprise, Don invited her. He thought it was a good idea that Patty see how bad a character Julio was.

Such anger drew her back into the war, binding her in a rope of memory, revisiting the prospects of loss. With her judgment clouded, she decided to accept Don's invitation.

Onboard, she sat in the co-pilot's seat beside Don, her camera resting in her lap. By half-past one, they were ready for start-up. Julio would be in the mountains. Don was certain he would have gone up the *Piquiña*, Route One, and would have stopped in Cayey, because Charlesville would have wanted to stop there for lunch. In the cockpit, Don seemed to Patty calm. She wondered what he felt, inside, and searched his eyes for signs. "Don't look at me," he told her, causing her to sit back and withdraw. So instead she stared out, straight ahead, out at nothing, like a person who wasn't there.

As always, the cockpit, having trapped heat through the morning, had become stifling by mid-day. But she didn't dare complain. The seat covers were almost too hot to sit on, and the control handles almost too hot to touch. But she kept her peace. When the checklist commenced, as call and response between Maxwell and Don, Patty was mindful of Mass, of the exchange between altar boy and priest, recalled from her childhood, on the hottest summer mornings in Baltimore. Then, Mass was still strange to her ears, as the checklist was now, and she could recall, now, vividly, the pew she sat in, with her eyes closed in concentration as she listened to the intonation of those words, and felt the perspiration tickle on her neck. How little had changed, except Don was the priest.

Don called out, "Clear!"

When the port engine started, Patty cradled her camera protectively, as she might have a child. She felt the very foundation of her sanctity shaken. Not only was the engine sharper and louder from within the cockpit than she recalled it having been from the day before, but the vibration seemed more immediate. Then the starboard engine started, and motes of dust appeared to levitate inside the cockpit.

During the runups, the sticks began to move. She felt the rotors moving them. She touched the right-hand stick with her fingertips and felt the pulse; a sensation she took as patently sexual. Perspiration had drenched her. She thought of men's things; of their words, the sexual connotations in their art, in the things they made with their hands, their machines, even more in their tools. There was, unmistakably, throb in the stick; or, better, in the yoke; tension, rhythm, cycling. There was *beat*, a certain music. She felt Don's steadying hand, not touching her own but present through the sticks. Outside the nose, Bill Pyrtle raised his arms above his head. Don acknowledged by nodding.

The throttle turned. At once, the engines raised their voices. There was a crease of concern in Don's brow. His eyes went out of focus as he listened, hearing, God knew, whatever she could not. She felt the pedals move, the sticks, the ship shifting, the rotor pitch changing, the engines working harder; and the ground just dropped away.

When she looked out she saw the rooftop of the hangar. She felt thrilled at the illusion that she belonged here. The ship was graceful in moving, no matter its appearance on the ground. The rotors beat a constant rush of wind, and it was cool inside the cockpit now. When the ship began to turn, and turn again, and climb, Patty felt omniscient, that she could see forever and understood what she could see. The ship could do no wrong in Patty's eyes.

Don flew out of the field to the south, crossing the coast and proceeding to sea. A hundred yards out he turned east. East of Ponce, they picked up the shore, which they followed for some miles to Salinas. There, Don turned northeast, overflying Route One toward the mountains. They flew by the Army's Losey Field. Don was taciturn, and Patty took her cue from his silence.

With the sea behind them to right, Patty looked back over her shoulder and saw *Caja de Muertos*, the coffin-shaped island off the coast. Ahead lay the Sierra de Cayey, inland mountains. The ship began to climb. They overflew traffic on the roadway below. The roadway began to rise into the foothills. Pressing on to the northeast, they crossed ranch land so desolate the highway traffic stood out, easily visible from the air. From a thousand feet above the road, they could see the road for miles ahead. In the lee of the mountain, the air became rough.

They had left behind a day of perfect weather. The Caribbean virtually sparkled. The sea seemed energized, enlivened by light. For the moment, Patty experienced the illusion of being joined to Don through the ship. Wherever he looked, she looked, for the world she was absorbed in was his. She wanted to see what he saw, feel what he felt, and be moved as he moved.

But apprehension never left her. Nor had Don wavered in that look of intent that meant to Patty he was hunting his prey. The mountains were crowned with great, towering cumulus that rose several miles. The ship closed on rising terrain, and the ridgeline rose beneath them. Though they were climbing, they seemed to be losing altitude. She glanced at Don quickly, but he was unconcerned with her. Then, suddenly, they lost their sunlight. And, in that moment, it was raining, too. They were in the mountains, and what been a fair day was now a deluge, low clouds and gray light. It shocked Patty how quickly things changed. Don dropped lower, keeping the ground in view by allowing the ship to be sandwiched between clouds and terrain.

"Are we okay?" Maxwell asked, using the intercom to Don.

"You bet," Don answered. The ship was buffeting. The ride was rough. But Don wasn't up here for Maxwell. He wasn't up here for Harry. He wasn't up here for Patty. He was up here to get Julio. Julio had sabotaged all their dreams. Julio had sold them all out. Julio had wrecked Don's career. Don knew how it was. Julio was passing for white.

Suddenly, he saw the green DeSoto, northeast of Cayey, poking along behind a truck on the two-lane road, unable to pass. From seventy feet above the ground, Don swooped down on them, quickly overtaking the car.

From the car, Julio looked out. He felt the ship's presence, then heard it, then saw the ship from the corner of his eye, above and behind him. The ship was on him so fast he looked up and saw Don. He caught Don's expression, Don's rage, like the gopher, catching the rage in the eye of the hawk.

"Damn you!" bellowed Don, to a man who could not hear him.

"Tu madre!" Julio shouted back at Don.

Neither could hear the other, for the ship drowned their shouts, and the rotors beat the rain across the windshield of the car. The truck driver ahead of Julio stopped, aware something was wrong. But the driver had never seen such a thing as the ship. Julio stopped. He couldn't get by. All the traffic behind Julio stopped. All the traffic coming the other way stopped. The mountaintop came to a halt. Charlesville was aghast, Walter grim.

Don touched the strut of the ship on the roof of the DeSoto and let the ship settle, just enough to dent the metal roof. Maxwell yelped. Patty wept and cried out, terrified. Don crunched the roof farther, to squeeze them all in. It felt good to him. It felt right. His insides were feeling warm. The doors of the car flew open, and Walter, Julio, and Charlesville all seemed to explode from inside. On the ground, people were scrambling left and right. Charlesville tumbled down an embankment; Julio headfirst behind him. Walter ran one way, then the other, hiding behind the car. Since nobody was left in the DeSoto, Don used a strut to smash out the windshield, and was fixing to push the car over the cliff, to let it just roll to its doom, but Patty was now beating on Don, screaming.

Maxwell jumped ship, since, today, for sure, Don had gone nuts. Maxwell leaped out the hatch and fell seven feet, got back up and then leaped down the bank after Charlesville and Julio. Patty screamed and beat until she turned Don away. "Don't hit me while I'm flying!" he railed at her, unable to remove either hand from the sticks to defend himself, as helpless before her onslaught as Julio had been before his.

"Stop it!" she screamed. "Stop it! Stop it! Stop it!" And she continued screaming at Don until Don did as he was told.

Don climbed, pulling the ship up higher in a hover, turning south toward the ridge and flying up into cloud.

From the ground, everyone looked. As suddenly as it had come, it had gone. The monster had disappeared into the gray morass of the sky.

Four minutes later, the aircraft broke out from cloud into sunlight, and now headed southwest back to Ponce. The highlands fell away and Don began a long, peaceful descent toward the plain.

Patty realized her worst nightmare had come to pass. The man she loved had turned into a monster. "You hurt me," she said, but he flew as calmly on the way home as he had on the way up, and her words did not reach him.

After the aircraft had touched down at Harry's field, and Don had shut down the engines, he and Patty simply sat, while the rotors, offloaded, spun down. Diego was outside, joining Lon and Bill Pyrtle. "It's over," Patty said, without rancor, her voice as flat and calm in her understatement of fact as Don had been in his flying. All had changed, she felt. Everything. She now viewed life in an entirely different way. Though she had seen rage before, Don's terrified her. It shook mountains, it was so sudden. And if Julio had betrayed Don, Don had more than made up for it by betraying Patty, by betraying her expectations for him. He was no hero. He did not belong in *Life*. Quietly, no longer having to shout to be heard over what she now felt was the relentless, insufferable thrashing of rotors, she asked, "Would you raise your own children that way? With such violence? Would you beat

your own child? Would you raise your hand to your wife? To
your daughter? Is that how you would teach your own son?"

"I don't know," Don admitted.

"Then you and I are far apart. You would have killed them."

"No," said Don.

"I saw you," she said, getting out of the seat. "I saw you. I
looked in your eyes."

She went aft. She had taken no photographs during the ride.
The camera had been vestigial in her lap. "Where's Maxwell?"
she demanded, thinking he must have gotten out. She was
unaware he had jumped ship in the mountains.

"I don't know," said Bill.

"He's up in the mountains," Harry said, arriving from the
house. "I've already had several calls."

She disembarked and walked off. Don moved aft and sat a
while longer, his legs dangling over the edge of the deck. Diego,
Lon, and Bill stood before him, glumly staring. "What *did* you
do?" asked Bill.

"No one sells us out," said Don. But whatever he had proved,
as soon as the others were gone, he felt depleted. She was right.
She had caught him enraged, and been hurt. She had seen Don in
his fury, and been hurt. He had displaced his own pain onto her,
and hurt her. She had wanted to see, and she saw. *El que ve es el
que sufre.* But Don was unable to walk away from himself, or his
rage, and that was a discovery for him.

In the parking lot, Harry called to Patty, and tried to stop
her. She had no car today, so she would walk into town, a long
hike. "I'll take you," Harry offered.

"You run a hard school," Patty told him, disinclined to accept
any offer from Harry.

In the cabin of the ship, still sitting, Don remembered an
incident all but forgotten from his childhood. When he was a
boy, barely six, his father had dragged him out into the Ohio
River, to teach him how to swim, out into water over Don's
head, and then thrust him still farther out, into water still deeper.
His father hadn't said a thing. Swim or drown, was the lesson.

Don had swum, somehow; frightened half to death, he had dog-paddled back. He had never assumed his father would have been there to take hold of his arm had he failed. "It's how I learned it," he said, out loud to himself. He had learned it, that life's lessons were final.

Driving Maxwell's car, Don caught up to Patty. "Ride?" he asked.

"Don't need one," she said, eyes straight as she walked.

"I'm sorry," he told her.

"It's too late," she said back.

"I didn't raise my daughter," he said. "I didn't strike her. Her grandparents raised her. As for my wife, she treated me worse."

"No good. Unacceptable."

"It's how I learned it," he cried, calling after, but letting her go.

"If that's how you learned it, you haven't learned it," she called out, never stopping, speaking to the sky. "You haven't learned it till you've learned to forgive." Though, for that, she hadn't learned it herself.

—

CHAPTER EIGHT

Despite being damaged, Julio's car ran, and Julio dropped off Charlesville and Walter in Cayey where they caught a *público* to San Juan. Julio and Maxwell then drove back to Harry's field, where, before Harry and the others, Julio insisted he had not spilled the beans. "My purpose was to hear Charlesville's offer," Julio maintained. Maxwell, hardly certain Julio was telling the whole truth, corroborated one important part of Julio's story. So far as Charlesville and Walter were concerned, neither man had given any indication that he doubted an air show would take place the following week, or that he doubted General Weggoner would be in Ponce.

"On the other hand," Maxwell said, "Charlesville thinks Don is crazy."

"He is crazy," said Julio.

"Shake hands," Harry said to them both.

"You would've told Charlesville," said Don.

"I should charge you for my car," said Julio.

"Julio," said Harry. "I'm the one who sent him."

That evening, at Alice's house, Alice was cleaning books in her den when Patty arrived. "Grab a rag," Alice joked, but, when she saw Patty had been crying, she became solicitous.

"Don is violent," Patty said. "I saw a side of him I never knew existed." Alice wanted Patty to go into this, which of course Patty did. "Today Harry got word from Antonio that Julio had taken Charlesville and Walter to San Juan. They slipped away around noon without saying anything to Harry, and so we figured Julio had betrayed our plans to go to Wright Field; that he had gone over to the French and would tell Charlesville everything. Harry was furious. So was Don."

"I can imagine," Alice said, appreciating what the disclosure would have meant to their dreams. Years of work, dashed.

"Don said he wanted the ship, and Harry asked him, 'What can you do?' Then Don said he could fly the ship up into the mountains to find them, to let Julio know that what he was doing was wrong. Harry said, 'Do what's best.' So three of us went: Maxwell, Don, and I. In the mountains it was raining. But Don kept going, and somehow we found Julio's car. Then Don tried to kill them. I could see the rage in his eyes. He actually tried to kill them. He was screaming at Julio the whole time." Patty had difficulty continuing. "He smashed in the roof of Julio's car with the landing gear. He broke out the windshield. He tried to crush them inside the car. By then, I was beating on him. I was frantic. I made him stop." Patty burst out in tears. "It was awful . . . ."

"I'm sure it was," said Alice, moved. "I'm sorry," she said.

"He seems so gentle."

"Oh well, no, honey, don't say that about Don. You've known him since Friday, and this goes way, way back . . . many years. A lifetime, perhaps. He blames Julio for betraying his dream. Did anyone get hurt?"

"Charlesville jumped out of the car when Don hit the roof, and so did Julio and Walter. Two of them went down in a ditch. Maxwell jumped out of the helicopter because he thought Don had gone crazy."

"So Julio's car is demolished?" Alice asked, though she recalled Julio's car was not much more than a wreck to begin with.

"No. The top is creased, and the windshield is gone. Then I stopped him."

"Well at least he was responsive to you. He couldn't have been out of control if you stopped him."

"He's violent," Patty said.

"Yes, I suppose that's true," Alice said. "So am I when I'm mad. I wouldn't have let Julio get away so easily as a dented roof. I wouldn't have let Charlesville get away either. Charlesville set up this whole thing. And this project is Don's life-long ambition.

Don waited his whole life to be a test pilot." Alice concluded that Patty was not woman enough to handle Don. She was perhaps too young. Alice could have handled him. "You should just leave him," she counselled. "Stay away from him."

"Why do you say that?" Patty asked, who, in order to *leave* Don, had to be *with* him.

"He threatens you," said Alice. "You can't be afraid of a man that you love."

"Love!" Patty was dumbstruck.

"Well, you do, don't you?"

She sat down. "Yes," she admitted.

"There. That's the issue, Patty. You have gotten yourself involved in a story you only came here to tell. But, nevermind, that's an old issue with you." Hearing her aunt, Patty was perplexed beyond accounting, but it was clear to Alice that, from the moment Patty arrived, she had thrust herself into the story, and was now preparing herself to pay the price. "Did the others agree with what Don did?"

"Yes."

"Like I say, it is too bad. But it goes way back. Brother against brother. Charlesville plays Harry against his men, and Harry plays Julio against Don."

Shocked by her realization that even her aunt knew her feelings toward Don, Patty also realized she had taken refuge in denial. It wasn't his anger, but the anger of her parents, were they to know that their daughter loved a Negro, that Patty found so disconcerting. To face their anger threatened her; to face her own anger she had no support whatsoever from her aunt.

Patty left Alice's for a walk. As she walked, she realized Alice was right about another thing: no one had died. Despite it all, at the end, Don had been under her control.

Across town, Don watched the sunset from the Roman Catholic cemetery, whose hilltop vista overlooked the western outskirts of Ponce and the sea. He enjoyed this quiet place, in a world he had mainly to himself. Over time, he had come to know who lay in the graves, especially the plots on the hilltop.

He knew who died younger than he was, and who at his present age. Except for the gathering dusk, he was mindless here to the passing of time, much as they were, who lay beneath his feet. And the dusk was a time he enjoyed, as he supposed they might as well.

The fact of the matter was Don lived so much in the past that he had given up much of where he was, as if the past were a nurturing meal, used to sustain the future, but requiring, for it to do so, that he give up the present to feed it. At one stage in Don's life, for many years, he had thought the past *would* sustain him. But, he had not done what he set out to do. By his own terms, he had failed. He was not the Negro Lindbergh of his dreams.

The fields called Don. They pulled him back. The fields and the camps of his youth. There had always been a place like Harry's, in his childhood's mind's eye, a field; and a place like this cemetery, set apart for rumination. There, in that coalescence of memory, a country of childhood, he had sat on the banks of Ohio's rivers: the Mad River, in Dayton; the Great Miami; the Little Miami, and, at his grandmother's, the Ohio itself. He never tired of watching rivers. The river was part of his life. He had never tired of looking out on the still life of Ponce, which, too, was part of his life. The dusk that gathered gave Ponce her sway, as if her current, and the breeze off the sea provided grace.

Someone had left carnations on a headstone. When Don's father was forty-one, Don's present age, he had been a farmer who farmed bottom land along the Ohio. Don's grandparents, on his mother's side, owned that land, well to the east of Cincinnati. When Don's grandfather had died, Don's aunts and uncles—his mother's brothers and sisters—offered a piece of that land to Don's father, who was too proud to accept it, and who soon gave up farming altogether, out of fear he might fail. Instead, he moved the family up to Dayton and into town. Don had come to think that, if a man suppressed all desire, controlled his own will, left nothing to chance, and never lost sight of his goal, he would attain what he wanted and succeed. He would never be his father. Unlike his father, he would survive on his ambition and be strong. He would not flinch, no matter his fear. He would not turn away at the offer of success. It was like crossing a desert; you took what you needed and set out. Then, you rationed and endured.

His mother had pushed him in youth; she had prepared him to endure, because she had seen in Don the one child of her five children who was destined to be dealing with whites. So she prepared him for the pain he would face.

But this pain was different. He had fallen in love with Patty Symms. It was unthinkable that this could happen, and yet it was exactly what had happened. The thought that he might never see Patty again was unbearable. No matter what else, the fact that he had disappointed her, and angered her, hurt deeply. Don was sorry. There was nothing he wouldn't do to win her back. He was no longer content, and never would be again, with the still life of Ponce, seen from the hill of the dead.

East of town, Patty walked to Ponce's grand and famous *Ceiba*, a kapok tree more than three hundred years old, and the largest, best known tree in Puerto Rico. Its branches were the thickness of a man, its crown, seventy feet in diameter, and its great, massive trunk ten feet across. The Ceiba's roots were gnarled protrusions, rising two to three feet above ground and ramifying yards from the trunk. The tree stood atop the bank of the *Río Portugués*, over-sheltering the old coast road at the entrance of the bridge into what was now Ponce's *Calle Comercio*, leading into the town from the east. For generations, lovers had carved initials and hearts in the trunk of the Ceiba, tourists had admired it, and, in earlier years, according to lore, highwaymen had hid in the crevices and clefts of its roots, there to spring upon the unwary passing by.

When Patty took shots, her camera and tripod attracted the attention of children who lived in the houses along the bank of the river. Before long, she had children around her, and for the only time in the last couple days, she felt happy. She took pictures of kids with the tree. As her outlook improved, she counted initials in the trunk, losing count at five hundred, and wondered, out of so many lovers, who survived? Were any of the lovers still living? Were any of the children before her the offspring of parents whose initials remained in the tree? Even after nightfall, she lingered.

When she returned to Alice's, she found Alice now at work on her typewriter, cleaning the characters with a swab. "Guess how many initials are carved in the Ceiba," Patty asked, knowing her aunt could not possibly guess. "As near as I can figure," she said, answering her own question, "there are five hundred and twelve."

"Remarkable," grunted Alice. She thought Patty had gone round the bend.

"I took pictures of people who wanted to be photographed by that tree. Passersby, children. I could set up a business." Patty was joking, of course.

"I'm happy to see you're feeling better," said Alice, standing away from the work to mop her brow. "Don came by." Alice caught the surprise in Patty's face at the mere mention of Don's name, even now, after all that fuss. "He came wearing his suit," Alice said, "or should I say, 'a suit'—he may have dozens—and I took that to mean he had come calling to apologize." She looked at her niece. Her niece seemed largely unaffected by this news. "I think he may have had more in mind than just an apology," Alice said. "He looked very fine, quite handsome, but, you know that already. He even brought you a token."

"A token?"

"A gift. It's in your room. I asked him to stay," Alice said. "But I think his nerve ran out. He said he would call in the morning. He seemed desperately afraid you might not forgive him. Dear me. You blame him for his rage, yet he's terrified of yours." Alice straightened her back. "It's your good luck I'm in my menopause," she said, but the remark was lost on Patty. "I really do think he came here to propose. In fact, I'm sure of it."

"He doesn't love me," Patty said. "He's married to ambition. He loves his work."

"You forgive him?"

"Yes, of course."

"Well I won't insult you by telling what to do."

"Thank you."

"Would you accept if he proposed?" Alice asked.

"He won't propose," Patty said. "It would kill my mom and dad."

"But would you accept, if he did?"

"I don't know," she answered Alice. "You ask a lot of questions."

"I know what I would do," said Alice, returning to work, and never one to be deterred by her ambition. In Alice's view, Don was a man worth pursuing.

"I do forgive him," Patty sighed, almost absent-mindedly, and went to her room to see the *token* Don had left, which turned out to be two sketches he had made of her. "Did you look at these?" Patty hollered out at her aunt.

"He drew them for you," Alice answered.

"That's not what I asked you. Did you look at the drawings?"

"Yes, of course," Alice admitted. "I'm only human, after all."

In one, Don had drawn Patty at the table at Harry's, and, in the other, he had placed her on the apron, outside the hangar, with her hand touching the ship. Against her resolve, Patty found herself flattered that he had drawn her, and, oddly, relieved. Dumbstruck, she saw the appeal, that he had been thinking of her at his side from the start. In the controversion of his thought, in which he could see himself as washed out yet fantasize her as being connected to the ship, he had managed, through his drawing, to do the improbable; first, to convince her the likenesses were real, which to Patty meant *that was her*, and, second, to persuade her to like the subject being drawn, the subject being herself, which was by far the more difficult achievement. Given the capture of expression, she was moved to wonder how he had paused long enough to record the visual data sufficient to his task, and it occurred to her that such was love. Had she never herself been so intent that a moment took forever, disclosing much? But she reasoned that, unlike herself, who made bold the camera for all to see, Don, in childhood, had learned the art of seeing a world in which he himself was seldom seen, a world at which he was rarely caught looking. She felt honored by the gift of such trust.

She returned to sit with Alice on the patio. Then, extremely sober with the thought of what was what, Patty told her aunt, "I can never marry him."

"So be it," said Alice, relieved to think that, in that case, Patty's parents would never know. Patty stared into the night, at the wall around the patio, at the edge of the roof, at the flowers, at the tree. She saw nothing of these things. She was thinking of Don. She was thinking of marriage. She wasn't really there, Alice knew.

That night, in bed, Patty wondered whether Don, too, lay awake in his bed, thinking of her. She wondered how he would be as a lover. She could only imagine. But, trying to imagine found her wanting to know, and wanting to know made it all seem worthwhile. She realized, she was her father's daughter, after all.

—

CHAPTER NINE

At *Tía's*, everybody seemed to know Don was on his way to see Patty. Of course, a man carrying a bouquet of flowers while wearing a three-piece suit might be viewed as dead giveaway.

Tía's—anglicized for "Aunt's"—referred to Magdalena Vieira, who was aunt to none of her lodgers, but who was, at seventy-one, the long-time owner of a boarding house known throughout southern Puerto Rico for its hospitality, good cooking, and the staunch moral fibre of Tía herself. Her house had been built when travel between towns of Puerto Rico constituted, more often than not, a day's journey, requiring the traveler to seek lodgings overnight, and so it had been a favorite for a generation of traveling salesmen and single gentlemen who stayed there from short to long-term. Bill, Lon, Maxwell, and Don all stayed at Tía's long-term.

The house, a large wooden structure, raised half a story, surrounded an open interior courtyard. Along the sides were the bedrooms, numbering eight, with the room farthest back on the right being Tía's own. In the back were also the kitchen and two bathrooms, and, in the front, the *comedor* or dining room, where, in the evenings, the men often played cards after dinner; and the somewhat larger *salon*, where guests, including females, could visit, and where the radio and phonograph stayed. The house was congenial, overall, spacious but not grand, and the high-ceilinged guest rooms had shuttered windows and transoms for ventilation. Over each four-poster draped a *mosquitero*, and two of the rooms, including Don's, had desks. Don had done some of the project's drafting at his desk. In the yard behind the house, Tía kept chickens, and under the porch in front slept her dog, Peluso, named ironically for his patches of bare skin.

Tía was teaching Don Spanish, *poco a poco*, and in her own struggling English they argued baseball, for Tía loved Ponce's team. She also had a keen interest in Harry's project, having gone to the field on two occasions to see the ship fly. Among Harry's men, she was closest to Don and thought he should marry and have children. Don, too, felt close to Tía, and had made her a present of a drawing that showed her, at work in her kitchen, Peluso sitting attentively at her side.

It was Peluso who barked when Don emerged Tuesday morning in his suit. "So," Tía said.

"We'll see," answered Don.

She gave him the flowers from her table.

As Don biked across town, he found to his consternation that it was impossible to visualize Patty's face. The amnesia grew worse as he neared Alice's house. If he couldn't recall Patty, perhaps he wouldn't remember what to tell her when he saw her, or perhaps it meant he didn't love her, or, far more likely, that she couldn't bring herself to love him. Perhaps, he reasoned, he should turn around and go. He felt terrible. Yet, capricious as memory was, recovering it was sometimes worse, for, in a flash, in a thrilling instant, with no effort at all on his part, her face would suddenly appear before him, at which point the giddy terror of proposing overwhelmed him, in all its grotesque exaggeration. To apologize was appropriate; to profess love, too; but Don had in mind the whole route, reversing his life to that moment. If ever a man needed counsel, it was he. But he was daunted by guilt, exaggerating the fear that he would live out his life without Patty; something only human sacrifice could avert. "What could be worse," he would mutter. To be without her was unspeakable.

Patty was up, but not dressed, when Don knocked. Alice was gone. Alice's maid, Teresa, answered Don's knock. Hearing someone on the way to the door, compulsively Don checked tie, cuffs, suit, shoes, and flowers. He had never, ever been this nervous before. If life had a hell, this was it. He wished he were dead, but he *had* been dead; this was death's alternative in life. He went over his lines: how to say he was sorry, how say he loved her, how to propose, all rushed, in one breath, and with reasons for each and an argument for all.

Teresa smiled, greeting Don. She showed him in, then led him to the patio in back, where, in Patty's behalf, she accepted the bouquet.

Patty was in her room, from which she overheard the exchange between Teresa and Don, which involved almost no words from Don. When Teresa showed her the flowers, and how lovely they looked, Patty drew on her robe and pushed open the shutters, looking out onto the patio and Don, whom she found sitting, more or less like a father, anxiously awaiting news of a delivery. He had worn a hat, amazingly enough, and now held it in his hands, turning it by the brim, as he rested his forearms across his thighs. The beige suit looked splendid on Don. Even the vest. She was charmed, done in, and said hello from the window to thank him for the flowers.

Her sudden appearance triggered his apology. "Patty, I am so sorry for what I did yesterday," he said, and would have kept talking, for days or weeks, for the words virtually tumbled from his lips, had she not stopped him.

"We'll talk," she said, and withdrew from the window.

He felt forgiven! He had survived the first step, but was unaware he need take no more! And she had smiled, accepting the flowers. "Thank you," he whispered to God. Forgiven, forgiven, the sight of her was tonic. There were so many things Don wanted to say to assure Patty he would never be violent with her, and to answer that question she had raised regarding how he would treat his own child. Would he strike his child? Never. Maybe he would've before yesterday, but not now. Would he strike *any* child? No! Would he find a better way to teach lessons? Better than the way he had learned? Absolutely. Teach with love.

As to marriage, he would propose that they be married and that they live on in Ponce. Of course, nothing could happen before they were married. He could not be with her, except to say in courting. In Ponce, that was a given, and he would abide by the code respecting the honor of a lady. But, then, he would have anyway, anywhere, for that was Don. He was his mother's son.

Ponce would be an excellent home, because, once they were married, Ponce would accept them. Dayton would not; Baltimore would not; perhaps France would, but there were few places: France and New York and Puerto Rico.

He would rather be with Patty than fly. He assumed that, no matter the flight to Wright Field, afterwards there would be little future opportunity for him to fly in Ponce. So his career as a test pilot soon would end. He owed the others and Harry whatever final measures were due. But Patty was worth giving up being Lindbergh.

If Don was ahead of himself, Patty, too, was at least *in a state*. She had spent sleepless nights, wrestling forces seeming beyond her control. Her fantasies were so real she believed she and Don were sharing the same thoughts. As she crossed the hallway to the bath, she looked out to the patio. He sat, bright in the sunlight of the garden, patiently awaiting her appearance. "I love you," he said, looking up, upon the sound of her footfall on tile, to catch her, in a frieze.

She had heard from him words that struck both terror and joy, the very thing she had longed for him to say, and feared he might, and she was caving in to the desire to hear more. "We could live here in Ponce," he said, having forgotten to propose. But that oversight contained a ton of his concession, which at once she recognized; an either-or concept, fly or love Patty; in effect, the succession to a still higher ambition, love for her, which he now saw as the highest ambition of all, and she now recognized he was seeing that way. To Don, she was worth everything, and not just everything, but all. Dizzily, she felt the same about him. Still, she clung to the shred of her control.

"Give me a minute," she said, and went on to her shower.

She had indulged him, of course, and he took it as yes, reflecting that, as a pilot, he had spent a lifetime being where he shouldn't be, going where he ought not go. That's what he did with his time, and it seemed now a rehearsal for here. Now, here, as in flying, taboo gave rise to the sense that he was being indulged by his fate, that what was present was more than its appearance, more than itself; that it was shadowed by ulterior meaning. Alice's house was more than just a house he had entered; the patio was more than just a patio he sat in; about him was more than just a garden, under a sun that was more than just a sun. Those things were propitious: they fulfilled a destiny. As a pilot, he had flown four thousand hours, and as a draftsman, toiled twenty years. If one started to run up statistics, they were awesome: what he had done to carve out his work. This woman was insane. If she indulged him, she would throw away her life as well. Both would crash. Taboo. But best of all, it all seemed all right. It seemed good. What he had labored to put together over years came unglued in her presence, years traded for a day, not a day, a morning; not even that, truth be told: just her passing. Just one look. Just the look in her eyes. Just one sound of her voice, and he would give up everything. Don was reeling, rehashing and rehearsing his own words. But it was a choice he had made, radical and extreme; not: both-and; *either-or.*

The contradiction in all things was that every moment with Patty was worth having, no matter its cost. Which moment would he have cut out or lost? Which sound of her voice? Which look in her eye? Which word or which smile or which glance? Just her presence, the promise of her presence, was enough. Damn tomorrow, and damn the future. He could imagine how she felt, and how she'd be. He could put himself inside her, and he had, mentally; inside her, by her side; day and night. He had vanquished his reserve, he had banished it. He could imagine her in every role: the comforting wife, the mother of children, and his lady. In thought, he had melted, like his heart. Inside, he had become like something molten, like the sea, awash. It was he who had crossed her course. He had put himself there, in harm's way, because he saw no harm in doing so, or accepted what there was.

And tomorrow? If she discarded him, to go on her merry way? If she rejected his offer? This one was not going to pass.

"I'm the loser," Don said.

But, no, that's not what she said. She said, *give her a minute.*

He had surrendered unconditionally before her, and she only meant she was about there as well.

In the shower, *she* was reeling, and half faint. To Patty, it was crazy that Don would quit his work for her; she had come here to boost his career, not end it. That was *her* work, the very thing that brought her. In the shower, she found herself wishing Don would join her. She wished this so fervently she peeked around the shower curtain to see if the bathroom door remained closed. But it had not been closed tight. As she did with most doors, she had left it open just a crack. His diffidence charmed her, stole her heart. He was so bundled up in his fears.

Such quaintness. He was swell but *sooo* constrained. First this and then that. What a proper gentleman was he. Goodness. Hop on in.

But he didn't. From the patio, he listened to the sounds Patty made as her shower and toilet resounded off the wall of the neighboring house. From somewhere, he heard children. Somewhere, in the maze of Ponce's streets, a vendor called out. Above him, he followed the mango tree with his eyes. He found the sun peeking through. He loved lordly Ponce, a place stern with custom and *seignorial* expectation. Here in Ponce, he had found respect that was missing in Dayton.

Through showering, Patty appeared at the door to the patio, wrapped in a large white towel. "So, you have made up your mind that you love me?" she asked.

"Yes," he answered.

"Yes what?" she asked.

"Yes, I've made up my mind," answered Don.

"Disgraceful," she teased, and went on.

In her room, where she dressed, he was immediately regretful of the sight he now missed, and so heard every move that she made, converting sounds into sights in his mind. She had exploited his defenses, just slipped through, exploiting the pleasure he took in giving in. Was it fair? It was not. Did he love her for being unfair? Did the victim love the thief? If the thief stole the heart, sometimes, yes. It was worth a life just to be in her way, that she might pity the fool as she passed. And if his plight made her smile, all the better. Then his entreaty would be simply to die.

She sat on the bed. Soft as silk. Drawing on this thing, and that. Don could smell the bouquet of her scents. Imagine that! He could see right through the walls of the house. Just imagine. Sound caressed her. When she touched herself, he felt it. He adored her. He would never understand such good fortune. God had smiled. He thought he was born for this moment, that his only true purpose was to be here, and he was, with all his heart. He could hear her feet slip into flats, and first one and then the other touch the floor. His mind became her carpet. He was devoted to her now.

Dressed, Patty appeared at the back door. "Will you zip me?" she asked. He zipped her. Steady Don was trembling now. "You look gorgeous," he said, so paltry a praise for a treasure.

"I have a request," Patty said.

"Anything."

"Would you sleep with me first?"

Lord, what a blow! He could not do that, and she knew it. She had asked him the one lethal thing. "We're not married," he stammered.

"And won't be," she said.

"We could go round and round on this."

"Just say yes," Patty said. She kissed him. She parted her lips. Then they were off to Alice's house on the beach.

—

CHAPTER TEN

Alice's beach house stood a mile south of the coast highway, east of town, and Don knew the way. It stood at the end of a narrow dirt road, beyond cane fields and mud flats, and the waterless *Río Bucaná*. Driving the dusty flats on the way to the beach, they passed cotton growing wild along the roadside. Though Don had been this way before, he had not noticed the cotton. And though he personally had never picked cotton, he found the sight achingly familiar. With Patty beside him, the sight of the cotton made Don feel ashamed, as if it were a pedigree. "My people were slaves," he confessed; hardly news. Beyond the cotton, stood the cane, green and tall as a man. He had never cut cane, either, but life had gone full circle: he was Patty's slave now. It was, all of it, achingly familiar.

Palms marked the beach, and, here, Patty's doubts began to rise alongside Don's, for on the beach stood a row of structures that in Patty's eyes were little more than shacks. At the end of the row was Alice's. Between the bungalow Patty had been envisioning and the shack she now saw, two points of view collided. "We're here," Don said. "That's it." The beach house was painted blue, constructed of wood, with ship-lapped boards, and it stood over the sand on brick piers. It had an outbuilding, as did the others in the row. Because it was shut up, it looked featureless, even smaller than it was. In Don's shamed view, this row of small wooden shacks lining, if not the sea, then some swamp, some river, or some dismal southern backwater was, all, hauntingly familiar.

Patty stared wide-eyed at the house. There were children about, half-dressed, barefoot, raggedy and brown; children who knew Alice's car but shied at the sight of Patty, who was a stranger, and Don, who was a stranger, too, though at least the right color. The children gave to both the blankest of stares, out of a curiosity so open it seemed solemn. Don viewed them as urchins. He had escorted Patty down to hell.

"My nerve came easier in England," she confessed, fingering her camera but releasing it again, profoundly depressed. There was nothing to shoot, nothing she found pictorially interesting, in a scene at once banal and yet strange.

"I'm sorry," he said.

"Don't be sorry," she said. Chickens roamed the sand, pecking in the margins between the modest homes and the cane. The sun was a tyrant, harsh, unremitting. The children were darker than Don. The people who lived here were cutters, descended of African slaves.

"Do you want to leave?" he asked.

"No," she said. Out of the dark sockets of windows of the houses she saw faces, peering out at them. Company coming, as it were. She thought again of her mother, who, like Patty, was honey-blonde. She wondered how many blondes had walked on this beach.

Having parked next to the hulk of a rusted green pickup, and between that hulk and the hulk of a doorless dead Buick, Don came around to let Patty out. He opened her door. She was clammy to his touch. Clothes flapped on a line. Husks of coconuts lay half-buried in sand. As she stepped out of the car, a goat stared at her. As Don took her hand, shards of glass caught the sun; brown bottles, and tin. She would go through life like this, Patty felt, now dredging up the dark bottom. She would force herself each step. She would endure it. She wished she were dead. "My parents eloped. They were sorry," she said. "I was supposed to marry the class president from Johns Hopkins." She was doing the thing her father had projected: outlining her failure on his map of success. "I was supposed to live in a big house on the north side of Baltimore. Be married in white. With a church full of friends." Patty wished she could jump to life's end. And then she yawned. The hell with it. They were here, like everyone else, for lack of resources to be somewhere else. So she wasn't so strange after all; as if the worst place on earth was this margin between the land and the sea, an evolutionary arrest from which the luckier, two-legged creatures went on.

She brought her camera, not for pictures, but out of fear it might be stolen from the car. As she and Don walked, the children, in a grim caricature of a wedding march, fell in behind them. She found the sound of Don's voice reassuring, as if silence were a curse and, by speaking, he dispelled it. "This is less difficult for me than for you," Don allowed, speaking rightly. "I already know where I am." She believed he did know much of what she felt. She believed in his intuition, in his sensitivity to pain. From the low crest of beach, the sight of the sea gave relief. He loved her, she could see that, and plenty more in his bright eyes, and she took strength from him.

Nobly, he volunteered, "Nothing has happened we can't stop."

"That's not true," Patty said, for she had fallen in love with him, as he with her. "But as far as this beach house goes, I'd say Alice could use a best seller."

The nearest neighbor, Joaquin, was a man in his forties who earned a few dollars as caretaker to the house during Alice's absence. Sporadically employed, Joaquin lived with his mother-in-law, his wife, and their three children. Other than Don, Joaquin was the only man visible on the beach. When he approached, scuffling in shoes full of sand, shoes broken down at the heels and untied, his dog stirred from under the house and emerged. The children stepped back and deferred. Joaquin had not expected Alice's return until the week-end, and was surprised to see people whom he didn't know driving her car. Don introduced himself by name as Don Perry, an introduction that, without connection to Alice, meant little to Joaquin. Then Don introduced Patty as Alice's niece, which meant much. Alice had mentioned Patty's arrival two weeks earlier.

Then, Patty, in a ruse of her own, introduced herself as *la Señora Don Perry*, and made sure Joaquin saw her ring, which she had borrowed from Alice, sans permission; or, more precisely, from the pouch in Alice's jewelry box in the dresser in Alice's room. The ring had belonged to Patty's great grandmother's, and Patty reasoned Alice would not need it right now. She stumbled for the phrase, *recien casados,* which Joaquin supplied. It meant newly married.

"*Se casaron hoy?*" Joaquin asked exuberantly, looking from one to the other for confirmation.

"*Sí,*" answered Don, knowing the Spanish for they had been married today. He seemed prouder to Patty than a man with a son; delirious, in fact, with her ruse. Joaquin assumed they had chosen this place for their honeymoon. The news also meant he would have to make hurried arrangements, for the house was not ready, and so, excitedly, he called for his wife.

Enriqueta came quickly, making much of Patty's ring, and of Patty, and Don, making them both feel at once welcome and at ease. Over Patty's protest—that no one go to any trouble—Enriqueta assured Patty she and Joaquin would have the house in order in no time. Patty promised them in turn a slow walk on the beach, and set off, ahead of Don. Don gave Joaquin the keys to Alice's car and cash for provisions in town.

"What are we doing?" he asked, when he caught up to Patty, who was wading along the shore in the surf, her back to the row of houses, her gaze on the unpopulated curve of the beach to the east.

"What are we doing? I love you," she said.

"I love you, too," he told her.

These simple professions they exchanged, not on the best tan beach in the world, but on a nice beach; not in the most wonderful surf, but in the sea, nonetheless; in the midst of a nice morning, a good breeze, under fair tropical skies, with warm sand underfoot, surrounded by countless green stones, in every shade imaginable of olive, jade, and teal.

When he kissed her, she tasted his mouth. She drew her fear out of Don. She drew her strength out of Don. She drew her love out of Don. He was lord.

When they returned, the house seemed transformed. Joaquin had raised the shutters and aired it out, and Enriqueta had summoned the children so that the newly married would be private. Joaquin had made certain the stove had white gas, the water jar fresh water, and the privy had paper. Entering the house, Patty found the table had been set. There stood an unlit candle, but a box of matches by the stove. A gingham tablecloth draped the table. Champagne stood in ice, and on a stand stood a bouquet of fresh flowers. There was block ice in the ice box, and a plate of fresh ham. On the table was bread and fresh cheese; on the sink, mangos and oranges.

She wept. Don held her. There were two back rooms in the house, both with a view to the cane, and in one there were linens on the bed. The bed was turned down. On the pillow, Enriqueta had left Patty a rose.

—

CHAPTER ELEVEN

Tuesday evening, Patty and Don went into town to the movies, where they found the effect of being away from lovemaking served mainly to heighten their desire to resume. In the movie, James Mason played *The Man in Grey*, a film Patty did not like. On the way out, they ran into Lon, who told them Harry was angry, because Don had missed flying. Don promised to show up in the morning, though flying was the thing farthest from his mind. Lon could see, plainly enough, that Don's apology to Patty had succeeded.

On the way out of town, Don stopped at the same *friquitín* they had passed two times earlier in the day and that Patty had passed on her way to and from the Ceiba on Monday.

The best advertisement for the place was not its name— *Piquito*—the name of a dish, but the aroma that wafted out over the street as a result of the stews and the spices. It made Patty ravenous. *Piquito* stayed open late, and at the window stood a male customer, talking to the woman inside, who had cooked the food whose aroma Patty was finding so enticing.

The menu in *Piquito* featured dishes based more on an African than a Spanish cuisine. "What is *piquito*?" Patty asked.

"Stewed pig's livers," Don explained, with a look that bordered on disgust.

"Good?"

"No," he said.

"You don't like it?" she asked, laughing with him.

"I eat healthy food," Don said. "Wheaties, not intestines. Eat fruit. Eat mangos. Eat papaya. Eat cheese from the country. Don't eat the innards of pigs."

"I like to try stuff," she said, smiling at the woman behind the window. The woman, squat and dark, in her fifties, welcomed Patty and Don both. "What's good?" Patty asked, in English not well understood. The menu items were exotic: alcapurrias, mofongo, gandinga, mondongo. "What's *morcilla*?" she asked.

"Sausage made of blood," said Don, disdainfully.

"*Rica*," said the woman, clearly proud.

Then the man at Patty's side interjected: *morcilla* was blood pudding—thickened blood, mixed with suet—he said in English, adding that he once had lived in Akron, which seemed sufficient in his mind to account for what he knew.

"Blood pudding?" Patty asked, eyeing the pan of crisp, black intestinal skins behind the window. Don hoped that would end it. Instead, Patty ordered morcilla.

"*A probar*," the woman said; just to taste.

Patty found the dish scrumptious. "Never ate chitt'lins?" she asked Don.

"No, never," he lied. He had, of course, but hadn't cared for them.

"He's been deprived," Patty told the woman, who agreed.

"You might like mofongo," said Don; mofongo being the least offensive of the items.

"What's mofongo?" Patty asked.

"*Éste*," said the woman, showing Patty the dish, which, the male customer then explained, consisted of grated plantains, cooked with rinds of pork.

"Something like cracklin'," said Don; another dish he didn't care for.

But Patty liked mofongo right away, and was established as the woman's favorite customer.

"Try mondongo," urged the man, upping the ante. Mondongo was stewed guts. The very sound of mondongo made Don queasy.

"You've forgotten your heritage," Patty kidded. "Something spicy," she said.

"Gandinga!" said the woman.

"Something saucy," said Patty.

"Gandinga!" said the man.

"Gandinga!" Patty beamed. "Something hot!"

"Gandinga!" both exclaimed. The woman radiated health and joy. The man looked proud. Gandinga was the prize, a spicy, rich, deep-flavored stew of heart, kidney, and liver of pig.

"*Deliciosa*," pronounced the woman.

"*Exquisita*," the man opined.

Patty savored and agreed. "You aren't eating?" she asked Don.

"Can you make me a grilled cheese sandwich?" Don inquired.

When they got back to the beach house, they went for a swim. While they were in the water, a strange thing occurred. Patty was standing in water to her shoulders, her back to the shore, looking out across the sea into the night, when she felt what she thought was Don's hand stroke her belly. Don had been with her the moment before, and she assumed he was still with her. But, when she turned to embrace him, she saw him on shore. That ended the night-swimming and the sex in the Caribbean after dark.

Later, she reflected that she had heard women say that they knew the moment conception had occurred, because it was like being stroked across the belly.

Don awoke Wednesday thinking of Harry, and thinking of flying, and he resolved to go to work. He had slept at some point, and while he wasn't sure whether it was a long or short time, he felt rested. Or, at least, he felt neutral; at home, and at peace, comfortable, and spent. She had made him glad. He had been for so long by himself, his good fortune now seemed boundless. The improbability of being with her impressed itself upon him as he lay, thinking, in the stillness before dawn. Again and again, he awakened to the shock of good fortune. Love began in the flesh, and ended in the spirit. Love had a beginning and no end. He trusted her. He loved her. He was accepted and indulged. In turn, she gave him her heart, her very soul. When she awakened, they embraced. They lay together. Their dreams seemed intertwined, as if they were married, somehow, and husband and wife were one flesh. "I have to go to work," he said, but made no move to leave.

The shore came to life. Gulls had arrived, and roosters in the margins of the field crowed. Perhaps Don would have a family. Then he too would be like Julio, looking out for the welfare of the wife and the kids. But for the moment, the thought of flying unnerved him. He was not ready after all. He heard the men in the row going to work. Gruff voices. He dozed. Patty cuddled in his arms. He heard the children go off to school. He had plenty of time. He took a warm bath of pleasure in the feel of Patty's closeness. "Can I stay home today?" he asked.

"Stay home," she whispered. He lay on his back, staring up at the underside of the roof. Throughout the night, mosquitos had bitten them both. He lit a cigarette. His body bore welts of *no see-um's*, insects named for the fact that no one saw them. She had dozed; he heard her breathing.

He heard the sea, washing ashore, receding. Of all sounds on the earth, sea sounds seemed most easily ignored, as easily as ignoring one's breath, or one's heart, excepting those times when the breath began to pant, or the sea began to slam the earth, or the heart began to pound; then would the terror of flying set things in motion? or the explosion of sex draw him out?

Through their neighbor, Joaquin, Patty and Don found a Dominican guide named Aluzame, and, through a local charter captain named Don Guille, Aluzame was able to find a launch that took them—Aluzame, Don Guille, Patty, and Don—out for a day of skin diving in the shallow waters over the reefs between the island, *Caja de Muertos*, and the south coast of Puerto Rico, east of Ponce. During the day, Don became fascinated with diving because, underwater, diffusion of light made the world seem luminous and, in that luminosity, he seemed able to fly. Prior to Tuesday, Don had never swum in the sea, and, prior to today, never so far from the shore. By contrast, Patty had swum often in the Atlantic and in the Chesapeake Bay, although, like

Don, she was still new to subtropical waters. Neither she nor Don had ever used fins or masks, articles Aluzame had provided.

Aluzame's deal was to guide them for free, but keep whatever he caught, which he then sold to local markets and restaurants of Ponce. From day to day, his bounty included conch, octopus, lobster, and a variety of edible fish. He caught the fish by spear. He had been fishing this way all his life, and the effects of a life of sun and saltwater made him appear wizened, older than his twenty-eight years.

For fun, Don competed with Aluzame in holding his breath underwater; Don's best time being just under two minutes, Aluzame's average time being just above three. On board the boat, Don made drawings of the fish he had seen during dives. But, when Aluzame offered to teach him to fish with a spear, Don declined. He identified with the fish. Patty, on the other hand, proved adept as Aluzame's student, and, since fish were fish and not people, by mid-day she was able to provide the party's lunch.

Ashore on *Caja de Muertos*, Patty fried *chillos*—red snapper—in an iron skillet over a fire on the beach. Then, the four: Don Guille, Aluzame, Patty, and Don ate fillets, salted and rubbed lightly with lime, while hunkering beneath a scorching bright sun on bright white sand at the edge of the sea. It pleased Patty no end to have provided the men so basic an item as their lunch. She took their compliments with gusto.

Caja de Muertos was deserted, apart from a lighthouse and goats, the latter of which were kept by the tender of the lighthouse, who had to bring them fresh water by boat. Except for scrub, the island consisted of rock and sand that, in profile, when viewed from the southern mountains and plains of Puerto Rico, suggested the shape and gave rise to the name, which in English meant coffin.

That evening, back in Ponce, Patty and Don lay on their bed in the dark of their beach house. Down the beach, their neighbors were singing. They heard the sounds of a cuatro. Burned by sun, tired, with eyes stinging with salt, they felt the bed gently rocking, like the sea. They felt their sleep, like a wave; their dream bright,

immanent, like a swim underwater. For Patty, the day had been
sheer exuberance. And Aluzame had been the marvel of the day.
Aluzame had speared *mero*, which were sea bass, *chillo*, and
capitán. He had snatched four lobsters and an octopus by hand
from the reef. He lived a simple life, almost literally hand-to-
mouth. Don, however, was perturbed, and lay awake to puzzle
over such feats, over the fact that, for Aluzame, catching fish
seemed altogether unremarkable. Don knew many people who
lived as Aluzame did. And did it matter if here the subsistence
was fish; there, some other food? Did it matter if a fish caught in
southern waters was eaten by someone from the north? Obviously,
the distinction was lost on the fish, except to say that if the
northerner stayed away, the fish might have survived. Don felt it
strange to have witnessed so much killing and partaken in the
feast, and that in itself was strange because killing resounded from
Don's youth. Country life had simple pleasures. He grew up
having heard the thud of the hatchet, the squawk of the chicken,
the thwack, the fatal blow, the shot; the music of slaughter, the
squeal, the thrash of death throes, panting, the slather of guts,
and the warm smell of blood. He had heard and watched his
mother talk sweetly to a chicken, even chide it to correct its
behavior, even as she chopped off its head. He had heard and
watched his sisters, too, learn the cruelty of beauty matched to
death. Such contrariety tore at Don, and always had. He had
grown apart from growing up, apart from his own past, moving
ever farther from flesh-eating and killing. Yet, he remained
transfixed, despite the years, as if subject to his mother's voice; as
if he were the chicken she beheaded. It disturbed him to associate
himself with Patty's prey, and to associate Patty with killing, but
it excited him, too, and what disturbed him most was his
excitement. "It's funny," he said, not meaning that it was. He
rooted for her to get the fish. Her willfulness made victimhood
seductive.

   In their absence, Maxwell had left them a message: "Show
up tomorrow or you're dead."

   Don's final words to the darkness, spoken eyes closed, on the gently rocking boat of their bed, were, "No matter." He fell asleep still wanting to go on.

On Thursday morning, they slept through the crowing of cocks and the departures of workmen who lived on the row. Once up, Patty swam and had breakfast, and afterwards indulged Don's propensity to look at her by allowing him to watch her get dressed. In turn, Don indulged Patty's propensity to show off by applying the most avid scrutiny to her fleetest and most casual gestures. His attention was a mirror and her deftness a charm, so she neither hurried nor teased. Outside, on the beach, the neighboring children played, and these Patty watched, unseen from within the darkened doorway, from which she projected the children as her own.

—

CHAPTER TWELVE

To a limited extent, Walter, back from San Juan, filled in for Don on Tuesday and Wednesday, but the real test flying, under extreme loading, had to wait Don's return.

Charlesville had stayed on in San Juan, but planned to return to Harry's Friday, in time for what he assumed would be the visit by General Weggoner.

And Alice, inspired by Patty, and perhaps a little jealous, had decided to begin writing again. She asked Harry if she might do a press release. At the field, Thursday, Minnie was about to serve lunch, when Alice arrived. With all of them present—Alice, Walter, Harry, the men, Patty, Elisa and Minnie, Harry announced, "Nobody eats until we've named the aircraft." He stopped Minnie from serving.

"I thought the ship *had* a name," Julio grumbled, since he and the others had been calling the ship *the ship* since the project was nothing more than a design, back in the autumn of 1942, when Harry had approached Julio and Don with tasks of computing and sketching outflow of two front rotors and a larger, rear, main rotor of a multirotor configuration. *That* had been the beginning of *the ship*.

"*The Ship* is generic," Harry said.

Harry pressed the point with Don. "What do you think we should call her?" he asked.

"*Nose Heavy*," said Don.

Harry was offended. "A name that speaks of her mission," he said.

"Which is what?" asked Julio.

"Shoot people of color in Asia," said Don.

"Don't serve them," Harry repeated to Minnie.

"We can't name an aircraft on an empty stomach," said Lon.

"You'll have to," said Harry.

"*At Your Service*," suggested Don.

"*Full of Fuel*," said Diego.

"Full of something," said Harry.

"*Stümpers!*" exclaimed Bill.

"What's a *stümper*?" Julio asked.

"A *stümper* is a *schlepper*," Harry said. "You guys are *stünkers*. You don't eat until you've named her."

"The food will get cold," complained Minnie.

"*Ready to Serve*," said Walter.

Harry liked that one. "Walter's got it," he said.

"No," Don said.

"No? What's better?" Harry challenged. Patty slipped her hand beneath the table and took Don's hand. "It comes down to the mission," Harry continued. "What's the mission?"

"Can we name her in Spanish?" asked Diego.

"Name her what?" Harry challenged.

"*La Ponceña.*"

"That's nice," Harry said. The men liked it, too. But Harry complained, "What if we had built her in Topeka?"

"*Air Worthy*," suggested Don.

"No," said Harry, but he liked what Don was doing. Don was thinking now, seeming to move in some direction. The room was suffuse with aroma. The men were in pain from the wait. Despite Harry, Minnie served them. Platter after platter arrived at the table.

"No one touch the food," said Harry.

Patty squeezed Don's hand.

"*Wait and See*," said Don, in a pun that slipped by Harry.

"*Weight and Sea* is excellent," said Lon, understanding Don's play on the words.

"Nothing on earth takes the place of a willing pilot," said Harry.

"That's very good," said Elisa, having picked up the phrase *Nothing on Earth*.

"If she won't get off at thirty-one thousand four hundred pounds, I suppose we should know about it," said Julio to Lon, for Julio had calculated the actual weight, revising Harry's figure of thirty-two thousand slightly down.

"So where *are* we flying?" Walter asked.

"We're practicing at Mercedita after lunch," Julio answered.

"I like that four-thousand-foot runway," said Don.

"There's a name that's worthy of your ship," said Walter. "*La Mercedita*." It was a name suggesting grace, a perfect name for an air ambulance.

Minnie hovered over Harry's shoulder. The food was teasing them. She had made them *empanadas*, fried chicken, rice and beans. She had served them plantains in cinnamon syrup, fresh bread, salad, and she had baked a guava tart for dessert, a tart whose crust was made with butter.

"Harry, are there any names that you really do like?" asked Lon.

"*Ready to Serve*," Harry answered. "But I'm still waiting." Again, he looked at Don. "You have one?"

On Tuesday, Patty had stood naked before Don, and, timid for a moment, had asked him not to look at her. For a moment he had honored her request. Then he had disobeyed. Charmed, he had glanced down and glimpsed the fine, yellow hair of her pubic arch. Now, his fingers curled inside her moist palm. Her hand was very warm. He began undressing her in his mind. "*Harry's Ark*," he blurted out. Lord, he felt young. He felt thirty-six.

"Good God!" Harry declared. "That's inspired!"

"Eat!" Minnie ordered, for all the men were poised over drumsticks and thighs.

During lunch, Alice spoke of her purpose in wanting to write a short piece. Excusing himself, Harry went out to the hangar, leaving the others with Alice at the table. "Did any of you happen to hear President Truman's speech to Congress last night?" Alice asked, hoping to solicit views about the new foreign policy doctrine the president had announced.

"I did," said Elisa, but Elisa was the only at the table who had.

"I wanted to get your reactions," said Alice, looking around and then realizing she had just gotten them.

"I'm sorry," said Lon Pyrtle. "What happened?"

"You all know that President Truman spoke to Congress in a special session last night?"

No one seemed to, except Elisa.

"You all know that we're having a crisis in Turkey, and another in Greece? Yes? Good. That's a start. Well, the president addressed those crises before the Congress last night."

"What did he say?" Bill asked.

"He said that the U.S. is to become the world's policeman," said Alice. "That wherever there is democracy in trouble we will intervene, even if it means sending troops. Even if *that* means having to fight. I should think," she went on, "the president's policy will make an eventual, important difference to the world, but especially to you and your project."

"I'm too old for the draft," Lon remarked.

"I should think," Alice continued, "that the new policy will open a market for aircraft such as yours, whose mission might be to help out in local situations."

"We've had a lot on our minds," said Lon. "I'm sorry you caught us uninformed."

"I didn't mean to intrude," Alice said. "It was a subject I thought you would take interest in."

"We do," said Bill, meaning *later*.

Alice concluded, rising, "The president's doctrine adds a world-view to your story. It places your work in a political context, which, in my view, raises it to a level of general importance."

"Does that mean without the president's doctrine we're not important?" asked Bill.

"I'm sorry. I didn't mean it quite that way," Alice said.

In the hangar, Alice looked for Harry. She called his name. He called hers back. She didn't see him. He was in the toilet in the back of the hangar, and had pulled the door shut. "I'm sorry," she apologized. "I'll wait for you outside."

"I know why you're here," Harry called out through the door. "It's in today's paper," he said. "You want a quote?"

"Yes."

"Global vindication for my ship."

Seeing Julio filling the ship's main fuel tank, Alice approached him. "Can you give me something to quote?" Alice asked.

"Sure," Julio said. "How 'bout: heavy is bad. Light is good."

"Very funny."

"Would you like to come with us to Mercedita?"

"Oh, yes, certainly," said Alice, assuming he meant would she like to ride along in someone's car.

"We'll be boarding shortly," he said.

"Fly?" she asked.

"Of course," he said.

She was suddenly frightened, but also thrilled, at the prospect of flying in the ship. "And Harry?"

"Nah. He's afraid. He'll take the car."

Harry had arranged through Ponce Cement for his men to scavenge the plant's yard for rejected pieces of precast concrete they would be using for ballast at Mercedita. For purposes of a test flight, they did not want the ship loaded with fuel. The Pyrtles, with Diego, had taken the truck to get the concrete. The day's plan was to simulate the fuel overload, as a rehearsal for Saturday, when the additional weight would in fact be gasoline.

By late afternoon, Lon telephoned to report he had the ballast, and Harry told him to take the truck to Mercedita to meet them. Then Harry and Walter left for Mercedita in the car.

After preflight inspection, Maxwell assisted Alice in boarding, and went so far as to put down a towel for her so that she wouldn't dirty her skirt on the deck of the cabin. He seated her in the hatchway, with the safety gate drawn. For Alice, the prospect of a flight in Harry's ship, even six miles in six minutes across town, held out the promise of more terror than pleasure. She preferred rail or steamship to flying. But she was determined to do a press release, at least that much, and she felt it her duty to fly in Harry's ship at least once.

When the port engine started, Alice nearly jumped. *A book,* she thought, she had been treating Harry as the subject of a book. Maxwell, having cleared Don for takeoff, brought with him on board two fire extinguishers he stowed in the cabin. Then, he sat beside Alice. When she rested her head against the safety gate, she could feel, as the ship's gearing engaged, vibrations and tremors in her hair and her skull. No, she was reminded, she would not embark on any book. This flight was merely research toward a press release, no more. Tonight, she would finish, knocking out the release in just one sitting.

The blades began to turn. She could see the left front and main rotors through the open hatchway. "We'll be going along the coast," Maxwell hollered.

Alice smiled to be agreeable. As to the route, she did not care what route Don chose, so long as it was safe. She reassured herself with the proposition that it would take the ship no longer to fly around town than it would take an average reader to finish what she'd written. With the runups concluded, Alice found herself absorbed in sounds. The sounds were not necessarily consonant, but they were somehow forged into consonance and she began to feel herself a part of them. The sensation was like listening to a firework display, at its finale, when the detonations seemed to come from within. When the rotors had run their pitches, she began distinguishing the sounds, counting ten in all, and asking Maxwell to identify each. He seemed amused to see her point in space and gesture, as if the sound could be located with her finger. Maxwell, of course, knew all the sounds that Alice wanted named. He hollered out the names of various things—turbos, bearings, planet gears, pitches being pulled and pitches being bottomed. The planet gears reminded Alice of the roll of summer thunder, and made her think of childhood. If she looked crazy, Maxwell didn't mind. She wondered might he be crazy too.

Nothing in life prepared Alice for the takeoff. It occurred in a swoop. There was no roll or lurch, but her belly went down, her heart went up, and she got a real flash, almost to the point of a precise recollection, of being swept off her feet by her father. The ship did not roll but was snatched, like a big bassinet. Nor was she prepared for the frenzy of wind that lashed against her face. When she realized that she was clutching at the bar, she saw that Maxwell was clutching at it, too; perhaps not so crazy after all.

The field withdrew from beneath her. She gaped as she flew over the top of her car. Before she half knew where she was, she was looking at the town from the southwest. She was seeing afternoon sun light the plaza, and the whole of Ponce seemed a giant swatch of colors. She knew every building she saw, and quickly lost count of all the buildings, and also her fear. She marveled at the tree tops, the crisp green crowns of laurels in the plaza, mangos and breadfruit trees along the streets. She marveled at the pastel blue of Don Antonio's house, the face of the cathedral, the roof of the *Plaza del Mercado*. A pocket of air buffeted the ship; she felt no peril. The town looked like a garden. She could see the school where she taught, and peek into narrow streets in search of her children. Even when Don altered course to northeast, and the deck beneath her slightly dipped, she felt no sense of danger.

From the southeast of town she began to see the shadows Ponce cast; the violet of bougainvillea. She saw the bakery on *Comercio* where she bought her daily bread; the pomegranate tree outside her own kitchen; and the roof of her own house, over which spread the thickly tangled branches of her own great mango. "I just saw why my downspouts are clogged," she shouted at Maxwell. Her rooftop was littered with dead leaves.

But Maxwell, himself absorbed as the ship flew east across the Rio Portugués, was taken by the sight of Ponce's great *Ceiba*. "Biggest tree I ever saw," he yelled. An old man, sitting on the *balcón* of his house, looked up at Alice. To her utter amazement, she waved, and to her utter delight the old man waved back. She was a child again, on a Sunday afternoon ride with her father. She wondered what that old man would think, were he to compare his experience to hers, as she did hers to her past. He could see the sky around her ship. But she could see the place where he was born.

When she looked over at Maxwell once more, the thought occurred to her that Maxwell seemed happy, too; that being here was sufficient. Alice didn't know where Maxwell came from, or anything about him. She didn't know anything about any of the men, and really not much about Patty. What had brought them all here? What kept them all together? There wasn't room for such information in a press release. Yet, as she looked at Maxwell, she thought, whatever it was that he had done with his life, from her point of view had he done nothing else but allow her to sit beside him, that was enough.

"Like it?" he asked, for the town receded and they were coming down.

"I like it," she answered. He seemed to understand; he seemed to know what she was feeling.

The touchdown was effortless, like a leaf coming down in a calm. And when the engines shut down, it was the silence that roared. She was sitting in *La Mercedita*, and, when she talked now, it was her voice that seemed loud. But Maxwell seemed to understand that, too. Alice told him thanks.

Julio understood. Many times in his life Julio had seen the look that Alice wore. When she told Julio thanks, he smiled.

Don certainly understood. How could he not? He'd been there all his life, and when Alice told Don thanks, he acknowledged with a smile.

Alice was so happy, she was flabbergasted. Yet what had happened? How could she explain it? She wanted to burst out in tears. She felt a longing to get to know Mr. Pyrtle, and Bill. And of course she ought to get to know Diego, who was not only a *Ponceño* but one with whose family she had been acquainted for years. And when she saw Harry, she gave Harry a hug, even Harry. And then she gave Walter one too. Why Walter? Why, indeed. She felt so grateful to be around those who knew. Who else would understand?

"It's your job to make them see us," Harry said, oh so wryly.

"It'll have to be a book," said Alice. "An article won't do."

"Alice," Patty called.

Alice heeled around. Patty took her picture from Don's window of the cockpit. Through the viewfinder Alice looked like a cheeky, blowzy, face-flushed kid, and Patty had evidence that once upon a time even Alice had been young. "Look to yourself," Alice chided.

But Patty had. Shooting Alice was her mirror.

—

CHAPTER THIRTEEN

Don was anxious. *La Mercedita* was Ponce's municipal airport, owned by the family Serralles, and Julio and Don felt that, to fly the ship at its maximum gross weight, they needed the rolling start that Mercedita's runway would afford. That was why they were here. At 3,900 feet, runway 12 was long enough to accommodate DC-3s and the small, four-engine de Havillands flown as shuttles by the island's carrier, Carib Air, and would be long enough to accommodate *Harry's Ark*. Normally a helicopter did not need a rolling start, but Harry's Ark would soon be overloaded.

The airport was deserted, except for Harry's company. At the tie-down, sat two local, single-engine planes, parked. But there was no-one at the fuel depot or on the parking apron, no-one in the terminal, and no aircraft arriving or taking off. The next arrival would be the Carib Air shuttle from San Juan, not due until nightfall.

Beyond the airport stood acres of cane, and directly to the north stood the Serralles refinery, which, along with the airport and fields, comprised the plantation *La Mercedita*.

At the west end of the taxistrip, where Don had parked the ship, Bill backed the truck so they could offload the precast. On the truck's bed rested the hundred-odd pieces of concrete Bill and Lon, with Diego, had culled from the yard of Ponce Cement. Seeing the precast triggered Don's anxiety, but the anxiety was something that had been building ever since they began planning a flight to Wright Field. *The ship's too heavy*, Don thought. For two days, with Patty, he had denied he felt that way, and now he knew he did. The pieces, measured and carefully weighed, ranged in size and weight from small to massive, from a few pounds to several hundred. To the extent possible, the men wished to simulate not only the weight but also the balance that, in flight, would be imposed on the ship by a load of nearly 12,000 pounds of aviation gasoline. To make better use of the cabin's space, Julio had removed the winch and winch motor. From the truck, one of the hoists taken from the field served to transfer pieces of precast from truck bed to cabin, there gently to be deposited on the deck and maneuvered into place. Transferring and loading precast was neither simple nor swift, since the requirements for balance were precise. In the heat of late afternoon, under the five o'clock sun, the ship was a veritable sweat box. Lack of breeze made things worse. Don just watched. He didn't participate. He felt doomed. Thirty-two thousand pounds was too much weight. So he turned his back on it.

He wanted to walk, to get away, to go anywhere. He now felt depleted. Two days on the beach had not refreshed him; they had depleted him. Two days of sexual adventure had left him spent. "The condemned needn't dig his own grave," he said to Harry, who stood beside the aircraft with Alice and Lon, watching.

"It's what happens when you mix a woman with work," Harry said; *old-school*, angry at Don for missing two days, and especially angry that Don would take off work to get laid.

Patty caught up to Don, who was walking down the runway. She planned to shoot the ship taking off, and so had to walk to the opposite end of the field.

"The ship's too heavy," he said, when they were far from Harry's men. But he was forging a connection between one burden and another, between the ship and its weight, and his equally oppressive memory of the support he had failed to provide to his daughter during the first ten years of her life. He spoke about his daughter, now twenty-one, three years short of Patty's age. "Her name is Antoinette. I was twenty when I got married. Her mother, Grace Phillips, was already pregnant. She had been married once before, but it ended badly. Then I came along, and that ended badly too. I thought twenty was old. But, of course, it isn't. I thought I knew everything. But, of course, I knew nothing. I wanted to be a father, but I had no idea what that meant. What I really wanted were high times. But those are dim now. The marriage lasted six years, then she divorced me. Out of the six years, I think only the first two years were what you might call, *really married*."

Patty looked on as he spoke, walking with him and listening. It was as if she were hearing his confession. But she could see he was bound up, iron-jawed about this business. He was afraid, after all, for the blame he would have to bear if he crashed, and no doubt he was afraid of being killed, though with Don the greater fear was always failure. Shame. Shame was worse. The runway had turned out like baked hell.

"It's my job," he said. "I volunteered for it."

"You're right," she said. "And if you back out, there'll be no flight, nor any story. Up to you." He wanted it both ways; she could see that: to confess but not be held accountable for confessing; to be heroic, but exempt from the burden heroes bore. Still, in the long view, pilots had been afraid of flying for as long as there were aircraft to be flown. It was no sin to be afraid. So they walked, together but apart. "How would it have been different had we come here Tuesday?" Patty asked. "Would the ship have been lighter?" Don laughed. "Are you sorry you had your time with me?"

"No," he said, but he had reverted to asceticism, a state in which he saw himself as responsible for everything, and for outlasting opposition. "Whether the aircraft flies depends mainly on me," he said.

"No, it depends mainly on weight," Patty told him. "Get the past off your chest."

"I didn't support her."

"I heard what you said."

"I wouldn't give up wanting to fly, and I wasn't earning steady money. Not till later."

"If you think the ship can fly at 31,400 pounds, then fly it," Patty said. It was simple as she saw it now. "Fly it to Miami. Fly it to Wright Field. Break those records. But if you think it can't fly, don't kill yourself trying. It's a better story if you live." Her conclusion should have been evident, but she doubted that it was. He was doing this for Harry. Was Harry great? Harry exploited his labor. Harry bet against himself. "You're my story," Patty said. "Do what you have to. Survive."

Don pondered, looking north at the refinery. Smoke rose from the chimneys in vertical columns. Dead calm. The fields seemed to sigh. The sun seemed to hang amidst clouds. It was the day's worst hour. In the distance, he could see men working, the pounds mounting. "Need a hundred pounder," he heard Julio's faraway voice. Another hundred pounds, and another. More and more. He felt Patty was right, and the thought of Harry enraged him. Harry gave no credit to anyone. All Harry wanted was for himself, and, when things went wrong, he blamed others. *Whip the nigger* was Harry's game. But, still, there was something inside: dishonesty on Don's part, too; hypocrisy, masking his own indulgence. He loved to be sought after, praised, and seduced. He loved his idle time. What he lived for, he would die for. How ironic. As Don thought back on his sins, especially his sin of having loved a white woman, he realized that, down the runway, given the distance, the men did indeed sound like a gallows crew, of riggers and diggers and carpenters, as raunchy and as punchy as any nightmare the South had ever produced.

The moment of realization was on Don. The flight he was about to fly justified the neglect of his child, and would punish him for Patty. And so he thought of it as duty, the wages of death for the sin of his life. Time and space were drawing to a close. "What should I do?" he asked Patty

Knowing he would do the opposite of what she said, she told him, "Don't fly. You said yourself the ship's too heavy."

Make it a good one," he said, referring to the shot she would get when he flew.

Patty set up her camera. She had reached the eastern bound, beyond the end of the runway. At the border of grass, a low wire fence separated the airport from the cane field. A few feet into the field, canebrakes stood at head height. The field seemed extended forever. A breeze stirred. It brought faint relief. She looked back, watching Don's figure recede and surveying the runway. Heat created a mirage, a black and silver shimmer down the distance to the men. The truck and ship looked ghastly. The men appeared to work at lake side. They were backlit by sun, in another country. The mirage had developed in a slight concavity of the runway's midspan. Longshadows cast out upon the waters. What Don had feared most was losing her, something certain to occur. In a white man's world, to love her could cost him his life. Tuesday, she had played for him, all her strings resonant; Wednesday, too. But today brought the change. She concluded life was kinder to the male. She could tell his story, that he cut a handsome figure, coming or going.

At the ship, Don confronted Julio and Harry. The men took a break, hearing his voice. "We're losing our light," he said.

"We're waiting for you," Harry told him. "Had you shown up Wednesday, like I asked you, then we wouldn't be losing our light. We'd have plenty of light."

"Let's get going," he said.

Lon Pyrtle felt thoroughly disgusted with how the loading had turned out. Not that it was wrong, but his idea had been to start with a lower weight and work up gradually, adding increments with each flight. But they had run out of time, and, so, jumped to the end, starting with the highest weight first. "It's what always happens to us," said Lon. "This is why our project is screwed up. We play Russian roulette, but, instead of using one round, we use two."

"Do what's best," Harry said, ignoring Lon's complaint.

"This is no way to run a test flight program," Lon continued.

"Who said it was?" Julio murmured.

"This is not why I came to Puerto Rico," Lon said, tossing his clipboard and going off in a huff toward the terminal. Alice, intrigued by Lon, tagged along. "Put it in your book," he told her, when he had finished explaining what was what.

"I intend to," she said.

As the sun sank, Patty, at the end of the runway, realigned her position, so that what she expected would be the track of the ship would pass between her camera and the sun. In keeping with her style of dramatic shots, she wanted the ship to be backlit. On the north corner of the runway, she moved back as far as she could from the threshold, then set the tripod at the edge of the cane. Glare was less a problem now, for clouds across the western sky absorbed some light. The sunset was glorious. She wished they would hurry.

Aboard the ship, Don and Julio took their stations. Maxwell drove the truck away, parking alongside Harry's car. As Don settled in, Julio stuck his head through the hatchway. "Wanted to tell you something."

"What?" asked Don.

"If the ship is overweight, I've got no problem with unloading a few hundred pounds, if that means live a few years longer."

"Little late for that," said Don. "Can we step up the rotor speed for takeoff?"

Julio quickly calculated the effects of a twenty percent increase on bearings, hinges and hubs. Centrifugal force would increase. The blades, stiffened, would resist pitch control. He thought of hydraulics, and then about engines. Valves would float. Tappets might not ride cam lobes. The engines would run hotter. "We can do it for a few minutes," he said.

"Long enough to clear the power lines," said Don. "I'll bring the nose up late on the take-off." Outside the ship, Maxwell placed the fire extinguishers in the back seat of Harry's car, then took the car around to face the runway. Don felt a great sadness, like a wave of great loss. He searched the distance for a sign of Patty, but could not see her.

Bill came onto the taxiway and stood before the ship's nose. He looked up at Don through the cockpit. "We're ready," he said. Don heard his soft voice through the window.

"Julio," Don called. Julio had returned to his station. To the left of the ship, Harry and Walter stood together. Maxwell remained in Harry's car.

"Right here," Julio said, using intercom to answer.

"Let's get going," said Don. Ponce's sky was emblazoned.

From the roof of the terminal, Lon looked out, at the men and the ship. The engines had started. Alice, busy with notes, looked up, first to the aircraft, then to the far end of the field. There she spied Patty. But she noticed Patty had moved to another location. "Isn't that dangerous?" she asked, for it occurred to her that Patty's new position placed her right in the line of the takeoff.

"Very much so," said Lon.

Down on the taxiway, with runups completed, Bill guided the aircraft. At the moment the ship began to taxi, Don felt the weight, right up from the tires. And deep in his bowels his intuition told him no. The aircraft was too heavy to fly.

"What do you think?" Julio asked.

"We're okay," Don replied.

When the ship crossed over the hold-short line and entered onto the runway, Don turned it upwind, then stopped. He looked down the runway. In the distance he spotted Patty, all but camouflaged among the canebrakes. At first, the sight of her was gladdening, then, when he recognized she was directly in his way, he shouted out the window at Bill. "Get her the hell off my runway!" And at first, Bill didn't comprehend what Don had said. He couldn't hear Don, but, when he turned, he also looked down the runway and saw Patty.

Alice posed what she thought was a stupid question. "What's happening?" she asked.

"Your niece thinks they're waving hello," answered Lon.

In the ship, Don paused to take stock of his moment. The moment was his; he had been here before. He owned it. The ship was ready; engines were running, rotors were turning at idle. Outside the aircraft, Harry was laughing with Walter. Things were okay. The sun was going down. Harry had the look of a proud man, a papa, a man confident of his success. It was as if his ship was about to be born. Walter, too, had the look of a man who was eager, for Walter wished to be sitting where Don was sitting now. Perhaps by next week his wish would come true. This moment was Don's; right man, right time, and right place.

The airport washed orange; a creature of refraction. Don thought of an oak tree he had seen once in autumn; home, in Ohio. Odd thoughts were converging. He went over his moves. The last light of the sun lay nearly parallel to the runway, extending the shadows of the rotors, constantly sweeping, forever. Light began to flicker around the arcs of each rotor's plane, and the thought occurred to Don that here was a moment like no other; for the first time in his life he was seeing sunlight strike the lower cambers of blades.

"Who's the first guy to arrive at the scene of an accident?" Julio asked.

"The pilot," Don answered.

"Just do what you do," Julio said.

The incredible moment—*it begins*—had begun. Don opened the throttles and began to wind engines. He felt the strange optical illusion, and the visceral sense, that the universe was drawn to his heart. It was as if his very power to attend had magnetized distance, bringing space close to him, bending lines, including the horizon, the runway, mountains, and sky. He had such energy, such vigilance, that through his will the ship began to roll. Every time he blinked he re-perceived the splice of space and time. Every instant was schematic. Time was eighty seconds. In eighty seconds was abundance. He could dream, reap fields, move the world in eighty seconds.

When the ship rolled by the terminal, Lon could hear the power was stepped up; how much he could not say. He further noted how slowly the ship was gaining speed.

Patty's second move, to her third and last position, put her just south of the runway, a concession she had made to all the frantic waving. She had not had a great deal of time for this particular readjustment, and she grappled with a sense that she would now have to rush to get her shot.

At a rolling speed of fifty-four, the ship's rear wheels rose from the runway. When the speed reached fifty-nine, Don was certain they would make it. She was airborne. Then the ship touched down again, and a bolt of fear went through him. At sixty-three, there seemed too little power, pitch was balky in changing, and the tilts of the rotors imprecise.

Patty saw the ship go into rotation. The nose come up.

Lon held his head.

Don tried to climb out at sixty-four. The ship crossed the threshold nose high, and he felt the retardation at the pylon, losing lift. He had never crashed a takeoff. "We're going down," he said.

Julio found Don's voice very calm.

Patty shot. The aircraft stalled. With a great whoosh it came down in a pancake, taking out fence and cane, and throwing up stalks in the air. Husks and tassels flew everywhere. Its nose crumpled, its belly caved in. Several tons of precast rammed the bulkhead, split open the deck, tore open the seams of the siding. The rotors had pranged with the weird reverse stress; went *boing* like diving boards, *da-dum, da-dum,* and still kept turning. One engine still ran at full speed. Hydraulic fluid burst a coupling. A steady stream of dust issued out of the earth and was chased around by the rotors. The air was a constant upheaval of flecks and leaves of sugarcane brakes.

Don thought of the end of his days. Armageddon. He was crushed but not hurt. He had suffered no injury whatever. Just the shock of his life and the worst wound he had ever inflicted. He hoped who came first would just shoot him.

Julio was pinned by the bulkhead. His whole panel had come back in his lap. The ballast had wedged him. He was numb, but he knew he had something wrong with his foot. It felt greasy and wet.

Patty was the first to arrive. She had been virtually at the site. She thought she smelled gasoline. Maxwell was second, in Harry's car. Walter couldn't get the truck started. Lon Pyrtle turned away from Alice. He had never in his life been so thoroughly fed up.

The ship's struts had collapsed, and some of its load had spilled out. Patty was afraid of the rotors, which turned much lower to the ground now that the ship had no legs. She went to the nose, where she stood outside Don's window. She screamed at him to shut the engine off. He stared at her, deeply shocked, then he cut the engines.

Getting Julio out took a couple of minutes, and Julio did most of the work. Don did nothing at all. Don crawled out forward through a break in the Plexiglas of the windshield to the right of the copilot's seat. Maxwell and Diego got to Julio through the cabin, first by climbing over precast and then by moving some of the smaller pieces from the pile. Julio could have freed himself, entirely by his own effort, but feared if he jerked he might pull his foot off. The wound gashed the top of Julio's left foot, and bled profusely. When he was free, with Diego's help, he crawled aft into the cabin under his own power, and when he reached the ground he started hopping on one leg.

Maxwell wanted to spray the ship with foam. Harry told him no.

No one else smelled gasoline. Patty was no longer sure if she had smelled it or not. Hydraulic fluid was every bit as dangerous. There was also oil beneath the cowling, aft.

Alice was greatly relieved to see Don. She outpaced Lon Pyrtle on the trot down the runway.

Harry assessed the look of things and concluded the end of the project had occurred. He could hardly speak he felt so ruined. Julio had to go to the hospital. Shock was setting in. He now lay on his back, staring at the sky. "Get a chain or something and hook it to the carcass," said Harry, referring to the ship. "Drag it off to the side somewhere. People have to use this airport. That's the end of it. The project's over. You all go home, you hear?"

"Julio's got to go to the hospital," Maxwell said.

Harry could get the Army to come over from Losey Field and the Army could bulldoze the ship and haul the remnants away. He didn't think it out. He didn't want to argue.

Julio went into shock in the back seat of Harry's car.

Harry told them just go ahead, do what they wanted.

Walter had begun inspecting the wreckage. He had climbed to the top of the fuselage. He had no intention of going anywhere.

He had no home to go to. "Going to be a long night," he said. Long nights were home to Walter.

"No it isn't," Harry snapped. Harry had seen wrecks before. He knew how fast this site could be cleared.

Diego climbed into the back seat with Julio. Maxwell drove. Off they roared in Harry's car. Alice noticed that Julio looked gray.

Walter came down. "This ship is still flyable," he said.

"Are you nuts?" Harry said.

"Are you okay?" Alice asked Don.

"I'm fine," said Don. He had never been hurt much in anything in his life, and had never been involved in an air crash before; ground loop being the closest he had come. The last hurt he had suffered was getting whipped by his daddy, and that was for not fighting whites. He looked balefully at Alice. He had remembered every thought in the sequence of thoughts, right up through the instant of the crash and beyond. "I wish I was dead," he told her.

Walter announced he felt certain the ship was okay.

Lon turned his back, refusing to dignify such nonsense. He offered Harry a ride in the truck. But Lon was angry, much more at Harry than at Walter. Harry needed to go to the terminal to call the Army.

Walter continued his inspection. He went into the cabin. He had located three leaks in the hydraulics and a leak in the oil. His principal concern was for the bent formers aft of Julio's station. He would need Bill's advice about the circuitry, but in light of the fact that both engines had continued running until Don shut them off, Walter was certain that critical electrical service had remained intact. Julio's panel was a mess; completely dislodged, but to Walter the future of the ship depended on whether mounts and housings for the points of support for the engines and drive trains had stayed in line. Any twisting, any torque at a point of support would spell the end.

"You all don't need me here," said Don. No one said yes, no one said no. But it wasn't a question so much as a fact. He got to his feet and brushed off his pants. It was such an idle gesture, really, purely reflex. "You don't belong," he said to Patty. "Damn your ass, you should never have come to Puerto Rico."

Patty said nothing. She appeared as if slapped, her eyes big and round.

When Harry returned with Lon in the truck, Walter pronounced the ship within reach of fast salvage. To Harry's bewildered, utterly dumbfounded look, Walter offered his expert assessment, which, he made certain to point out, was based on some years experience on the Russian front. "We have made aircraft fly that were in far worse shape than this," Walter said with some pride.

"You lost the goddam war," said Harry.

"You're screwy," said Lon, who knew very well it would take days to check tolerances and welds, to say nothing of the time for readjustments and repairs.

"I called the Army," Harry said, addressing Bill. "They won't come until morning. I want you to sit with the ship for the night."

"Why?" asked Bill.

"Because I want you to," said Harry. "I don't want the townspeople here."

"Good enough," said Bill.

"You don't understand," said Walter, persisting with Harry. "You really don't. We could have this ship flying by sunrise. At least as far as your field, where we could do the remaining work."

"You don't understand either," said Harry, at last fed up and willing to deal with Walter head on, if only to get him to stop. "The project is over and done with. Finished. In the morning we will clear the field at O eight hundred hours. And by ten hundred hours she'll be gone. This is an airport. We're blocking traffic with our wreck."

"Utterly foolish," said Walter.

"Americans bury their dead," Harry said. "The project is dead. Bury it." Then he was finished. He had a lot of things to do at the office; a thousand tasks; call Antonio; call the mayor; and, certainly, call the police. Not a thing was keeping him here, certainly not a need for debate. To Bill he added, "I'll have someone bring you supper."

Bill turned to his dad. "What are you going to do?"

"Get a plane ticket," said Lon. "Head back to Cincinnati."

Walter asserted his claim. "I can take possession."

But this was ridiculous. "Sue me," Harry said, who had nothing to lose.

"At least leave me the scaffold," said Walter. "I need the chainfall. I need some flashlights. I need some tools and hydraulic fluid."

"Forget it," Lon told him.

"Let me have the scaffold," Walter insisted.

"The hell with it," said Harry.

"Let him have it," said Bill. "We're going to have to clear out the concrete anyway."

"Take it," Harry said.

Walter at once climbed up on the truck. They offloaded the scaffold to the ground.

Lon left them a flashlight.

"We can make this aircraft fly," said Walter.

"You said that. Let it go," Bill murmured, not altogether unsympathetic.

"I just need a few spare parts."

Alice and Patty climbed onto the bed of the truck. Lon drove and Harry sat beside him. As the truck started up, Patty leaned over to Alice. "Why does he blame me?" she asked.

"Because you're his partner," Alice answered, dismayed at the naivete of the question.

On the road into town, Lon pulled over for Don. When he stopped, Don looked up at Harry. "You want a ride?" Harry asked.

"No," said Don.

"I blame you!" Patty said to him, and, as the truck went on, Don caught Patty's glare.

At Mercedita, Walter walked to the terminal and called long distance to Charlesville's attorney in San Juan. On his return,

Walter heard an aircraft approaching. The aircraft was coming from the northeast, which meant from San Juan. It was too dark now to see the markings. "He's going to land," Walter said to Bill. But the airplane's gear remained up and the downwind leg was flown much too high to be entering the pattern for landing. As the plane flew by, Bill could see it was a passenger plane. Walter went aboard the ship and tried the radio. To Bill's surprise, Walter was able to raise the plane and alert the pilot to an encumbrance. The pilot confirmed that he knew what had happened; the Army had advised him to reroute to Mayagüez. He was just flying over, to see.

—

CHAPTER FOURTEEN

When Julio's shock subsided, the doctor at *Clínica Doctor Pila* in Ponce instructed Diego and Maxwell to take him home and put him to bed. Julio would need at least a day's rest, after which limited walking would help the bone in his foot to resect. An X-ray had disclosed a break in the third metatarsal, and the doctor had put in stitches to close the gash. As Julio left, the nurse provided him with crutches.

At the sight of her husband being helped up the steps, Carlota Rodriguez became hysterical. Julio recoiled at her shrill, biting voice. But, as soon as Diego explained what had happened, Carlota calmed. She had known it would end as it did.

At Harry's, Patty tried making herself inconspicuous in the corner of the living room. Alice felt reminded of times she had visited homes in which an untoward death had occurred in the family. There was telltale intensity of purpose in all Harry did— Harry, the central bereaved—against a background of hush. His busyness seemed measured against the larger sense of loss, which only added to the contrast between what seemed inherent silence and the muffled issuance of minor communications. For lack of expectation, there was no continuity to what was said, nothing to connect the things Harry did. First, calls went out, as Harry broke the news, then the calls began arriving, as those to whom he broke it spread the news to others.

Harry wanted no help with his tasks; they were, as it were, *the least he could do*. He took the calls and made them. He seemed to need to fight back silence, which, if he let up, would engulf him. More than just a ship had crashed, Harry knew. Alice noted that, with each call Harry made, he shaped his version of the subject. Harry loved information, even under present

circumstances. He spoke of the ship as if its loss had made him a
widower, or as if its loss had killed him too.

When Minnie arrived, she brought *pan de Mallorca*, a light
pastry. Elisa came accompanied by her husband and one daughter.
Harry's call had interrupted their supper, and Elisa would not
drive after dark.

Patty was glad at the sight of these arrivals. More people
meant the sorrow could be shared. Don had blamed her, and
now she blamed herself. She had pushed him to try. He had
done it for her. The thought she might just disappear, a thought
she had not experienced since England, seemed appealing, much
as it had been then. "Do you want me to take you home?" Alice
asked.

"No, thank you," Patty said. Alice could see she was waiting
for Don.

Maxwell and Diego brought in news about Julio. But they
had stopped at a bar and came drunk.

Lon went out to the hangar to pack tools; not only those he
personally owned but those belonging to Bill, who he assumed
would accompany him home to Cincinnati.

Antonio arrived.

By rehashing for Antonio the last few seconds of the flight,
then backtracking to the conditions preceding it, Diego, Harry,
and Maxwell competed for a definitive analysis of why the ship
had crashed. In each telling, however, the crash itself was pushed
farther toward abeyance. To watch denial at work intrigued Alice,
who stood on the outskirts of the coterie and listened. She
recognized that, by expanding upon the conditions leading up to
the moment the crash had occurred, and by enlarging upon the
moments just prior to the occurrence, the men would never quite
reach the event. If they got too close, they could always backtrack
and start over. This retelling and enlargement upon last moments
stood for a future they had lost. She turned to Patty. "Do you see
what they are doing?" she asked. Patty nodded but hadn't been
paying much attention. "By repeating the story," said Alice, "they
are in effect saving time. By augmenting, they are slowing the

clock." But Patty didn't care. "Well, it's a writer's observation, I suppose," Alice said. Alice had always viewed her niece as being *picture oriented.* Thinking of Don, Alice doubted he would come.

What Alice found impressive was Harry's management of what surely was despair. She wondered if that was something inbred, or was it something life in the Army had taught him to do. Although the life Harry had known seemed ended now—for where would he get funds to start a new project, at his age, and in his physical condition?—and although activities pursuant to that life were now narrowly defined by the scope of a few final chores, the worst Alice had heard Harry say was the matter-of-fact complaint that pilot error had caused the crash. This he said without rancor, as simple fact. About such fact there was nothing he could do, no one to whom he could turn, no remedy, redress, or appeal. She did hear him complain, though, that the house seemed too dark, but for that, at least, he had a cure. He went around and turned on all the lights.

At *Mercedita*, amidst tools Julio kept in a box beneath his jump seat, Bill found a second flashlight. He said to Walter that if he could get his hands on test equipment he could determine what the status of the electrical system was. The breaks seemed to be at terminals pulled loose from the panel. Aft, he found impact had dislodged residue from the positive plates of the batteries, which led to shorts in a number of cells. One battery case had cracked, spilling acid.

From the cabin, Walter unloaded ballast. Bill noted that some of the bottom pieces now appeared farther aft than he recalled. Walter thought the same was so. Bill guessed, then, that, when the ship rotated in order to climb, rotation had caused the load to slide aft. If that was the case, the resulting imbalance might have driven up the nose of the ship even higher, and thus caused the stall that in turn led to the crash.

Walter also enjoyed finding clues to a wreck, and had seen many more wrecks than Bill. When they stepped outside for a breather, he offered his own observation, not as to why the ship had crashed, because, in Walter's experience, that's what ships did, but, rather, as to why it had survived the crash the way it had, for by now Walter was convinced the ship had survived. To illustrate, he pointed out that at the moment of impact the ship had little forward motion. It crashed flat; otherwise, it would have crumpled fore to aft. Also, on the basis of assessing damage underneath, Walter inferred from what he could see that the rate of descent was between eight and ten feet per second at impact, a rate sufficiently low that Walter could term the mishap a "controlled crash."

"Controlled?" Bill asked, incredulous.

"I believe so," Walter answered. "It was controlled in that the pilot was still flying, even at the moment of impact."

"But how do you know?"

"Because the front rotors at takeoff were tilted, and the front rotors right now are horizontal." As Walter spoke, Bill looked to confirm that was so. "Don was making every effort to stay with her," Walter said. "As a result, he cushioned the descent. He flew her down."

At Harry's, Patty moved from the house to the porch, there to sit by herself on the rail, staring out. The darkness consoled her. The house was filling with people now. Colonel Brooks from Losey Field had come, and, with him, Captain DeCelis. The mayor of Ponce, Andres Grillasca, arrived, and, with him, Ponce's police chief. A photographer and reporter from *El Día* had come.

Tired of hearing Don blamed, Alice, too, went out to the porch. "Every pilot wants to fly," she said, her response to the people who blamed Don. She only meant that Don had been doing what he was paid for, what he had come to Ponce to do. Her own recollection was that Harry—not Don—had come up with the idea of so much weight, and that Julio had championed the idea. But of course, neither of them was the pilot.

In Patty's lap, she held her camera, whose contours her fingers idly traced. The scent of *empanadas* escaped the house, but to Patty the thought of eating was repugnant. Inside, the reporter was trying to get a lead out of Harry, and Harry, in turn, was leading him on. Patty heard conjecture from the reporter that, had the pilot not been Negro, he might not have tried such a stunt. She felt her blood freeze. She felt ready to attack, to tear at someone, to make someone pay. But that's what they were doing to Don, making *him* pay. The photographer complained that he had been to *Mercedita*, but that a flashbulb wouldn't light enough of the ship. The talk went on.

Patty's thoughts reverted to England. "I weigh too much," she said to Alice. Weight frightened her. Food repulsed her. She wished to be infinitely light, the stuff of an image on film. On the flanks of her imagination, she could pare her own flesh, and she could stand the thought that she would never again eat. Death held that promise of lightness, and, were starvation but faster, it would be otherwise ideal. "Your life is not over," said Alice.

Inside, Antonio explained that the extent of Harry's civil liability with regard to Caribbean Atlantic Airlines amounted to the cost the airline had incurred when it hired a *público* in Mayagüez in order to get three Ponce-bound passengers, who had been aboard the flight that had been diverted from landing at Mercedita, to Ponce from the airport in Mayagüez. The cost for those damages was twelve dollars. Hearing that, the men laughed. Maxwell said the hospital bill for Julio amounted to eighteen dollars, and that included crutches, but, hearing that, the men were solemn.

According to Mayor Grillasca, now holding court, Ponce was responsible not only to the Serralles family, which owned *La Mercedita*, but, equally, under federal regulations, responsible to keep the airport safe. The mayor wanted Harry's ship removed before noon. Regarding damages to the cane field and fence, the mayor had been in touch with the Serralles family, which asked only that the fence be restrung. Lon Pyrtle noted that this was the second fence that Don had wiped out. When the mayor resumed, he indicated that if Ponce incurred no other damages, it would assess none to Harry. Colonel Brooks, referring to the cost of removing the wreck, doubted that the Army would be charging anyone for what he considered an exercise in good will toward Ponce. Captain DeCelis assured Harry and the mayor that the Army would be there at O eight hundred hours with bulldozer, trucks, crane, and men; and would have the site cleared in thirty minutes. On a more delicate issue, though, the captain said it was not the worst wreck in the world. He had been out to the airport to take a look for himself. "Bad enough to finish me," said Harry.

Politely, the captain persisted, mentioning that one of Harry's men, of the two Harry had left to stand guard, had expressed a similar opinion, to the effect that the ship could be saved. "If that was your wish," said the captain.

"It's not a matter of wishing," said Harry, "and the man you saw was Walter Schmidt. He's not one of mine."

"The tall, lanky German," Lon explained to the captain.

"No, no, not the German," said DeCelis, who had seen Walter. "I mean the one with brown hair, from Wright Field."

Alice looked past Patty to the parking lot. Don had arrived. Then Alice looked at Patty, who in turn was fixed on Don. But Don did not come toward the house. He got his bicycle, and pedaled off.

Alice watched the expression change in Patty's face, from suddenly hopeful to finally hopeless. "Maybe next time," she consoled.

"There is no next time!" Patty cried. "I love that man!" With that, as if to share Don's grief, she hurled her camera to the ground.

At *Mercedita*, Lon took Bill and Walter their supper, but he missed Walter, who had hitched a ride into Ponce in the company of one of the policemen who had been patrolling the airport, on and off, throughout the evening.

Bill and Walter had completed the first step of their work, which was to unload the ballast, since nothing much could happen until that. Sitting next to his father to eat, Bill ran through the items he and Walter had determined they could fix. But Lon took little interest.

Repairs were pointless. All evening, Lon had been thinking about Cincinnati, and what he and Bill might do there. "Your mother will be happy to see you," he said.

"I don't know when that will be," said Bill, for among Bill's options was the likely prospect that repairs to the ship would take a few weeks, and Walter, if he stayed on to run the project, would also want Bill there to help him.

"I made reservations for both of us," said Lon, who viewed Bill as having no interest in Ponce. The Eastern Airlines flight was to leave San Juan for Miami tomorrow afternoon. Lon had arranged connections in Miami for Cincinnati. "I brought your tools," he said. They were in the trunk of the car, with his own. Bill had been needing his tools. "This time tomorrow we'll be home," Lon added.

"You will be," said Bill, who put his plate down to go look in the trunk of the car.

"I spoke to Antonio," Lon said. "He said he would sell this car for us. We just sign it over and he'll forward the proceeds."

"Sign your half to me," said Bill, "and I'll hold the car till I'm ready to leave Puerto Rico. Then I'll split the proceeds with you."

"You'll change your mind in the morning," said Lon. "This aircraft won't fly."

Bill returned with the box and shined the light in to see what was there. "You know," he said, "we're rebuilding Europe. Why not rebuild the aircraft?"

"Well that's silly," said Lon. "That's one helluva analogy. Besides, the guy's a Kraut."

"We're rebuilding Germany, too."

"Here's your paycheck. One thing has nothing to do with the other."

"No? I think everything is connected." Bill shined the light on the check. The old man had gotten him his back pay. In defeat, Harry turned out to be more forthcoming than he had been when times were good, although Bill could not recall Harry ever having admitted that times were good. He thanked his father.

"Don't thank me. You earned it," said Lon.

"Thank you for getting it," said Bill, finding it difficult to say anything to Lon without fighting with him.

"Elisa said that if she were you, she'd cash that check first thing in the morning." Lon figured he had gotten that money out of Harry mainly because the mayor and Captain DeCelis were there in the room when Elisa presented the checks for Harry to sign.

"I'm surprised you missed Walter," said Bill. "He was heading back to the field."

"I just came from the field," said Lon. "But I've crossed paths with enough fools for one day."

Vindictive, Harry spied Walter coming in from the parking lot. "Walter's here," Harry said, primarily to the mayor and Antonio.

When Walter entered the door of the house he looked peaked, harried. He took no notice of the Army, Alice, none of Patty; he went right by the police chief and did not recognize Mayor Grillasca, who was, in any event, a nondescript man, short, in late middle-age, with hair center-parted in an old-fashioned style. The *Wehrmacht* rolled on. Walter ignored Minnie and Elisa, and Elisa's husband and child. He ignored Maxwell and Diego. "Harry," Walter said, putting the focus of his entire being on Harry. "You have been sued! Charlesville has sued you in U.S. District Court! The attorneys have obtained an injunction in San Juan. The federal marshall is on his way here with the Order."

"You ass," Harry said.

"You're very stupid," Walter answered. "I could have saved you this trouble."

"Who are Charlesville's attorneys?" Mayor Grillasca asked.

"Wakefield and Goyco," said Antonio.

"Is Charlesville with them?" asked Harry.

"No," Walter answered.

"Is Goyco in his office?" asked Antonio.

"He's waiting for your call."

Fernando Goyco was well known to Antonio, who had faced him on occasions in the Municipal Court of Ponce. Goyco the litigator was a very strong attorney. Mayor Grillasca, too, knew the names Wakefield and Goyco: Wakefield, the business counsel, and Goyco, the trial lawyer, who had represented contractors in disputes over the construction of buildings in Ponce. The mayor was not pleased to hear mention of their names.

"What an idiot," Harry said, about Walter.

"I asked only for the use of your truck and some parts, and just some time, overnight," Walter said.

"Gentlemen," said Antonio, leading the parties down the hall to Harry's office. When they assembled inside—Mayor Grillasca, Walter, Harry, and Antonio—Antonio closed the door. Without deliberating, but as a matter of course, Antonio chose to sit at Harry's desk, leaving Harry to sit on the bed. To his friend Andres Grillasca, Antonio offered the one other chair in the room, but when the mayor chose instead to stand with his back to the window, opposing Walter, Antonio offered the chair to Walter. Walter too preferred to stand, but with his back to the door, as if to block the escape.

For Walter's sake, Antonio introduced him to Andres. "Walter, Andres Grillasca, Mayor of Ponce. Andres, this is Walter Schmidt, who is here as Charlesville's agent."

They shook no hands. Walter looked right across the room and right through the mayor.

Andres returned the stare at him through wire-rimmed spectacles.

"Harry forced me to do this," said Walter, matter-of-factly to Antonio.

"Events have forced us all," said Andres.

"We'll get to the bottom of it," said Antonio, very calmly, able to picture Charlesville's balls on a skewer.

"You ought to be ashamed," said Harry, still at Walter.

"I'm ashamed of you," said Walter.

"I suffered loss, of everything," said Harry.

"What does the Order say?" Antonio asked.

"It says Harry is to keep his hands off the ship."

"Harry only?"

"Who else?" Who else but Harry had invited the Army to the front room of his house? Who had threatened to bring the Army in? Who intended to demolish the ship?

"But I mean, no one else is named in the Order but Harry?"

"No one is," Walter said, seeing no use to the question.

"Where do you fit into this?" asked Antonio.

"I don't fit into it now. I've done my duty," Walter said. "The lawyers are running the show. They wanted me here to make certain you were told."

"Is there a Complaint attached to the Order?"

"The Complaint was not filed," Walter said. "We are to maintain the status quo until Monday."

"Charlesville has extended Harry's contract pending the air show next week," Antonio noted, for the sake of Andres, who merely acknowledged that he had heard. "After that, the ship belongs to Charlesville. It is his collateral on a loan."

"What is he in all of this?" asked Walter, referring to Andres.

"He is a party," said Antonio, drawing out Harry's paper and pen to take his notes. "So you have not been in touch with Charlesville?"

"Not since Tuesday, when he left for New York," said Walter.

"Have *they* been in touch with him?" Antonio asked, careful to distinguish Walter from a reference to Charlesville's attorneys.

"I don't know. They say they know what he wants," Walter answered.

Visibly the coolest head in the room, Antonio was able also to be affable. "What *does* Charlesville want, if you know?"

"He's as greedy as Harry."

"Of that I am certain," Antonio said. "But if he determines the ship can be made airworthy?"

"That's not up to me anymore. He'll take it to France."

Walter's presence in Ponce addressed the doubt Charlesville had about Harry. But, in Antonio's judgment, by the same token, the fact that San Juan lawyers were retained implied the doubt Charlesville had about Walter. "If I were you," Antonio suggested, "I think I'd be angry."

"I am angry," Walter said. "I am furious." For the lawyers did not care about the aircraft, and had no sense of the problem.

"You did explain the situation when you called them, did you not?"

"Of course. Many times," Walter said. Walter now viewed himself as excess baggage. "I am a free man," he added, sarcastically.

"I envy you that," said Antonio.

"I could save that aircraft. Charlesville will likely say otherwise, that the ship should be destroyed. They want to bring in experts, but who am I? I'm an expert! They don't trust my judgment, yet it was my judgment that I call them. I can get that aircraft to fly. I can repair it tonight. If I could have one chance, by morning I could fly it back here."

"It is unjust," Antonio concurred.

"Utterly foolish," said Walter. "Worse than war."

"It *is* war," Antonio corrected. "But, these matters rarely go so far as a trial. The Order draws a skirmish line, nothing more." With that, Antonio picked up the phone for *Central* and San Juan.

When Fernando Goyco answered, Antonio greeted him amiably, identifying himself and those around him in the room. "Walter's been telling us about the Order," he said.

"Yes," said Fernando, "I think the Order is fair."

"How long do we contemplate maintaining this Order?"

"Well, certainly until contract expiration," said Fernando, "and thereafter for as long as we need in order to determine which course of action will be best."

"One moment," said Antonio. He covered the phone. To Walter, Harry, and Andres he said in a low voice. "Many days."

"Way too long," said Andres.

"I'm the expert," Walter said, holding up one finger: one day.

Antonio returned to Don Fernando. "Fernando, I think you should know that I represent the city of Ponce in this matter." A silence ensued. Antonio continued. "I am sure you realize that you have not named Ponce in the Order." Antonio thought he heard a grunt. "I would like you to speak with Andres Grillasca," said Antonio. But the phone seemed to be dead. "Will you speak with him?" Antonio asked. When still no response was forthcoming, Antonio prompted his opponent. "Fernando?"

"All right," said Fernando.

Antonio handed over the phone.

Andres Grillasca had been Antonio's friend for many years. Andres Grillasca also had been Ponce's mayor for many years. Antonio himself had represented Ponce many times. Once, Andres could recall, Antonio represented Ponce in a lawsuit involving construction of a municipal building in Ponce, in which the contractor who built the building and thereafter sued the city happened to be a San Juan company represented by Fernando Goyco in court. Goyco won. The contractor made a lot of extra money, at the expense of Ponce's taxpayers. "Listen here goddam your ass," began the mayor.

Antonio pictured Fernando's expression. Of course nobody in the world had a right to tell Ponce that Ponce could not operate its own municipal airport—*Mercedita*—simply because somebody's private property, which was there by trespassing in the first place, and had no business being there, and was expressly forbidden from being there, and was a nuisance in a public place, and had no business being in any other public place in Ponce, happened to be there in spite of those proscriptions. It was such a pleasure to listen to Andres. And no doubt it was too bad about the crash. But the fact was Ponce was going to exercise its right to get rid of that piece of shit that was sitting out on the end of the runway at *Mercedita*, and was going to do so tomorrow, regardless. Never mind the Court Order. Antonio would be in San Juan first thing in the morning and be in court, entering his appearance in behalf of the City of Ponce, and would get that Order lifted. Because no court would see it any other way. Charlesville had no rights; he was a trespasser. But if he did have rights they fell to Ponce's right to maintain the safe operation of its airport. Was all this clear? Very clear? The public weal outweighed the private right, which wasn't right to start with. "We'll have the Order lifted," Andres barked. "We don't care who moves the aircraft but we will move it if you don't.

"We are a major city," he continued, hardly pausing for the beat. "You cannot shut us down, and won't."

Then Andres gave Antonio the phone, but kept on talking very loud, while Antonio turned the mouthpiece out to catch the sound. "Tell him," said Andres, "that once we lift that Order, that you will be filing in Municipal Court here. We will have a trespass warrant out against Charlesville. We will have a complaint for disturbing the peace. A complaint for nuisance. We will have a civil action going against the Frenchman for destruction of public property. And we will impound that aircraft. Ponce will impound it and it will stay here until all these matters are resolved, which I might add may take years. The family Serralles will want indemnification for damage to its cane field. They have lost the business use of their commercial property. Our tourist trade has suffered. Our citizens are suffering. We will look to Charlesville to indemnify us. We will look to him for all those damages. He moved for the injunction; he will pay for all those damages. Hear? Or that ship will stay here in our impound lot till hell freezes over. And he will pay for the towing to get it there and for the impound costs as well. Charlesville will pay for everything. Hear?"

"Did you hear all that?" Antonio asked.

"I heard," said Fernando Goyco.

"He heard it," said Antonio.

"It's crippling my city's economy!"

"He wants to know what we suggest."

"Tell him," said the mayor, "that any contractor represented by Wakefield and Goyco will never again build a building in Ponce."

"No, you can't say that," said Antonio, who had deliberately allowed it to be heard. "I don't know what you think you just heard, Fernando, but if you think you heard a threat, I'm certain you were wrong. The mayor would never have said that your clients will never work again in Ponce, if that's what you thought he just said. On the other hand, there is a way out."

"I'd like to hear about that," said Fernando.

"We thought your man Walter presented a very good proposal," said Antonio.

Fernando answered that he did not want to hear Walter's proposal.

Relaying to Walter and Andres, Antonio said, "He does not want to hear Walter's proposal." Then, to Fernando, he said, "Walter is disappointed."

"I have a proposal for you," said Fernando.

"We would like to hear *your* proposal," said Antonio.

The first thing Fernando proposed was that there would be no need for an injunction if Charlesville's man, Walter, was running the project. Then, Charlesville's interests would be served. Antonio thought that proposal was astute, and he relayed it to the others.

"But that's exactly what *I* proposed," said Walter, astonished.

"Such things go round," Antonio admitted. "We all must earn a living."

Fernando proposed, further, that, if Charlesville came in the morning to Ponce to see how things looked, he might find that there was no need to call in outside experts.

"He might, indeed," agreed Antonio, who passed this on to Walter, who was, by now, beside himself.

"After all," said Fernando. "Walter is something of an expert."

"He thinks you are something of an expert," Antonio told Walter.

Fernando then proposed that if Harry could see fit to lend Walter his equipment and tools, and maybe some manpower, then maybe there would be grounds for a settlement between Charlesville and Harry.

"May be," Antonio agreed.

"If Harry would cooperate with Walter, then we would not have to file to replevy the aircraft, or compel specific performance," Fernando noted.

"No, you wouldn't," said Antonio, "and it would free Harry to honor his contractual duties to provide the as-built drawings your client requires, subject, of course, to Walter's direction."

"Perhaps the mayor would then see no need for Ponce to come into this?"

"So long as there is progress," said Antonio, "Ponce would view that as reasonable."

"Charlesville will be there early," said Fernando.

"Then he will find me," said Antonio.

"Ponce is a wonderful city," Fernando concluded, for he had a brother living in Ponce, and reminded Antonio of that; also, Fernando's daughter-in-law came from Ponce. And, of course, Fernando counted many Ponceños as friends, not the least of whom was Antonio himself.

"We are honored," Antonio said.

At the end of the phone call, the mayor gave Walter a cigar.

"What do I do if the federal marshall tells me I can't work on the ship?" Walter asked.

"You are not named in the Court Order," said Andres. "Nevertheless, I will have my police protect you through the night. San Juan does not tell Ponce what to do."

Returning to the front room, the four men rejoined the group. Antonio suggested to Captain DeCelis that in the morning he bring in his men to stand by. Harry interjected by beginning a tirade, launched primarily for the benefit of the reporter, on the subjects of self-sacrifice and personal honor. Well before he was finished, however, people began leaving. Harry asked, rhetorically, what did he ever get out of the sacrifices he had made, during his long life of service to his country. He wanted them all to stay and hear him out. But, they were leaving. Colonel Brooks had to go. Captain DeCelis left. Minnie left. Elisa was going. The chief of police went. The reporter and photographer did stay, however, and a flashbulb erupted across the room. Harry maintained that he gave up everything for people like Julio and Don, and concluded by saying that all he ever got out of life was to be kicked in the face for his troubles, and stabbed in the back by the very people whom he helped. Mayor Grillasca went home. Walter left the house to get the truck, which he drove from the parking lot to the hangar.

Harry sat down on the sofa. The house was now quiet. Alice and Patty came back in. To them, Harry looked awful. The anger had taken its toll. Since the matter had reverted to family, as it were, Antonio asked the reporter and photographer, politely, to leave.

When they had gone, Antonio began to summarize what had happened, for the benefit of Alice and Patty. "Walter is going to be using the truck," Antonio said, "and any tools he needs."

Harry looked up.

"I don't want to argue this with you, Harry. If you're going to argue, get another lawyer."

"I'm an old man," Harry said.

"Walter will take whatever parts he needs. If the men are willing to help him, they will help him. You will not obstruct anything he does. You will assist in any way."

"Baloney," Harry said, in a voice that barely whispered.

"Walter will now take charge of the project, and, until the matter is resolved, you, Harry, will assist in whatever Walter says. You will follow Walter's directions, and you will positively complete a set of as-built drawings for Charlesville. If all goes well, God willing, all of the foregoing will be stipulated in writing at *Mercedita* tomorrow and carried back to San Juan to be filed with the Court. I hope you are satisfied."

"What does Harry get out of this?" Alice asked, for it seemed terribly unfair to Harry.

"A chance to see his work survive," Antonio answered.

Later, when Harry had departed for his room, Patty ventured to ask what it meant to replevy something. She had heard the word used, and didn't know. Before Antonio could answer that, and much to Patty's surprise, Harry hollered from the room. "It's what you do when you piss on someone's grave."

At *Mercedita,* by half past three a.m., Bill and Walter had entered an absorbingly personal world that was, for each, fervid, intense, and nonverbal. They broke silence only to ask for tools or lend an occasional hand with a task. Bill worked out of resentment toward his father. He worked out of pride in his own best achievements, which likely surpassed Lon's. But, with every item he inspected or repaired, he clashed against the figure of the father who had taught him.

For Walter, memories harvested another field. Walter recalled the Russian Front, the times he worked in snow. His memory gravitated to the winter of the first campaign, 1941, 1942. There was a time in that winter he had begged God, let him die. The German advance, long stalled, had turned into a rout. Seemingly unending divisions of Russians attacked from the east. Everything that could have gone wrong had gone wrong, all at once, but the worst of it all was the cold. Walter had watched how quickly morale deteriorated. He had made a judgment, an observation, that the safeguards assumed to be in place in our lives were chiefly those borne by our assumptions. They were fictions. Indeed, it took only a modest confluence of commonplace events to convince us, to the contrary, that all would be lost.

He recalled seeing men blown off their feet by winter wind, and then being unable to rise. He recalled a night the temperature dropped to fifty-five degrees below zero, during the course of which night he had serviced an airplane. He saw inconsequential events become fatal. He recalled his own panicky feeling when he knocked his cap askew, exposing his ear and part of his scalp to the cold; his dread when he could not remember how to tuck the ends of his scarf inside the collar of his coat. He remembered losing a glove and being too busy to pick it up, then the fear that accompanied his inability to find it. How easily metal cut into cold flesh. They had laughed at the wooden planes the Russians flew, but ceased to laugh when their own no longer could fly. He remembered bending over for a tool he had dropped, only to be plagued for some hours because his shirt had pulled up from his waist. He recalled a bootlace that had snapped. He recalled taking off over bumps on a field and mistaking those bumps for the holes left by shells; only to find, at the thaw, they were bodies frozen in snow. He remembered taking off so close to Russian lines that at the point the aircraft raised its nose in rotation he was exposed to enemy fire.

Blame was everywhere, those days. He used up his own energy in rage. Finally, outright, he begged to die, taking the easy way out to beg for warmth. He bargained with God, to persuade Him it was not so truly banal if he froze, for he had seen men withdrawing by degrees, beyond pain, and knew that one could find, at the end of freezing, warmth. It was a kind of dream; the Russian winter, a nightmare. He thought of them now, bringing to life again his dead friends as he worked. Perhaps he served Harry, by showing Harry's men that things were not really so bad. Perhaps he served God; God had listened after all.

"Did you know that when you freeze you get warm, at the very end?" Walter asked. Birds called through the night, and the sound of crickets filled the field. In the Russian winter there was gunfire, sometimes silence, sometimes wind. For the first time on the island, Walter heard the *coqui*. "Did you hear me?" he asked.

"I heard you," said Bill. "Could you pass me a three-quarter inch socket?"

"It's a pity," Walter said, at ten past four.

At four fifteen, Bill answered. "What?"

"She's a very good ship."

"I don't know."

Shortly past six, the dawn began to break.

"I hate my old man," said Bill. "I'm checking his work. He never screws up."

Before the sun rose, they left off. Without either having said so, sunrise meant, for each of them, an execution.

"Let's see if we can start an engine," Bill suggested. In the distance, roosters crowed. The dawn air was as sweet, as balmy and tranquil, as suggestively soft, as any help that Heaven ever offered.

—

CHAPTER FIFTEEN

Friday morning, Alice reached the airport shortly after seven. The Army wasn't there yet. She expected to see Harry but couldn't find him either. At the far end of the runway a small group had gathered to watch the operation. As Alice drew near the group, she realized the ship had not moved. Two local police held people back at the threshold of the runway. Near the ship she saw a U.S. marshall. In the cane field just outside the airport's fence, the truck had pulled up to the ship. Bill and Walter looked bedraggled. Concrete ballast lay about the field. The situation in broad day led Alice to think things looked worse than what she had remembered from last night. When she asked what was going on, the man beside her said that they were trying to start the engines. When she asked were they having a problem, one of the policemen explained the batteries were dead.

The ship's batteries would not provide amperage to crank the starter. Neither would they take a charge. Bill had rigged a harness, then, using the generator Walter took from the field, a replacement battery, and cables. The old batteries, vestigial now, remained trapped inside their aft compartment, where damage to the frame prevented Bill from moving them.

Walter boarded, entering the cockpit through the shattered window at the nose. He took Don's seat and consulted Don's startup procedure. Many functions had been terminated. Many items were of no use to check. Bill and Walter had done the best they could, given the damage aft in the engineer's station and elsewhere in the ship. Bill went to the truck and hand-started the generator. He walked back to the ship and stood outside the window. "Good luck," he said.

Walter switched on the master switch, the fuel switch, and

pump. He primed the port engine and checked closed throttle. With no more ado, he hit the starter button. The engine engaged and within three turns was running. The ammeter showed charge. Bill signaled thumbs up. Walter held up two fingers; not for victory, but to start the second engine. Bill agreed. Walter started number two.

The sound was one Alice was accustomed to hearing. Yet even at a distance of nearly two hundred feet, the sound was more than she expected. Above the din of the engines, she had heard the small crowd cheer.

Bill stepped away from the ship. The exhaust manifold was cracked. His ear told him that. He meant to indicate to Walter that there was nothing of particular importance, no cause for alarm, but Walter, disregarding him, shut down both engines. "What's the problem?" Bill asked.

"Can't move the sticks," Walter said.

"Alice said they got the engines running!" Elisa exclaimed, having received a phone call from Alice and relaying the message across the hall to Harry.

"Makes no difference," Harry said, and as he spoke he looked out the window at the empty apron by the hangar.

"Talk to Alice," begged Elisa, still excited, for Alice was still on the phone.

"You talk to her," Harry said.

"She says you should be out there."

"It's a travesty," Harry said.

"Please talk to her," said Elisa.

"It's a travesty. Tell her that."

"It's a travesty," Elisa said, telling Alice she was quoting Harry. "He doesn't want to go." There was silence from Alice's end.

"Well?" Harry asked. "What'd she say?"

"She said you're too proud."

"I'm not going," said Harry, with the air of a petulant boy.

"He's still not going," said Elisa. After a pause, Elisa murmured no, but Harry turned, catching this, and looked across the hall at her.

"No, what?" he asked.

"She asked if I was coming," Elisa said, sadly.

At Mercedita, Antonio greeted Charlesville. Antonio read the stipulation that Charlesville's attorney, Fernando Goyco, had drafted. "It looks right to me," Antonio said, and completed the execution, following Charlesville's own signature and date. "I can have it filed for you."

"That will be fine," Charlesville said.

The crowd at Mercedita, swollen to eighty people, continued growing. The U.S. marshal, disturbed by the overnight presence of police, was even more anxious at the sight of the Army. The Army stood by, with three trucks and a complement of twenty men headed by Captain DeCelis. The men had torches, crane, bulldozer, hawsers. Finally, when Ponce's police chief arrived, heading straight to Antonio, the marshal decided to join in. Captain DeCelis followed the marshal, and took two sergeants with him. At a loss what to do, the captain told Antonio that the Army was there to help but could not stand by forever.

Antonio summoned Walter, and Walter summoned Bill. Alice followed them, with Minnie, while Diego went off to find his father, who was chatting with the airport manager. "What's going on?" Walter asked Charlesville.

"You tell me," said Charlesville.

"No controls," Walter answered.

"Charlesville expected the ship to be . . . farther along," said Antonio. To Walter he posed the question, "If you can get her off the runway, can you finish what you're doing?"

"You mean, if we keep working, will she ever fly again?" Walter asked.

"Yes," Antonio said, not wanting to get tangled in niceties.

"I expect she'll fly today, if not this morning," Walter said.

"There's your answer," said Antonio to the others. He searched for Colonel Brooks, but the colonel hadn't come. Then he spoke to Captain DeCelis. "Is it permissible for you to help?"

"Certainly," said the captain, repeating that the Army had come to be of service.

"Unless it's against your rules," Antonio said, "you could treat her like a boat that's run aground."

"How's that?" asked Captain DeCelis.

But Walter saw it immediately. The ship had engine power but no control. It could rise from the ground but not fly. The Army had men and steel hawsers. If she rose, they could pull her. There was no need to wait for high tide.

At ten past nine, Walter started the engines again. With the ship now tethered to cables on all sides, and men in place to tow her, Walter put power to the rotors and the ship came off the ground. On seeing the extent of her damage, Antonio reconsidered Harry's judgment. The undercarriage was crushed, and her belly flattened. Scabs of metal, some half-torn, flapped and banged beneath the torrent of wind. For the men farthest into the cane field, footing was bad and the cane itself was flaying them. As they struggled, the ship seemed to wallow, reminding Antonio of a dinosaur, or whale. Men stumbled and fell. Even the noise now seemed monstrous and cruel. Antonio turned, and, finding nobody about him but Alice, spoke to her, shouting, "Maybe Harry was right."

"Harry's jealous," Alice shouted back, pleased to have been consulted. In her view, it wasn't Harry's show, so Harry wouldn't come. Reluctant to break off from Alice's company, Antonio inquired as to Patty, for he had been watching Patty's rival, the photographer from *El Día*, out and about, shooting. "Still in bed," Alice shouted, for Patty suffered Don's grief.

The air filled with chaff, which carried to the spectators, most of whom retreated. More than once, the craft banged down. From a distance, Walter's expression in the cockpit looked pained. After ten minutes, the men had towed the ship some yards. "At least it makes the airport safe to use," yelled Alice, who thought the sight of the ship lying, as it had been, in the cane field would surely have discouraged any pilot coming in, and even more so any passenger who had a window seat.

In bed at home, upon awakening, Julio knew he had stayed in bed too long. He had slept around the clock. He knew the

kids had gone because, hearing them go, their departure made
sense to him in dream. Now he wondered where they went.
School, he thought, although it had seemed too long ago that he
heard them. Then, he found the note Carlota left, which read, "I
took the children to my mother's." The thought of the ship came
to him. He remembered the crash, but felt stricken by an old
sense of abandonment. His father had died when he was seventeen,
and his mother's poverty had thrust him out into the world.

At the dining room table he called *Central* and asked for
Harry's field. While the connection was being made, he
remembered being treated for his foot. When Harry answered,
Julio remembered coming home. Carlota had screamed at him,
cursing him, Harry, the ship.

"Harry," said Julio, his own voice sounding strange.

"How do you feel?" Harry asked.

"I'm all right. How's the ship?"

"Walter sued me," Harry said. "I wanted to have the Army
demolish the ship, but Walter got an Order from the court to
stop me. Now he's running the show."

Julio's head seemed about to burst. The headache had set in,
as always, at the base of his skull. He recalled last evening he felt
no pain in his foot. Now his foot seemed on fire. He felt sick to
his stomach. From the moment he had risen from bed he felt
dizzy. On the table he saw the half-empty cup Carlota drank
from this morning. With sudden affection, he touched the cup
with his fingertips, and for a moment his fingertips lied and told
him the coffee was still warm.

"Is she finished?" Julio asked.

"She's a total wreck," Harry said.

Julio suddenly remembered Don walking away in a daze
outside the cockpit. He was glad Don walked away. "I guess we
were lucky," he said.

"If that's how you want to think of it," said Harry.

Julio longed to be held by Carlota; in turn to take hold of his
children and hold them. "They've all run off," he said.

"Then you must know how I feel," Harry judged.

When Julio hung up, Harry remarked to Elisa that Julio was as much to blame as Don. No, he thought, on second thought, Julio was more to blame than Don. Julio had played both ends against the middle. "You know," Harry said, "if I had put my career ahead of theirs . . . ." At this juncture, Elisa knew exactly where Harry was going: he would work himself into a dither again; self-pity and blame, in the victim's frame of mind. "In other words," Harry continued, "had I done to them what they've done to me, I'd be a celebrity in world aviation, and most of those guys would be *schlepping* with brooms. The aircraft was loaded wrong. It was aft-loaded. I know it. And that's why it crashed. It wasn't too heavy; it was out of balance."

Elisa found it pointless to argue. She just stared at Harry until he stopped. "How's Julio?" she asked.

"He said his wife and children left him."

With the hope that Harry might offer to drive her, Elisa asked if Harry would like to go to Mercedita. Instead, he disappointed her, yet again. She could borrow his car, he said, as he handed her the keys. "Stop by Julio's first," he asked her. "You might as well take him his last pay."

At Mercedita, in the office of the airport manager, Antonio and Charlesville summoned Walter. The ship had been flown, but, while it was under its own power to stay aloft, it had required twenty men from the Army to tow it, and it took an hour to go the fifteen hundred feet from the runway to the ramp outside the terminal, where Walter, exhausted, had set it down. Now, the ship lay on its belly on the tarmac, and although the runway was technically clear, the airport was still the site of a wreck.

Sopping with perspiration, Walter stood before the two men. His hair was tangled, his face was gaunt. "I want the ship removed from here as quickly as possible and taken to San Juan," Charlesville said. "To do that, shouldn't we disassemble it now? I could arrange for trucks to haul it overland, or for a freighter to make a stop in Ponce's harbor."

Walter sat down. He was so tired, he sprawled. He could not close his lips. His frustration and fatigue at dealing with the aircraft overwhelmed him. Antonio, quick to note exasperation, offered him a cup of cool water. Finally, Walter spoke. "If all you want is a museum piece, to take back home to France . . . ."

"No. I want more than that," Charlesville said. "I want a ship that flies."

"If you disassemble the aircraft now, it will never fly," Walter said. "And there will never be an accurate set of drawings to show how it was built. Inaccurate drawings are worse than none."

"I see," said Charlesville. "Than what do you propose?"

"Let me get her to Harry's," Walter answered. "If we can do that, we can make better repairs. It may take a little longer, but then we'll be able to fly her to San Juan, right onto the deck of the freighter. That way, when we get her to France, she'll still be an aircraft; not an assembly of parts. We'll have something to work with, and we'll have drawings we can use to build another aircraft."

"How long will this take?" Charlesville asked him.

"A few hours here."

"And at Harry's?"

"Perhaps a few days."

"Okay," Charlesville said. When Walter had gone, he watched a few moments longer while the men returned to the work.

"Not a good place to work, is it," Antonio noted.

"No," Charlesville agreed. "I'm going back to San Juan. At least up in the mountains, it's cool."

At the edge of the cane field, the U.S. Army was picking up debris and pieces of precast, and loading their own trucks. Antonio, outside now, summoned the marshal and stood with him as the marshal read the stipulation. Antonio wanted the marshal to see the injunction would be lifted. When the marshal finished, Antonio summoned Alice, for he wanted her to read it as well.

According to the stipulation, Harry would write a letter to Andres, apologizing for having violated a prohibition against flying the ship at *Mercedita* and for having disrupted *Mercedita*'s operations. Harry would cover any damages. Ponce would forbear from any action. Walter would run the show. Harry's men would now work under Walter's direction, but Harry would pay them their salaries through Sunday night at midnight. Harry would make his field available for use by Charlesville, including all equipment and tools, for as long as Charlesville needed. Starting on Monday, Charlesville would sublet the field from Harry. Also on Monday, Charlesville would own the gasoline in the tank buried outside the hangar, and would own all the spare parts for the ship. And, of course, Charlesville would own the ship itself. Charlesville could hire Minnie, Elisa, and all Harry's men, assuming they chose to work for him. Harry would have to move out. The one exception concerned as-builts. Under the contract for the loan, since Harry had promised a set of drawings, Harry would pay Don's salary for as long as Don was needed to produce as-builts. The exception to the exception was that, if Don had flying to do, after Sunday, then Charlesville would pay him for that. It was down to dotting "i"'s and crossing "t"'s.

When Elisa arrived at Mercedita she spotted Minnie, then Alice, and, beyond them, Diego, Maxwell, and Bill, all of whom were meeting with Walter by the ship. The Army was about, and people from Ponce as well. But the sight of the ship struck Elisa. Owing in part to what she had imagined, and in part to what she had heard, she had come expecting to find the wreckage catastrophic. But the reality was subtler. Not mashed, but somewhat flattened underneath, the ship reminded her of a brood hen, come to roost on folded legs. Elisa felt her eye drawn to its contours, as if, by caressing them, sympathy could effect their repair. Baffled by this strange appearance, she also thought of funerals attended in which the body of the deceased was that of someone she had seen just prior to death. The ship, too, looked much the same now as before, but, like any corpse, it did appear changed from the last time she had seen it alive.

The men were exhausted. "Is Julio coming?" asked Bill.

"No," Elisa told them, sorry to deliver more bad news. She had not made it to Julio's in time to hand-deliver his check, and so had left it on the table. "Julio went to San Juan to get Carlota. She left him and took the kids."

The morning grew hot. Walter asked Bill what they needed most. Lemonade, Bill answered. Outside of Julio, the help they most needed was Lon's. It was Lon who chiefly designed the mixing box and hydraulics, now bashed and misaligned beneath the flight deck. Walter guessed they also needed as-builts.

"Even incomplete as-builts," Maxwell said, in a sarcastic reference to Don.

"We'll need Don anyway," said Walter, for, after all, he admitted, who else but Don had enough feel for the ship to know if it was fixed. The comment was wry and self-mocking.

Alice volunteered to go look for Don.

"He's at the ballpark," Maxwell said.

"Terry Stadium?" Alice asked.

"He wanted to watch Ponce's team at their last practice," said Maxwell.

"He wanted to be by himself," said Bill. Alice felt in sympathy with that.

Colonel Brooks had arrived, and Antonio brought him into the group. "The Army has to leave within the hour," Antonio said. "Can you manage by yourselves?"

"We can manage," Maxwell answered. "If it comes to that, I'd frankly rather it be us who busts her down." And to Colonel Brooks he added, "No offense intended but we built her."

Alice called her house from Mercedita. "Here's your chance," she told Patty. "He's at the ballpark."

Dressed to travel—home—Patty left the jacket of her wool winter suit, the same being the suit she had worn when she arrived in Puerto Rico, at Alice's, and she walked to Charles H. Terry Stadium, six blocks under Ponce's blazing sun. When she arrived, perspiring, she was shocked to find the stadium was no more than a minor league ballpark. In such humble surroundings, Don was easy to find. Given the championship series, in her mind she had built up the stadium virtually to the scale of Ebbetts Field.

From the edge of the tunnel, inside, she saw Don, sitting by himself in a box along the third base line, directly behind the visiting team's dugout. Out on the field, Ponce's players were taking batting practice. From the deep gloaming of the grandstand, the contrast of noon sun on the field was abrupt. Don looked relaxed and at home. He even wore a sport shirt with a floral print, which fit right in with the sport shirts other men were wearing. Don was sitting among children playing hooky from school. He was sitting among men out of work. And he was out of work, too; regressed to childhood, to youth, also playing hooky.

Afraid to go forward, her heart in her mouth, Patty feared his rejection. She reasoned that her presence was another instance of intruding, and that it was she, not Don, who was clearly out-of-place. Only by reminding herself that she had come to deliver a message could she summon the nerve to face Don. Even so, she resolved to speak to him and leave.

Don's recognition, though instant, was confused, because Patty had approached just as Ponce's great slugger, Pancho Coimbre, hit a shot out to center. The ball bounced off the scoreboard, while Don was half-turned to greet Patty. In center, Felo Guilbe played the carom. "That's your friend," said Don, referring to Coimbre, whom Patty had professed to admire. "*El Toletero*," he said, when he saw that she was puzzled. The phrase in English meant "the one who hits lines drives." But she was puzzled mostly that Don had acknowledged her presence right off, as if she were right to be there and had been there all along. She recognized that it was Don who had been thinking of her, and so, in that sense, she *had* been there all along.

On the next pitch, *El Toletero* drilled a rising liner into left. Appreciative whistles and laughter rose from players and the thirty or so fans scattered throughout the stadium. Everyone loved watching *El Toletero*. Even the batting practice pitcher seemed awed. "*Jonron Don Q!*" someone shouted, a reference to a homer in honor of the rum distilled at Mercedita. As if seeming to oblige, Coimbre hit the next pitch so hard that it seemed destined to go to Mercedita.

Having stood to applaud a great hitter, Don remained standing, now to record the appearance of the woman he loved.

Although Don had not seen her the day she arrived in Puerto Rico, he did not miss the reference to her pending departure implied by the wool skirt she was wearing, for no one in Puerto Rico wore wool, and only someone about to travel north in a northern winter would think to do so. From a strap over her shoulder hung a small boxy camera. Don smiled. Neither she nor he was dressed for work. "They've got the ship running," Patty said. "They want you to fly it to Harry's Field."

A sense of redemption gladdened Don's heart upon hearing this news. As the news sank in, he smiled. "When?" he asked, as much surprised as moved.

Patty told him what little she knew, which was simply that Alice had called from Mercedita to say they had got the ship flying. Don had assumed that by now it was demolished. His remorse had been so great he spent the last night in a sleep so deep he got no rest at all; a sleep that merely took him away, as death would. Even his appearance at the ballpark was a throwback, to a time that seemed happier. There was only so much guilt a man could bear. Still, the ballpark was an admission of defeat, not of happier times, for lack of responsibilities and lack of prospects went together. Don hadn't thought he would see Patty again. She was not even wearing her great grandmother's ring.

El Toletero popped up. Don confessed he doubted he would ever fly again; but, then, he had not expected Patty's news. He had kissed off *Life*, and the dream of the Negro Lindbergh. "This is where people come who have nothing to come to," Don said.

"I love you," Patty said, risking one more try.

His pleasure was hers to see. Her face was flush. Such good color. Her brow perspired. And, when he smiled, she seemed to him approving the very smile that her smile had evoked.

"I cursed you. I'm sorry," Don said.

"I owe you the same apology," Patty answered.

Coimbre took a cut, and this time connected so hard the bat broke in two. The ball shot out of the infield so fast, Burgos declined to make a stab at it, not wanting to risk breaking his hand. When the ball bounced off the wall, the return bounce

HARRY'S ARK 163

brought it all the way to the infield, and Burgos fielded it after
all. People laughed. Don took Patty by the hand, then embraced
her. Coimbre smacked another pitch, with a report so loud it
sounded like a thunderclap. He hit a shot out to right field, then
pulled one to left. Every time he swung, he connected, sending
the ball to the fence, or out of the park, where the longer shots
hit roofs, en route to the *Río Portugués*.

Outside, the world looked different. The sun was colorblind.
"Did you hear about Jackie Robinson?" Don asked.

Patty hadn't heard about anybody. She didn't know Jackie
Robinson from Adam.

It had been on the radio, all the news about Jackie Robinson,
all morning.

"Slow down," Patty said.

"He got called up," said Don.

"Who?"

"Jackie Robinson."

"Who is Jackie Robinson?"

"A baseball player," said Don. Robinson played for the
Montreal Royals. The Dodgers were going to try him at first.
"He's Negro."

Now, she understood. Okay, now it was clear. She could
reckon; she could think like Don. Who batted fourth in Ponce's
lineup? Coimbre. Coimbre was best, but not first. She had arrived
at Don's distinctions. He was the best, but not first. "How good
is Jackie Robinson?" she asked.

"He's the best," said Don. "More than good enough to make
the Dodgers." He had all Robinson's stats. Robinson had won
the batting crown. He had stolen the most bases in the
International League. But Patty had never even *heard* of the
International League, and the numbers didn't matter.

"A third of Ponce's team could play the Majors," Don
declared. "And they would if they were white, and if they did,
they'd all be great." She suspected he was right.

She rode the bar of the bike, between the handlebars and
seat, as he pedaled. When she leaned back, it was against his chest,

surrounded by his arms as he reached around her. She smelled his
fragrance, cologne, bath soap, perspiration; woodsy and male;
she was near to him now. As he pedaled south, to *Calle Comercio*
and the bridge, the warmth of midday began to reach him. "Why
do you like me?" Patty asked.

"I see us together," Don answered.

Since he might equally have answered that he saw them not
quite together, or that he loved her, she led him on. She let him
breathe her hair and stroke her behind as he pedaled.

As he turned east, toward *Mercedita*, he just loafed, just
huffing along, at an easy pace, allowing the bike to drift from
one side of the street to the other, in and out of noonday traffic,
seeking the streetside shade of the trees. "Pay attention," Patty
warned.

But Don felt he *was* paying attention; his attention was
entirely on her. The street reminded him of the runway at
Mercedita. He had weight on the tires. There was hard feel to the
pavement. He recalled the gladness he had felt when he first
spotted her, far down the runway, near the cane, where she had
taken her position to shoot. The sight of Patty had made him
glad. Still, now, he noticed the sensation he felt each time his feet
went around through a cycle as he pedaled. To propel the bike,
his knees, of course, were pumping up and down. He found it
pleasing when his thigh rubbed her bottom. The manner in which
she was sitting brought his right leg into contact with her cheek.
Stroke for stroke, he could rub her. His left leg rubbed her thigh.
Such pleasant sensations had a life of their own. Her very posture
encouraged his legs. Never nearer, never farther, he kept his place
behind her.

Up the ramp to cross the river, Don found the pleasure self-
exciting. Pumping harder spread the fire. On the downside, far
from coasting, he kept pedaling, even faster. The street became
Route One, heading east to Mercedita. Propelled, she shared the
motion he imparted to the bike. Whether led, or simply
following, he realized that the woman he was chasing he would
gladly call his wife, gladly support, and gladly protect, through

all else. To accomplish such ends were his purpose. Had she not moved when Bill had signaled, yesterday; had Don not seen her when she backed against the cane, the ship would have killed her when it crashed. It would have landed on top of her. That thought harrowed Don's mind, until, each time he realized she was alive, he thanked God.

From one horizon to the next, he'd ever be behind her, her support. He lost sight of where he pedaled.

Don pulled up short, in the middle of Route One. In the middle of noon traffic he dismounted. Another minute, half a mile, a little farther, they'd have reached *La Mercedita*. But, he had blown himself out; his passion had consumed him. Breathless, excited, and on fire, Don dropped to his knees on the highway to beg. "God," he cried, "please marry me."

"I don't know," she cried.

He'd do anything for Patty, even die. She longed for him, as well; and, not immune in the least to the spectacle he created, for cars had stopped, horns were blowing, locals were whistling and razzing, Patty now saw him as hers. She saw them belonging together, but in bed. Aware that, oddly, his pleasure crippled him, and left him dazed as to the outside world, and unresponsive, she made an alternate suggestion. "Let's go to Alice's," she said.

—

CHAPTER SIXTEEN

Catty-corner to Harry's ship at Mercedita sat a De Havilland, parked for boarding, and Lon, early for his departure, stood beside it as he watched Harry's men. Lon could see the men were working on controls. They had torn up the deck in the cockpit, removed seats, yokes, and fuselage panels along the nose. But their immediate problem seemed lack of access, because, as Lon viewed it, the best access to the flight controls was up from underneath. It was a vicious cycle, of sorts, for, unless they got the ship to Harry's, where they could mount it on blocks and work from underneath, they would not get access to the controls, and, unless they got access to the controls, they would not likely get the ship back to Harry's. Lon was glad he was no longer a part of this. It was all too common a dilemma. He noted that Julio was not around, nor, for that matter, Don.

Finally, he approached them. "I understand it took an hour to fly her from where she crashed," he said.

Lacking seclusion where they worked, Harry's men were indifferent to onlookers. But on hearing Lon's voice, they stopped. "Actually, it took longer than an hour," said Bill, though to round off the number seemed charitable. The sight of his father merely served to remind Bill that the gulf between them was never greater, for Bill was covered in grease and soaked in his own perspiration, while Lon wore his white linen suit, and his hat, and looked the part of a traveler.

"I don't suppose you'd like to join us?" Maxwell asked.

Lon concluded he was kidding. "I'm glad to be out of it," he said. Even if they got the ship flying, he knew it would never fly well, nor ever be airworthy as before. The danger of residual damage would lurk in every flight. Impact stress was insidious;

cracks in metal, so minute. Bearing wear and bushing wear might suddenly occur, with little warning, like a heart attack, and bring her down. Like Harry, at least in one respect, Lon could appreciate a dignified exit. He might never recoup on his losses; a year-and-a-half of his life had been wasted. But, at least, Lon knew when to quit.

"Could you look at this, pop?" Bill requested.

Lon peered in through the nose and down through what remained of the flight deck, at the mixing box Bill had uncovered. Inside that box, mechanisms differentiated collective pitch between front rotors. There, lay the rosette of cam lobes on pitman arm shafts—Lon's original design and best contribution to the project—without which the pilot could not combine two functions in one blended motion of the stick.

Touching the ship for the last time in his life, Lon advised Bill what to do. "The pitman arm to the sector shaft should be torqued to a hundred fifty foot pounds," he said. "And the pitman arm to center link attaching nut should be torqued at thirty-five."

When Bill looked up, the pilot of Carib Air was signaling time to board. "Say 'hi' to mom for me," Bill requested.

"I'll do that," said Lon.

"Hey, pop, I enjoyed it."

"I did too," said Lon. Moved but for a moment, Lon recovered his composure. "I left the car in the parking lot. Keys are over the visor. Title is in the glove compartment. My part's signed." Then, to include the others, he added, "Hey, if any of you guys are ever in Cincinnati . . . ."

"Yeah, we'll look you up," said Maxwell. "Absolutely." They were welcome at Lon's, they all knew.

"It's been my pleasure," said Walter, understanding the reluctance on Lon's part to shake his greasy hand.

"*Adios*," Diego said.

After Lon had boarded, the men persisted in staring at his aircraft. Walter knew, however, from long experience on the front, that when you're dying you don't stop to watch another man's farewell. "Back to work," he ordered, including himself in the order, and, upon the spell being broken, all four of the men went back into the pit.

Minnie went to Harry's and returned with lunch for the men. Alice, too, having gone to Harry's, returned soon after with the drawings and the spec. book. Elisa, having helped Alice look for things, stayed at Harry's. The drawings Alice returned with included some from among the as-builts, but, more importantly, all of Lon's original shop drawings for his work on the controls.

"Where did you find those?" Bill asked.

Alice explained that they were lying in a bundle on top of Don's desk in the hangar, so that not even she could miss them, and, when she said that, the men had their laugh, because they knew that Lon had put them out for her. The sketches were labeled "Controls," and each sheet bore Lon's initials, "LP."

While the others ate, Bill created a shed by removing fuselage panels from the sides of the cabin. The aluminum roof remained, reflecting the sun, but now they enjoyed lateral ventilation. When they brought in the pilots' seats, which had been removed from the cockpit, and placed those on the cabin deck, then they had a place of relative comfort, where two could sit on seats and all could eat in shade. The temperature on the tarmac had hit one hundred.

After lunch, Minnie left, and, soon after, Don and Patty arrived. Greeting them, Alice resumed her afternoon's chore, which was to read aloud from the morning's paper, *El Día*. There were news pieces about Ponce's ball team the men liked hearing while they worked. And Alice was getting a chance to improve her skills at Spanish-to-English translation. When she faltered, Diego helped her. The paper also carried news of Harry's ship, and, dominant on page one, a four-column photograph of the ship, wonderfully backlit by the sunset, shot with a perfect sense of timing as the ship was lifting off, its nose way up in the sky, conveying all that power, and uncertainty, in a fierce struggle to get airborne. Beneath the photo read the credit, "Patty Symms."

In mid afternoon, Alice asked what she feared was a silly question. She had been watching the men work on the pedal and master cylinder assemblies that drove hydraulic fluid through lines to the pylons for cyclic control of the front rotors. Her question, which she directed to Maxwell, concerned use of those assemblies. "Not a bad question," Maxwell answered. "Without the assemblies, the front rotors wouldn't tilt."

"Oh. Well, the reason I ask," Alice said, "is because the assemblies, as you call them, look like the brakes in my car."

"No," said Maxwell, "Your car is a Dodge. We stole these assemblies from Fords."

Diego likened the progress they made to that of a surgical procedure, in which the patient's stomach was being operated on while the patient was lying face down.

At three o'clock, another Carib Air flight came in. Two people got off, not counting the pilots. At four-fifteen, the plane departed.

At five-fifteen, the trade winds subsided.

At five-fifteen, Bill went over to the east wall of the terminal, which now cast a long shadow on the apron, and sat there, with his back to the wall. At five-fifteen, Don gave up on the as-builts. At five-fifteen, the airport manager quit work for the day. Alice folded her paper, and Patty no longer jumped when she was called.

"Where are we?" asked Don.

"I think we have arrived at your turn," Walter answered.

"Where is that?" asked Don.

"No front rotor control," said Walter. "Only throttle."

"Aft?"

"No collective, no hydraulics," Maxwell said.

"We're talking tolerances of four-thousandths of an inch," said Diego, apologizing for their efforts to realign pivots with shafts. No one could say what would work in the air.

"So I may not have any aft cyclic?" Don asked.

"You may not have much of anything," Maxwell said. "Whatever's under stress is subject to binding. If the tolerances close, then the pivots will jam."

"Aft cyclic and two throttles," Don concluded.

Bill confirmed.

"Aft cyclic, manually controlled, within a limited range, and two throttles," Diego corrected.

"If you're up forty feet, and you lose it . . . ," said Walter.

"I won't go up to forty feet," said Don, who knew he was facing his own death. He asked whether they might get him something more if they continued working until sunset, but no one seemed to think so.

"It'll just add to your problems," said Maxwell. "On top of everything else, then you'd be flying at night."

"So you're saying do it now?"

"Now or never." Maxwell couldn't avoid pushing Don, by serving that ultimatum.

Diego walked over and got Bill. They had done their part. What else could they do? "He wants more control," said Diego.

"Don't we all," said Bill, having watched the fear begin to gather in Don. Bill rose and walked over to the ship, where Don and the others were gathered. "You just have to try her, Don, that's the best I can say. We've done all we can." In Bill's view, Don was responsible, largely, for their being in this situation.

Don felt gripped by his fear. Just like yesterday, fear wrenched his guts. He knew, and they all knew, that, trying to fly that aircraft, they could dig a blade in; that aircraft could break up in flight, catastrophically. He couldn't hide how he felt. He couldn't conceal it from Patty. The war within him still raged, forcing him to another moment of truth. "You guys don't know how much I'd like to walk away from this one," said Don.

"Yeah, I think we do," said Bill. If the ship would do to Don what he had tried to do to it, it would kill him.

"All right," he said, now the humblest pilot on earth. "I'll take her as slow as I can, and keep her as low as she'll go."

It was six o'clock and close to sundown before they started the engines. Tossing cables onto the bed of the truck, Bill asked Patty where her camera was. She had taken up a shooting position among fuselage panels, but she was shooting with a Rolleiflex and he was accustomed to seeing the Speed Graphic.

"I traded it for dirt," Patty said.

When the ship lifted off, Don held it, barely, in a hover, then slowly brought it around to face the sun. Behind the truck a caravan formed, with Walter and Alice in Alice's Dodge, Maxwell in his Buick, and Diego in his Ford. Painstakingly, Don nudged the ship forward; to and fro, barely inches off the ground. He was rocking it around the longitudinal axis, using throttles. By revving the engine that ran the aft rotor, the ship came up a degree at the tail, and moved forward. No sooner did it exceed the speed of an amble than Don revved the engine that ran the forward rotors, and eased off aft. The nose came up, retarding the ship. Since he was constantly adjusting throttles, he was constantly combating yaw. He had just enough cyclic to hold heading.

"Take forever this way," Walter griped.

"Give him his chance," said Alice.

By fits and starts, Don maneuvered the ship across the runway, heading south by southwest toward the coast back to town.

"Must be hard on him," said Alice, some moments later, when the ship had cleared Mercedita.

"Hard on me to watch him," said Walter.

Patty got a picture, shooting at one one-hundredth of a second through a filter, and stopped down to f:11. Though it tore at her to see Don struggle, she had to admit the ship's slow progress did make for an easy shoot.

"Lord," Walter groused.

"Well what would you do?" Alice asked, piqued at Walter.

"Just let her go," said Walter. "Fly."

"Because you don't care," said Alice, deciding to test Walter, to see what mattered to him. "Did you know they were going to fly this ship to Wright Field?" she asked. Her words surprised Walter. "That's why they were practicing at Mercedita," she said. "The air show was a ruse, to cover their departure from Puerto Rico."

"I'll be damned," Walter said. "They should've just told me. I *like* that idea."

His answer surprised Alice. She had never realized *he* was crazy.

Don picked up a spur road to follow to *Punta Cabullón* to the south. The sun was in his eyes. To see anything at all, now, he had to turn his head away, squint and peek from the corner, first from one eye then from the other. Because he kept both hands on throttles, he had no hand free to shield his eyes. He had not thought of bringing sunglasses. He lost sight of the caravan that trailed him. The sun flooded in from the right side front of the cockpit. The Plexiglas made it worse; made the light smear into glare. No one had thought to wash windows. For lack of clear vision he nearly ran the ship into a tree. The cane fields ended. He nearly snagged a boundary fence. He flew by two houses, then almost clipped a third with the starboard rotor. No matter which way he turned, the sun was blinding him, all but obliterating a field of view. He felt so frantic, he landed. The ship ground into scrub. He let the engines continue idling, and, in a gesture of utter relief, removed both hands from the throttles to cover his eyes.

The Dodge pulled up and Walter got out. Then Maxwell pulled up behind Walter. Walter walked across the field toward the ship. Maxwell trotted after him. Diego pulled up behind Maxwell, then Bill and Patty in the truck, behind Diego. "I can't see," yelled Don, when Walter stepped up to his window.

"You're doing fine," Walter yelled.

"Come with me," Don yelled. "I can't see." Even as he sat, the cockpit was garish in sunlight.

"What's to look at?" shouted Maxwell, as Walter boarded the ship and sat next to Don. From outside, Maxwell handed in a pair of glasses. "At the rate you're going," he shouted, "you'll die of old age before you crash."

With Walter beside him, Don took off again. He flew another half-mile. At the edge of the marsh he could make out the reflection of sunlight off water. They were heading into coast. "He's right," Don yelled. He brought the ship around. The sun lay at the horizon, seeming to grow larger. Walter put his head out the window, searching the ground ahead of them. He looked back and saw the road recede, the truck turning around to drive off. Don put his own head out the window, emulating Walter, but found he was looking into glare. Ahead, he made out silhouettes of ships in the Port of Ponce. He changed heading, northwest. The new heading was no better. The sun's lower rim appeared to touch the sea's surface, then to melt. Don had taken an hour to bring the ship just four miles. "He's right," Don repeated, when Walter retracted his head from the window.

Walter was uncertain to whom or what Don referred. "Who's right?" he shouted back.

"Maxwell," Don yelled. "It's too slow."

"Then go faster," Walter yelled. He could see what bothered Don. At root, Don was less fearful about dying than he was about losing his job, and, while that phenomenon might seem odd, Walter had seen it before, often enough, among men in Germany during the depression following the First World War.

The sun, half set, appeared fervid orange. "Go on," Walter urged. All Don seemed to need was permission. Walter gave it. Looking above as they flew, Walter enjoyed the spectacle of cumulus, piled high into the evening sky, illuminated from underneath by sunlight. Left of Don, smokestacks, bridges and mastheads of ships remained in daylight. As they passed *Playa de Ponce*, the last of the sun sank seaward, and the dazzle on the sea's surface abruptly ceased. Tops of coconut palms shone gold. It took all kinds to make a world, but Walter thought that Don must know that too.

Don opened the throttles. The ship began climbing. Ahead lay the thoroughfare, *Avenida Hostos*, connecting downtown Ponce to its port. From among the cars, Walter picked out the truck, which, having gone the long way around by road, had arrived to meet them. At a height of seventy-five feet, the ship flew over houses, then powerlines and roadway. Walter waved at Bill. From the truckbed, Patty shot a picture. The other cars arrived. Don kept climbing. When the ship reached eighty-five feet, the top sector of the sun reappeared. Walter waved to Alice in her Dodge. Don kept climbing. Once again sun shone through the cockpit. Once again, Don squinted. He kept climbing. "How high?" Walter yelled, with a rush of splendid excitement.

Out of the sea came the sun, intact and entire. It rose as resurrected. A reversal of time and of dusk. The race delighted Walter, thrilled him. They were racing with the sun! At three hundred feet, Don topped out the climb. Up there, it was bright as broad day. Beyond the foreground of trees, Ponce proper emerged. Beyond Ponce, rose *El Vigia*, then the foothills, draped in sun. Beyond the foothills, rose the mountains, the *Cordillera Central*, whose skyline ran west for many miles. "Oh my," Walter said. "We *should* take this ship to Wright Field."

"Say what?" Don yelled, having proven once again he was a man.

"I said, give this ship to your Army," Walter yelled. "Because, by nineteen sixty, she'll be your nation's top performer."

At the field, Harry hadn't shaved all day, which was unlike him. Since he had been up most of the night, *being up* became his excuse for letting things slide through the morning and into the afternoon. But, no more. Not into the evening. Harry was strong, and he drew upon that strength. He knew the difference between self-pity and rage. Rage was what a man felt when insulted. But, self-pity, well . . . . If a man felt bad, he should at least look his best. The worst thing to do was to let appearance go down just because feelings were hurt. Feelings could be fixed. Feelings were easy. But, to sit bleary-eyed, with a growth of gray stubble, wearing nothing but an undershirt, that was for losers. Harry was no loser. Things were taken from him, but he hadn't lost. He hadn't weakened his resolve. He wouldn't grovel. He wouldn't beg. And when he was right, which he was, he wouldn't say otherwise, and lie.

Harry remained true to the Army despite adversity, despite his bad heart, despite disloyal men; despite ailments, edema, near-sightedness, diabetes, enlarged prostate; despite his arthritis in knees and both hands; despite being hearing-impaired, *he* was true. He could still dress and look his best for the evening. Harry had resolved, in fact, to drive into town to see a movie. Why not? It was his regular routine for Friday night, and he had resolved to eat in town, too, though Minnie had left him some supper. There was so much to be said for a man's pride. He could shave, brush his teeth, comb his hair, do those things. Put a fresh shine on his shoes. Wear a fresh shirt. Fake a smile.

The first intimation Harry had that his ship was flying again occurred with the roar of vehicles racing onto the field. First the truck, skidding onto gravel and making no bones about noise, then the cars right behind it, brought Harry to the porch. But he thought the men were drunk, that they had come to revile him, to piss on his grave. If they were going to do that, he would just take out his service weapon and shoot them.

Harry returned to the bathroom. Then, the sound of rotors, compounding a general jubilation, whooping, and car doors slamming told him, upon the instant, that his ship was coming home. When the ship flew over, the entire house shook. The house shook, but Harry's hand did not tremble. No fool, he could hear she was damaged. Don was flying her with throttles. Harry drew down the stropped razor so artfully, and shaved around the mole beside his ear. The sound of the aircraft seemed like leviathan, like a great, wounded beast. Too bad! Although Harry's heart would have liked to know gladness, his pride said never lie. The damage had crippled the ship, and he knew it. It had left her bereft of any promise. Pathos pulled compassion out of Harry. Were the ship a horse, he would shoot it, as he once had done to his mare. But that was years ago. The ship's return now was a taunt, meant only to insult Harry Baird.

When the engines shut down, *then* Harry's hand began to tremble. He heard Walter and Don disembark. In place of engines, the field resounded with clamorous celebration, with joyous laughter, with redemptive dancing, and with glee. He would have thought there were fifty people out there. A cotillion. But, there were only his people, truth be told. He heard Alice's voice, Patty's. He heard Diego and Don; Maxwell, Walter and Bill. He went to his room. From the window, he watched them: each joyous in the company of the others. Such tidings meant nothing to Harry;

hypocrisy, if anything. Ultimately, it was he who was the laughingstock. They were not celebrating life. They were laughing at him. They had come back to taunt him, to flout the ship in his face. The war continued. They were vultures at his corpse. Harry's house was his grave; his office, the coffin.

Yet, an abiding, small voice spoke to Harry. In spite of everything, it persisted. Like the voice Elijah heard atop Mount Horeb, a small, still voice said, "*Harry, you have built a great ship.*" Grief was unendurable. Unhappiness pierced him. He could not believe his life would end this way, desolate and bare. Under the clatter of duty and blame. Ripped apart. Yet the small, still voice spoke the truth: the ship had flown, and he was wrong. It had passed the test of every great ship to carry its crew safely home.

No one came to the house.

The men conferred by the ship.

Then two of them approached. One was Walter, the other was Don. They came in quietly. The festivity had subsided. Don led the way, respectfully back to Harry's office. "Sir, could we see you?"

"Come in," Harry said.

With Harry's permission, they sat on his bed. The contrast in appearances struck Harry, for, here he was. He looked fresh, fit as a fiddle, and he felt rotten inside. And here they were, they looked like hell; and yet, their faces shone like glory. "I envy you," he told them. "Whether you're right or you're wrong, I envy you."

"We came here to ask your help," said Walter.

"There's nothing I can do for you," said Harry.

"Sir, with all respect," said Don, "if we could just get her up on timbers, a drydock, we could work on the controls from underneath."

"To what end?" asked Harry.

"There's plenty we can do," said Walter, speaking sharply. "Many things."

"Do what you must," Harry said. "You don't need me."

"We thought, maybe, you could get Julio to come back," said Don, "and maybe call the lumberyard, to see if they would let us take timbers, for our drydock. Also, if you could arrange with the Army, so that when we get to Miami . . . ."

"Miami?! You're insane," said Harry.

"We're still going to take her to Wright Field," said Don.

"No," said Harry. "That's absurd."

Don looked down. Then, Walter took over. Walter was afire now. "I know about your stupid ruse," he told Harry. "Now, you will do what *I* tell you. We *need* you to help us, and we *will* fly that aircraft to Wright Field. We *will* set a world's record. Your aircraft *is* still capable of that."

"Think it over," said Don, for, with Harry or without him, they intended to go forward, and he and Walter rose to leave.

"Wait," said Harry. "I can talk with Julio, at least." And he rose to follow them, having decided to give life another shot.

Julio had been to San Juan, and there entreated his family to return. They had agreed, but he had to make some concessions. He had promised to take any job Charlesville might still offer, promised to get his back pay from Harry, and promised that, once he was paid, he would tell Harry good-bye. But those promises were made without anyone realizing that, at their house, the back pay was waiting, delivered in the form of a check by Elisa earlier in the day. Nor did Julio realize that the ship was flying now, or that it had flown from Mercedita. But there was a note from Alice saying that it had.

So Julio showed up at the field, in the company of Carlota, where he saw not only that the ship had flown, and flown to the field from Mercedita, but that now the men had it up on timbers, allowing them access to work on the controls. Because the distance from the parking lot was too far for him to walk on his crutches, Julio drove directly onto the field, right up to the apron and the ship.

Harry, Maxwell, Alice, Walter, Diego, Bill, and Don were there. They had turned on floodlights from the roof of the hangar, and had rigged more floodlights on the scaffolds. Trouble lights shone up from underneath the ship. They had even pulled the truck in, and were using its headlights, and those of Diego's Ford, to add to the illumination. It was a strange sight to Julio; men stripped to the waist, perspiring profusely, glistening in the beams of so much light. They looked garish, but, then, they were exhausted, all of them.

The company broke from its work. As the DeSoto parked, motor running, adding its light to the light of the others, the men and Alice gathered around to see how Julio fared. He had his crutches, of course, and hobbled, and his foot was still in wraps, but otherwise he looked the same. "I'd say that's a miracle," Julio said, referring to the flight of the ship from Mercedita. Of course, he knew the work that went into making that miracle occur; evidence of it showed in the strain in people's faces.

To Carlota, the miracle was money. She could almost forgive Harry his sins, for Harry had paid what he owed. She got out of the car to stand with her husband, even to take a closer look at the ship. Carlota wanted to remind people that Julio was the only one injured; and that, of all people, he was the one raising children.

"We know," Harry said, solemnly, hearing Carlota's sharp words.

"He's through working with you, Harry," Carlota said.

"I think they need me," Julio said softly, correctly assessing what he saw. Not all the bargaining chips belonged to Carlota. Julio looked at her as he spoke. In San Juan, she had gone to her mother's, but her mother was overwhelmed by the sudden arrival of her daughter and five grandchildren, and had been relieved when Julio came to fetch them. The matter was delicate.

Julio enjoyed playing the role of the comrade, returning to the lines after being wounded in combat. He showed off his agility on crutches. He was ceremonious, in clean clothes for a change, and in stark contrast to the others. The crutches made Julio seem noble. "Can you work?" Maxwell asked.

"Of course I can work," Julio said. "I drove to San Juan and back. The question is: do I want to?"

"How's your foot?" Diego asked.

"It's better," Julio answered. "We got your note," he told Alice.

"So are you here to work?" Maxwell asked more pointedly.

"A shock like that does make one appreciate," Julio said, without needing to identify what it was he appreciated. "All day long I've been worried, worried about what working for Harry has done to my life." He was careful to avoid tripping over cables. "I've been worried about what I'm going to do with the rest of my life. How I'm going to provide." He enjoyed how he focused their attention.

"We're going to cut off the struts," said Maxwell.

But Julio could see what they were going to do; there was nothing they were going to do that wasn't obvious to him.

"We formed a partnership," said Don.

"What does that mean?" Julio asked.

"We're not working for Harry now," Maxwell said.

"Is that right?" Julio asked Harry.

"I'm afraid so," Harry said.

"Harry's part of our partnership," said Don.

"We want you to become part of it, too," said Walter.

"Are *you* part of it?" Julio asked Walter.

"Yes," Walter answered.

"And Patty?"

"Patty, yes," Don answered for her, for Patty was sleeping in the hangar.

"And Lon?"

"No. He went to Cincinnati," said Bill.

"A partnership," said Julio, still not knowing what that meant. He looked at Diego. "And you?"

"No, I'm not either. I have to go back to M.I.T," Diego said.

Julio looked at Alice.

"'Fraid not," said Alice.

"So it's Walter, Don, Harry, Maxwell, Bill, and Patty," said Julio.

"But not you," Carlota told Julio.

"Not me," Julio agreed. "I lose in these things, every time."

"We have a different offer for you," said Harry.

"What does that mean?" Julio asked. He peered in through the nose of the ship. "You've got no pitch control," he noted. "It took a lot longer to build her than crash her. But, you know that." Moving to the side, he found what he was looking for: his own dried blood in the ship. There were splotches at the base of the panel. "Dangerous work," he observed.

"We don't want you to die," said Walter. "We are proposing that you not fly again."

"Where are you going to fly?" Julio asked, as he looked through the frame, in one side of the ship and out the other.

"Wright Field," said Walter.

Julio smiled at the irony that Walter had come over to Harry. Neither a wrinkle nor a dent escaped Julio's eye. Looking at the panel, he could see where Bill had capped circuits. He could see where the weight of the precast, having bounced on impact, had slammed forward. He could see how easily it had jammed the panel back in his lap. He could see the bends that were produced in the airframe when forces of impact and inertia combined. He could see how close he had come to being killed. "And you think this thing can make it to Wright Field?" he asked Don.

"We think so," offered Don.

"Pleated," Julio noted, wryly commenting on the deformation of the frame. He wondered aloud, "If we leave the frame the way it is, we'll have to build crooked to accommodate the bend." He found that prospect amusing. "But, if we try to straighten her, we might misalign some upper mount . . . ." He let his eyes travel up to the engines; forward to the transmission; to the drivetrain. He looked across, again through the ship, at Maxwell, Don, Walter, Diego, Harry, and Bill. "So you really think you can make it to Wright Field?"

"We think so," Don repeated. "But our chances improve if you help us."

Julio thought for a moment. "And Charlesville? Doesn't the aircraft belong to him?"

"The hell with Charlesville," said Walter.

"You guys really are the buccaneers," Julio said, referring to what Bill had called them the day the plan was hatched.

"All we want is your advice," said Maxwell.

"Yes, we don't even want you on board," said Bill. "We don't want you to touch anything."

"You don't have to get dirty," said Diego. "You don't even have to change your clothes."

"Get that," Julio said to Carlota.

"Julio," Harry said, "Listen to our offer. We know your situation. We know what Charlesville was willing to offer you. And we can match and beat Charlesville's offer."

"Yes? I would like to hear that," said Carlota.

"I would too," said Julio.

"The men wanted to make a concession to you and your family. They wanted to make sure you're provided for. We are offering you sixty-five dollars a week as lead engineer. That's the offer. But, there's more: it's a guaranteed salary. That's the concession. You get a one-year's guaranteed salary, no matter what happens to this project. It means you start tonight. You help us do what we must, advising us only, nothing hands on. And then, if nothing comes of it, you will have done your part, even if it's only one night's work. You will continue to draw sixty-five dollars a week, for one year, no matter what else you do. You can go work for Charlesville, or you can go fishing, we don't care." Harry took stock of Julio's response, and Carlota's, which seemed favorable, albeit puzzled. "There's more," Harry said. "I'll have Antonio come out here tonight to establish an escrow account. Guaranteed income," he repeated. "These are your witnesses, and you'll have it in writing."

"So, even if I get another job?"

"Even if you get another job, even if you go to work for Charlesville, so long as there's no more work for the partnership."

"Guaranteed?"

"Guaranteed.

"You have that much money?" Carlota asked Harry.

"I do," Harry said. "And I want you to come to the house and see it. Then, once you've signed on, Antonio will hold it in escrow and will be in charge of paying you. I know you trust him." The cash Harry spoke of was sitting in a strongbox on the dining room table in Harry's house. The others had seen it, and agreed with what Harry said.

"This would be for one night's work?" Julio asked, compelled but incredulous.

"No. For one night's work *if we fail*," Harry said. "That's the minimum."

"And if you succeed?"

"If we succeed, you're in it with us. You're a partner."

"Yeah, you have to work then," said Maxwell.

"But not fly," Harry said. "Not fly. Just work, do your share."

"As a partner?"

"As a *general* partner in the Baird Aircraft Company," Harry said, "along with the rest of us. Shall we go to the house? I know you want to see the strongbox and cash."

"Well?" Julio asked Carlota.

"Wait a minute," she answered. "I'm not staying in Ponce."

"You won't have to," said Harry. "We're going to relocate the company to New York City; headquarters in Manhattan, plant on Long Island."

"This is better," she said, meaning *better than Charlesville*. New York was her favorite place in all the world.

"Time's a wasting," said Bill. Harry had sweetened the pot, in his own, inimitable way, and done the impossible in charming Carlota.

When Antonio arrived, he drafted the partnership agreement, including the guarantee of weekly paychecks for Julio. Antonio personally acted as the escrow agent, and took the money in Julio's behalf.

"Any chance of getting the first week in advance?" Carlota asked him.

"Not in the agreement," Antonio answered.

Just past eleven, Carlota left to go home; Antonio, too. Julio stayed. The men told Don to knock off. If the work went well, he would have a day's flying ahead of him to get the ship to Florida. He slept in the hangar next to Patty.

Alice had decided to stay up. She made a pot of coffee. Harry was sitting at the table, the open strongbox, now largely empty, before him. He stated his misgivings. "Julio sold himself," he said flatly. "He sold himself like a whore. I can't stand a man who will sell out his ideals."

"You're going broke," Alice noted. Harry had used his life's savings.

"I hate a man that sells his loyalty," said Harry.

"How will you live?" Alice asked.

"Well, I can't," he admitted.

"I didn't think so," she said.

"I need him for tonight," Harry told her, "When you're in a fight, you do what you must, no matter the cost."

"'My kingdom for a horse?'" Alice quoted.

"Exactly," Harry said. "I'm Army. Army! Julio doesn't understand that. I'll pay for one night of his expertise. We do what we have to." But, when Harry undertook to carry the box back to his office, he found his strength had ebbed. "Help me with this," he asked Alice.

She had no problem with the strongbox. It weighed less than her typewriter. Harry followed her, and in the office pointed toward the floor beneath his bed. "Who gave you the rose?" Alice asked, for she had seen a pressed rose inside the book of Tennyson's poems inside the box.

"None of your business," Harry told her. *Dakota* had been playing in town at the Fox Delicias. Harry missed it. He said he was sorry. He liked movies; he approved of John Wayne.

Harry took in this woman, Alice, with whom he had shared so much of his day. "They won't make it to Wright Field," he predicted. "I didn't have the heart to tell them not to try."

"I hope you're wrong," Alice said.

"It's out of my hands. I'm not the doer anymore."

Harry took the coffee to the men. For a while, he watched them work. Past midnight, he returned to the house. At half past twelve, Harry died.

—

CHAPTER SEVENTEEN

Awakened by the telephone, Antonio learned abruptly his friend Harry had died. "*Dios mio*," he gasped, all of a sudden recalling the moment in his own childhood when he had looked up at the heavens, and felt himself being pulled toward the stars. That moment had been his intimation of death, or perhaps of his own soul. Still, language formed, even then, reducing wonder to cause. "How did it happen?" Antonio had asked.

"It just did," Alice answered.

On his way to the field, Antonio stopped for Harry's will, which he kept in his office.

Ahead of him at the field, his friend, Joe Gándara, who was Harry's personal physician, had been first to arrive out of those Alice had called, and Joe had pronounced Harry dead. Still to come were Elisa, Minnie, and the *Funeraria Santa Marta*. As Antonio entered the house, he greeted Alice, Harry's men, Patty, and Joe, remarking that, except for Joe, the people whom he was seeing now he had just seen two hours ago, including Harry, who was at that time alive.

The men had placed Harry's body on his bed in the back room, and Alice led Antonio down the hall to see it. In dying, Harry had fallen in the doorway between his office and the hall. Accompanied by Joe and Alice, Antonio stood at that doorway now, looking in upon the body. Harry lay supine, jaw agape, eyes partially open. In the throes of death he had become clonic, a condition accounting for what appeared to be anguish in the expression of his face. Joe was sensitive to the fact that Antonio was horrified. "Antonio," he said gently, "it was only a spasm of muscles that gave him that look. He felt nothing."

But Alice took issue with Joe's reassurance, for she had been with Harry when he died. Again she told the story of Harry's final moments. "I was across the hall," she began, "typing. And Harry was there, at his desk. I wasn't paying him any mind, but I do remember he seemed restless. He got up and sat down several times. Then, one time he got up and came to the doorway, right here . . . ," and, saying that, Alice put her hand to her throat. "It was as if he were going to speak to me, as if he were waiting for me to look up. Owing to the silence, I did look up, and I saw that he was stricken. His face was ashen. Perspiration was beaded on his brow. 'I can't breathe,' he gasped. I tell you, I was shocked. I jumped right up. Shock went through me like a current. I couldn't believe this was happening. Then Harry fell; I tried to hold him, but he fell, not straightaway, but slowly, sliding his hand down the door frame. He was on his knees, right there, looking at the floor. He was gasping. I was beside him. I heard his last words. He said, 'I didn't know it was so hard to die.' I got up and ran. Outside, I called the men."

"She called us, all right. She woke the dead," said Diego.

"Well, not quite," quipped Bill.

"There was nothing we could do," said Walter, who had been the first to arrive. Walter knew the look. He had seen the look on many men. Harry was gone.

"Yeah, done for," Maxwell agreed. "Even by Kentucky's standards, we all knew he was dead."

Elisa and Minnie arrived. Soon, their tears proved contagious, for Alice and Antonio began weeping with them. Then, Alice told the story, one more time, how Harry had died.

In the front room, afterwards, with everyone gathered, the company drank to Harry's memory, using Harry's Cutty Sark. Pending the arrival of the *funeraria*, they took coffee afterwards. The surviving partners had business, and conducted it then and there. They had been planning to fly in the morning, but a morning flight was out of the question. Harry's death had drained them, to say nothing of disrupting their work. "The real question is, should we even try it," Maxwell said.

"Harry's death changes nothing," said Don.

They voted, whether to go forward with the plan for the flight to Wright Field, albeit at a later time. Julio voted yes, try it. Maxwell voted no, don't. Bill concurred with Maxwell, voting no. In his view, the repairs had not gone well enough. Don asked Patty. "Yes," Patty said. "Go."

"With you onboard?" asked Bill.

"Certainly, with me on board," she said, "in place of Harry."

"Walter?"

"Yes," voted Walter. "But I will be your flight engineer. Patty can help with navigation."

"A crew of three. The 'ayes' have it," said Don, whose vote was well known as an aye. "We'll leave Saturday night," he said. "And Saturday night is tonight." He checked his watch. It was one forty-five Saturday morning.

"A night flight will be a lot more dangerous," said Bill.

"Yes, and another full day of delay adds to the problem of going at all," Don judged. No one argued. Even Antonio, who opposed them flying, though he had no vote in the matter, admitted that Charlesville was certain to come to Ponce following the news of Harry's death, and Charlesville's presence back in Ponce would make their flying impossible.

"We need to keep him away eighteen hours," said Don. "Once we're gone, what can he do?"

Harry had wanted cremation, but cremation was not practiced in Puerto Rico, and there were no crematoria on the island. So the men decided to have Harry's body flown to south Florida, to be cremated there, which would allow the remains to accompany the ship on the final leg north to Wright Field. It seemed poetically just that Harry come *home* on board his ship.

Concerned that his thirteen-year-old son Leonard would wake to the news that he would never see Harry again, Julio excused himself to go get him. Leonard loved Harry. Everyone knew that.

In Julio's absence, Antonio read portions of Harry's will, including the provision that Harry's remains be scattered on

Huffman Prairie, which was land outside Dayton that had been used once by the Wright brothers in their early efforts to fly, and was now owned by the AAF within the domain of Patterson Field.

"Will there be a service for Harry at Wright Field?" Alice asked.

"Oh yes," said Bill. Harry was very well known.

"And will you all take part in it?" she asked.

"Definitely," said Maxwell. "Everybody in U.S. aviation will be there."

At the Rodriguez house, Carlota awoke. "Harry's dead," Julio whispered. "He died at half past twelve."

"Oh no," Carlota cried, confused and dazed by the news, and, for the moment, sorry for Harry. She looked at the clock: it was after two. She blinked in amazement. "Is our agreement still good?"

"It's still good."

"We get money?"

"We get money."

"How did he die?" she asked, sitting up.

"He had a heart attack," Julio told her. "I came to get Leonard."

"Why?"

"I want to take him to see Harry before the funeral parlor comes."

"I'm not going over there."

"You don't have to."

"Can't you take him in the morning?"

"No. They're going to take the body tonight. We're going to have the body flown to Florida; in fact, all the way to Wright Field," Julio said, choosing carefully how he worded this. "Let's make love," he said.

"No," she said, indignant. One human had just left this world, and already Julio wanted to replace him. But, that was how Julio was. He thought out things through love-making and children. That was why they were always in debt. That was why they had no money. Now she was awake. "He caused us grief," she said, not precisely justifying Harry's death tit-for-tat, but, in essence, reminding Julio it was just. The world did not need Harry's immediate successor to come forth. The world could do without another Harry for a while.

"Okay," Julio said, though he loved to make love to Carlota. "We're all going to Wright Field," he told her. "There'll be a big service for Harry."

"I'm not going to Wright Field," she said.

"You don't have to," he told her.

"You guys are screwed up, you know that? I'll never go back to that place."

"He was like my father," Julio said.

"I hated it there," Carlota told him.

"You don't have to go there. It's for Harry, not for you."

"He wouldn't go there for you."

Julio was going, that was that.

"You could bury him in Ponce," she said. But she wouldn't dignify Julio now. She turned away. He watched her breathe, then gave up. As he left the room, she rolled over and stared from the bed. The children were awake; at least Leonard and the girls. "*Pendejos!*" she said, cursing all Harry's men. "You waste my money, I'll take my children to my mother's." She rolled away again and hurled herself back into sleep.

In the boys' room, where Leonard, Tim, and Daniel slept, Leonard sat up. "Cucho," Julio whispered, calling to Leonard from the doorway.

"*Que, Papi?*" Leonard asked.

"Harry died."

The words, like the rain, took their time to sink in. Like the rain on baked earth, on dry earth, the words took their time. "I can see him," Leonard said. Leonard could see Harry. Harry was full of light, riding a mare, and the mare flew.

"You see him?"

"Uh-huh." Harry waved to Leonard.

Julio understood from what his son was saying that Leonard did not relish going to the field. He understand from what

Leonard was telling him that Leonard was not accepting Harry's death. So, he gave Leonard a kiss. He loved his *Cucho*, his Leonard. He understood that Leonard saw Harry as happy, or felt happy in thinking of Harry alive, and therefore could not see Harry dead. Leonard did not want the world to change. He had moved too many times. He did not relish the seasons. Julio did not for one moment think Leonard really did see Harry, because of course nobody could see someone who was dead: there was nothing to see. "It's okay," Julio said. He loved his son.

"*Papi*, I think you're sadder than Harry."

"It's okay," Julio repeated. Someday, Julio knew, his son would have to face up to death, which, like endings in general, meant *vacío*, empty, everything over and done with. But that need not be tonight and would not be tonight. Julio did not wish to inflict the reality of guilt in addition to the reality of death on his son. "God will grant Harry his peace," Julio said, trying to recall what the priests would have said.

Leonard was sad, and his sadness came from far away; not for Harry, who was relieved of duty and jubilant now, but for his father, who could not see.

Carlota was up now and stopped Julio on the way out. "Do you want coffee?"

"No."

"He's not going?" she asked, referring to Leonard, who, normally, jumped at the opportunity to go to the field.

"I don't think he's up to it," said Julio.

"I'm sorry," Carlota said. "I know you thought of Harry like a father."

"No matter, it's okay," Julio told her.

"I know you think I'm crass."

"No."

"It's just that he hurt you."

"I understand how you feel."

"I can't forgive that."

"No need to. I understand it," Julio said.

She sighed. She sighed as her husband went down the steps to the street, and on her own way back to bed she stopped to look in on her son.

When Julio arrived back at Harry's, the hearse was there. To facilitate loading the body, the mortician had backed the hearse to the porch. In the house, the mortician, Ricardo Torres, anticipating the visit of a child to view the corpse, had closed Harry's eyes and mouth, and massaged away the grimace. Elisa and Minnie had placed Harry's uniform and personal effects on the table in the front room, and the men had placed Harry's body onto the stretcher in the hall.

"No Leonard?" Elisa asked.

"He's having a hard time accepting," Julio said.

Julio identified the decorations Harry had won, including the Meritorious Service Medal, Legion of Merit, and Distinguished Service Medal. "That latter," Julio said, referring to the Distinguished Service Medal, "you get for doing something the Army considers truly important. In Harry's case, it was for coming out of retirement at the outbreak of war to take up the post he served: technical liaison between Air Matériel Command and private industry." By comparison, Julio had gotten only a Meritorious Service Medal for his own work in engineering design.

Joe Gándara remarked that Harry was one of the toughest patients he had ever treated. "He was tough, because he never complained about his ailments," Joe said, "Despite the fact that he had a ton of them."

"Harry was tough," agreed Maxwell.

Holding the volume of Tennyson Harry kept in his strong box, Antonio recalled that the first time he met Harry, fifteen months ago at a dinner party, Harry had recited a long poem, by Tennyson. "He recited *Ulysses*," Antonio said. As it happened, *Ulysses* was Harry's favorite poem, one of the few poems he knew, and the only one he could recite. "I thought," Antonio said, "before we say goodbye to him, you might like to hear the final verses." Thus, Antonio read:

Tis not too late to seek a newer world.
Push off, and sitting well in order smite
The sounding furrows; for my purpose holds
To sail beyond the sunset, and the baths
Of all the western stars, until I die.
It may be that the gulfs will wash us down;
It may be we shall touch the Happy Isles,
And see the great Achilles, whom we knew.
Though much is taken, much abides; and though
We are not now that strength which in old days
Moved earth and heaven, that which we are, we are;
One equal temper of heroic hearts,
Made weak by time and fate, but strong in will
To strive, to seek, to find, and not to yield.

Moved by Antonio's reading, and no less by the verses themselves, Alice suggested that if anyone else had something to say about Harry, this would be a good time.

"There were a lot of men like Harry in England," Patty said, "and many of them were officers. He was the kind of man you liked to have breakfast with."

Minnie said she liked cooking for Harry, because he ate with gusto. "I would leave him his supper," she said, "and the next day he never failed to thank me, and to tell me how much he enjoyed it."

Elisa, too, added something, but apologized to Harry, wherever he was, for wanting to say something a little *critical*. She regretted the fact that Harry was difficult to work for, because, as a boss, he was never wrong. When she said that, the men chuckled. "But," Elisa went on, "Harry always asked after my daughter, or, if someone was sick in my family, after their welfare. The one time I invited him to my home for dinner, he could not have been more gracious, not to my family or me. I think he was terribly lonely and did appreciate the small things of this world."

Diego spoke. "I think some day when you guys have a famous aircraft, then I'll be able to tell people, 'Hey, you know, I worked for Harry Baird, way back when, back in Ponce, in the beginning.'"

Maxwell told the story of the dog Harry owned. This story went back a few years, to the time when the men were at Wright Field. Harry's dog was a tawny and white, mixed-breed Collie and Shepherd, and, according to Maxwell, Harry was devoted to it. "But the dog had grown feeble," Maxwell said. "It couldn't walk anymore. It had arthritis and cancer, and couldn't control its bowels. So Harry took the dog out to the country and shot it. I happened to run into Harry later that day. I also like dogs and Harry knew that I did, so he told me he had killed his dog. The moment he said that, he broke down and bawled like a baby. And I believe for every one of those tears Harry shed, he reserved himself a place up in Heaven."

"He treated a dog a whole lot better than he treated a man," muttered Bill.

"No doubt about it," Maxwell agreed. "Men are a dime a dozen, but a good dog is hard to find."

"This is Harry's Bible," Alice said. "Would someone like to read from it?" When no one volunteered, she asked, "Do any of you know if Harry had a favorite passage?" Again, no one spoke. "Do any of *you* have a favorite passage?" Still, no one volunteered.

Julio spoke. "Many times I've said that I hated Harry Baird. I didn't. I loved him. My father died when I was young, and Harry was the father to me that he never was. Harry *was* difficult, but it was ultimately to make us better men."

"That's hogwash," said Don. "Harry used us. He promoted himself by using us."

"I see it more or less the same way," Bill concurred.

Saying nothing, Alice considered how, moments before Harry died, he had blamed Julio, and called Julio a betrayer, virtually a whore, who had sold honor for money. Elisa, too, recalled to herself that, during the day, Harry had blamed Julio for the crash, and, last evening, Don. She could think of many similar occasions; there was no end of them.

"I don't have any stories to tell," said Bill. "And I'm not much for religion. All I can say is I met Harry at Wright Field for the first time in 1942. In looking back, I don't think he was a great engineer—in fact, I know he wasn't—not in the sense we mean when we say Sikorsky is a great engineer, or Cierva was a great engineer. Harry was what we call 'results oriented,' which is good, in that he knew what he wanted. I don't think he understood what we were doing, or even how we got there. I know he did not relish getting his hands dirty. You never saw Harry with grease under his nails. On the other hand, when things went wrong he could let you know you screwed up. So, naturally, it will be a long time before I have a warm memory of Harry. I may never. Julio may think of him as a father," Bill continued, "but I had enough to do with my own father here. It seems to me that Harry took advantage of people, by playing on their pride and their ambition. Whatever you feared, he would find out about that and use it against you, even if it meant just to threaten you. He used our ambition and our fear of failure, and Don is right: he couldn't have done it had he not taken misfits."

"Harry was a misfit," Maxwell said.

"Yes," agreed Bill. "The Army passed him over. He retired a lieutenant colonel in '39. Had it not been for the war, he would never have made full colonel. I think at bottom, he saw himself as a victim. It was a miracle we got as far as we did. And I say that in light of the fact that my father and I did the best work of our lives, right here in Ponce, working for Harry, on that aircraft."

"We Germans," said Walter, at length, "have our problems with fathers." At this, he paused, until the snickering subsided. "After the war, I started reading the works of the Swiss psychoanalyst, Carl Jung, because that gave me solace." Walter looked around, but could see that none of them, excepting Alice, was aware of Carl Jung. "Patty mentioned that men like Harry were common in England, or in the Army. Well, I tell you, in the thirties, men like Harry were also common in the Reich, and, thank God, most of them are now dead. Harry was not the type of man who would have been SS, mind you. He was not small and sniveling, or small and arrogant. But, neither would he have been a line officer, or a field-grade officer. He was not great and daring, or bold. He would have stayed behind the range of the guns. To give you someone you know, for comparison, I liken Harry to Goering, or even Hitler. Harry would have been the one who demands everything from his men, and blames his own side for defeat. Like Hitler, he sanctioned death before dishonor, so long as it was your death, not his. Because I am so much a part of a culture steeped in blaming others, I rely on Carl Jung, who reminds me that what I see to be true of Germans is true of Harry as well; that we look magnanimous in victory, but only by projecting onto others those flaws whose existence we deny in ourselves.

"Jung said men like Harry are torn between the pursuit of perfection on the one hand, and the quest for completion on the other, and are unable to reconcile those irreconcilable extremes. Such men, Jung found, lack compassion, foremostly for themselves. They neither forget nor forgive. But, then, neither do I. We Germans have ruined our nation. We have dishonored our culture. We have set Europe back to the Stone Age. And we have defined the new meaning of disgrace.

"Harry spoke often of the Jews, and claimed identity with them. But Harry was no Jew, it seems to me. Nor was Harry a true gentile, except to say that, like Christ, he was pulled in opposite directions, on his cross. Harry never saw perfection. But, he never reached completion, either. Nor will I. Nor will any of us here. It just goes on and on until it ends. May God have mercy on his soul."

So stark was Walter's view of things, that Don, to retreat from it, began speaking to Julio about the rate of fuel consumption for the engines. "About a thousand pounds an hour, at the outset," Julio said.

"Please," Patty said.

"This is important," said Don.

"You've got the rest of the night to discuss it," she replied.

"I'm the one who will be out there," he said.

"Actually, I'm going to be out there, too," Patty said.

"So am I," said Julio, now speaking to everyone. "I've changed my mind. I am going to go. Walter, I'm senior. You stand down.

I'm going in your place." No one argued with Julio, much to Alice's surprise. But the reason no one argued was that no one knew the ship as well as he.

"I don't think that's wise," said Antonio, finally speaking up for the welfare of Julio's family.

"I don't care what anyone thinks," Julio told them. "I have a son I want to look up to me. And I know how he looked up to Harry Baird."

"It's okay," said Walter, not objecting to Julio's pre-emption. "It will be bad enough in Charlesville's eyes that I betrayed him. Let him not think I also led the charge."

"Actually, I can fly alone," said Don.

"Still playing Lindbergh?" asked Bill.

"No one else has a stake in the ship," Patty said. "Only Don."

"He's taking over for Harry," said Maxwell.

Don felt the contempt rising like gorge in his throat. He felt the rage and resentment: against Harry, against authority, against whites, against God, against being preached at, being lectured, being told, being taught; especially being taught a lesson, and especially being taught one by Harry or any woman. "To hell with you!" he shouted.

"'Behold,'" Alice whispered, citing St. Paul, "'I show you a mystery.'"

"I show you one too!" Don railed. "You should be praying for me!"

"We are," Alice murmured.

Don went out.

Harry had triggered Don's rage. Mortality drove him, bringing the hatred to the fore; hatred that had ruined Harry, and threatened, now, to ruin Don; but, in any event, hatred that had bound them both. "Damn you all!" he roared from outside.

"We accept your apology," Patty whispered, though none was given.

"He gets angry," said Bill.

"Until we learn compassion, we don't have much of a choice," Alice said.

Through the remainder of the night, Patty worked with Julio on navigation, using wind data Harry had compiled as a basis for calculating speed, headings, and times; all part of the dead reckoning they would do.

At daybreak, everybody convened in the hangar, Don included, to confirm plans and assess the status of repairs. They gathered around the drafting table with charts of the area their flight to Miami would cover, and Patty presented their intended route. "The course we plan to fly begins at Mercedita," she said. On the chart, she ran her finger from Mercedita west along the southern coast of Puerto Rico to the lighthouse at Cabo Rojo, which stood at the southwest corner of the island. From there, she traced a line west across Mona Passage, making landfall at the eastern-most tip of the Dominican Republic. Her course-line proceeded northwest, then west across the northern coast of the Dominican Republic into Haiti. It went on, as she traced it, to the northwest tip of Haiti. From Haiti, again Patty traced the course over open water, this time the Windward Passage, heading west to the eastern-most tip of Cuba. As before, she traced the course from point to point along the coast, northwest, then west, following the long northern line of the Cuban coast. Eventually, the course jogged, in its final leg, almost due north, across the Florida Straits, to south Florida, and on, continuing its line, to Miami. "From Ponce's Mercedita to Miami Air Field," Patty said, "is one thousand one hundred sixty-eight statutory miles; or, roughly, one thousand nautical miles."

"A record," Maxwell judged.

"A very long flight," Antonio opined. "I still urge you not try it."

"It's for Harry," said Julio.

"No, it's for all of *us*," said Walter.

Since they did plan to use Mercedita as the point of departure, Antonio agreed to ask Ponce's mayor for permission. For their reception at Miami Air Field in Florida, they hoped Colonel Brooks of Losey Field would involve the AAF. Maxwell, Walter, and Bill would rendezvous with the ship in Miami.

As to the flight controls, Julio cautioned they wouldn't have the luxury of a lot of check rides to make sure the controls were now functional, but he thought everything was okay. "We'll know if it isn't," he cracked.

Maxwell described changes made to the undercarriage, which everyone seemed to know about except Alice. He and Walter had cut away the ship's struts and landing gear assemblies, and, in their place, had fashioned crude steel skids, which would leave the aircraft lower to the ground. Since there would be insufficient room to nest the auxiliary tank underneath, for purposes of takeoff, Maxwell's new plan called for them to hover over the tank, which was now fitted with a cradle and wheels, and attach the tank on short tethers to the ship. Then, with the tank in tow, the ship would haul the tank airborne, and fly with it suspended.

"Will that work?" Alice asked. No one seemed to know.

Among other changes, Julio had decided to reclad only the forward half of the fuselage with panels, a decision saving weight. Still other matters concerned restoration of electrical functions, replacement of the Plexiglas panel broken out of the nose when the ship crashed, and the decision to leave unstraightened certain deformities no longer thought critical in the airframe. In short, the men had done what they could, and no one said it was anything other than makeshift.

Antonio brought up the matter of christening the ship. Harry had wanted the ship to be christened. Don was willing to try his hand at a stencil, to paint *Harry's Ark* on the ship. Antonio volunteered champagne from his cellar. "Who will do the honors?" Patty asked, assuming she would. After all, she was *flight crew*. She had even been thinking about what to wear.

"Wouldn't the fairest thing be to draw straws?" Maxwell asked, acknowledging not only Patty's candidacy but Alice's, Elisa's, and Minnie's.

"Yes, of course," Patty agreed, with some chagrin.

Don had not forgiven Harry for Harry's many imperfections, and at the end of the meeting he felt himself apart from the group. Sorry, not for Harry but himself, and finding forgiveness impossible, Don felt as though he had eaten Harry and choked. His hatred for Harry turned sour. It festered inside of him. It seemed nothing in the world, now, could make things right. Such was the aftermath of Harry. Don walked slowly away from the group, crossing the apron to the parking lot. Patty ran to catch up, and, as Don raised the kickstand on his bicycle, she invited him to breakfast. "Minnie thought we should all be together," Patty said.

"Not hungry," said Don.

"It'll be the last time we can all sit together," Patty requested.

"No, thank you. Maybe in Heaven," he added.

"How can you talk about God, and yet hate one of God's human beings?"

"I can be true to myself, I suppose." He said that, pedaling off, all alone, back to town, a man no longer young, no longer a man among men, no longer of this world, or even in it. He was a man deader than Harry. Patty took a photograph of Don. But, to do so, she shot through a long-distance lens. Turning away, she thought of her own mother, who, like Don, took the bath of self-pity.

"Don's not staying?" Alice asked, as she, Antonio, Elisa, Minnie, and Patty sauntered toward the house.

Used to covering for her mother, Patty covered for Don. "He wanted to rest before flying."

"Antonio's going to Dayton," Alice said.

"You should too," Patty told her.

"Perhaps I will," Alice mused.

They heard the phone ringing, even before they reached the porch, and it was the first of many calls, as word had spread.

Beneath a mackerel sky, a formation most unusual for Ponce, Don pedaled to Tía's to settle the rent, gather what he needed, and rest. He had made more friends in Ponce than in any other place he had lived, and he judged that, if the air seemed sweeter, it was because, as the Lord had ordained it, our breaths were numbered. Where better to have them numbered than here? He decided he would leave his bicycle with Tía, and to pack only what he would need for the flight. Packing meant weight, and weight was the thing Don most feared.

Tía's radio, playing in the parlour, broadcast news of Harry's death, whom the broadcaster referred to as *"el famoso inventor, Harry Baird."*

"You look sad," Tía said, come round to see Don.

"Death is lonely," said Don.

—

CHAPTER EIGHTEEN

At a reasonable hour, Saturday, Antonio called Charlesville to tell him Harry had died. In the course of his account, however, Antonio dissembled, telling Charlesville a series of half-truths. He said the men had succeeded on Friday evening in bringing the ship from Mercedita to Harry's field, but he did not tell Charlesville about their having formed a partnership for the purpose of flying the ship on to Wright Field. He described how Harry had died, and the likelihood of a service for Harry at Wright Field, and even went so far as to say that Harry's men would be accompanying the body to Wright Field, but he certainly did not mention Harry's remains would likely be aboard the ship when it arrived there. At the end, Antonio invited Charlesville to the ball game in Ponce on Sunday.

"I will come, and I thank you," Charlesville answered. "And tell your men I am sorry."

After the call, Antonio joined Alice in the front room. "How'd it go?" she asked.

"I'll be disbarred," Antonio answered.

In late morning, MPs from Losey Field brought over equipment for the flight, including a raft, Mae Wests, survival gear, flares, tools, and a Foley bag for the pilot. Then, *Funeraria Santa Marta* notified Antonio that Harry's body had left Puerto Rico, bound for Miami aboard an Eastern Airlines flight. Arrangements to receive the body and cremate it in Miami were firm.

Scores of people visited the field during the day, and Losey's MPs stayed on to direct traffic and keep them away from the ship. Minnie, Elisa, Antonio, and Alice received visitors all morning and well into the afternoon. When Mayor Grillasca came out, Antonio spoke with him in private in Harry's office, precisely the place he and the mayor, with Harry and Walter, had met Thursday night, when the mayor had spoken to Fernando Goyco over the phone. Mayor Grillasca objected now to the new plan to use Mercedita again, and would not relent in his objection until Antonio assured him the ship would not crash a second time, or, in the alternative, if it did crash a second time, that Antonio would never say the mayor had given his permission. Antonio, of course, agreed to this condition, and promised to keep the mayor's name out of it.

Alice, too, placed calls during the day, because she wanted people outside Puerto Rico to know Harry had died. She called Harry's sister, the widow Mrs. Anna Milnes, in Bayonne, New Jersey. She called Colonel Anderson of Air Matériel Command, Wright Field; and certain periodicals, notably *The Washington Post*, *The New York Times*, *The Cincinnati Enquirer*, *The Cincinnati Post*, *The Cincinnati Times Star*, the *Daily News* of Dayton, the *Columbus Dispatch*, and *The Baltimore Sun*. She also called the United Press and the Associated Press.

In all, by one p.m., Minnie had counted sixty-one visitors, and Elisa said more than forty had called. "Over a hundred, altogether," Alice noted, feeling Harry would have been proud.

By three, the number of visitors had dwindled, and the men began returning. Julio brought Leonard, his son. They inspected the ship together, observing the repairs. After much thought, Julio confided what the plan was to Leonard, and told him that he, Don, and Patty would be aboard the ship for the flight to the mainland U.S., and on to Wright Field. Wright Field was Leonard's favorite place in all the world. "Could I go?" Leonard asked.

"You can go with Antonio, maybe," said Julio, who intended to give Antonio money to cover Leonard's ticket.

"Why maybe?"

"We need to ask Antonio, don't we? And we need to ask your mother."

'Ask-your-mother' was a death sentence for that proposal, Leonard knew. Carlota would send her child to the devil before she sent him to Wright Field. "She won't let me," Leonard said.

"You may be right," Julio admitted.

"Did you tell mamí you were going to fly?"

"No, of course not," Julio said. "I told her that *we* were going to Wright Field, because that's where Harry's ashes would be scattered."

"So mamí doesn't know?"

"No. And you're not to tell her."

A secret was as bad as a lie, Leonard understood. A half-truth could be worse than a lie. Now, he would be in trouble because, eventually, Carlota would want to know *had he known his father was going to Wright Field aboard the ship.* Then, he would have to lie, or be punished. Papí, you shouldn't have told me. I have to lie now," Leonard said.

"The problem is," said Julio, "there are things that do come up in your life that you have to do, and it may not always be possible to ask somebody's permission. You just do them. Sometimes you know nobody will let you. Sometimes you know it's wrong. Sometimes you go ahead and do what you have to do, even though you know you will be in trouble."

"I understand about trouble," said Leonard, who was considered a problem child by his teachers.

"Then that's the answer," Julio said. "If you tell your mother I'm leaving, you'll be in trouble with me. But if she figures you don't know, who knows? Maybe Antonio will take you to Wright Field."

"You say to lie?"

"I didn't tell you what you had to do."

"Okay, papí."

"Thank you."

Walking by them, Maxwell observed they looked glum.

At Tía's, Don awoke in mid-afternoon, past his anger. His thoughts were now focused on flying.

At Alice's, Patty had tried sleeping but couldn't, and so stayed up. Anxious to do her part, she resumed her study of navigation. Finding it difficult to concentrate, she nonetheless recognized that in flight it would be that much more difficult. She was tired, but she would be tireder that night. If she didn't sleep, she shouldn't go, and she knew that. But, she was going, she had resolved. They needed three people in the crew, and nobody else wanted to go except Don and Julio and her. So she worked on her assignment, though nobody told her to give up rest for the work. They would expect her to be prepared.

On the floor with charts, protractor, compass, and plotter, she worked on devising wind triangles, and solving for wind correction angles to get her true headings. For supper, she ate leftovers, cold from the refrigerator. She resumed her practice, then, even before she had finished eating. Obsessed with fault-free performance, she practiced calculations in the shower, while brushing her teeth, on the toilet, getting dressed, and while packing.

Day waned. She left her shot log for Alice, most of her clothes, her grip, and most of her gear. She half-expected to be killed taking off. She would go regardless. Immensely depressed and ever so tired, she folded the charts, put away her materials, and prayed that if she crashed she not burn. Never mind that there was no God; still, she prayed. In England, when they crashed taking off, they burned, or blew up. Don had been lucky, so lucky. The ship would be loaded with fuel, carrying fuel underneath it, too, as well as on top. She wrote a will, just a scribble, leaving it all to Alice. How much did a memory weigh?

Before leaving, she turned pages of the albums once more, a last time, and saw the faces of those wonderful men: eighteen-year-old gunners in turrets. Twenty-year-old pilots in cockpits. She loved them all. She had danced with them while there, and missed them, now. Soon, she feared, she would be among them again, as a ghost. She returned Alice's ring—Alice's grandmother's ring—to its pouch in the drawer in Alice's bureau. She found solace in the thought that, live or die, she would be in the company of someone she loved.

When Patty returned to Harry's field, the setting sun was so much in her face that, for a moment, squinting to see, she missed the fact that the ship had departed. For a moment after that, the agonizing thought that they had gone away, abandoning her, plunged her into desperation. From the parking lot she could see that, except for one jeep and two MPs from Losey, there was no one else around. "What happened?" Patty asked.

"They took the ship to Mercedita," said a soldier.

"Did they christen it?" she asked.

"Oh yeah. Couple of hours ago," said the other.

"No!" She couldn't conceal the dismay. "Who?"

"All of them."

"No. Who?"

"The lady. Alice Symms."

In the pilots' lounge at Mercedita, Julio, Don, and Walter met to brief Colonel Brooks, who had come from Losey Field, and Major Joe Girard, who had come from Air Transport Command. Major Girard served as navigation officer at Borinquen Field, located in the northwestern tip of Puerto Rico. As a courtesy to Mayor Grillasca, Antonio also attended this meeting, as did Mercedita's manager, Pedro Melendez, who had opened the terminal for the men. No one greeted Patty upon her entrance; people looked up, saw who it was, and looked back. She was late. They were absorbed. "Sorry," she said, muttering. Major Girard had the latest weather forecasts, and forecast winds aloft, which were applicable to the night ahead and indicated that, although the winds remained favorable, the strength of the wind would subside during the night an average six, maybe seven miles an hour.

When Patty heard these new figures for wind, her heart sank. She had been using obsolete data, Harry's, and realized suddenly that she had calculated all the ground speeds based on figures for forecast winds that were greater—figures that applied to winds during the daylight hours and that Harry had gotten in a briefing the night before, when Harry was assuming the ship would fly during the day. Major Girard, unaware of Patty's calculations, nevertheless knew where Harry had gotten his data. "He got his weather briefing from me," said the major, looking at Patty. What Patty had not known was that, at night, winds did typically subside. Her inexperience had caused her to err.

"Lord," she murmured. If her wind speeds were wrong, her ground speeds were wrong, which meant the time in the air would be wrong, which meant the amount of fuel needed would be wrong, which meant, then, that the ship would be heavier when it flew. But Julio was wrong, too. It was Julio who had prepped her all night.

"That's the way it goes," said Julio.

"Bad judgment," said the major, not meaning merely that a fundamental error in navigation had occurred, but that their judgment was wrong concerning the very premise of the flight, which ought not to be occurring at all, given the inexperienced flight crew and the condition of the aircraft.

Patty tried hurriedly to recalculate, to catch up. But Julio had already done that. "Here," he said. They would average a groundspeed just under seventy-six miles an hour; not the eighty-two miles an hour Patty had originally calculated. They would be in the air an hour-and-a-half longer than she had thought. Which meant they would carry another thousand pounds of gasoline. Patty's face burned with shame.

"It's too much weight," said Don, and everybody knew that.

"Stand down, people. There's your answer. Your answer is obvious," said Major Girard. "If you must fly, fly tomorrow, when the winds pick back up, and we'll be available to track you." Colonel Brooks concurred in the major's judgment, for in the colonel's opinion Major Girard was the best there was. During the war, Girard had been awarded the DFC for leading the longest Allied bombing raid in the European theatre: B-24s from Italy to Berlin and back to Italy. If anyone knew how it felt to make the last leg of a flight flying on fumes, it was Joe Girard, and if he saw no need to take the risk, there wasn't any. The colonel could reschedule the AT-7 he had arranged to pick up Walter, Maxwell, and Bill to fly them to Florida.

"We could land at Guantánamo Bay and refuel there; forget the record," Julio said.

"If we wait until tomorrow, by then Charlesville will stop us," said Don.

"It's too far to go to Florida," said the Colonel, who, by lighting his cigar, seemed to indicate that the matter was closed. Don did not think it was closed, and stood his ground, though he didn't see precisely what he could do, and realized that, in standing his ground, he was confirming the view Colonel Anderson had put out to the world: that he was a pilot lacking in good judgment. Patty looked about. Julio was wearing a baseball cap. Don was wearing one, too. "Where's mine?" she asked, to break the tension. To her surprise, Major Girard handed her a baseball cap.

"Let me take a walk," Don said.

"That's a good idea," said the colonel, seeing the value in face-saving. It was not the colonel's intention to embarrass Don, or any of them. To the contrary, he liked Harry's men. "We appreciate how hard you've worked," he said. "And we know you're under stress. But we also feel that you're missing your best options."

Outside, Don walked by himself down the same runway he had walked on Thursday, in the moments before they had crashed. Staying back, to let him go by himself, Patty went to find Bill. In the event they would fly, she wanted to practice on the ADF before they left.

"They trust you," Bill told her. "Julio and Don both trust you, or they wouldn't have you on board. Don't worry about the mistake."

Leonard stood next to Alice by the ship and watched the fueling. "Are they going to go?" Leonard asked.

"I don't know, child," Alice answered.

"Do you know what ADF stands for?"

"I have no idea," Alice said.

"Automatic Direction Finder," said Leonard.

"Very good. And you know about such things?" Alice asked.

"Oh yes, my father taught me everything."

"Your father loves you very much," said Alice.

Walter walked over and joined them. "The Atlantic Ocean is bigger than the universe," he said. "It is unimaginably big. You can not even begin to fathom how big it is. Truly, it is without limit."

"Oh, I don't know," Alice said. "My father drowned in a pint. So let's go forward, or let's dance."

Darkness settled in. Having walked to the end of the runway, Don stood before the cane field. The cane lay flattened and dried where the ship had crushed it on Thursday. In that crash, Don had almost killed Patty. He had almost killed Julio. He had almost killed himself. He had nearly destroyed the ship. And, indirectly, he had contributed to Harry's death. But, now, his own pain was sufficient. Tired of hating, Don forgave. He forgave Harry, he forgave himself, and he asked God for grace.

As if Heaven were responding to him, there appeared in his mind's eye the image of a great, one thousand twenty-six millibar high pressure system, spreading its immense arms over the Atlantic. It lay centered to the northeast of Puerto Rico, a horse latitudes high that had held on for days. He saw the course he would fly, out of the arms of that spiral; the high that touched Venezuela and Colombia, that touched the Slave Coast of Africa, that cradled the entire Caribbean. That great high that bathed Puerto Rico, that bathed the Windward and the Leeward Isles; that coddled the mountains and would sweep Harry's Ark. It would carry them to Florida. *We can make it,* seemed its words. From Africa to Miami, it was all in one span, like a bridge.

When Don returned, he told them they were going. Julio stood beside him in affirming that decision; Patty, too. To the disbelief of Colonel Brooks and Major Girard, Don pointed to the charts that lay opened on the table. "We didn't compute it the other way," he said.

"There is no other way," Girard countered.

"Sure there is," said Don, who, with unerring hand, drew a new rhumb line for a course from Cabo Cabrón on the northeast coast of the Dominican Republic straight across the ocean to Miami. "How far is that?" He measured the distance himself and answered his own question. "Total distance, one thousand twenty-eight statutory miles," he said. "We just saved one hundred forty miles," he said. "We *can* make that."

"But son, that's over open ocean," said the major. "And at night."

"We'll make it," said Don.

"It's nuts," said the major, for it was clear to him, if not to Don, Julio, or Patty, that if they went down in the ocean at night, out at sea, they were finished. That aircraft would sink like a rock. None of them would get out of it in time, and, even if they did, the Army Air Forces would never find them.

"At least fly by day," pleaded Colonel Brooks. "So we can track you." The colonel had arranged for day-time escort aircraft the whole way over to Florida.

"Ever fly the ocean?" Major Girard asked Don.

"No, sir," Don answered.

"Is the ship equipped with instruments?" the major asked.

"ADF," Julio answered.

"Done night flying?" the major asked.

"Not a lot," Don confided.

"But none over water."

"Sir," Don maintained, "I can do it. I wouldn't go if I didn't know that I could do it."

The major and the colonel looked at him, and then at one another.

"Same with me," said Julio. "My kid's proud of dad."

"They're my story," Patty said.

The major almost laughed. It was a joke, of course, and, in its way, almost funny. It had been years since the major had seen a flight crew so foolhardy as this one. It went all the way back to before the beginning of the war, before people understood what was happening.

Patty telephoned Manny Gutierrez of Ponce's *El Día*. "Manny," she said. "Patty Symms."

"*Que pasa?*" Manny asked her.

"Want a story?"

"Always."

"Mercedita. Come right now. Bring a photographer."

"Why?" Manny asked.

"Don't ask. The ship's flying. We're leaving for Miami, then Wright Field."

By seven-thirty-five, the ship was ready. People said their good-byes, gathering to go over last things.

—

CHAPTER NINETEEN

Walking between Julio and Don, on her way to the ship, Patty strutted her stuff. *Befitting flight crew*, she thought.

From among the few spectators, someone shouted, "*Que bombon, y yo con diabetes!*"

"What'd he say?" Maxwell asked Alice.

"He said Patty's a 'bon bon' and he's got diabetes," Alice said.

On board, Julio and Don decided on a fifteen percent increase in the speed of the main rotor to compensate the rotor's tendency to cone under loading. They figured that by forty minutes into the flight they would have burned off enough fuel to reduce the rpm to its normal one-ten. On an issue related to balance, to shift the center-of-gravity forward and help offload the main rotor, they planned to draw fuel from the main tank but replenish the tank by transferring fuel from the auxiliary tank into the main tank. They decided to go with full boost, thirty-eight inches, both engines, at takeoff. Don had practiced the departure at lesser weight in two trial flights, and felt confident he knew where the phone lines were, since the third time he would be flying in the dark. The phone lines were strung above Route One, the highway they would cross turning south toward the coast.

Helped by a team of men, including two sergeants from Losey, Maxwell, Diego, and Walter set out to push the auxiliary tank, now holding 5,300 pounds of fuel, toward the downwind, western end of the runway, where, when they got there, the ship would fly over and tether the tank. As the tank rolled on the small, makeshift wheels Maxwell had installed, the men could hear the fuel inside, not quite a full load, sloshing back and forth through the baffles. The grounding strap dragged along the tarmac.

Aboard the ship, Julio recapped the takeoff weight, which would total 31,300 pounds, including the auxiliary tank in tow. That total consisted of the empty weight of the ship, 17,395 pounds; the 'useful load,' which included 11,300 pounds of fuel, 650 pounds of oil, the auxiliary tank, whose empty weight was 1,023 pounds, the winch, including the motor, 345 pounds, the flight crew, 465 pounds, and tools, equipment, and supplies totalling 110 pounds. They would be lighter by 700 pounds than when they had crashed, and, equally important, the ship's balance was improved. Don thought he had margin enough, and nobody but Don had that call.

At startup, people moved back as if pushed by the noise. Don had Patty mark the time, 1951 hours. At Don's instruction, she set the altimeter to the station elevation, thirty feet above mean sea level. At his instruction, she set the directional gyro. When she looked out, she saw Alice and several others—Leonard, Antonio, Sr. Melendez, Manny Gutierrez, Elisa, Minnie, Colonel Brooks, Major Girard, Bill—all of them watching the ship; watching her, as it were. She didn't feel flattered. She felt it was too late to change her mind.

Don flew the aircraft up off the tarmac into a hover, swung it around toward the western end of the runway, and flew out to the threshold, where Maxwell, Walter, Diego, and the sergeants were now waiting, having pulled the tank out onto the runway. Now hovering over the runway's threshold, Don turned the ship upwind, maintaining the height of the skids three feet above the ground. Diego went around forward, to a position in front of the cockpit, so that Don could see him and he could signal Don. By spreading his hands, Diego indicated the relative distance between the skids and the ground, and the distance between the skids and the sides of the tank the ship now straddled. Julio went aft. Maxwell boarded, to lend Julio a hand. Don flew so precisely that he felt the ship sink beneath Maxwell's additional weight, and at once he corrected for it. From inside the cabin, Maxwell and Julio secured the tank. Given the danger the ship might settle on the tank, crushing it, Don kept his attention fixed on Diego, who matched Don's precision with his own.

With the tank's lifting lugs now tethered to spreader bars on the winch line, Julio coupled the fuel feeder line to the tank, and Maxwell locked down the winch drum. "Secure," Maxwell yelled.

"That's it," Julio said, calling Don. Maxwell jumped ship. Don felt the tow lines tighten. Outside, Diego signaled thumbs up. Walter and the others cleared out. The lines were tense. The tank was fast. It would roll when Don pulled it. It would fly when the ship had enough power to haul it aloft. And if the ship couldn't make it, it would go down with the tank still attached.

"They're starting," Alice said to Leonard, who stood in awe.

On the threshold of the runway, Diego waved Don on. "We're going," said Don, acknowledging the wave with a nod. The ship moved forward, lurching slightly as the tank beneath it rolled.

"We're going," said Julio to himself.

"Mary," Patty prayed. The transfer of power grew smoother, the power of the aircraft seemed enormous. The ship accelerated and the tank lifted off. Suddenly, with the tank airborne, the ship became much heavier, and Patty felt helpless, in something beyond her control. There was nothing she could do now to affect how things were. Yet, the tank was airborne. The ship was flying sixty-five miles an hour. The terminal went by. The bystanders went by. Then, when Patty looked down, through the Plexiglas nose, she saw seemingly the shadow of her own past self, looking up from the place where she had stood Thursday, the position she had held the night she escaped being crushed. It wasn't herself she saw. It was the photographer from Ponce's *El Día*, shooting her. "Pray to *that*," Patty said, meaning *fate*.

At the terminal, they cheered when the ship cleared the fence at the end of the field, and kept cheering as it went on, remaining airborne. Then, Bill reminded them they had the phone lines ahead. Farther and farther, the ship receded, visible by its running lights but flying very low to the cane field. "Get it up," exhorted Bill, as if someone could hear him onboard. Then, as if in compliance with his demand, the running lights on the aircraft rose in perspective, as the aircraft climbed, and they appeared asymmetrical, with the red slightly higher and the green slightly lower, as the aircraft banked into its turn. The ship crossed the highway, and cleared the phone lines. Again, people cheered, and happily, a moment later, they lost sight of the ship at the coast. In the absence of a fireball, they concluded the ship had cleared the palms and gone to sea.

"They made it!" yelled Walter, from out at the end of the runway.

"They made it!" yelled Bill, from the terminal. They all yelled. Everybody cheered.

On board, Julio pulled back on the boost. They didn't need all the power. Even turning, out over the sea, sixty-five percent was all they needed.

Four miles out, to the south of Puerto Rico, Don established his course to the west, rolling out of the long turn on a compass heading of 271, which allowed for a nine degree correction for wind, on a true course of 270, and ten degree west variation. He was holding sixty-five miles an hour true airspeed, at an altitude two hundred feet above the sea. On the way to Cabo Rojo he wanted to make no turns other than to correct for the wind. "Note the time," he told Patty, for Port of Ponce, to the north, marked the first leg of their course to Wright Field.

Past Ponce, west, as Patty looked back, the coastline of Puerto Rico was dark. The stars appeared more prominent, the sense of night, deeper. Inland, the mountains were not visible as such but as massed darkness, lacking features or terrain. Below the ship the sea was not visible as such, either, but seemed to suggest its presence, near shore, by a pallid, faint blue.

The ship flew too low for Don to rely solely on instruments, and he strained to make out what was ahead and abreast. Far to the south, there was a ship on the horizon. Ahead, but to the north, appeared the bubble-like canopy of light marking the town of Guánica, although the town itself lay hidden within the gorge of the bay.

In his station, Julio had been thinking, intermittently, about getting Leonard to Wright Field. Toward that end, he had given Antonio the air fare.

With the tailwind, they were clipping right along, at a groundspeed close to eighty miles an hour. Ahead of them, at length, Patty saw the lighthouse at Cabo Rojo, and was pleased to have spotted it before Don. Her night vision was perfect. The lighthouse stood at land's end, the southwest corner of the island. She predicted they would pass it at eight thirty and her dead reckoning proved correct to the minute.

At the lighthouse, Don changed heading to 309 degrees, which put the wind almost precisely behind them, a steady seventeen miles an hour from the southeast. They would fly a true course of 303 degrees for eighty-seven miles over the Mona Passage to the Dominican Republic, at whose eastern-most point Don hoped to make landfall.

With the new heading, the town of Boquerón came into view from the right-side windows of the ship. Boquerón was a fishing village, at the head of a three-mile-wide crescent bay, the last town on the island's southwest coast. Julio had gone there, once, on his one free week-end, with Carlota. Over the distance he could see the string of boats at moor; houseboats lit up in yellow light, the light rippling over the surface of the water. In fifteen months in Puerto Rico, Julio and Carlota got two days to themselves, and spent them both at Boquerón, where there was nothing to do but wait for the fisherman to come in with their catches, pick oysters among the mangrove roots, make love, spend forever at dinner, sleep too long, and walk the beach. Two days they had like that. The kids were in San Juan. Harry had given him time off. At night, sounds carried over water; the houseboat rocked and water lapped along its water line; the hammock rocked; the chair leg scraped the deck; a quatro strummed; someone dropped a fork, somewhere; and, somewhere, someone laughed. Boquerón was out-of-touch, like Julio himself; quaint. Royal sunsets blazed along the coast.

Don had been climbing. To give himself some breathing room, he wanted six hundred feet. They were pulling away from Puerto Rico now, putting to sea. Looking at the panel before him, he knew that, without instruments, he could no longer distinguish up from down.

At sea, there was nothing, and Patty grasped better what Walter had meant when he said the sea was immense. Its immensity was half the world. And the night was half of time. Directly, she realized she was relying on Don, and on Julio, if not for her sense of purpose on this flight, then, far more basically, for her survival. "You all right?" she questioned Don.

"Fine," he answered.

"You all right?" she questioned Julio.

"Yes," Julio told her.

After the excitement of the takeoff, the exuberance of flying along the coast, she was relaxing; she felt decompressed.

"Start taking rough fixes," Don told her, not concerned that he would miss the Dominican Republic if she didn't, but concerned that she acquire a feel for the navigation that lay ahead, for, to Don, now, the friendliest things in the night were the glowing green lights of the instrument panel and the signals of the beacons she would tune.

For Julio, the chief task was monitoring engines, running now at normal temperatures, and the consumption of fuel, including the transfer of fuel from the auxiliary tank to the main tank. Having run the transfer pump from Ponce, Julio had caused the balance of the aircraft to change, and by mid-way to the Dominican Republic, he allowed Don to reduce rpm on the main rotor.

Don's world became increasingly interior, limited to the gauges of the panel. When he checked outside, which he did routinely, there was nothing to see: no sense of horizon, no lights, no ships, no moon; stars but, below, just the blank, empty space; not even space, void. There was no surf, no crests of waves, no reflection; no nothing, as if it had never been, as if to say light brought all things into existence. He watched the panel; in the panel there was life, the gauges a busy community of friends. His eyes were like bees and the gauges like flowers, and he went from one to another on his rounds. He went from the airspeed indicator to the altimeter, from the altimeter to the turn-and-bank indicator. He looked for the telltale rise in the airspeed, signifying descent; he listened for the change in the pitch. He checked the tachometer, then the manifold pressure, then started his rounds again, one thing to the next, bee-like. He swept the compass. He touched on the directional gyro. His eyes moved ahead of his mind, like the beat of the conductor half-a-beat before the players. The ship was a symphony to Don. His eyes retained what they saw until his mind could interpret. Indications related like siblings, needing no numbers to signal what was meant; merely the position of the needle on the face of the gauge seemed sufficient. Air speed and altitude related; rotor tach and manifold pressure; oil pressure and engine temperature; directional gyro and compass; turn indicator and artificial horizon; artificial horizon and altimeter; directional gyro and turn-and-bank. Again and again and again, back and forth across the panel, over his rounds like the bee. Don wondered if Harry was with them. *Harry* he called, in his thoughts.

Patty watched Don intently. In the most minute ways he controlled the aircraft with his hands and his feet, but all she could see of his movements were the movements of his eyes, gauge to gauge, the intelligence that played in his eyes. She wondered how could he produce results without moving? Yet, the results he produced served to keep things from changing; or, more precisely, to compensate for their changes so subtly, as the fuel burned away, as the weight of the aircraft subtly changed, as its balance changed, that she felt nothing changing at all. She likened what he was doing to the dance; to lead perfectly, anticipating all that came forth; to the dance and to God, sustaining the heavens.

"I can't find stations," she confessed. Don glanced over at her, his concern apparent. "I tuned Miraflores but I couldn't hear anything. Then I tuned Bowen Field but I didn't get anything there either." The radio facility chart lay on her lap. She had the call signs before her. She had tested out the ADF. It was on, it was working. "Call Julio," said Don.

She felt dismayed at herself. Julio came forward, sticking his head into the cockpit. "I can't get stations," Patty said. "I'm sorry."

Julio looked at her chart. "It's out of date," he told her.

"But I took it from Harry's," she protested. "It's the one that I've been using since last night."

"It's out of date," said Julio, simply. The AAF had dismantled some of its facilities. There had been major reorganization since the war.

She felt the sting of a blush; mortified, deeply embarrassed. Why had no one stopped her? No one had. It was her responsibility. She was the navigator.

Major Girard had brought a chart to Mercedita. Don had assumed Patty took that.

"How was I to know?!" she said, thinking: *You left the one that we need, and you brought the one that's obsolete,* and, in thinking that, she could hear her own mother, scolding: *You foolish girl!* "I'm sorry I'm here," she confessed. "Lord, but I'm sorry." They would be lost over the ocean without radio navigation, and that was their only means for navigating at night. She would cause them to fail. All things wrong were her fault.

"Tune San Juan," Julio said. "It's still there. So is Miami, and Havana."

Don leaned over, to bolster her. "We need you," he said. "Don't let this get you down."

"Yeah," Julio yelled. "If you had a nickel for all's Don's mistakes, you'd be rich."

And Don yelled, too. "If you had one for all of Julio's mistakes, you could retire."

When she tuned in San Juan, the ADF indicator deflected to the beacon, showing the relative bearing to the station from the fore-aft line of the aircraft. If ever God had a Voice, it seemed to Patty San Juan's beacon, in Morse Code, Saint John, *SJA*: S for Sierra, three dots; J for Juliett, a dot and three dashes; A for Alpha, a dot and a dash. "Thank heaven," Patty whispered.

Before reaching the Dominican Republic, Julio called forward, asking Don what was what. Julio had immediately sensed the engines begin to load.

"We're going up in the world," Don said. He wanted to climb to two thousand feet.

The change in altimeter gave Patty quite a show. Like a clock, it had two hands, the big hand on a scale of hundreds, the small hand on a scale of thousands. There was also a stubby indication of ten-thousands, but that made no detectable movements. For all that, she could see no movement in the hand that showed thousands; even the hand that showed hundreds virtually crept, six to seven, seven to eight. When she was growing up, the treat of the week came on Saturday night. Instead of going to bed at eight-thirty, she was allowed to stay up until nine-thirty. When she went to bed at nine-thirty, she was allowed to play the radio. What magic! She would lie under the tent of her covers and listen, in the dark, seeing only the red glow of the radio's inner tubes, and the faint red light on the dial. There was one other light in her room, which was the crack of light from the hall spreading beneath the bottom bevel of the door. There might be a moon, and, if there was, she would watch it traverse its slow arc in the sky. The moon in winter shined its beam on her pillow. It seemed to her, of the many times she had lain there, hearing the radio and watching the winter moon cross the sky, that the sweetest sleep in all her life occurred with the moon's light on her. "It's Saturday night," Patty said. Of course it was. Just so.

In summer, she would hear the crickets, but all year long the trains. The Baltimore and Ohio? The Chessie? No doubt. Far away. The songs on the radio made her cry. The noises, simply microphone effects, terrified her: a creaking door, footfalls, the clop of horses. She liked the summer sounds best, and of those, the trains, especially at night. How often she would fall asleep counting cars; the clatter starting up, miles away and carrying. Still, even in winter, silence became a sound, too, during a snowfall, a hush.

Don saw land. Excitement. There was something to do. She could hardly contain herself. They had crossed Mona Passage, where the Atlantic Ocean and the Caribbean Sea met. She noted the time. It was now twenty-seven minutes to ten.

There was something to do. The world had become complex

once again. Don had turned to a new heading, 318 degrees. They had overflown the coast of the Dominican Republic and flown inland some distance. He hadn't seen the coast line when they crossed it. But the time agreed with their estimated time of arrival, even though he did not know precisely where it was they had come ashore. Near Cabo Engaño, Don guessed, which was the eastern-most tip of the island. As with the southern coast of Puerto Rico, the eastern chain of mountains of the Dominican Republic rose not far inland from the coast, reaching peak heights almost as high, 2,400 feet, as the mountains of Puerto Rico. The mountains concerned him, of course. He saw no habitations, no lights, no roads. The land was deserted and dark. And even as the ship climbed, passing through 900 feet on its slow ascent toward 2,000, he feared flying into a mountain. He needed Patty for course-keeping. He needed a rough fix of their location.

A moment later, staring out the window to his left, Don realized there was a mountain blotting stars. Julio saw it at the same time. "We're too close," Julio warned.

Don turned the ship right. "Where's my fix?" he asked Patty.

"I can only find you one station," she answered.

"One's no good." Along the way, below, he saw two lights, way down there; one a lantern in some shack, the other the headlights on a car. Then, Don sensed they were over water again, having flown out from the coast across the *Bahía de Samaná*, a passage that, had they been on course precisely, would have taken them thirty miles to *Cabo Cabrón* to the north. But, they were southwest of their course, he could reckon that, six to eight miles, and had flown a few miles farther than they planned, erring in the right direction, at least, for the error put them closer to Miami.

Don was intolerant of her struggle. She struggled under exigent conditions. But, they all did. She felt him suppressing his anger, as she suppressed hers against him. He had no feel for what she was doing, none. She had no prior qualifications for navigation. She had never held herself out as an expert. She had no room to move about in the cockpit. She couldn't move from her seat any more than he could. The wind was blowing and she was having to use goggles to read anything that needed illuminating by flashlight; goggles because the light was infra-red. At least she had one chart, the aeronautical chart, that was current, although that one was too big for the piece of plywood she lay on her lap as a desk. More, the edges of the chart tended to flute in the winds that weren't supposed to be in the cockpit but were anyway. She would press the chart down but it also tended to puff. The air came into the cockpit from a dozen different places. And then she would have to change from one thing to another and then back again; the aeronautical chart to the RF chart. And she kept dropping her plotter, which she would have to grope around to try to find on the deck.

"It's okay," said Don.

"No it's not," Patty said. Logging the time and logging the distance; logging this and logging that. One thing was certain. They had gone a long way into the course, and had an even longer way to go. They had gone a hundred seventy miles and had hardly scratched the surface. "We should pick up land in twenty minutes," she finally judged.

"Why do you say that?" he challenged. "I think we'll pick it up in fourteen," he said.

"Fine," she muttered. "You think what you think and I'll think what I think. But I'm telling you it's twenty. I'm here figuring it out. You're there in the dark. It's twenty." She wondered what Don did when he couldn't control what he was doing? Who did he rely on when he was lost?

He didn't hear her. He couldn't. She spoke too low and he wasn't listening. "What'd you say?" he asked.

"Nevermind."

"Okay."

But it wasn't, it wasn't okay, and she didn't let things go when they weren't, or even if they were. "Do you know everything?" she demanded.

"No," he answered.

"Who's got the chart?"

"You do."

"Well, you're off course, and you should correct to the right."

"Fly what?"

"Change heading to Zero-two-zero."

"Why?" he argued. "We're erring in the right direction, toward Miami." He was arguing, because that was his way, and he did not quite, truth be told, trust her. "Correct your numbers," he said. "Instead of having me move the ship over to suit you, change the numbers."

"No," she said, refusing to give in. "In six minutes we're going to run into a mountain."

"Call Julio," said Don.

"You call him. The mountain is higher than we are."

"Julio," Don called.

"What's up?" Julio answered.

"Come here and settle this." From his station, Julio went forward. Patty showed him what she had done. "Are we going to run into a mountain?" Don yelled.

"Yes," Julio said, "change course."

"Oh," said Don, stung. "To what?"

"Zero two zero."

"Thank you," said Patty.

"Not at all," Julio told her, and withdrew.

"I'm sorry," Don said, a moment later.

"No problem," she said, hardly gloating.

At ten thirty-five, they departed the coast of the Dominican Republic on a new heading of 309 degrees, setting out now on the longest leg of the trip, 819 miles direct to Miami. The ship had burned off 2,500 pounds of fuel, and for much of their course, ahead, though they figured not to see them, they would be flying parallel to the islands of the Bahamas.

Don became increasingly absorbed in his communion with the aircraft. Turned in, absorbed by the instruments, Don lived in each moment, and time, outside its sole function of flight, did not exist for him. He no longer thought of the past, much less of the future, except as it related to the ship's position on its track. Attuned, thus, the ship extended him, its flight his meditation.

Patty was accustomed to the shimmy and sway of a helicopter ride, but, here, in smooth air, the ship seemed not to be moving at all. The attitude did not change. There was no sense of anything going by. No sense that time passed. The minutest of changes were the lightening of weight as the fuel burned away, which resulted in Don throttling back. The greatest work seemed none at all; the greatest effort to seem effortless. Don seemed almost to smile, to take pleasure in this stasis. He looked like the Buddha in the book Alice had written. Patty looked upon his placid face while his eyes remained at watch; his life ever centered in his eyes.

Puerto Rico seemed another life, gone now, a million miles, far behind. Patty hadn't expected that so soon after leaving Puerto Rico they would be so far from the world she had known. Visibility was unlimited, because there was nothing to see. Did Creation look like this to God, in the moment just prior to His wish to begin? In the curve of space, was the universe a conch shell? She wondered if a conch shell reflected God's intent; unfolding at one end like a lip, and, at the other, turned in on a point. If a conch shell was the universe, she wondered where they were on it, between the cold relativity heading out, and the tight quantum spiral turning in.

She reflected on the little time it took, just a step out into the ocean, to go from civilized to desolate. Mere moments ago. Only miles. And yet, now, Alice and Antonio, Maxwell and Walter, Diego and Bill, Minnie and Elisa and Leonard, the whole group she had left was gone. They seemed never to have lived. The crash Thursday night seemed a dream.

To Patty, even Harry's death was far away, and that was, when? Today! He had died Saturday morning, and it was still Saturday! She thought back to the beach, her first night together with Don. Another life. Even the war seemed closer. But the war was global. The war was cosmic. She was no more than an asteroid in its field. Her first flight in the ship? Or meeting Charlesville? Her childhood seemed sooner than that. Perhaps it was. Perhaps she was born on the seventh of March, this year, and, like an insect, measured her lifespan as days. Had it been a good life? It seemed so. Long? She could remember every moment, and it seemed she hardly had slept.

The air grew cooler in the cockpit, a change reflecting the 2,000 foot elevation they had reached. Again, Patty tuned the beacon at San Juan, taking the fix, cross-referencing Havana when she could tune that, or homing to Miami, whose signal fluctuated. As a child she had loved radio most of all. Real life was never quite so engaging as radio, which *was* real life. Even during the war it was radio that held one's attention and broke hearts. In a contest between sound and sight, sound pulled. Sight could catch the attention but sound could pull it, and take one away to someplace else. She wondered if Don could hear voices as he flew. Sound lived forever. The question was dumb and she was glad she hadn't asked it. Voices could travel; those she heard never ceased. Don heard a symphony in the ship. She found it ironic that one who liked sound more than sight had chosen photography to pursue for her work. The ADF gave its relative bearings. The ocean was enormous, creation immense, and the track of *Harry's Ark* like a bug, like a trickle of water on the face of a glacier. The winds were stronger at two thousand feet than down near the surface of the sea. Still, at eighty-seven miles per hour for their track, it would be hours before they reached Acklin's Island.

She would while away hours converting magnetic to true and reciprocals of bearings from the ship to the station. What a hospitable thing were the beacons; Don had called them *islands of sound in the night*. Years ago, at her grandparents, her father's parents, she would sometimes spend the night. On those times, she shared their bedroom upstairs, but had her own child's bed and quilts. Her grandfather liked windows left open at night, for the air brought health, he would say. Year round! On Saturdays, she could hear the drunks outside, stumbling home on the cobbles. The gas lanterns cast light that reflected from the pitch of the ceiling in the room, casting a shadow in flickers. On the wall,

Mary smiled, babe to breast. The wallpaper was pink and beige stripe, like the dresses of Renoir's women. Sometimes, in winter, when it snowed, snow mounded on the stool of the windows, and, if the wind was blowing, it drifted to the floor. No matter. Sometimes, she rose at night to look out. Her grandparents snored. No matter. Throughout the night, they farted and snored. How she giggled. Growlers and howlers. She wondered if heaven heard farts. If somewhere in space farts were still going, like the dim echo of creation, the early gas. The clock in that room was the loudest she heard, and grew louder the later the hour. Odd that neither grandparent ever noticed. But, then, she never saw either get up, in the morning, though she always awoke to their voices coming up from downstairs, as they argued over how to fry eggs. "I've been remembering," she said.

"Sure," said Don. She thought she saw him smile, but, if he did, then the smile came and went like the bloom of a peony; here in an instant, gone in the next.

Patty closed one window and half-closed the other. The second hand moved and the minute hand crept. Don was wearing a jacket. He had put it on in Ponce. She put on her sweater. There was a ton of excitement on board. Saturday night! At least, closing windows was something.

She could not remember when she drifted off, or why he did not wake her. She dreamed she was keeping him awake. But he was awake for them both. Like Job, he was praying for them both. Can you pray for another? Can you say another's prayer? She understood every thing Don had asked, but while being asleep. She had some consciousness reserved for listening, even then. Were they where they should be? Absolutely. But where was that? Anyplace, because anyplace seemed right to her. She could discuss it. She would deny she was asleep. Even while she was sleeping she would deny that. But, if the universe was a conch shell, she was pretty certain they were on the outermost lip, now, and not in the quick, hot, start of the beginning, where everything happened, like in babyhood, through tiny fragments too short to remember, but where brightness made the segments seem to blend. "Every twenty," were his words. Twenty minutes were an awful lot of time. He meant every twenty minutes take a rough fix. She could see the stations, out in space. She could see the ocean, like the ether, like the void, pre-Creation, what God saw in starting out, and perhaps the reason He did start out. She could see, she could see . . . where they were, and where they were going, farther and farther. The bearings tracked them. The bearings kept crossing as they flew. She did the numbers as she slept.

The aircraft gently swayed. On a reflex, Patty put her hand against the panel. The sway was so gentle that she had noticed it only because the flight had been otherwise so smooth. "Are you going to introduce me to your family?" she asked.

"If you want to meet them," he said.

"How will I be received?"

"That all depends on who you are," he said. "If you are there from *Life*, you'll be welcome." Indeed, Don reckoned that his oldest sister, Abigail, would covet Patty's attention, and want Patty to shoot *her*, and *her* children, and *her* house.

"What if I'm there as your mistress?" Patty asked.

"That will be different," he said.

"And as your fiancée?"

He shook his head. There would be little distinction between mistress and fiancée. She'd be reviled as either. "You'd be viewed as bringing disgrace on my family," Don said, "and so would I."

"Heartache is what I feel now," Patty murmured. But, she understood. It'd be no better in her own family. "What a world," she said. "You won't go back to Ponce now?" she asked, a moment later.

"There'd be no work, especially now." He shook his head.

Well, of course, there would be, she thought. Not as a test pilot. Not as a pilot. Maybe not as a draftsman. But, then she reckoned with his words. What would he do? He had no college degree. He had no background in business. His Spanish was deficient. Like Don had said, Puerto Ricans themselves were leaving the island. "You have a great reputation in Ponce."

"That's about all," Don said.

In Ponce, it wouldn't necessarily be any better for her than for him. What would *she* do? Teach school, with her aunt, or work for a paper. "What about Dayton?" she asked.

"I can always find work around Dayton," said Don. For that matter, they might still go to New York.

The ship did not seem to be moving. They seemed to be an island, bonded to darkness, self-contained. No gauges seemed to move. The altimeter did not move. The airspeed did not change. The tachometers remained fixed. The directional gyro did not vary from the compass, nor the compass card slide before the lubber. The artificial horizon reinforced the turn-and-bank, which in turn showed no turn and no slip. What moved? Fuel gauges, too imperceptibly to notice. And the clock of integration. Time slowed down, out in space. Relativity reigned. It was kind of a turning nut, Patty thought. From one point of view, the wrench went right; from the other, it went to the left. She felt she understood. Things seemed wrong, no matter what they seemed or how they looked.

Thank God there were stars. The ship was floating inside stars. "Are we moving at all?" she asked. But, perhaps she hadn't asked that. She thought she heard her voice but it seemed a long time back. They were level in the cream, the deep velvet. The wind owned the sea. Air produced the stillness. She would have to tell her mother. That seemed right.

Don nudged her. She woke and took a fix. "I'm sorry," she said, but the exhaustion and the lack of sleep had overtaken her, and her trust in Don's flying was complete. The ADF showed a relative bearing to Havana of 324 degrees, a relative bearing to San Juan of 117 degrees, and she marked the time at 1:05 in the morning. The ship's heading remained 309. Magnetic variation was seven degrees west. She came up with a true bearing from Havana that was wrong and a true bearing from San Juan that was right, but she was unable to distinguish which was which. The two lines wouldn't cross. She couldn't remember, magnetic to true, or what to do with the 360 when the number got too large. What angle was she dealing with, after all?

"Take a break," Don said.

"What?"

"Go aft. Bring me an RC."

"Do we have any RCs?" She pushed herself up and backwards from the seat. Aft, she decided to visit Julio. She took the jump seat beside him. With a smile, he looked over. "Just took a rough fix," she told him.

"Yes?"

"Came out we're in Madagascar."

Julio laughed. He enjoyed her little joke.

At his side, she watched the panel for a moment. He wanted to know how Don was holding up. "Okay," she said. "Better than me. I fell asleep."

In her mind's eye, she saw her grandfather. He had a shock of white hair, like Harry's. She remembered how his hands felt. Rough, with the character of boards. She remembered the smell of sawdust in his clothes, and pipe tobacco. She remembered that pipe, which he would allow her to carry, because he was always setting it down when he worked. She doted on him. As a child, she had adored him. She could hear his voice. If she spoke to him, he spoke to her. She could hear the intonation, the very stuff of his sound. "Grandpa?" She could see his forehead so clearly she could count the gulls' wings in the furrows of his brow. To delight her, he used to strike great wooden matches on the sole of his boot, or sometimes the rough twill of his pants. She may have been her father's daughter, but she was her grandfather's granddaughter even more. And even now she could look into his eyes.

"When did he die?" asked Julio.

"Who?"

"The person you're thinking about."

"I guess never," she said.

"That would be him, wouldn't it?"

"Who?"

"Whoever."

"Yes." And it was, of course. The very same. She wondered if Alice knew that too.

Aft, she found sodas. But, she also smelled gas. She left the sodas and went forward. "There's a strong smell of gasoline in the cabin," she told Julio.

Julio got up and went aft. Because the cabin was open at the top and the sides, he found it hard at first to pick up any smell, and thought she was mistaken. The rotorblast and the slipstream whirled through. But, then, the smell came and went, and he found the plywood deck was wet with gasoline. He rubbed his fingertips together. The gas had been dribbling down the fuel line from the coupling at the transfer pump overhead. The coupling had worked part-way loose. One more turn, and it would have parted. Julio tightened it. He reached down through the belly hatch, next, feeling the other coupling, at the tank. That, too, was working loose. Vibration had caused that one as well. He looked up at Patty. "Vibration," he yelled. They had never flown so far with the hose connected. It was something he hadn't thought of. Using safety wire from the tool box, he secured the couplings. The repercussions of what had nearly happened sank in. Patty gave him a rag. He wiped off his hands. "Don't even start the 'what ifs,'" Julio warned her, grateful she had had presence of mind to tell him. He shook his head. What if? What if?

Life was dear. Death was eternal. She went forward, almost sick with the thought that she might die, and almost had. Far worse than the fear that had accompanied the takeoff, which was active like *whoopee!*, was the fear of being swallowed by the night. That was the fear of the misstep, of darkness, of the thing that lies waiting. Ultimately, it was the fear of chance. "Dear Lord," Patty muttered, helpless to do better than mutter. *Not tonight, and not here. Please. And she would do whatever He said, if He said anything at all, she agreed.*

She told Don what had happened. "Would there have been a fire?" she asked.

"Not for long," he said sarcastically. By the same token, though, he knew there might have been no fire at all. They simply would have run out of gas, and suddenly and silently glided down to the sea.

She held the bottle for Don. In England, she had done the same for airmen in the hospital: hold the bottle for them to suck the straw. There was a difference, to be sure. Don was not bound by his wounds, and she did not need the airmen to survive.

The equivalent of being helpless, bound hand and foot to controls, exacerbated Don's thoughts about death. He thought again about the fish Patty had speared. "How would *your* mother react?" he asked.

"Different from yours," Patty answered. "She'd want to kill you, I think." For it was the mother who protected the cub.

Later, over what she thought to be Acklins Island, Patty tried her hand at giving a position report; something that until now Don had been doing. "Borinquen tower, this is *Harry's Ark*," she called.

"Go ahead," crackled the voice of the controller.

The response delighted her, for there was really someone out there. "Our position as of . . . ." she was about to say *as of two thirty-three in the morning*, when she caught herself. She would need to use the twenty-four-hour clock system, which was okay; she was accustomed to that. That would be *zero two three three hours*.

"Give Greenwich time first," Don reminded her.

"What?"

"Greenwich. Give Greenwich time first."

"Eh . . . Borinquen tower, our position at . . ."

"Zero six three three hours . . . ."

"Zero six three three hours . . . ." She broke off. "Don't interrupt me," she scolded.

"Talk to the man, not to me," countered Don.

"Borinquen tower, at . . . ."

"Zulu," said Don.

"What?"

"Zulu. Give the time as *zulu*. Greenwich Mean Time."

"At . . . uh . . . zero six."

"Zero six three three, Zulu."

"Just fly the damned ship," she snapped back. "I'm sorry," she said to the tower. "Borinquen tower, our position at zero six three three, Zulu is . . . shoot. Now I've lost my place on the chart."

"Acklins Island," said Don. "Just tell him Acklins Island."

"You shut up! On a true bearing from San Juan beacon of two seven seven degrees . . . ."

"No, no, no," said Don.

"Let me!" she hollered back. "Er . . . ," she resumed. "Okay. A true bearing from Havana beacon of one zero six degrees."

"Acklins Island," said Don.

"Acklins Island," said the Borinquen Field controller.

"Yes," she said, turning red as a beet. "We're at two thousand feet, on a true course three zero one degrees . . . ah . . . mm . . . ."

"ETA Miami Field?"

"Yes!" A moment went by.

"Do you read?" asked the controller.

"Yes," Patty answered.

"ETA Miami Field?"

"When?"

"Lady, you tell me."

"Oh. Sorry. Just a minute. Stand by." She broke off. "He wants to know ETA Miami Field. Don't we have a time change?"

"Yes," Don said, "So give the time as Zulu."

"ETA Miami . . . ," she resumed.

"Say again. You're breaking up," the controller answered.

"ETA Miami, one two three six, Zulu . . . ." Patty said.

"Roger. Go ahead," said the controller.

"That's all," said Don.

"That's it," said Patty.

"Roger. Out."

"You do it next time," she said.

"No, you do it next time, but better," said Don.

At seventy-five degrees west longitude, they lost an hour.

At three forty-seven, the moon rose. Don saw a ship, far to the southwest. Soon after, he saw another aircraft, way up there, flying what appeared to be the same heading. Two distant neighbors, as it were; one on the vastness of the ocean at night; one in the vastness of heaven.

He let time slip by. He began to think thoughts of sleep. He thought of calling Julio on the intercom, but didn't. He thought Julio might be asleep. He rationalized not calling him because he didn't want to wake him. They all needed sleep. At his side, Patty dozed. He thought of waking her but didn't. It was seductive to let her sleep. She could sleep in place of him.

But Julio was awake, thinking about the collapse of his marriage. The worst hour of the day, the darkest hour of the night, was upon him. Julio found it ironic that Don and Patty were just starting out, while he and Carlota were just about to end. Harry was there, with Julio. Julio could feel Harry there.

The shape of Don's thoughts wrapped in wind, embedded in wind, in the turning of rotors, engines, the fire of exhaust. The engines were awake. Don's heart was awake. God was awake. Don withdrew, withdrew from his own limbs. He withdrew from his feet, from his knees and his legs, which grew numb. Breathing was harsh, so he withdrew from his chest and his arms. He felt warm. It was like taking a bath. It was tingling. He could bathe in the wind. He withdrew from his own face. He could listen to the wind howling in the cave of his thought. Beyond words, utterance took the visual part of form. He could see what he thought. He could see what he heard. He could see the very shape of his thought, how it looked, and, beyond the form, something else seemed waiting there, deep inside, and so he went in there, to see. Brightness drew his attention, a light of no source and no heat. Free from his heartbeat, like many sounds all at once; free from the coursing of blood, like rolling thunder; free from the rumble of breath; free, at last, of thought itself, he occupied a small, still point. There, he found Elijah, at his vigil on Mount Horeb.

"Where are we?" he asked.

"Where?" She awoke. She had not logged their position in many miles. She had not been watching the numbers, the lines, the positions. How many times could she take their position, even though she could not force herself to move. She had to ask six times: move, arm. Move, hand. She had to dream herself awake. In the space of a second, she could think two full thoughts; each a well developed sentence, each with meaning, if expressed. Had she said anything to Don? That was one. Had she spoken? That was two. What was really down there? A third. Could she look? She was half of him. Could she see?

She looked. She bent forward in her seat and peered down. She looked up, or over, and was fully astonished. Patty saw the ocean beneath the ship. It was dismal, it was cast in gray, but she could see it! She could see the splash of waves! And, momentarily, crests and troughs.

She tuned the ADF to San Juan; her gesture now so reflexive no thought or will conveyed it. Her hand moved as Don's, automatically and sure.

"Getting light," Julio said, over the intercom.

It was wonderful. It was the greatest news! The bearing indicator said 225 degrees. The needle pointed there, so it must have been right. Two two five, and it was 5:35 in the morning; 0535 hours, local; 1035, Zulu. She tuned Havana. The needle pointed to 260. "Are you confirming those?" asked Don.

"Yes," she said, but she didn't know where she left off; she wasn't certain she had left off. She didn't remember the moon having risen. Thus, how did it get in the sky?

"Confirm those stations," Don repeated.

When she thought about that, she laughed; about his ordering her, she laughed, not raucously, not even visibly, but to herself. She had controlled this flight. She had directed Don to hold a heading. And she had trusted him to do that. He had controlled merely the ship. Who was boss? The one who controlled the ship, or the one who controlled the one who controlled the ship?

Although she hadn't noticed it, they must have crossed over Andros Island in the dark. They had fewer than a hundred-twenty nautical miles left before reaching Miami. At seventy-two knots they would be there in an hour and forty minutes. Had it not been dark she would have seen Andros Island. Andros was a large island, but deserted and flat. For that matter, for most of the night they had been crossing over, or passing near to, islands, and she hadn't seen any of them.

The sun came up. First, it lit them, then, at 6:03, the ocean turned blue. It came to life. Life had color. Clouds and haze obscured the distance, but she could see, and it was warm.

"We should have seen Andros Island," said Don. Andros Island was not a speck on the chart; it was a huge land mass.

"We're on course," Patty told him.

"We're behind our course," he said, thinking about it. The bearing from Havana showed them over Andros Island.

"We crossed the island in the dark," she said. She searched out his face as she spoke. "We're ahead of time," she said.

"Wake up," he told her.

"I am awake," she said, rudely stung by the tone of his voice. Just because there was a two-hour gap in the paperwork . . . . which Patty was now beginning to see . . . .

"How can the bearing show us over Andros when there's no island underneath us, unless we're way off course?" Don demanded to know.

It was a helluva good question; so good she couldn't immediately answer it. Then, she thought of what the answer was. "You said yourself, the signals will deviate at daybreak. It's *night effect*," she told him; at daybreak and at dusk.

"Tune Nassau," said Don.

She tuned Miami.

"Tune Nassau," he repeated.

On the chart, Nassau was marked *MRA*, which she knew meant something, but she didn't know what. It was not a code for an identifier. She called Julio on the intercom. "Julio."

"What?"

"What's 'MRA'?"

"What do you mean, 'MRA'?"

"On the RF chart for Nassau's beacon."

"Middle Right Anterior."

"What's that mean?"

"It's an Adcock Range. Means 'Medium Range Adcock facility.'"

"How do I tune it?"

"From the channel number, then you listen."

"Listen?"

"Ask Don."

"I'm asking you."

"You'll get a hum. Nevermind. Tune Miami."

"Julio."

"What?"

"He wants me to tune Nassau."

"I'll come help you."

She tuned Miami. But Miami did not jibe with San Juan. "Night effect," Patty echoed. In a few moments the signals would normalize. Miami showed them north. San Juan showed them north. Havana showed them east.

"Where are we?" asked Don.

"We're on course," she said.

"Where are we?"

"We're on course ahead of time, and we're waiting for the signals to normalize."

"No!" he yelled. "We are *not* on course!"

Julio was there. She tuned Nassau and got the Nassau Morse Code, *dot dash*, and then the *hum*. Then Julio listened, and he realized it was really *dash dot*; not the east-west quadrants but the north-south quadrants! He tried to explain, and then she understood. "It's all screwed up," she told Don. The north-south quadrants couldn't be right. She would have to figure things out. It would take a minute.

Julio checked what she had done. Her method seemed right. If what she tuned was the quadrant, and what she tuned was the station, then Nassau showed them north of New Providence Island, which was well off their course. Julio assumed she had been tracking their progress all night long. It was likely, then, that Nassau's indication was incorrect. "It sometimes happens," he said.

"Look!" said Don. "Northwest." He was looking out at a lighthouse, whose beacon pecked the horizon some nine or ten miles abreast to starboard. "Hold up that chart so I can see it," he demanded. She was glad to do that, glad to be relieved of responsibility. The wind fluttered the chart but she was not offended in the least to have her chief responsibility removed—to be relieved of her duties, as it were—because she really didn't understand what had happened, or whether anything had happened. But things were not *coming together*, as they should. "Try to find that lighthouse on the chart," Don said.

"You think we're off course?"

"We have to be. There is no lighthouse near our course. Find me that lighthouse."

"How could we be off course?"

"We've gone between islands."

"Which islands?"

"That's for you to tell me! Andros and New Providence, probably. Now, maybe Andros and Chub Cay."

"That's impossible," she said, doing her best to keep up, but, she could feel the icy panic start to grab.

"Call me when you need me," said the prankster Julio.

"Don't you dare!" she yelled at Julio, meaning: dare not leave. And he stayed. Julio could be a barrel of laughs. She was sweating. She was cold as ice, but sweating. The fact of the matter was they were LOST. LOST AT SEA! Her heart beat furiously. How could they be lost, having flown a single heading? They had been flying one heading since the Dominican Republic. She unfolded the chart, looking back over all those early fixes. Nothing made sense anymore. Convert what? What into what? Subtract or add what? She heard her stupid mother calling her: *come die with me.* None of the indications on the ADF made any sense. Nothing did. It was all scramble. Everything was. She had worked all her life just to screw up this one flight. If somebody had told her a month ago that a month hence she would be fulfilling her destiny to screw up the navigation on a transoceanic night flight in a helicopter, she would have screamed. She would have told the guy he was nuts. And it would have been a guy, for certain. No woman would be so stupid to have said that.

Switching over from the sectional to the WAC and from the WAC to the RF chart, she vowed if she got through this— this nightmare—she would never do it again; she would quit. This was the end of it.

"You were sleeping," Don said.

"Were you?" Julio asked.

"Yes," she admitted.

"Let me see," Julio said, quickly assessing her past work. The gap of missed fixes was too big to reckon with. Things could happen in much less time than that. "Why didn't you wake her?" he asked Don.

"I should have," Don admitted.

"You could have called me."

"I should have," he admitted. "I thought you were asleep too."

"Well I wasn't," Julio said, indignant. Their quandary was clear. Not only were they *temporarily misplaced*, but they could flounder in the Bahamas and miss the state of Florida. They could run out of gas, short of land, especially if they were positioned north on Florida's coast, which tended to recede to the west.

For one moment, Patty reverted to the hope she could be right. For one silly moment, she persisted, thinking they were west of Andros, which they had crossed in the dark, and were closing, even now, on Miami. Then, with Julio to watch her, she took the rough fix, ending with the chill of her life. Miami showed them 353 degrees; Havana, 303. She plotted the fix on the chart, then tried Nassau again, to confirm. Nassau's station was behind them. She had heard stories of aircraft disappearing out here, in the Bahamas, disappearing without a trace. And she began to see how that might happen, for it might happen to them. Frantically she searched the chart. And there it was! On the chart, abaft to starboard from where she plotted them, a lighthouse! The lighthouse Don wanted her to find! "We're an hour late, but I know where we are," she confessed. "We're sixty miles east and forty miles north of our course."

"Flew between the islands," judged Don.

"Yes, we did," Julio said, ruefully. If they headed due west, they'd go straight to Miami. In forty minutes or so, they'd go across the cays south of Bimini.

"We can home to the beacon," said Don, meaning the range on Miami Beach. He had changed the ship's heading, heading west.

Sick with guilt, Patty tuned Miami's station. Barely registering in the welter of her thoughts was the thought that they did not have as much wind from behind as they had figured; the wind had changed in the last couple of hours. And, too, they had had a little more wind from the south than what they reckoned.

"It happens," said Don.

"It does," Julio agreed. "The weather can change. The forecasts can be off."

On a heading of 270, Don saw the ADF deflect to a relative bearing of 11 degrees for Miami. She punched the ADF receive button, and a voice broadcast identified the station, and gave winds, which, east of the station, were south at fifteen knots, enough to account for their drift. "Do we have enough fuel?" Don asked Julio. Even without the fuel log in front of him, Julio suspected they did not, and went aft to check. When he returned, Don asked him how close it would be.

"We have an hour and twenty minutes in the tank," Julio said.

"How long before we reach Miami Field?" Don asked Patty.

"Ninety minutes," she answered, and felt her soul sinking. She never felt so bad in all her life; not even the night the ship crashed at Mercedita.

"So we're short ten minutes," said Don. "We might make it to Miami Beach."

"Other options?" Julio asked. It was true Miami Beach was about ten minutes short of Miami Field. Ten minutes was ten minutes.

"Bimini," said Patty.

"If we can find it," Julio said.

"I vote to gamble," said Don. "Miami Beach."

"I say gamble, too," Julio said.

"No," she said. Although she knew what the record meant to them, they might lose the ship. "Bimini's safer," she judged, holding herself responsible in full.

"Let's dump the aux tank," said Julio, working at full tilt. The tank had been pumped out hours before, and jettisoning it would lighten the aircraft by more than half a ton, although the more important relief might prove to be the reduction in the drag that towing the tank had induced. Joined by Patty aft in the cabin, Julio uncoupled the fuel line. Then, with the tank hanging from the winch line, he sawed the line with a hacksaw, while Patty, wearing gloves and goggles to protect against whiplash, stayed the cable where he cut. When the line snapped, the tank dropped away behind the ship, sailing for an instant like an airfoil, then rolling slowly in the wind as it fell. Fascinated, they watched it spin to the sea. It hit with a splash, and, last seen, remained afloat. Still hustling, Julio disassembled the winch, winch motor and drum, pushing each in succession out the side hatch. "Spring cleaning," he joked. The winch assembly by itself accounted for three hundred forty-five pounds. Then, they broke out Mae Wests and the raft. "Want me to jump too?" Patty asked, only partly in jest.

"You saved us hours ago," Julio said. He was referring to her detection of the leak in the fuel line, which, had she left it unreported, would have pre-empted their present crisis. "It all works out in the end," he told her. When she returned to Don's side in the cockpit, Don asked that she call Miami tower.

"Can you feel the difference?" she asked him.

"Yes. Like night and day," he said. "Now call." The tank had been a powerful drag, and it had been a dead weight, as was the winch.

"What should I tell them when I call them?" Patty asked.

"Start by telling them we're late," Don replied. "Then tell them we'll need help. Tell them our fuel situation is critical. And last, tell them we *think* we can make Miami Beach."

"Uh, Miami Tower. This is HB One, *Harry's Ark.*"

Came back a man's voice, "Ark, go ahead. Miami Tower."

"We are ninety-two nautical miles east, on a true bearing one zero one to the beacon. Revise destination: we can make Miami Beach. New ETA: one three one zero, Zulu. Will need assistance. We are critical on fuel."

"That's a roger. Confirm destination."

"Miami Beach."

"Roger. Say where."

"We can put down on the beacon if you want." She broke off the transmission and looked at Don. "Is that all?"

"That's all."

"Shouldn't I tell him we got lost?"

Don laughed. "Patty, he knows that already."

When the ship was ten minutes from the Florida coast, the needles on the fuel gauges of the main tanks indicated empty. "Won't be long," Don said to Julio. Julio had his own set of gauges aft, and his read marginally higher than Don's. Either way, it wouldn't be long, nor possible until they actually ran out of gas to determine which of the two sets of gauges proved the more accurate.

A moment later, Patty wanted to know if, at the end, the ship would just drop from the sky, the way the tank had dropped when they cut the cable.

"No, not like the tank," Julio explained, because autorotation would brake the descent and the ship would glide down. But, as soon as the ship ditched in the ocean, it would sink, and the rotors, turning overhead, would continue to turn until they struck the water. It was possible the blades might break off at that point. "What you and I have to do," Julio yelled, "is jump ship, before the ship touches down. We have to jump when Don flares."

"Why?" she asked.

"We don't want to jump when the ship's in the water and those rotors come down on our head."

She understood then. They would have to be ready, aft, in the cabin, wearing their life vests. "What about Don?" Patty yelled.

Don would wait until the ship was under water, until the rotors had stopped turning. "I'll be all right," Don yelled. By the time he got aft, the ship would be heading toward the bottom. The cabin would be fifteen feet down by the time it was clear for him to swim.

"Are you sure?" she asked him.

"I have no choice," he assured her.

"Let's go," Julio said, pulling Patty from the seat, for, when things began to happen, they would happen very fast.

"Don't worry," Don yelled.

"I love you," she yelled, worried. She saw him smile. He loved her too.

Aft, Julio confessed to Patty that he couldn't swim. He was clearly terrified. She helped him tie on his Mae West.

"Florida!" she said, looking forward at the hazy coast ahead on the horizon.

Even the aft gauges, on the engineer's panel, displayed needles pegged to the empty line now. "Down to the fumes," Julio said.

A Sikorsky R-5 came out to track the flight. The co-pilot waved. The R-5 stayed close to the ship. "Our competition," Don said over the intercom, referring to Sikorsky. A moment later, he spotted the Coast Guard, out too. "When we go down, we'll be in good hands," he remarked.

Four miles out and still flying, Patty could distinguish features of Miami Beach, including hotels and a skyline.

"She's been a good ship," said Julio, feeling certain they would lose her.

"Everything ready?" asked Don.

"We're set," Julio answered. He hoped Don could make the flare smooth. At one mile out, Don began to descend. Still, the engines were running. He throttled them back. Neither engine missed a beat. The shore drew nearer. Patty felt so tense she thought she would explode. Julio was as tense as she was. So was Don. Don's jaw was clenched.

The beach came up on them fast. There was a party awaiting them at the beacon: two jeeps, brass; some sergeants. Still, the engines were running. Don flared. Then, he settled. Neither engine even sputtered. At eight twenty-five in the morning, on a grass-covered dune Don had chosen, Harry's Ark landed.

The engines continued running. The party on the ground held back. The R-5 flew by and waved off. A sergeant lowered his camera, having shot them. "I want one too," Patty yelled, jumping ship.

Since he still had power, Don lifted back up into a hover, limiting the height to one foot off the ground. The ship was light as a feather. Patty shot. He landed again. Even so, to kill the engines, he had to cut the switches.

It was done. They had made it to Miami.

"What on earth happened?" yelled the Miami Field C.O., Colonel Bradenton.

"Defective fuel gauges," Julio said, with a grin.

Lt. Colonel Glen Anderson, the colonel who had witnessed the ship crash through the fence at Baird Field and who had called them all clowns, had come down from Wright Field, and was part of the landing party anticipating the arrival of the same ship he had told General Weggoner not to buy. Joined by Colonel Bradenton and five other commissioned and noncommissioned officers of the Army Sixth Air Force, Air Transport Command, Anderson welcomed Harry's Ark to Florida in a very unofficial ceremony taking place one hundred-sixteen feet from the radio beacon on the southern tip of Miami Beach. The flight had established a new world's record, 1,028 statutory miles of unrefuelled, linear distance in a rotary wing aircraft. The ship had flown even farther than that, but got no credit for the miles flown off course. The record was one Harry had coveted, but no more so than Julio or Don.

In establishing one record, the ship had also set another. It had carried aloft a record 31,300 pounds, more than any other rotary wing class aircraft ever flown.

To answer the question how much fuel was left in the tank, in view of the indication of the gauges, which had agreed there was none, Julio climbed to the top of the ship and measured, using the dipstick and a flashlight. He estimated between five and six gallons in the sump. "Oh, hell," joked a sergeant. "With that, you could have gone another . . . mm, three minutes." Colonel Bradenton, a former wing operations officer with the Eighth Air Force, recalled like occasions when B-17s, B-24s, and their escorts, returned to fields in East Anglia, arriving empty and seeming to fly on the basis of prayer. When Bradenton looked to Lieutenant Colonel Anderson to confirm, the lieutenant colonel admitted with a shrug that he had heard, but couldn't say. His flying experience had been in the Pacific Theater with Sikorsky helicopters.

The maiden flight was over now, and, according to Bradenton, the world had two more heroes and a heroine to cheer. That was good news for the AAF, he thought. And it was good news for the rotary wing program at Wright Field, Lieutenant Colonel Anderson admitted.

Patty discovered she was unable to walk without staggering. She had *air legs* said the men.

Colonel Bradenton informed them that the others—he meant Walter, Bill and Maxwell—were being flown over in a Beechcraft AT-7 *Navigator*, which had departed Ponce when people on both sides were fairly confident the ship would reach Miami. "If they only knew," Julio said.

Over coffee served from a thermos, Lieutenant Colonel Anderson reminded people that on March first a North American P-51 Mustang "twin," *Betty Jo*, flown by Lieutenant

Colonel Bob Thacker and Lieutenant John Ard, had flown 5,051 miles, nonstop, from Hickam Field in Honolulu to La Guardia Airport in New York. "Just to put it in perspective," he said, "that flight took fourteen hours and thirty-three minutes, which was only about an hour longer than yours, but it covered five times the distance."

"So it did," Don agreed.

Anderson went on, relating another anecdote of yet another recent, nonstop flight, this one again involving a Mustang, only from Burbank, California to La Guardia. "Three hundred ninety-five miles per hour, average speed, the whole way across," said the lieutenant colonel. "You all averaged what? About seventy-nine or so?"

"If that," Don said.

"Pretty poky," said the lieutenant colonel.

"Yes sir, we were making time the hard way."

Anderson felt that higher and faster clearly paved the road into the future, which was an odd attitude, Julio thought, for a man committed to rotary wing development.

"We live in interesting times," said Colonel Bradenton, thinking more of the mix of people on board *Harry's Ark* than of the pending technical developments in the world of aviation. The plan of the moment was to provide the ship with thirty gallons of fuel and have it fly over to Miami Field, where it could be refuelled, refitted as needed, and sent north. "It's not you aren't welcome to stay with us," said the colonel, "but your other people tell me you have business in Dayton."

"We do that," said Julio.

"We'd like to get there," Don agreed, who also felt it might be nice to have some rest, and mentioned that in passing.

"By all means," said the colonel. "Rest, by all means. No point in flying tired."

Patty had been thinking it might be nice to conduct a press conference. And Julio had been thinking it might be smart to call Carlota, since by now she would be wanting a divorce.

After setting down his tin cup, Don went behind the dune to empty his Foley bag. Already the colonel's men were pouring gasoline into the ship's tank. "'Keep 'em flying,'" said Don, when he returned.

"That's right. Keep 'em flying north," said the colonel, with a twinkle in his eye. Aside, he spoke with Don. "Son, we're going to isolate you at the field. I'd hate for matters unrelated to your flight to rear their ugly heads. I don't want to ruin things for you, or, by the same token, for the AAF."

"No, sir," said Don. "I appreciate that." He knew the colonel would have to keep him under wraps, or keep *them* under wraps—them being the Negro, the white girl, and the Puerto Rican, although the colonel seemed not to have picked up on Julio's situation, in which African blood was mixed with Spanish.

"Of course, it gets worse farther north," said the colonel. "So, the faster you all get through north Florida, Georgia, the Carolinas, Tennessee, Virginia and Kentucky . . . well, you see."

"Yes, sir," Don agreed.

"It ain't me."

It never was, or anyone else, and Don knew that. "I know that, sir," he said. "I appreciate you allowing me to come in, and I appreciate your advice." Out of the corner of his eye he watched a man trounce the tin cup he had drunk from; crush the cup into the sand out of view. "I owe the Army quite a bit," said Don. "And I consider it my good fortune to have had the opportunity to fly this aircraft."

"You used to work at Wright Field?"

"As a civilian, sir, yes I did."

"Good," said the colonel, who loved to see a pilot whose brains could match his balls.

Lieutenant Colonel Anderson had sided with Patty. "Old Harry died, eh?" he said.

"He did," Patty answered.

Then, looking around at Julio, specifically at Julio's crutches and the bandage on his foot, the colonel said, "I understand you all crashed again?"

"Thursday," Julio said.

"Pilot error?"

"No, it was *my* error," Julio said. "I messed up weight and balance calculations."

"Too bad," said the lieutenant colonel, not liking Julio any better than Don.

Returning, Colonel Bradenton again marveled at the combination that had produced such an unlikely event. "Sweet Jesus," he said. "What an oddball assortment for a crew. One crippled. One a woman. A Negro flying. And a crippled aircraft. Nobody with much experience. A little whimsy and some derring-do. You all got pluck. Did you think you would make it?"

"Sir, I wouldn't have left Ponce otherwise," said Don.

"Good for you," said the colonel.

The sun had grown warm. Off came sweaters and jackets. "Any of you fellows like to fly with us, you're welcome," Don said, ready to go now, and fairly certain no one would accept his invitation. He was referring to the short hop across Biscayne Bay, which would take them to Miami Field.

"I'd like to go with you," said Colonel Bradenton, a response surprising Don.

"Be honored to," said a sergeant, joining the colonel.

"So would I," said a captain. In a moment, six out of the seven men who had met the ship's arrival boarded the ship to be carried to their field. The one who didn't was Lieutenant Colonel Anderson, who, it turned out, with no one else around, got assigned by the colonel to guard jeeps.

—

CHAPTER TWENTY

As of Sunday morning, Ponce remained preoccupied with its championship series against Caguas, and few people knew about the flight of *Harry's Ark*. Ponce still trailed Caguas three games to two when the sixth game began at ten a.m. Charlesville had joined Alice and Antonio, and several thousand people, in the grandstand of Ponce's Terry Stadium. He had no idea Harry's men had left Puerto Rico aboard his aircraft, or that his aircraft had already flown to Florida.

The stadium announcer announced that paid attendance had surpassed the old mark of 5,538 and established a new record, 6,710. In festivities prior to the start of the game, the Honorable Andres Grillasca, Mayor of Ponce, standing on the diamond with other luminaries of the city and with players of both teams, welcomed the visiting *Criollos* of Caguas-Guayama and all others who had come or tuned in. Following the mayor's welcome, Ponce's famed singer, Ruth Fernandez, sang the Star Spangled Banner followed by *La Borinqueña*, Puerto Rico's national anthem. Alice explained to Charlesville that Ruth Fernandez happened also to be married to Ponce's starting pitcher, Juan Guilbe. But Alice seemed subdued, a condition Charlesville attributed to the shock she must have experienced at Harry's death.

At the conclusion of *La Borinqueña*, the mayor returned for a solemn announcement, reminding everyone of the untimely passing of one of Ponce's leading citizens, Colonel Harry R. Baird, United States Army Air Forces, Retired. As the mayor put it, Colonel Baird died "early Saturday morning, at his home, in Ponce."

"It is a shame," lamented Charlesville. "Things turned out so poorly for Harry at the end." Charlesville felt certain that the mishap with the ship had broken Harry's heart. As the mayor continued, providing background about Harry and Harry's project, Charlesville, well aware of that background, inquired about Walter.

"Walter is with the men. They are en route to Wright Field," Antonio answered.

"All of them?"

"All of them." Charlesville was surprised that Walter had chosen to go. But, then, Charlesville had weighed the prospect as well; not for Harry's sake, but out of curiosity, to meet some of the people at Wright Field.

On the diamond, Mayor Grillasca elaborated on the innovative nature of the ship Harry had built and the indebtedness of society toward those who serve as pioneers. Charlesville, only half-listening, asked Alice about Patty.

"She went to Wright Field," Alice answered.

"Really!" Charlesville responded.

Near the end of his remarks, Mayor Grillasca noted that, like its namesake, *Noah's Ark*, *Harry's Ark*, too, had crossed the fathomless sea, as part of its great voyage.

Hearing that, Charlesville sat up abruptly. What *fathomless sea*!? What *great voyage!?* And what was he talking about: *Harry's Ark*. Had the men named the ship? "What is happening?" he asked Antonio.

Antonio held up a finger, to stay him as the mayor continued. "Last night," the mayor said, "Colonel Baird's ship set out from Ponce's Mercedita airport, and flew non stop across the Atlantic Ocean to Florida." Charlesville, dazed, shot a damning look at Antonio, then one at Alice. The mayor concluded, "This morning, just moments ago, we received word from the United States Army Air Forces that Colonel Baird's ship, *Harry's Ark*, piloted by Don Perry of Ponce, accompanied by Flight Engineer, Major Julio Rodriguez, US Army Air Forces, retired, and navigated by *Señorita* Patricia Symms, has landed safely on the beach at Miami, Florida. Their flight has set a new world's record of one thousand six hundred fifty-four kilometers for a helicopter flying unrefuelled."

Hearing this, the stadium's crowd erupted into a thunderous ovation, rampant with stomping and cheers. "I'm sorry," Antonio said, though his words were drowned out.

"Damn you!" Charlesville told Antonio. "It's not over," he threatened, and left.

"Play ball," yelled the ump, as the applause over the announcement subsided.

"Just so," Antonio said.

On the mound, the elegant Juan Guilbe glowered down at the centerfielder from Caguas, first up.

At Miami Field, Don asked directions to the colored men's latrine, and a captain pointed him "yonder." *Yonder* proved to be too great a distance for Julio on crutches, and Julio decided he would try passing in the terminal instead. Patty went with Julio. "I Spanish," Julio joked.

A mile from the ship, in the southwestern corner of the field, backed so close to the field's fence that it bordered on swamp, stood the facility Don sought. The building combined functions of washroom, locker, supply closet, and lounge, serving the Negro civilian population attached to the field as porters, custodians, maids, kitchen, and laundry help. Since it was Sunday, most were off duty, and since it was the middle of a shift for those who were on duty, Don found the place empty.

Constipated from flying and stress, Don pored over sports from last week's *Miami Herald*. A custodian his age, heavier and gray, arrived. Mistaking Don for a hire, the custodian asked, "You be the new man?"

"No, I'm not," said Don.

"Be lookin' for work?" the man asked.

"No." Don looked up. "Not here."

"Where y'all from?" the man asked.

"Dayton," Don said.

"Wright Field?"

"Uh-huh."

The man checked his face in the mirror. "You work?"

"Pilot," said Don, sorry at once he had said that. He could feel the man's scrutiny.

"Bull—shit," the man said, fixing Don in the mirror.

Don laughed. "You're right. I'm a draftsman," he said.

"Know what I git?" asked the man.

"It's posted," said Don, referring to the poster on the wall that showed the wages the civilian staff earned.

"Forty-six fifty a week," the man said.

"I saw that," said Don, who had himself earned forty a week from Harry.

"Damn good, I'd say. But I work overtime. Sunday's my day. Yas suh. I got it made, Sunday."

Later, after the man had gone, Don calculated backwards and figured the man worked a seven-day week, off a base pay of forty-eight hours, to get to overtime on the seventh day, Sunday. Even so, he figured that the man was doing better than he was.

Stretched out on the cot that stood against the back wall of the annex, Don looked up at the rafters and felt he was airborne, still flying. Above the cot, the window was latched open. Someone had tacked up bright yellow curtains, which had little green flowers in a print. The curtains furled very pleasantly in the breeze. The window faced west and the breeze came in from the Everglades, bringing sounds of birds. Although the rustling of the curtains was peaceful, although he felt himself seduced by the sultry air, Don reminded himself that, despite what he said to the custodian, when he got back to Dayton he would have to find work, and finding work as a draftsman would be tough. Wright Field had scaled down since the end of the war, and no one knew him anymore. He could carry mail, pull trash, use family connections to get a janitor's job; or work as a porter on a train. He wouldn't do better than the man who was here, because that man spent little on clothes. The thought of unemployment gnawed at Don. Had he gone on to college, he would have been able to find something; in that case, teach school or do something. As it was, he faced work in a ditch.

When he woke, he felt cheated. In Ponce, though it was March, it had felt to him like June, especially if the weather was judged by the standards of Ohio. Now, in south Florida, the soft air made it feel like September. It felt like the end was coming on. *I've been cheated*, Don thought, *my summer jumped over to fall.*

When Julio stumped out to the ship on his crutches, he found Patty had returned ahead of him. He sat with her on the edge of the deck, and they dangled their legs out the hatchway. The sun was lovely. "I called Carlota," he said. "She said we're famous. They announced our flight on the radio. Now she wants me back." He was happy.

"Good," Patty said, glum, tied up with worry.

"What's the matter?"

"I want to marry Don."

"Good for you."

"I must be crazy."

"You are."

"Would you do it?"

"Would *I* marry Don? No, I don't think so," Julio joked.

"If you were me?"

"That's a tough one," Julio said.

"Yeah."

"Yeah." He paused. "I'm glad I'm not you."

"It will absolutely, and positively, crush my parents," she said. "They will never see the good in it, ever, ever. The same is true for all my old friends. All of them. And it's true of my other relatives as well, except Alice. I bring their world that pain." She put her hand to her brow, and rubbed the bridge of her nose. "I can't let him go, and he proposed. I love him. He loves me. If he were jilting me, I'd have to cope with that. But he wants kids. He wants a new life, settled down."

"Interracial children will face hell in Ohio," Julio said.

"I know that," she said.

"Better they not be born at all."

"That's terrible."

"Patty, your children will be Negro," said Julio. "Even if they're white, they'll be Negro."

"I don't care," she said.

"They'll have to be as tough as little soldiers. Who will accept them? Who will accept you? Not the white world. Not the black. For the rest of your life, you will be the white woman with the nigger, and Don will be the nigger with the white woman. You'll be at home in each other's arms, but nowhere else. And your kids will be like soldiers." She hung her head, hearing Julio, thinking over the import of his words. But Julio wondered, did she know what she was doing? Did she really understand? Don's own people would reject them: him, because he was too good to get a black woman; her, because she must be damaged goods, else why would she like Don? "You'd have a better chance if Don were light skinned," Julio said. But, Lord, man, Don was dark.

"Wow," she said, when she looked up.

"Shall I leave you to your misery?"

"It's too bad we can't live back in Ponce. Or maybe France is the place. Or New York."

"May be," said Julio. "If we make Wright Field, maybe Charlesville will forgive us. Maybe not. If the Army offers to buy the ship, perhaps he will. Don's major worry will be how to support you. He already knows about the wars."

"I don't want soldiers for children," she said.

"Who does," Julio said. But the insults were only part, Julio knew; the confrontations, only part. It would be worse than she imagined. "There will be half-insults," he said, "along with full-fledged insults. There will be snide remarks, slow service in restaurants and stores; 'maybe' insults—looks, quiet refusals, silence, snubs. Apartment leases inexplicably not available. Promotions gone elsewhere. Loans that disappear. The 'you people,' and the 'such people,' that will be your lot. What a beating."

"It's already started," she admitted. "Inside the terminal, I went to the WAC's quarters to use the bathroom, and some WAC was there while I was washing my face. She knew who I was, so she started asking me questions. Foolish me, I started answering them. Then she said, 'Ain't you married?' I said, 'No.' She said,

'How do you let yourself *do* that?' 'Do what?' I asked her. Stupidest question I ever asked in my life. 'Fly next to a nigger,' she said." Patty blushed. "I told her, "'Dolly, I swing with the pilots.'"

Afterwards, Julio gave his advice. "Don't fight every battle," he said. "Love is a secret. Sometimes, it's better just to pass."

"I hear you," she said, having learned it herself.

By the time Don returned to the ship, the others who had flown over from Puerto Rico reached the field. Walter, Maxwell, Major Girard and Captain Morales, who had flown them, were there. Bill had come too, but gone into town to the crematorium to see about Harry's remains. Maxwell broke the news that was most pressing to Don, "Ponce's leading, three to two in the eighth," and Don was delighted to hear it.

The Army brought out lunch, and the men ate, in quarantine as it were, at the ship. Ponce rallied, and, by the time Don filed the flight plan for the second half of the flight, Ponce's slugger, Pancho Coimbre, had doubled, capping the rally and driving in three more runs. Now Ponce led eight to two. The men were getting the scores from the tower, which in turn was getting them from Borinquen Field.

Don's flight plan for the 994 mile flight to Wright Field had the ship arriving by midnight. From Miami on, they would no longer have the benefit of the tailwind that had helped them reach Florida, and from the Blue Ridge north, they expected headwinds. They also expected a squall line, associated with the cold front that trailed south from a low over the Saint Lawrence Seaway. "Life's been easy," said Maxwell, a comment causing all of them to laugh. Temperatures in the north were forecast near freezing.

Walter, Maxwell, and Bill would continue their flight, too, again courtesy of the AAF, and again with Captain Morales as their pilot and Major Girard as company. The major had 'adopted' Harry's company.

Bill showed up with Harry's remains in a cardboard box that weighed twelve pounds. The men, curious, cut the box open.

Harry's bones were no more than nuggets now, many with the color of nacreous, mother-of-pearl, which Patty likened to the hues of magnolia blossoms in a Baltimore spring.

Before boarding, Patty had a word in private with Don. "Do you still want to marry me?" she asked, her heart pounding furiously and her voice tight with emotion.

"Yes," he answered, trying to search her intent.

"Well, I'm willing," she said. "I accept."

Don was stunned. He never thought he'd hear those words. "Okay," he said. "I mean *great!*"

Beyond the ship, a small group had gathered to watch the departure. Don started the port engine. Patty entered the log: Sunday morning, quarter past eleven, March 16, 1947, which entry served also, without it being said, to record the moment she considered their engagement to be official. A moment after that, Don started the starboard engine. Over the radio, he requested clearance for the takeoff. The controller, not at first responsive, asked Don to stand by, then, instead of the clearance, he relayed the ball score. "Eight to two, Ponce. That's a final." There would be a seventh game. "*HB-1*, you are cleared to go," the controller said. "Watch the C-54 to the north of the field."

The ship was much lighter than it had been taking off from Mercedita, and was able to climb and accelerate quickly. At six hundred feet, holding an airspeed of eighty, they flew north along the edge of the Everglades. Below them lay jungle, and to the west of them, swamp. Winds were west at twelve. The air was choppy. It was sunny but hazy, with visibility in a slant-range of four to five miles. To the north, a line of cumulus was beginning to build on the horizon. "It's a sun-shiny, balmy, seventy-six degrees in Miami," Julio said. But the ride would turn bumpy, he knew that; it would not be like the night above the sea.

They hit the squall line at the shore of Okeechobee, and said nothing for an hour-and-a-half as Don struggled to hold a heading. By the time they emerged, through the front and out its back, they were northwest of Vero Beach, back in sunlight. Visibility was better, and the winds, for a while north-northeast, became westerly again. Don resumed an airspeed of eighty, after having slowed down through the squall. Near Melbourne, they saw checkpoints of small lakes.

They had been aloft three hours twenty minutes, and had lost half an hour due to weather. The air had become dryer, but the temperature had dropped twelve degrees. Julio reported they had burned less than half their fuel, 2,176 pounds, and he noted they were 237 miles into their flight, with another 200 to Camp Oliver.

Patty looked east, beyond Daytona's lagoon and beach, toward the ocean. "Back to sea," she murmured, reluctant to go out there again. From her point of view, Florida's coast appeared to go due north and the course of their flight appeared to go northeast. That view was illusory, solipsistic. It was the coastline of Florida that was retreating to the west. She was skewing the world to fit her conception. Below, along Daytona's famed beach, she watched a car race over sand, dodging waves and splashing through some. "Looks like fun," she said. The grandeur of the beach impressed her, and the fact that the beach appeared deserted seemed enticing. "Julio," she called over the intercom. "There's no one down there. Just one car."

"Too cold for the natives; too soon for the tourists," Julio responded.

In Ponce, the seventh and deciding game of the series erupted into a slugfest almost from the start. But it was a slugfest that went Ponce's way, and throughout the island realization dawned that Ponce had done what no other team in history had done, what no one in fact thought it possible *to do*, and that was to come from behind in a best-of-seven series after having been down three games to none, and then win. Alice had left early with Antonio to go to Harry's Field. In the car, over the radio, they heard the final score, ending the series and the season: Ponce eleven, Caguas-Guayama two. Ponce was champion! Ponce had won! It was over!

During the day, Alice had answered so many inquiries about the flight that she extended an invitation to anyone interested to drop by Harry's later, where there would be, she imagined, a vigil to follow the progress of the ship. Normally, such an invitation would attract a sizable crowd. But, today, the invitation competed with the celebration of Ponce's victory, and no one immediately showed up. All Ponce seemed in the midst of its own party. The city was a party.

At the field, alone with Antonio, Alice was moved by the sight of the truck and the Plymouth, and the sudden thought that Harry's death meant she would never see him again. She recalled an evening she and Harry had sat together on the steps, in front of the house, enjoying the sunset. She looked out across the field at the empty apron. The timbers were still in place but the ship would never again stand on that apron. In early evening, poor Harry's spirit had the sky to itself. "We're all who's left," she noted, as they entered the house.

"If nobody else comes, I won't be sorry," Antonio said, for he was reluctant to indulge Alice in melancholy. "Ponce is full of life. Our lives are full. This is but one part of the story."

Antonio's connection to the news of the flight had remained Colonel Brooks, whom he continued to call, almost hourly, for updates on the ship's progress. As Alice made drinks, the colonel reported over the phone that the ship was approaching Camp Oliver. "They're almost to Camp Oliver!" Antonio repeated to Alice.

"Where is that?" Alice asked.

"It's in Georgia," said Antonio.

"South Georgia," the colonel amended, overhearing Antonio call to Alice. "I'll be here till they get to Wright Field," he added, in effect promising attendance past midnight.

Joining Alice on the porch afterwards, Antonio kept looking toward the parking lot for cars, half-expecting the arrival of Minnie, or Elisa, or Diego, or the mayor. But, Alice seemed to focus her vigil in the opposite direction, again toward the apron, where the absence of the ship continued to define what she missed. "It's not the same at all," she said.

"No," Antonio agreed. "It never will be the same."

"I miss Harry."

"Yes."

"He *did* make a difference."

"Certainly, he made a difference. Absolutely," Antonio said.

"It's not that I'm jealous," said Alice, after a moment, "but when it comes time to write the book about Harry and his men, I'm going to remove my niece from the story."

"You can't do that," said Antonio. "It's too late."

"She put herself into the story."

"And so she has become part of it." Antonio was amused by Alice on this point. Alice had no reason to be jealous, but she was. "You know," he kidded, "it's murder if you kill a character."

"I'll not kill her," said Alice. "I'll just not put her in. Then it's fiction."

"Oh. Well, if it's fiction," said Antonio, "then make me forty-one."

"I'll do that," she promised. "And while I'm at it, I'll be thirty-five." Thirty-five, she recalled fondly, had been a wonderful year.

On approach into U.S. Army Camp Oliver, Don noticed how crisp the air had become, reinforcing his sense that, somehow, he had skipped forward in time, from summer in Puerto Rico to September in Miami, and, now, on to the fall. Ahead of them, by that reckoning, lay winter, up north. A year had passed since Don had seen barren trees, or seasonal foliage, or the uncanny magnolias, which had shed not for winter but spring. When he remarked on his sense that the day had gone forward like a life, Patty agreed. She felt the same thing. There was, indeed, something missing. "Where are my children?" she asked.

Don overflew the field, then descended, entering the pattern. Parked by the hangar sat the AT-7, there ahead of them, and, not far from it, Walter, blonde hair visible at a distance, was watching them land. Patty saw Maxwell and Bill, then Major Girard and Captain Morales, and three others whom she assumed to be Camp Oliver's personnel.

On the flight line were helicopters. "R-6A's," Julio noted.

"More competition?" Patty asked.

"Sikorsky," Don answered, meaning yes.

On the base leg of the approach, Patty moved out of the cockpit and went aft. On final, she was sitting on the jumpseat beside Julio. The aircraft came down and flared out. She would have liked to have looked out the window, to have smiled for the men, the few there to see them arrive. But, what she had done by moving aft was deny to those watching from the ground any visible evidence of an association between a white woman in the cockpit and Don.

On the ground, in a snub lost on no one, Corporal Bluett headed a delegation of three, the other two being privates, in welcoming the *Ark* to Camp Oliver. "On behalf of Colonel William Witherspoon," said the corporal, who struck Patty as being all of twenty, "welcome to Camp Oliver."

By ten after five, the ship had taken fuel. For the flight north, they broke out scarves, gloves, hats and coats, and a fresh set of batteries for the flashlight Patty would hold. Don was happy Ponce had won. Joe Girard gave the weather, which promised to be clear to the mountains, cloudy and cold, with headwinds thereafter. They had 551 miles still to fly. Someone from the mess brought them coffee.

At five-twenty, the ship took off.

A hundred miles north of the camp, Patty got a shot of the Georgia sunset, which caught them just west of Augusta. Beyond Augusta, the AT-7 flew by, Captain Morales overtaking close to port to give Major Girard and the others a chance to take pictures, which they did. Then, from Julio's window, Patty took pictures of them.

North of the Savannah, in Georgia's last light, Don looked down and saw forsythia in bloom.

By nightfall in Ponce, Leonard Rodriguez had so nagged his mother that Carlota gave in, loading not only Leonard but the four other kids into the car and driving them all to join the vigil at Harry's. At the field, people had been dropping in, some to stay, most to visit briefly and go, beginning in the late afternoon and on into the evening. There were plenty of families and many kids, including those of Minnie and Elisa.

Antonio noted that the field likely had never seen so many children as today. The children played everywhere, running and squealing. The field was a wonderful playground, the more so at night, when it was spooky, too.

Leonard, disdaining the company of *children*, remained with the grownups, who, if not supervising children, seemed centered around the food and the drinks being served on the porch of the house. Many who had come thought to bring something with them, and the vigil had evolved into a feast.

In a local conversation, Antonio asked Carlota if she was going to Wright Field. She told him no. Antonio asked if she would let Leonard accompany Alice and him to Wright Field. "We can't afford that," she said simply, still meaning no.

Her answer caught Antonio off guard, for he found himself in the middle of a domestic dispute. "I'm sorry," he said. "I did not understand, then. You see, Julio gave me money, with which to buy a ticket for Leonard, of course subject to your approval, in the event you were personally not going to go."

"I just told you we can't afford it," Carlota said. "So you should be giving that money to me."

"And of course I will do that," said Antonio.

"I cannot afford side trips to Dayton."

Antonio tendered Julio's check, written to him, to Carlota.

Leonard, standing by, was crushed at this outcome, and privately resolved to go stealing.

"So, you are going too?" Carlota asked Alice.

"Yes, surely," Alice said.

"How long will you stay?" Carlota asked.

"At least a few days," Alice said. "It's not certain." As Alice viewed it, the people who would attend the memorial at Wright Field would be locals as well as manufacturers who had built aircraft. They would come from all over. Alice felt certain the rotary-wing industry would be represented. She felt equally certain the Army would want people there, and, to that end, she had continued calling papers. "Harry *was* prominent, you know," she added, as a counter to Carlota's resentment.

"I know that," Carlota conceded, giving the devil his due.

Leonard began scheming to rob cars, a bank, a drugstore, but he kept his plans to himself. "Piasecki!" he exclaimed, abruptly and without warning, as he suddenly thought of an aviation pioneer, for Leonard knew all of their names and what each had accomplished. It was his pantheon of heroes, an epic catalog.

"Frank Piasecki, yes, that's a name I've heard of," said Antonio, who had heard Harry mention it.

"What did Harry steal from him?" Carlota asked.

"Control configuration," Leonard said. "Placement of the rear rotor relative to the forward rotors. Airframe design. Plus ideas about the center of gravity."

"Now, they will accuse Julio of stealing, since Harry's gone," said Carlota.

"Sikorsky!" exclaimed Leonard.

"Yes. Him, too, of course," said Antonio, referring to his recognition of that name.

"Cierva!" Leonard said.

"Juan de la Cierva, and what from him?" asked Antonio.

"Tri-rotor," Leonard said.

Alice took an interest now because she was hearing something new and of potential use to her in writing. "What did Harry steal from Sikorsky?" Alice asked, playing devil's advocate.

"Everything," Leonard said. "He stole from Sikorsky most of all. Off-set hinge design. Rotor design. Mast design. All-metal blades. It's like the S-51 Sikorsky's building."

"Is it now? How do you know Sikorsky's building something?" asked Alice.

"Papí told me."

"Trade secrets," said Carlota. "They'll say Harry infringed on their patents, that he took advantage of being in their factories to see what they were doing. But they all look over their shoulders at each other anyway. That's the way that industry is."

"Howard Hughes!" Leonard exclaimed.

"Howard Hughes, yes, that name sounds familiar," Antonio

agreed, having recalled the name principally in terms of seaplanes but, also, he thought, helicopters.

"You see, Harry had access," said Carlota.

"Platt / LePage!" Leonard exclaimed.

"Harry went to every company involved in rotary wing design and manufacture. He saw what each one was doing. He looked at their plans."

"Arthur Young! He's a genius!" Leonard said.

"They're all geniuses, aren't they?" asked Alice.

"Yes," Leonard said. "Every one. Papí knows. He's a genius, too."

"So what will happen?" asked Alice, returning to the subject of the theft of trade secrets, or infringement, or breach of a fiduciary duty; whatever was the case.

"Harry stole from the best. What will happen? They'll all want to sue him," said Carlota. "So they'll come to Harry's service at Wright Field, and take a look at the ship Harry built, and they'll sue Julio instead." Carlota laughed, but she clearly imagined this prospect as real.

"But, did Harry really steal? is my question," Alice asked.

"Talent borrows. Genius steals. Of course he did," said Carlota.

"Did he?" Alice asked Leonard.

"Pay for my ticket and I'll tell you," Leonard said.

"That's extortion," said Alice, enjoying every minute of this. "This kid's on his way to the top."

"I'll pay for him," Antonio offered. "Definitely, he should be at Wright Field to see the honors paid—or the subpoenas served—to people he loves."

"I can't let you do that," Carlota protested, not too strongly, although in protesting she faced the prospect of having Leonard nag her to death; in which case her protest had almost no force at all. Besides, she was afraid of looking cheap.

"Surely," said Antonio. "To pay for this child's trip would be my pleasure."

"Yes!" said Leonard, "Yes! Please, mamí, please!"

"Oh all right," said Carlota, "if you insist. Say thank you," she told Leonard.

"Thank you, thank you, thank you," Leonard told Antonio.

"My pleasure," Antonio said.

Alice looked over at Antonio. "Did you discuss all this, this *stealing* of proprietary data, you and Harry?" she asked.

"Harry was my client," Antonio said. "We discussed many things."

"That means you're not going to tell me," said Alice.

"My dad is smarter than Sikorsky," Leonard said.

"After Harry showed him how," Carlota added.

—

CHAPTER TWENTY-ONE

The C-54 returning General Thomas and party from Spain landed across from Wright Field at Patterson Field. Included in Thomas' party was his assistant, Brigadier General Bernard Weggoner, who served as Acting Chief of the Procurement Division within Thomas' Deputy Command of Supply. Deplaning, General Weggoner was mildly surprised to be met at the steps by Lieutenant Colonel Glen Anderson—the same colonel he had sent nine days ago to Ponce—surprised because Anderson did not serve under him and would not in the normal course have come out to meet him. "Anderson?" General Weggoner asked, returning the salute. "Everything okay?"

"Sir," Anderson began, walking the general to the car, "Harry Baird's helicopter is on its way to Wright Field. It's presently over the Blue Ridge and we expect it to arrive at Wright at 0030 hours."

Weggoner stopped short, accustomed to surprises but not pleased about this one. "How did that happen?" he asked the colonel pointedly, for he recalled Anderson's report that Harry's project was not viable; and that in fact it was little more than a joke.

"I misjudged," the colonel said, knowing he had to take the hit. "The ship left Ponce last night and flew to Miami nonstop. They came in this morning onto Miami Beach, bone dry, at 0825 hours. They had a flight crew of three people, and had to send a Mayday on the way in. I went down last night, as soon as I found out what was happening. I was there, with Colonel Bradenton's party, when we met the ship's arrival at the beach."

General Thomas was de-planing and Weggoner turned to him. "Al, you've got to hear this," he called, turning back, then, to Anderson. "That's a thousand-mile flight."

"Yessir, it's a thousand twenty-eight miles. They set a world's record," Anderson said.

As General Thomas approached, Weggoner turned to him again. "We missed a call, Al," he said. "A group of our people just set a world's record." He turned back to Anderson to hear it confirmed.

"Sir," Anderson said, speaking to General Thomas, "Some of Wright's people flew from Puerto Rico to Miami, a thousand twenty-eight miles, nonstop, in a helicopter, and they set two world's records: one for distance and one for gross weight. They took off from Puerto Rico at thirty-one thousand three hundred pounds. I say they're our people, but they're all retired now. It's a private enterprise."

General Thomas laughed out loud, for everyone knew it was not possible for a helicopter to fly at 31,300 pounds, let alone to fly a thousand miles unrefuelled.

"They built their ship in Puerto Rico," Weggoner explained to his boss. "I sent Glen down there to assess what they had done."

"I didn't think their ship would be capable of significant flight," Anderson admitted. "But there's more to that story, I'm afraid."

"What?" Weggoner asked.

"To begin with, Colonel Baird died, and now they have his ashes on board, and, second, there are newspaper reporters all over Area B."

"Get in the car, son," Thomas told him. "You've got some explaining to do."

On board the ship, in the air above North Carolina, for some minutes, Don had been losing his ability to fly, and Patty her ability to navigate. As the ship proceeded through the gap in the Blue Ridge northwest of Asheville, Don was chasing the needles. "I'm freezing," he said, trying to maintain straight and level flight; an altitude of 6,500 feet, an airspeed of 80 miles an hour, and a compass heading of 336 degrees.

"I am too," Patty said. She found the cold excruciating, and she had seen Don's performance deteriorate. The air through the pass was rough, but that wasn't the cause of his poor flying. He was no longer alert.

Cold, Julio said, or thought; he wasn't sure, he who was sitting on gloved hands, as he peered at the panel before him. He had never been so cold in all his life. The thermometer outside the aircraft read ten degrees Fahrenheit. They were heading toward the Tennessee valley, with Asheville behind them and Greeneville, Tennessee, ahead, but it seemed half the arctic air of Canada poured through the pass, opposing their progress, and Don was losing it, all knew.

"Keep going," Patty urged him. Don could not let down from altitude, for they were blind, flying in cloud, in tricky air currents. They could always turn back to Asheville and put down for the night. That would be the end of it. But it was better, she thought, to track the beacon on over; make Greeneville, and keep going.

She tugged Don's wool dutzel, to protect his ears. She tucked in his scarf, and stiffened his collar; things he could not do for himself. He was bound. His hands were bound to the yokes. She looked at his face: he seemed so determined, so grim; his eyes so apprehensive.

They should have heeded Major Girard, but they hadn't. The major told them send the ship north on a train, but they didn't. Now, they were in danger for their lives. Now, they were suffering the consequences.

"I want to quit," Don confirmed, dully, slow to respond. He was stuporous from cold. He had put on all the clothing he could, but it was not enough. It was too cold, and he had been too long exposed to that cold.

"Make you a deal," she yelled. "Get us to Delaney beacon and we can let down two thousand feet. If we can see the valley floor, we can land there." It was the best she could offer. Twenty miles. Every once in a while, the clouds in the pass broke and she could see headlights and taillights of the roadway traffic below.

From his childhood, Don remembered something terrible. Once, in summer, a boyhood friend had set out to swim the

Ohio River, leaving Don and other friends behind on the Ohio shore. Don's friend was certain he could make it to Kentucky, and he did. From the Kentucky shore, having made it, he waved back. Then, he must have realized his predicament, for he would have to swim across the river again. There was no other way to get home. Don remembered seeing the show of bravado his friend had put up, in the far distance of the Kentucky shore; bravado how he would undertake the swim home. Half-way out into the river, he floundered, as Don and the others watched helplessly from Ohio. Don watched him go under and drown.

Don was floundering. He would go under and drown. The ship felt as if it were floundering. His strength was giving out. He had gone beyond what he could effectively do, he had pushed it, he had tried, but he was tired, like his friend. His reactions were slow. His fingers were too cold. His concentration was slipping. He had taken on too much of a task. An old story. He had over-reached. Now, he was not anticipating his dilemmas; not correcting them sufficiently to recover. "I'm behind on the curve," he announced, admitting defeat.

Shivers spread through his body. His teeth were chattering. Like a man with fever, like a nation broken in strife, his body shook in parts of the body politic. His arm shook, then his shoulder, then one leg, and then the other. The more he quieted one part, the more another erupted. The more the ship required of him, the more he cramped, and shook, and tore at himself, and the less he had to give. Tension and cold seemed in concert; one to burn, the other pillage. He thought of the racism he had faced in Miami, the preview of what was to come. He saw the lieutenant colonel—Anderson—whose face rose before him, like a face out of hell. He thought of the snub he had faced at Camp Oliver, and a thousand-and-one snubs that would follow. Life would be hell for Patty and him both. Insults and threats were their due. Pain. A legion of past hurts arose in his mind, hurts clumped in thought, all resident in one fury, like the flakes of a blizzard, too numerous to count. Hate warmed him inside. He was losing it, succumbing to hate. His belly felt warm. "It's not worth it," he cried. "What's the use?"

Pitch and yaw. This was no ride like the ocean.

"Gonna lose it," Julio said.

"Can't help it," said Don. He rose and came down in his seat. He lifted completely in air as the ship fell away.

"Turn around," Julio begged.

"Hafta' quit," Don said, facing Patty. "Have to."

He wanted to lie down by a fire. He begged to relax; free of his body; free of the cold that had burned him. Don rejected himself as no good; equating self-worth with the norm of despair. He was no good as a pilot, no good as a man. He was, at best, stubborn and hung on. Stubborn could be mistaken for steady. *Stupid* could be mistaken for steady. What had Don done with his life? He was not as good as any white pilot, but he drew pictures of the airplanes they flew. He had abandoned a daughter. Failed a marriage. Crashed *Harry's Ark*. Dear Lord, what could he do? "Oh hell," he cried out. Had he ever been kind, with so much hate in his heart? Loving or kind? He had lived for himself, yet had *hated* his life.

Patty could see the dull rage, and she prayed. She could feel the heat of that rage, and she prayed for her husband, for Don. They were trapped in a Plexiglas bubble, like two blind fish in a fishbowl covered by a blanket and placed in a dark room on a night without stars or the moon.

There was nothing to see, but, even if there was, they couldn't. Humidity had frosted the perspex. Condensation had frozen on the panes.

She prayed harder. "Don't quit," Patty prayed. She prayed for herself and she prayed for her man. There were things beyond *quitting*, she prayed, sending support from her heart. God was there. With pain so great, God had to exist. "Help my husband," she begged. Don would hear it from every white pilot. There would be no end to the comparisons with the pilots who flew cold, flew tired, flew hurting, or injured; the pilots who flew open-air cockpits, way up there, in winter. *Never quit* was Harry's lesson. Don knew it was so.

She called Julio on the intercom. "Don's in trouble," she said.
"So am I," Julio said. "Turn back. Try tomorrow."
She drew close to Don's ear. "Delany Beacon," she yelled.
"How far?" she heard him ask.
"Ten miles," she lied, for it was more like fifteen.
"Ask Julio," he said.
"He said yes," Patty lied.

Don saw himself an old man, old in winter. Yet, for all that, he saw her beside him, giving him care. She would tend him to the end, no matter how she suffered too. "If we make Wright Field, that's the end of it," he swore, the words coming ever so slowly, passing lips made insensible by cold. That was his bargain, his promise to God. There was no point to anything further. He was shedding his dreams, peeling away his ambition. "No test flying, no more colonels, no more Army."

"I don't care," Patty yelled. If hate would warm him, hate would do. "They're not all like that colonel. Suit yourself." Some were, and some were worse. But worse was relative. And some were better. She was better. In her experience, flying through clouds over the mountains at night, in an unheated aircraft, with a pilot who was losing control, and a flight engineer who had lost it, was no more gruelling than the dread she had faced discovering the fuel leak over the ocean, or the sick, panicky dread of discovering she had gotten them lost. If moments lived in eternity, those lived too. Those moments had singed Patty's soul. She yelled at Don. "Any bargain you make, I forgive and accept. But I think if you quit, you'll be sorry." She had spoken her piece. He glanced over, with tears of physical pain in his eyes. The sight of his pain moved her heart, but they would be facing an ordeal their whole life long. And, with children, they could not easily back out.

"Someplace warm?" Julio begged, clicking into the intercom.
"Hang on," Don told him. "Delany beacon."

At Wright Field, at the Weggoner's house, the general's comely wife, Jane Weggoner, served the men coffee. "How was Spain?" she asked General Thomas.

"Spain was fine," Thomas said.

Jane Weggoner played bridge with the wife of General Thomas.

When they were alone, again—Glen Anderson, Bernie Weggoner, and Al Thomas—Anderson brought out the photos he had taken in Miami. He wanted the generals to see the damaged aircraft, to vindicate his view that Harry's people lacked judgment. "They crashed this aircraft on Thursday night," he said. "Ran it into a fence on a busted takeoff. That's the second time, and you can see they should never have been flying it now. Bad judgment. They got a nigra flying."

Weggoner recalled Anderson's report of a similar mishap, though less serious, nine days previously, when the truck crashed through the fence at Harry's Field. For the benefit of General Thomas, he mentioned it.

Thomas wanted to hear about that.

"They were trying to demonstrate the ship for me," said Anderson, explaining. "But they hadn't thought it out. They tried lifting their own truck with the ship. Only thing was, nobody knew how much their truck weighed. It turns out, it weighed too much. And they ended up crashing through the fence. Pilot error."

"Same pilot?" asked Thomas.

"Same pilot," Anderson said.

"Man loves fences," said the general. The generals laughed.

The two generals passed the photos back and forth. Thomas was impressed by the configuration of the aircraft; Weggoner by its size. Neither disputed the obvious fact that the ship appeared damaged. "They took a fearful risk," said Thomas.

"How did the newspapers find out about this flight?" asked Weggoner.

"A woman named Alice Symms has been calling them, and she called here," Anderson explained. "She lives in Ponce, and she's the aunt of the girl who's flying with them. She not only got to the papers, but also every radio station from Florida to Cleveland." General Thomas was apprehensive at the prospect of so much publicity. There were too many unknowns to the story, and too many events outside the control of Air Matériel Command. "The reporters have been calling and showing up here all evening," Anderson continued, then ticking off the list for the generals. "As of half an hour ago . . . the *Columbus Dispatch*. The Dayton *Daily News. The Cincinnati Post. The Cincinnati Times Star.* The Cincinnati *Enquirer.* Some rag from Middletown. Another from Hamilton. The AP is here. The *Plain Dealer* is sending someone from Cleveland. We've had queries from the Chicago *Tribune,* Boston *Globe, New York Times,* and the Washington *Post.* Some of those papers carried news of Harry's death in today's editions. As far as the flight, the ship is so slow that the news has caught up to it."

Anderson had also brought files; Harry's, and those of all Harry's men—Julio, Bill, Lon, Maxwell, and Don—all of whom had served in some capacity at Wright Field. Thomas' recollection of Harry was sketchy, and when he looked at the file he confessed he had forgotten about Harry's heart attack. Thomas didn't know Don, Julio, or any of the others.

Although the news of Harry's death shocked both generals, Weggoner in particular knew and liked Harry, and felt Harry's death as a personal loss. "I served under Colonel Baird in the thirties," he said. Not only did Weggoner like Harry, he admired Harry's *chutzpa,* a word he had learned from Harry. Nobody ever had to tell Weggoner that a man needed balls to survive, but, with Harry, there was also the matter of style. Harry had balls, but Harry could *break* balls. Weggoner was sorry, truly, that Harry had not lived to see his triumph, and sorry that *he* had not had a chance to see Harry once more. They had grown distant during the war, but there was always a fondness. If Harry had once thought of Weggoner as protege, Weggoner had allowed it to be so, or encouraged it. And, if he had surpassed Harry, that was because teachers were often destined to be surpassed.

Anderson, on the other hand, did not relish the career dent he would suffer on account of a nigra or an old con like Harry, and so he went on the offensive. "With all due respect, general," he said to Weggoner, "I stand by my report to you, sir. The aircraft's not airworthy. It's not a viable project, and I say that despite the fact that they made it to Miami."

"You said they told you it was Colonel Baird's dying wish to have his body flown home aboard his ship?" Weggoner asked.

"Sir, I said he was planning to fly as engineer," said the colonel.

"Same thing," said Weggoner, erasing the distinction. "Perhaps I like my way of putting it."

"We can see who we've got to deal with the newspapers," said Al Thomas. They had Weggoner, of course.

"Yessir," said Anderson.

"I need to know about the flight crew," said Weggoner, who had the files in hand but no sense of the people.

"The flight engineer taking Harry's place is the Porto Rican major, Rodriguez, who served here seven years, in Engineering. He's their lead man, don't ask me how. Then, there's the nigra named Perry, who was a draftsman here for twelve years. He was their draftsmen there, too, but they also made him their pilot. Real bush-league, back-barn type operation, if you ask me. Perry's not instrument-rated. Until this flight, he had no over-water experience. He has no rating for multi-engines. And he had no experience flying at night. So what's he do? He chose to fly the course at night, and not stay along landfall, which is relatively safer, but to take her out over open waters, far from landfall; and this, in a crippled aircraft, with a green crew. The girl's not cockpit-qualified, and the flight engineer just got out of the hospital, which is where he landed after they crashed on Thursday. Even so, he's on crutches. These people are something. They're really something. The pilot's a clown, a minstrel darkie. He's flown Piper Cubs; that's all. And the girl got hired for publicity. She had a picture in *Life*. Nobody else will fly with the nigra, so she's there in the cockpit, at his side. They can't do celestial navigation, and all they had to guide them was one ADF.

"So, of course, they got lost," Anderson continued. "It's a miracle they survived. Truly is. How they ever made it. God favors children and fools, 'n them damn darkies."

"Hang on, colonel," said Thomas. "How do you know nobody will fly with the pilot?"

"Sir, I believe nobody else in that company would fly with him, but, they wouldn't admit that to me when I asked them in Miami."

"Maybe it's how you asked them," said Thomas.

"Maybe so, sir. I let it be known I disapprove."

"If you'd put the 'e' back in Negro you'd get a better response."

"Sir, I did look up the girl's work," the colonel said, changing tack. He had stopped by the Public Affairs Office and taken the issue of *Life* dating from October, 1943. He showed the magazine to the generals, opened to the page displaying the picture Patty had shot. The picture recalled for the generals the worst debacle Allied air power had suffered in the war. The generals remembered the picture at once.

"Of course," said General Thomas.

"Harry hired her?" asked Weggoner.

"He did, sir," said the colonel.

"*Black Thursday*," said Thomas, referring to the nickname of the mission to bomb Schweinfurt. Patty's picture showed an airman eating alone in the mess. It was titled *The Survivor*. All the other plates around the airman, all the other place settings, were untouched.

"Patricia Symms?" Weggoner asked, seeing the credit.

"She goes by Patty," said Anderson. "As I say, it's my personal belief that after Harry died none of the men wanted to fly with that boy, so she filled in, and, as I say, there's more to that, too. They got lost." The disclosure that Patty was on board was unsettling to both generals, because it ran counter to the tradition each held sacred, that flight crews were qualified not by gender but skill. It seemed bad judgment for her to be there, when there were qualified engineers in the company, who could have navigated, certainly. It meant the issue, at bottom, really *was* bad judgment, or race, as Anderson had been insisting, especially since Don, as ship's captain, had the right to say who flew. For a long moment the three men simply sat, no longer speaking, each lost in his own thoughts.

"Why *did* they fly at night?" Thomas asked.

"Bad judgment," Anderson said.

Here, however, Weggoner interceded, for he had been briefed once before by Anderson, some weeks back. "If I recall, they have a loan agreement with a French manufacturer from Marseille, and under that agreement Harry keeps rights to produce the ship, if he can sell it, but only if he can find a reasonable offer before the contract expires."

"Something like that," said the colonel.

"Please continue," Thomas told Anderson. "What else?"

"I think I covered most of it, sir," Anderson said. "They still don't have a completed set of as-builts, but that's the . . . *Negro* . . . again. So they're out there, over the ocean, at risk, with no as-builts, and there's only one prototype of the ship."

"I know that pilot," said Weggoner, finally. "I've been trying to place him. He threw me out once, when I was trying to stretch a two-bagger into three. The guy could hit like you wouldn't believe, and he had an arm like a rifle. He would have been a lead draftsman here had it not been for his color."

"His claim to fame as a pilot is he's flown a Cub for four thousand hours," said the colonel, deprecatingly.

"I spent time in a Cub," said General Thomas.

"Yessir," said Anderson. "I just meant he's not instrument-rated."

"I'm not instrument-rated either," said General Thomas.

"Sorry, sir."

"You only get old being good," said the general.

"Yessir," said Anderson, in full agreement.

"We're taking the high road here," said Weggoner.

"Yessir, I see that," said Anderson. "I just meant the pilot seemed something of a hotdog."

"Actually, *I'm* something of a hotdog," Weggoner said.

"Yessir."

"We'll hold a memorial service for Colonel Baird," said General Thomas.

"He was a forty-year-man," said Weggoner. "It'll be one heck of a service."

"So it will be," agreed Thomas.

"The men christened their ship *Harry's Ark*," said the colonel.

"*Harry's Ark*?" Thomas laughed.

"Baird knew everybody," said Weggoner.

"So we'll invite everybody," said Thomas. "His career went back to Signal Corps days. He went back to the beginning of flight."

"Yes. He did," said Weggoner. "He was friends with both Wrights. Whatever else you might say, Colonel Baird was devoted to aviation, to the Army, and to Wright Field."

"Good man," said Thomas.

"Maybe a great one," said Weggoner.

"Well, let's not get carried away," said Thomas.

Weggoner laughed.

"Sir, if I may, there's a problem we haven't dealt with so far," Anderson said.

"Go ahead," said General Thomas.

"It appears they stole their ship's design from others," said Anderson. "Mostly, from Sikorsky and Cierva Autogyro in Great Britain, but also from Platt / LePage, McDonnell, and Piasecki. Whoever had good ideas, Harry took them, with the worst stealing being designs for the mastheads, which he got from Sikorsky, and perhaps rotor configurations from Cierva."

Thomas looked at Weggoner, and Weggoner back at Thomas. Neither was amused.

"Let me ask you something," Thomas said to Anderson. "Does the Cierva Autogyro Company have an aircraft that can fly at a gross weight of 30,000 pounds?"

"No, sir."

"Will they ever?"

"I don't know, sir."

"How about Sikorsky? Have any of Sikorsky's helicopters flown a thousand miles unrefueled?"

"No, sir, none has," said the colonel.

"So Harry did something they didn't?"

"Yes, sir."

"Maybe they should be stealing from him."

"Maybe so, sir."

"Speak your mind," the general ordered.

"Sir, I spoke it," said the colonel. "But perhaps I misspoke in saying 'theft.'"

"Thank you," said Weggoner.

"Go on," said General Thomas. "And the ship?"

"It will prove expensive, whoever owns it," said Anderson. "It's very large for a helicopter, as you have seen from the photos. The ship was not only difficult to build, but will prove difficult to test, difficult to develop, difficult to fly, and difficult to maintain. In short, very expensive. Not a good value."

"What else?" Thomas asked, wanting everything out.

"That's about it, sir," said the colonel. "The man who lent them money called the loan, I believe, or was about to. Everything they did was patch and piecemeal; catch-as-catch-can. They had no program of their own."

"When you were there you told Harry we weren't interested?" Weggoner asked.

"Yes I did, sir," said the colonel.

"Did you tell him to fuck off?" asked Thomas.

"Words to that effect," said the colonel.

"Then you fucked up," Thomas told him. "Never dash a man's hopes."

"No sir."

"Never tell a purveyor 'no.' You tell him, 'Well, perhaps,' or, 'Well, we'll see.'"

"Yessir."

"I think the colonel's beginning to understand that all he

did was get Harry mad," Weggoner said. "Had you been a little kinder," he said to Anderson, "Harry might still be alive, but, also, very likely, they'd have held off their attack."

"I'm sorry, sir," said the colonel, who believed in being plain. Still, he said nothing now in defense, for he knew he had no opinion to be heard.

"Anything more?" Thomas asked.

"Yes, sir," he said. "Three of the men who worked in Harry's company are on the way here in an AT-7, flying with a navigator from Air Transport Command and a pilot stationed at Borinquen Field."

"Let's make the most of it," said Thomas. "They're our people. Why, it all hangs together, doesn't it," he added, deadpan.

"Sure does," said Weggoner, wryly concurring.

"*Harry's Ark*?" said Thomas. "It has a certain ring."

"Vintage Harry," Weggoner said, for, to him, positive publicity for the procurement program at Wright was, within the confines of strict budgetary constraints of the post-war air forces, a crucial issue, sensitive, one whose outcome promised to determine which of the corporate offerings of the rotary wing industry stood to gain. They would make no fuss about Harry's presumed intrusions on intellectual property. "I need a shave," Weggoner said, for he had been flying for hours with General Thomas, breathing piped air and the smoke of cigars, and his face, unless he washed it and shaved, would photograph with a shadow and show up oily in a black-and-white print.

General Thomas, comparing Harry to Sikorsky, rose to go, and asked which of the two, Harry or Sikorsky, had something left to lose. "You see?" he asked Anderson, who rose also to go with him. "Leave the press to Bernie. Bernie understands." Thomas waved to Jane Weggoner, who looked out from the kitchen. "We'll have a memorial for Harry, and Bernie can handle the press," he repeated, for General Weggoner knew a stunt when he saw one, and a hotdog pilot when he saw one, and a grandstand play when he saw one, especially a play like Harry's, naming the aircraft *Harry's Ark*, which was intended to move the story into myth.

"Sorry I was harsh with Colonel Baird," said the colonel.

"Don't fire the first shot when you're surrounded," Thomas said. "Good night," he told the Weggoners.

"Good night, general," said Jane Weggoner.

"See ya, Al," said Bernie.

At Tennessee's Delany beacon, Don landed the ship. They were near the town of Greeneville. He shut down the engines. Then, for fifteen minutes, he lay spread eagle up on the engine nacelle, where the temperature of the metal was a hundred twenty degrees, and he could bask, like a crocodile, in that wonderful heat. Below, Julio puked. Patty acknowledged there was God, thanking Him profusely. On Tennessee's ground lay His snow.

"How 'bout Knoxville?" Julio pleaded, when Don climbed down. Knoxville was the nearest big city.

"Long Hollow," Patty said, pointing north. She was now directing the flight. "If we make it to Long Hollow, Clinch Mountain."

They took off at nine twenty, having lost twenty minutes. Don turned to his heading, 346. He called Knoxville to report their position. "Amazing," he said, at the end of the call.

"What?" Patty asked.

"The controller said he got a call from the Cincinnati *Post and Times Star*, asking where we are and when we'd get to Wright Field."

———

CHAPTER TWENTY-TWO

At nine thirty, the phone rang in the Pyrtle's home on Kenwood Hill, overlooking Cincinnati to the northeast of the city. Millicent Pyrtle, Lon's wife, found to her pleasant surprise the caller was Bill, their son. He was calling from Dayton, from Wright Field, where he had just arrived; and he told her that Harry Baird had died, early Saturday. She grew disturbed, hearing things like "cremation," and "flight," and "ship to arrive," so many things at once that she could not digest all she heard. Harry's remains would soon be arriving, she understood. "You best talk to your father," she said. It seemed Harry's remains were on board.

"It's your son," Millie said, as Lon came thumping down the hall, his sock feet hard on the planks of the ancient oak floor. Lon had heard her exclaim, he had heard her commotion and surprise, so he knew it wasn't their daughter who had called. "Harry died," Millie said, handing over the phone. The words shocked Lon. He stopped short. It was the third oldest house in Hamilton County, never warm, and he felt, suddenly, the force of the chill.

"Hello," he said, at last.

"Yeah, pop. Harry died," said Bill.

Hearing that, part of Lon died, too. He was fifty-eight. He knew the sound of the knock.

"We're at Wright."

"Who?"

"Walter and Maxwell and me. The Army flew us here. The ship made it to Miami, and it's heading up from Miami now. We just saw them in Georgia. They're in Tennessee somewhere now."

"Slow down," said Lon.

"The ship left Ponce last night, and flew all night to Miami and then this evening . . . ."

"Slow down."

"Sorry, pop."

"Tell me about Harry."

"Harry died."

"That's what I want to hear."

"Tell them all to come here," said Millie, standing by.

"He dropped dead, pop," Bill explained. "He was at his desk. It happened a little past midnight, Saturday morning. We had gotten the ship to fly, and flew it back to the field Friday night, and Harry had persuaded Julio to come back. But, right after midnight, Harry died. Alice was there. We were all there at the field. He just died. Heart attack."

"I'm sorry."

"We sent the body to Miami, and had him cremated there. Harry wanted his ashes to be spread at Wright Field, and Don and all of us wanted to bring Harry home on the ship. So his ashes are onboard in a box."

"You're all to stay here." Lon was shaking his head. It dismayed him, the things they had done. Flown the ocean. "Your mother says . . . do you hear? That you're all to stay here."

"The ship's not due until midnight," said Bill. "Twelve thirty, at Wright. Julio's with them; Patty, Julio and Don. They just called Knoxville, so we know they made it that far. It's snowing in southeastern Kentucky."

"I want you all to stay here," repeated Millie, with a loud voice three feet from the mouthpiece Lon held. The Pyrtles were proud of their house. The house was built in 1840, and during the Civil War had served as a point of terminus for the Underground Railroad, accommodating refugee slaves who had fled north across the river from Kentucky into Cincinnati. It was the second oldest house in the county.

"I'll come up," Lon told Bill, meaning to Dayton.

In flight, crossing Clinch Mountain, the ship cleared the ridge with six hundred feet to spare. Don fell asleep while flying. Patty woke him at once. She kept watch on his eyes.

"Where are we?" Julio asked, over the intercom.

"We're still in Tennessee, coming up on the ridge to Mulberry Gap," Patty told him. "A little farther, then we look for the town of Ben Hur."

Julio subsided into torpor. He remembered what he had forgotten about living in the north, and cold weather was it.

Walter found himself a minor celebrity at Wright; in part, because the mystique developing around the flight of *Harry's Ark* included him, and, in part, because he was yet another German aeronautical engineer, and in his case, a former pilot with the Luftwaffe, here visiting the citadel of world aviation. In the months following the war, so many Germans had come that field personnel constructed barracks to house them. As Bill explained, "We ended up with fifteen tons of your paper." The paper Bill referred to consisted of technical papers on rocketry and aeronautical subjects, including plans and project specifications, treatises and logs, even prospectuses for flights to the moon. Wright's intelligence personnel, T-2, were still digesting it all.

But Walter's role at war's end had been modest. Owing to his education as an engineer and family connections, he had been transferred from logistical flying on the Eastern Front to engine research in a laboratory in Bavaria. He spent the last year of the war in an enclave, hidden in the Bavarian Alps.

At liberty to go outside, at least to the edge of the flight line, Walter stood in front of Hangar One for a breath of air. On the flight line he could see the new jet fighters America was developing, and he recalled that the B-17s that so relentlessly bombed Germany were refined at Wright Field. So, too, the fighter escorts that ultimately proved so effective; right here. The radar, right here. The great engines, right here. The turbosuperchargers, here. The radio navigation. The electronics. The gun accuracy. All here. B-29s. B-24s. Mitchells. A-26s.

Mustangs. Lightnings. Jugs. All of it. All of them. "Mother of God," Walter whispered. Had the war gone on, German cities would have faced annihilation.

"You're the German?" asked a sergeant, who had come out for a smoke.

"Yes," Walter answered.

"That's a helluva thing you guys did."

"They did most of it," Walter said, understanding the reference to be that of the project.

"Care for a smoke?"

"No, thank you."

"So, what do you think?"

"I've been looking at that one," said Walter, referring to the aircraft whose tail was so tall that it rose four stories into the night sky. The ship dwarfed everything in sight.

"That," said the sergeant, "is a Consolidated-Vultee XB-36."

"Awesome," Walter said. The airplane had six engines; each propeller was the size of a helicopter rotor. The wingspan was two hundred thirty feet.

"It has a round-trip range of ten thousand miles," said the sergeant. "It can fly from Canada to Berlin, drop a load of bombs, and then fly back to Canada."

"I hope not," Walter said, relishing the cold air. If anyone asked, Walter could tell them how much like Germany it felt here in Ohio. No one asked, so he stared out at the flight line of the future, which featured airplanes a block long and four stories high; bombers that could fly oceans, round trip, and fighters that could fly faster than sound. "I do thank God it's over," he said.

In the middle of a briefing, Lon arrived, entering the ready room and surveying the scene. The briefing was being given by Captain Fiore, senior officer on duty in the tower, who, a few moments earlier, had received a call from controllers at Lexington tower in Kentucky, who in turn had passed on the position report provided to them by the ship. Lon listened for a moment, but had to ask a reporter. "I came in late," he apologized.

"They called in their position sixty miles east of Lexington, at ten fifty," said the reporter.

"Oh," said Lon. "What time will they get here?"

"Twelve forty-five." The reporter, having answered Lon's question, then wanted to know who Lon was.

"I was part of the team that built the ship," said Lon. "That's my son, over there," he said, pointing to Bill. "He's part of the team." And he pointed to Maxwell. "So is he. We all used to work here," he explained. He felt some pride. "All of us came from Wright Field."

"You must be Lon Pyrtle," said the reporter, having deduced Lon's identity from notes identifying all the people in Harry's company.

When the briefing ended, Bill hailed his father, then resumed exhibiting the as-builts to three engineering officers from the rotary wing branch. The officers, off-duty each of them, had come in because they had heard about the flight. One, looking at the drawings with Bill, claimed he was able to see what he termed *the obvious influence of Sikorsky* on the design of the ship's rotor hubs. "Wrong," said Bill, indignantly. The other claimed he saw Piasecki's influence in the engine mounts and gear trains. "That's crazy, too," said Bill. Then, only half kidding, Bill asked if the third guy was going to say that he could see that the controls had been copied from Cierva. "No, they appear to be original work," said the man.

A reporter came up. "You ought to close that," said the first engineer, referring to the breach of security in leaving open the folio of drawings for a reporter to look at.

The reporter scoffed at this precaution. "Gentlemen," he said, hands open to disavow any thought he might spy, "what do I know about helicopters? What I wanted to know is: is it true the guy flying is colored?"

Maxwell borrowed the Chevrolet belonging to the lieutenant from Public Affairs, and went out into Fairfield to get burgers at the Blue Dell. For a year-and-a-half, Maxwell had been savoring his memories of the Blue Dell, whose cheeseburgers were good enough that he could justify the exaggeration that he had flown all the way from Puerto Rico just to eat one. "Maxwell," said MacGregor, who owned the Blue Dell, "if the newspaper people ask you, tell them how good my cheeseburgers are." Maxwell had known MacGregor for years.

While the order was walking, Maxwell called Don's mother, who lived with Don's younger brother, William, in the family homestead on the banks of the Little Miami, southeast of Dayton. Don no longer lived in the homestead, but during the war he had taken Maxwell there several times for home-cooked meals. Only William, among the five Perry children, actually lived there with Mrs. Perry, and she was delighted to hear from Maxwell, whom she remembered fondly. She told him she had indeed heard about the flight, because her oldest, Abigail, had called her to tell her to put on the radio. She was thrilled, of course, but really not surprised. After all, it had been her son.

"If you like, you can be here when they arrive," Maxwell offered. "I'll be happy to drive down and get you."

"Thank you all the same, Burton," she told him, referring to him by his given name, as she did with most of Don's friends. She was neither austere nor formal, but wary in her way. "It was kind of you to think of me," she said. "But, Donald will call when he's here."

"Yes, ma'am," said Maxwell, who would not dream of addressing her other than 'Mrs. Perry' or 'ma'am.' The woman had taught school fifty years. Not only could she unnerve a man with one look, but, now eighty-three, she had been alive when President Lincoln was shot.

Returning to the counter, Maxwell looked at the cheeseburgers. He had ordered for the others as well.

"How 'bout chili?" MacGregor asked.

"Good idea," Maxwell said.

"Apple pie?"

"Sure."

"And coffee?"

"Oh yes. Whole big pot."

The people of Kentucky began retiring, Sunday's worship at an end. As the lights went out, the countryside became a blanket. "Ohio River," Don announced, seeing reflections of the ship's lights on the surface of the water.

"How much farther?" Julio asked.

"Eighty-two miles," Patty answered. They had flown by the town of Maysville, Kentucky, at eleven forty-six. Don was slightly west of his course. "Wright Field at maybe twelve fifty," Patty guessed.

"Thank God," Julio said, chattering.

Downstream of Maysville, the river bent north and for a mile ran parallel to their course. Heading directly away from them, out in the channel, a sternwheeler pushed barges down the river. Don pursued it, overtaking to starboard and descending to pull up abreast. He was thirty feet above the river, hovering, creeping forward, eighty feet away from the pilot house. She was the *Josiah Morgan*, running coal down from Pittsburgh. She pushed six barges, two abreast, and the barges ran low in the water. Aft, she was powered by her great wheel, which churned up the water in her wake and set the river to rolling. Even aboard the ship, over the ship's engines, Julio could hear the thunder of the great paddlewheel, and was held, fascinated at the sight. The helicopter frightened the *Morgan's* pilot and watch, and Don saw a lantern swing from the bow of the lead barge, a hundred yards down the river, alarming everyone. Then, out of the pilothouse, out of the bunkhouse, tumbled crew, all hands, onto the deck, for no one on the *Morgan* had ever seen such a craft as *Harry's Ark*, and the river was a desolate place.

They put on the arc light, training it from the bridge onto Harry's ship, a light so brilliant it felt warm on Don's face. It obliterated his night vision. The ship stood out in the night sky, fixed as a garish, white target. "Let's get out of here," yelled Julio, afraid the *Morgan's* crew might open fire.

Against the sounds of the engines, the ship's exhausts, and the rotors, even so, the thunder of the paddlewheel rose. In boyhood, Don had saluted such vessels with the oar of a rowboat.

"Old friend," he yelled over, knowing full well no one heard, for to the *Morgan*, *Harry's Ark* seemed Armageddon. Roil against roil, blast against blast, from one ancient thing to another, Don saluted, sashaying the ship in a sassy Dutch Roll, right on down, right back up: *Honey, catch that.* Then, from the *Morgan*, they returned the salute, with a mournful, deep blast from her horn, the most mournful sound in all creation; a blast splitting time, north and south, whose echoes caromed off the hills of Kentucky, and off the shores of Ohio, down to Ripley, and beyond.

Near midnight, Wright Field's off-duty personnel began showing up to witness the ship's arrival. Only some of these people had previous connections to Harry or Harry's people. Most worked or served in the Engineering Division. Nearly everyone involved in rotary wing development had arrived. Several pilots from the Flight Test Division also came.

At quarter past twelve, General Weggoner entered the ready room and quickly sized the crowd at seventy people. Going at once to the front of the room, he called people to attention. Weggoner had a strong, tenor voice that easily commanded the room. As he spoke, Colonel Anderson collected the as-builts, rounded up the Pyrtles, Maxwell, Walter, Major Girard and Captain Morales, and took them all down the hall to a separate room.

"The ship is due here in thirty minutes," Weggoner announced. "Right now, they're west of Wilmington, Ohio, approaching at an altitude of two thousand five hundred feet. Their groundspeed is seventy-four miles an hour. We do not yet have them on radar, but we are in radio contact from the tower. They are in good shape overall, but they have been suffering from cold. Their aircraft is unheated. They have had a long ordeal. For the record, it's twenty-nine degrees here at Wright, and visibility is fair; eight miles in slight haze. We have overcast at four thousand five hundred, and winds north northwest at nine."

At this point the general introduced a new subject. "I'm sure by now all of you know that the remains of Colonel Baird are onboard, and I'm sure all of you know that the colonel's wishes were that his remains be scattered at Wright Field, a place he considered to be home. Many of you may be wondering whether Wright Field is planning some sort of service to honor the memory of Colonel Baird, whose service career spanned forty years. The answer is yes. We have not yet had time to contact all the people who would attend such a service. Colonel Baird knew many major figures in aviation; not only military personnel, but in the private sector as well. In recent years, Colonel Baird worked closely with the rotary wing industry. We are in the process of getting in touch with people, and will keep you posted as plans take shape.

"On a personal note, I know many of you here knew the colonel. I also knew him, and had the good fortune to serve under him from 1933 to 1935. I remember him not only for the fact that he was a brilliant engineer, and a visionary, but because he was an excellent teacher, and a mentor to young officers. His true love was the United States Army, and what has evolved as the Army Air Forces. We were all fortunate to have had such an officer among us, for he was a good friend and a loyal patriot, who served his country well. Indeed, he served until he died. There was no retirement for Harry."

The easy part of his presentation over, Weggoner looked around at all the cameras, for the hard part was at hand. Abruptly, he changed tact, establishing his authority. "Gentlemen," he said, "we need to go over the ground rules for the arrival of the ship. First, the flight of Colonel Baird's aircraft is a military undertaking and is being handled as such. Our rotary wing program is closed to the public, and material relating to it is classified, regardless whether the material originated in the private sector or here. Accordingly, as to photographs, the press takes no photographs whatsoever of the aircraft, and Captain Cleary, whom you see by the door—Captain Cleary, stand up." The captain stood up. "He will collect your cameras. That's final. Sorry. No bends in that road."

The murmur of disapproval arose immediately, but Weggoner was inured to it and proceeded. "Service-connected personnel with clearances and civilian personnel with clearances may take photographs of the ship, but not of the ship's masts, mast heads, or rotors," he said. "There are no exceptions to that. Wright's own photographers will take authorized, official photographs of the arrival of the ship and the ship itself. As to you who represent the press, I'm not turning a deaf ear to you. I know you need a story. You will be given at least one print-quality photograph of the arrival of the ship, or the ship and its crew, that you may take with you when you leave here tonight and use for publication in your papers. We will develop those prints here, in house, tonight. Kindly see Lieutenant Archer. Lieutenant Archer, stand up." The lieutenant stood up. "We have security at stake, and the national interest. Period. You understand it.

"Next," Weggoner said. "Interviews. The press will have a chance to conduct a group interview of the flight crew, with all of the flight crew attending. Before that interview takes place, however, we are going to debrief the flight crew. So you may ask *no* questions until *after* we have had an opportunity to meet with the flight crew, and then, during the group interview, I ask that you refrain from questions of a technical nature about the aircraft. We are preparing a one-page summary of data and flight information that you may take with you when you leave, and that summary will suffice for your purposes. You've met Colonel Anderson; see him for that summary."

"Are you going to censor the interview?" asked a reporter.

"Yes," Weggoner answered. "Any other questions?" In the doorway, two MPs appeared.

"Do we even get to see the ship and the crew when they arrive?" asked a reporter.

"Yes," Weggoner said. "From a visitors' area outside. You will be escorted. Those two gentlemen will be your escorts." The reporters looked over and saw the MPs.

"When do we get to view the bones?" asked a reporter.

"Not until we've had a chance to inspect them," Weggoner said, not breaking stride for that one at all. No more questions seemed pending. The general thanked them, and excused himself.

A moment later, Captain Fiore appeared in the room. "Patterson Field has them on radar," he announced.

In a room down the hall from the ready room, Weggoner sorted out Harry's men, greeting Bill first, Maxwell, then Lon, and, after Harry's men, Walter. Although Weggoner had read the file pertaining to each of Harry's men, he insulted no one by pretending to remember any of them. Not all Weggoner's wartime duty had been at Wright, and, even had it been, there were over forty thousand people working at Wright Field during the peak period of the war. On the other hand, the more the general looked at Lon Pyrtle, the more he thought he did remember Lon. Lon was distinguished by his age, poor posture, and the appearance of his graying Van Dyke. "Did you have that beard during the war?" Weggoner asked.

"Yes, I did," said Lon.

The general nodded. He smiled. He offered cigars all around, but no one smoked them. He congratulated all of them on the work they had done. Then he came to his point. "I know you've been talking with the newspaper guys," Weggoner said. "And what's done is done. But no more, okay? I put the press on a leash, but I want to put a muzzle on you. No more. You've gone far enough. You have a limited range of things you can discuss with the newspapers, and here's what that limited range of things is . . . ." The general made quick eye contact with each of the four people he addressed, for he was not interested in Major Girard, Captain Morales, or Colonel Anderson. He was interested in Walter, Lon, Maxwell, and Bill.

"Say nothing more to the press about anything technical," he said. "No matter what you've said to date, that's the end of it. Nothing about rotor dynamics. Nothing about masts. Nothing about rotors, rotor blades, rotor pitches, or controls. Not control systems. Not engines. Not drive trains, mounts, or transmissions. Not secondary gain in a tandem rotor configuration. Not about the airframe. Not about the crash in Mercedita. Not about as-built drawings. Clear? Say nothing about your loan agreement with Mr. Charlesville, who called to say he will be here tomorrow. He was in New York and will travel tonight on the train. Say nothing about him. I don't want to hear the name Sikorsky. I don't want to hear the name Piasecki. I don't want to hear the name Cierva Autogyro. I don't want to hear Platt / LePage. Getting the picture?

"In time, we may change how we're doing this, but, for now, what I just told you is it: you can talk about Porto Rico and how Harry died, and you can talk about how your company got started, in general terms: what your goals were. You can certainly talk about your years at Wright Field; except, I don't want to hear anything about whether Harry may have been in breach of good faith with private industry. I don't want to hear about stealing trade secrets or proprietary data, or infringing on copyrights or patents. Whatever you'd like to say about the war, you can say. I assume you are loyal to the Army Air Forces and Wright Field." He looked about. He saw no challenges. "Talk about the AAF, talk about defense, talk about air power, talk about freedom; talk about what a great guy Harry was, and mention that we're building an arsenal for peace. What else? You can talk about how you named the ship; how you decided on that name."

"In other words, we're stupid," Maxwell said.

"Not the flight?" asked Bill. "We've already been talking about the flight. They already know about the flight. We've set records."

"You have, and I'm glad, but no," said the general. "You're not stupid, but you can't talk about it. The flight's over. What you've said, you've said, but nothing you've said is confirmed. Thus far and no farther."

"Then there's nothing we can say," said Bill.

"There's plenty you can say," Weggoner said.

"Not how much the ship weighed at takeoff?" Maxwell asked.

"No," Weggoner said.

"But I already told a reporter."

"Unconfirmed and speculative," said Weggoner. "Not official. I can't rewrite history, but the information is unfounded."

"How about: how we built the ship?" asked Bill. "I mean, that's part of our corporate endeavor."

"Limit your 'endeavor' to the dream of vertical flight," Weggoner said. "Talk about Leonardo Da Vinci, because how you built that aircraft is now classified." Weggoner looked around at solemn mugs. "I'm sorry, fellas," he said. "I'm just asking your cooperation until we've had a chance to sort things out. You guys just show up like some orphans. Like some Indians off the range. Here we are: bang, bang, bang. Beat that drum. We had no warning, no idea you were coming. Now, you're here. And you've got a big problem on your hand with proprietary data that belong to sources Harry had access to. Manufacturers trusted Harry with trade secrets. The United States does not want to get sued because it appears we sponsored *Harry's Ark*, at the expense of the industry we buy from. The Army is supposed to keep a confidence, especially when a manufacturer opens his files. Did Harry breach that trust? I don't know. But with all that material at stake, national security is my theme. I don't want Russia to have our news on page one."

Finally, Weggoner turned personal. "I knew Harry, too," he told them. "Before any of you knew him, I knew him. Every damn thing Colonel Baird was associated with turned out strange somehow, or screwed up. Why do you think the man never got promoted beyond lieutenant colonel, until the war came along and we needed all the people we could get? The reason is because Harry screwed up everything he touched. Because he couldn't take orders is why. Because he fought with authority. He wouldn't listen. He struck out on his own, time and again. He was a grandstander and a maverick, and he cost the Army plenty. The miracle is he made it as far as he did. The miracle is he made officer at all."

"Kill the dead," Walter said. "Just like Germany. Blame those who died. Blame them all."

"Where's your star?" asked Weggoner. Weggoner's parents came from Prussia, and Walter's from Bavaria, but Weggoner's parents emigrated before Weggoner was born. And, now, the German American and the German, the general and Walter, stared across that great chasm. Walter's parents had struggled to make do, and stayed on to raise a family through the depression in Germany, then the war. Walter went to school in Heidelberg.

And Weggoner, born in New York, attended West Point. Weggoner never spoke German at home. Walter rarely spoke anything else.

"I am Walter Schmidt," said Walter, in German, "Proud to have served my country, and been a friend of Harry Baird."

En route, the ship overflew Caesar Creek. Looking down, Don could not see the creek, but knew it was there, somewhere, for he needed no more than the few scattered lights of the countryside to orient his approach to Wright Field. The outskirts of Dayton lay ahead, and out Patty's window lay Xenia. To the left, Waynesville and Corwin. "Route 42, the federal highway," Don yelled, seeing cars snake along it to Mount Holly. They were fifteen miles out from Wright Field, and would be down in twelve minutes. It was twelve thirty-seven, Monday morning.

Julio went forward. As he had done so often, he stood on the catwalk aft of the bulkhead, thrusting his shoulders and head forward into the cockpit. "Well?" he yelled.

"Well?" Don yelled back.

"I've flown backwards the whole way," Julio yelled. "Thought it would be nice to see the end." To Julio, the end was what one could not see looking back.

Though the flight had been an ordeal, the three were inseparably bound by that ordeal, and each felt the others knew it too. "It's an end, not an ending," Patty said in an effort to explain. But it was an ending as much as an end, and she might have reversed her own words, for what she dealt with was finally beyond explaining. *Nothing ends*, Patty thought. *There is a beginning but nothing ends.* It didn't matter. She didn't need to speak of this. Julio knew what she meant. Don knew what she meant. The three of them could look out the window together, together in the same direction, rolling off the final moments. They had been alone in the world, together, insulated, and aloof, and together had faced painful, exhausting moments, some terrible to bear. They had known things no one knew, or ever could, except themselves, and that knowledge was their bond. "If the Army does not give you full credit," Patty yelled, meaning

Don, then meaning Julio, then meaning both, and both at once, "if you do not get the credit you deserve, then I *will* shout it from the rooftops. I swear. I will make people see."

"See what?" Don yelled back.

"You are the greatest black pilot," she yelled.

"That honor belongs to the Tuskeegee Airmen," Don yelled back.

"Love is a secret," Julio yelled. "Remember what I told you in Miami. Start saying how great someone is, and people will think you've got something at stake."

"I do!" Patty said. "You are the world's greatest engineer."

"You're right," he agreed. "You can say that."

"It's not the Army," yelled Don. "I love the Army. I love Wright Field. I love flying. I love you."

"I love you too," she said, fighting back tears because it *was* an ending, and she always cried at endings; in a minute things would change and would be different evermore. "Are you going to speak for Harry?"

"Sure, if they ask me," yelled Don. "A pioneer. A genius. He told me so himself, very often. Who's to say? He was right."

"Hey. You want to hear a joke Harry told me?" Julio yelled.

"Tell it," Patty yelled.

"I'll have to yell," said Julio.

"Yell," said Don.

"Ah, the hell with it," said Julio.

"I'll tell you one he told me," said Don. "Guy's down in Kentucky, right? runnin' moonshine. He sees a guy on the road, late at night. Deserted road. Picks him up. They're going together in the car, a hundred miles an hour through the back roads. The driver says, 'Want some whiskey?' The man says, 'No.' The driver tells him, 'Reach under your seat, get that jug.' The man says, 'No, don't want any.' The driver says, 'Do it.' So the man pulls up the jug. Then the driver says, 'Take a drink.' The man says, 'No, don't want to take a drink.' So the driver takes out a pistol, aims it at the man's head, and says, 'Now, I told you, take a drink.' So, the man drinks. He's scared half to death. When he finishes, the whiskey starts to burn and burns so bad tears come to his eyes. Then the driver hands *him* the pistol and says, 'Here, now you hold the pistol on me and I'll take a drink.'"

Patty laughed, delighted with Don's story.

"I think Maxwell told Harry that one," said Julio, who thought he had heard it from Maxwell, but, who knew? All the jokes they told in Ponce went around.

Wright Field's approach controller called, with instructions for a straight-in approach. "We're cleared for straight-in," Don yelled. They could see the field's beacon, and Don began to let down. "That's Wright," he yelled at Patty. She said nothing, nodding. He was glad it was straight-in. He professed to be too cold to move the sticks.

But she was moved by his words from the moment before, that he loved her. She would tolerate no bar against Don, no prejudice, none at all; not from Wright, nor anywhere else, for ultimately she could not lie about her love. She could not keep it secret, and would not try. "My mother lives down there," he yelled. "She lives there with William, my brother." The ship had just crossed the Little Miami, the river that fed the Ohio. To Don, it was home.

Five miles from Wright Field, the lights of the great triangle of runways of Area B came into view. Don reported to the tower, "Field in view."

"Roger that," said the tower. "We see you. Runway thirty-four is active. Proceed to the second taxi turn-off and land your aircraft."

"Roger," Don answered. A mile out, he saw men in the tower.

The ship overflew the reservation boundary, entering Area B between Page Manor and Gate twenty-two. "Wright Field," Don announced, barely heard.

Six hundred feet below them stood the array of aircraft representing the mission of Air Matériel Command. Closing in from the right stood the bank of structures, in a city-like grid of an industrial park, which comprised Area B; the labs, shops, and facilities that had developed the world of aviation. "That's what we needed in Ponce," Julio yelled, waving at the enormity of the installation, which in sum enveloped not only the brains of air power but much of its inspiration.

Don pulled back on the power. *One step at a time*, he was thinking. *First things first*, went his thought. He allowed the ship to come down, but then misjudged the glide slope and overshot the second taxiway turnoff. He circled around. "I've forgotten how to fly," he said, feeling that the more he thought about it, the less able he was to do it. *Just do it for me*, he prayed to God. *You've been doing it for me till now.* Then, out there, were all those people. He could see them. Test pilots from Wright Field. He knew who they were. Top Brass. And, in his heart, he felt Harry.

He worked the pitch, the main rotor cyclic, the left rotor collective. The ship came round. To be seen from the ground, it was graceful. It swooped down. And it flared. The touchdown was like smoothing on cream, or a leaf that had cradled to earth.

"Cut the engines," Julio said.

Don reached forward and cut the engines. "Don't think I could have gone much farther," he said, overcompensating loudly in the sudden silence.

"Of course you could've," said Julio. "You could have gone another thousand miles."

"Yeah?"

"A guy like you will never stop."

Out came the force, eighty strong, of enlisted personnel, officers and civilians. "Here they come," Patty said.

"Before they get here, thank God," Don said.

"*Gracias a Dios y La Virgen*," Julio prayed.

"Lord, thank you," Patty prayed, although, unfortunately, as she saw it, the really hard part now began.

They were in no hurry to climb out, despite the field's personnel, all a clamor, and Wright's own people using cameras, using flashes. Don's back was too stiff to move fast. "Permission to board her?" asked the general, saluting Don from outside, as six or seven cameras popped bulbs.

"Permission granted," said Don. "She's all yours." *Harry's Ark* seemed Harry's gift, to all the world; *coming home*, the gift of God, to mainly Don.

—